ANGEL
OF LIGHT

OTHER BOOKS BY JOYCE CAROL OATES

NOVELS
Bellefleur
Unholy Loves
Cybele
Son of the Morning
Childwold
The Assassins
Do With Me What You Will
Wonderland
them
Expensive People
A Garden of Earthly Delights
With Shuddering Fall

SHORT STORIES
A Sentimental Education
Night Side
Crossing the Border
The Goddess and Other Women
Marriages and Infidelities
The Wheel of Love
Upon the Sweeping Flood
By the North Gate
The Hungry Ghosts
The Seduction
The Poisoned Kiss (Fernandes/Oates)

CRITICISM
Contraries
New Heaven, New Earth: The Visionary Experience in Literature
The Edge of Impossibility: Tragic Forms in Literature

PLAYS
Miracle Play
Three Plays

POEMS
Women Whose Lives Are Food, Men Whose Lives Are Money
Anonymous Sins
Love and Its Derangements
Angel Fire
The Fabulous Beasts

ANTHOLOGIES
The Best American Short Stories 1979 (edited with Shannon Ravenel)
Scenes from American Life: Contemporary Short Fiction (editor)

ANGEL
OF LIGHT

Joyce Carol Oates

E. P. DUTTON   New York

"The Storm" first appeared in *Cosmopolitan* © 1981.
"Anatomical Studies" first appeared, in slightly different form, in *Chatelaine* © 1980.

Published in the United States by Elsevier-Dutton Publishing Co., Inc., 2 Park Avenue, New York, N.Y. 10016

Library of Congress Cataloging in Publication Data
Oates, Joyce Carol
  Angel of light.
  I. Title.
PS3565.A8A79   813'.54   81-730
AACR2

ISBN: 0-525-05483-9

Published simultaneously in Canada by Clarke, Irwin & Company Limited, Toronto and Vancouver

Designed by The Etheredges

This novel is for Robert Fagles,
in honor of his service in the House of Atreus;
and for our lost generations—

What we call Evil in this World, Moral as well as Natural, is the grand Principle that makes us sociable Creatures, the solid Basis, the Life and Support of all Trades and Employments without Exception: That there we must look for the true Original of all Arts and Sciences, and that the Moment Evil ceases, the Society must be spoiled if not totally dissolved.

—MANDEVILLE, *The Fable of the Bees,* 1714

Contents

I. The Seduction

Eyre, New York,
March 1980

The Children
of Maurice J. Halleck

It is on a windy morning in early March, a day of high scudding dizzy clouds, some nine months after their father's ignoble death, that his only children, Owen and Kirsten, make a pact to revenge that death.

Not revenge. Not revenge but justice—that's what we want.

But how will we know . . . ?

Who his murderers are, you mean?—we know.

No. If it's justice. Or only revenge.

A morning of falling tumbling shadows, high above the river. The raucous and distracting noise of birds—blackbirds, grackles—in the leafless trees. Owen finds the birds' cries distinctly unpleasant and when he finally pauses to look around he is struck, even a little alarmed, by the vast numbers of birds: a spring migration, evidently? Hundreds upon hundreds. Thousands. A ceaseless din, fluttering wings, cries, screams, virtual shrieks. He cannot remember ever having seen so many birds flocking at one time. There is something repulsive about them in addition, even, to their unholy noise—something blackly snakelike about their necks, their heads—he thinks of dream-serpents—a scuttling and slithering in the dark, out of the range of his vision—an incoherent memory, perhaps, from his troubled sleep of the previous night.

Thousands and thousands of birds, and his sister is barely conscious of them. She blinks, she stares, looking around where he is pointing with a hand that trembles just perceptibly—her pinched anemic face and her slate-gray eyes with their contracted pupils, their look of glassy stupor, cannot seem to register the din—the nuisance—the panicky outrage that Owen feels.

After a moment Kirsten says, slowly, with a subtle air of re-proach, *They* can't interrupt us.

Less than two weeks after Owen received, and never acknowl-edged, a certain singularly disturbing—and singularly ugly—"mes-sage" from his sister in an ordinary manila envelope addressed to him at his dormitory, their mother telephoned. Toward midnight of a week-day. Not quite as if nothing were wrong—for of course a great deal was wrong—but as if the issue, the problem, the pathology, had primarily to do with Kirsten.

Is she sick again? Owen asked, lowering his voice though cer-tainly no one could overhear—his suitemates were not even home yet, as far as he knew. (Kirsten had been ill earlier that winter with a mild form of pneumonia. "Ambulatory" pneumonia. She had told no one at her boarding school, assuming it was merely the flu, or a severe cold; she had had a temperature of 103 degrees; then one day she fainted on a staircase and would have injured herself badly if another girl had not caught her. Even then, confined to the infirmary, she had insisted over the phone that she was *not* sick enough to come home.) —Or is it—well —more of the same—?

Isabel was telephoning from Nassau. From the handsome white villa on the ocean owned by her old and dear friend Mrs. Lleyn, the ambassador's widow. A widow for some six or eight years now, and surely comfortable with her altered status, and surely with the money inherited from her husband. The very best company, Owen thinks, the most *therapeutic* company, for the new and still-grieving widow of the late Maurie Halleck.

Isabel began the strained conversation by mentioning, by repeat-ing, the fact that Claudia Lleyn has warmly issued invitations to Owen and Kirsten to come down at spring break—though of course they are welcome at any time. And when Isabel goes to Mexico at the end of March, to stay with Jack Fair and Martha Degler at Mrs. Degler's place in Guadalajara, they are welcome to visit there too; they are *very* wel-come. Owen murmurs yes, thank you, I mean thank them for us, at least for *me*—but I don't think I can make it. I'm overwhelmed with work. . . . If I want to graduate . . . I think I'll just stay here in the dormitory where it will be dead quiet and . . .

You know you're always welcome, Owen, Isabel says. Her voice sounds both distant and breathy; Owen shuts his eyes hard to summon her face.

Yes, says Owen, I know, that's fine, but I don't particularly enjoy people feeling sorry for me. Even if it's very discreetly done.

No one feels *sorry* for you, Isabel says, as if piqued; and then, reconsidering, she says, I mean in the sense of pitying you. Of pitying any of us. Claudia is an old friend and Jack Fair likes you and you've seen snapshots of Martha's place in Guadalajara, you know how immense it is, part of an old monastery in fact, I should think you and Kirsten would be grateful to spend a week or ten days there, in the sun. The past eight or nine or however many months it's been haven't exactly been easy for any of us. . . .

Owen coughs, cupping his hand over the receiver. More than nine months, I think, Mother, he says; but so quietly, so courteously, that Isabel does not hear. She continues talking, her voice remote, grieving, then musical and "Latin"—for Isabel Halleck is, after all, Isabel de Benavente, and quite exotically half-Spanish—chiding Owen for not having driven up yet this term to visit his sister though the Eyre Academy isn't far away—surely he isn't busy *every* weekend—and doesn't he have a friend, a girl friend, at Connecticut College? He could, Isabel points out shrewdly, combine a visit. Unless he and the girl—what was her name?—Sandra?—have broken up?

Her name is Lynn Fischer and we haven't "broken up," Owen says. We weren't affiliated in any sort of partnership—we both have a lot of other friends—and so it isn't quite possible for us to break up.

All right, Isabel says placidly, but you get my point, don't you.

I get your point, Owen says.

Considering the fact that Kirsten won't allow me to visit her, Isabel says.

She won't allow you to visit her? Owen asks, startled. Since when?

You must know about it, Isabel says. I assume the two of you are communicating.

But we're *not*, Owen says. No—we're really not.

You've always been close, Isabel says.

No. Not really. Why do you say that? Owen asks, distracted. I mean—does it look that way to you?

The two of you have been close, Isabel says. In certain respects. But we don't have time to discuss it now.

We're not close, Owen says, protesting, I can't talk to her any more than you can and I'm bored with her and I don't want to drive up to see her, it will only be Daddy this and Daddy that, and at Christmas she looked like hell, I don't have time for her emotional blackmail any more than you do, Mother, I have my own life and I'm up to my ass in work—

I do have time for Kirsten, Isabel says sharply, interrupting, I think you've misunderstood: the fact is she doesn't want me to fly up.

She's made that quite clear. And when I telephone—I've been telephoning a great deal lately—she refuses to come to the phone and her roommate Hannah talks to me, the poor girl practically stammers with embarrassment, she's such a *civilized* child, and has such a mature sense of social tact, obviously Kirsten is in the room and listening and she has forced Hannah to lie, telling me that everything is all right, everything is fine, when of course I've been talking to the dormitory counselor and the dean and the psychologist—*she's* been helpful, a Dr. Haslet—and the president of the damned school when she has five minutes to spare —and I know very well that Kirsten is skipping half her classes and sometimes she sleeps all day and sometimes she doesn't sleep at all but wanders around the dormitory at night, and goes outside—that sort of thing. Do you see my point now?

Owen thinks carefully before he replies. He says: But Kirsten has always been rather self-conscious about being Kirsten, hasn't she?— rather *deliberate*. She had trouble at Picketts and it wasn't altogether clear if she was involved in that secret club at Hays—

She was not involved in that club, Isabel says. She was not involved in any secret club.

All right, Owen says quickly, my point is simply that none of this is new, she's gone through spells before, not working in school or working too hard in one subject, refusing to eat, sleeping most of the day and staying awake at night. . . . She was going to Dr. Pritchard a long time before Brean Down—you can't blame it all on Father.

I'm not blaming anything on him, Isabel said, why do you express it that way? That's a curious way of expressing it.

Then who are you blaming it on, me?

I'm not blaming anyone, Isabel says, I'm not even in the kind of self-pitying mood in which I'd blame myself, it's just that I can't talk with her any longer—I mean she doesn't allow me to talk—to see her —she behaves as if I didn't exist—as if I were dead: she doesn't know it, but she's behaving as if I were dead. I know it isn't for the first time, but in the past our disagreements weren't so extreme, they weren't so —I dislike the word pathological, but, well, yes, *pathological*—they were the usual mother-daughter problems—frictions—in fact even you and I didn't always get along perfectly, and you and Maurie—mothers and daughters, fathers and sons—it's quite normal—I know it's quite normal during adolescence, up to a point. Maurie could lose his temper too, it wasn't just me, with Kirsten especially, she has always tested us, you know how she's been, except that now—since Christmas—it's gotten much worse—I think her behavior is deteriorating—I think she's seriously disturbed and maybe even dangerous to herself, she seems so *angry* with me and I don't understand, I have enough grief without her hostility—

I don't think she's necessarily *angry*, Mother, Owen says cautiously, I mean angry with you—

—enough to think about without her hatred—neither of you gives a damn about *me*—

Don't say that, Owen murmurs. Mother?—look, don't say that.

For a moment the line falls silent. Then Isabel begins again, in a calmer voice: So I'm calling to ask whether you won't help me. Whether you won't take the time to visit her, to see how serious it really is, if maybe she does need treatment of some kind—really good professional treatment—Charley Clayton was telling me he could get Kirsten in that place outside Bethesda—Fair Hills or Far Hills, I don't recall the name —the Moultons' son was there for a while after that terrible business in California—and Bianca Marek's daughter, I think you know her, the one who almost died on some sort of brown rice diet, and her liver was affected, and her eyesight. It isn't a hospital exactly, there aren't any walls or fences or anything so visible, in fact they're said to have an excellent tennis pro, he's Mexican, and wonderful to work with, I know because he takes part in the tennis clinic at Claudia's club and she happened to mention him—but it isn't important: the important thing is that Kirsten might need help if she's going to come through this normally—

Owen finds that he has been gripping the telephone receiver hard. Very hard. And his forehead is uncomfortably damp with perspiration. But he manages to make his voice light: Come through this "normally," or come through this "normal"—which do you mean, Mother?

Owen, it's late, Isabel says angrily, I don't have time to argue with you. If you don't give a damn about me you might at least give a damn about your sister. Surely you could spare an hour or two. . . . Just to talk with her, just to check on her. You could take her to lunch at that old inn, the stone inn, you know.

It's more like five or six hours, Owen says.

But you could visit the Fischer girl. She's a very attractive girl— I liked her.

It's still five or six hours, Owen says, a little wildly. He isn't altogether certain what their conversation is about; but he has begun to feel the usual disquieting symptoms—a slowly accelerating heartbeat, a certain dryness in his mouth. Unless he is mistaken Isabel wants him to spy on his sister and is offering him, not very obliquely, what amounts to a sexual interlude by way of an enticement.

Or *is* he mistaken? Isabel so rattles him, he cannot be certain of

anything except that he is becoming increasingly upset. . . . An enticement, a bribe? Unknowing Lynn Fischer, who is so "attractive"?

He stalls, he speaks more calmly, he hears himself asking Isabel
if she *had* planned to visit Kirsten, in any case. If she had been prepared
to fly up to New York, and take a train out to Eyre. In any case.

Of course, Isabel says at once. What do you think we've been
talking about?

But Kirsten won't let you come?—she's said you *can't* come?

She has told Hannah and the dormitory counselor and Dr. Haslet
that she won't see me if I show up there, Isabel says, her message is that
she isn't angry with me—ah, no!—who would have thought *that*—and
she doesn't of course hate me—but she'd rather not see me right now;
that's all. She'd "prefer" not to see me right now. I assumed you knew
all about it.

I think she'll change her mind, Owen says, still stalling, swallowing with difficulty, I mean—*did* you have plans to fly up?—if—

The Silbers have been asking me to spend a few days with them,
Isabel says, they have that lovely big brownstone now, you know, or
maybe you haven't seen it, on East Sixty-eighth, it would be no trouble
to fly up and stay with them and I could hire a car and go to Eyre and
get Kirsten and we could spend a while in New York together—see some
plays, the museums—buy her a few things—Hannah did admit once
when I called and Kirsten evidently wasn't in the room that her clothes
don't exactly fit now, she's lost so much weight—and I assume—dear
Christ, I *know*—that they're in shameful condition anyway—Kirsten
simply isn't a *clean* person—even before the trouble with your father
—she's been a disturbed girl for years—I don't know what to do with
her—I might have to insist that she leave Eyre and get some professional help—I might have to have her committed—

Don't say that, Mother, Owen begs. But in an undertone. His
husky voice trembling. Hey look, Mother, I mean—you were saying—
a psychologist at Eyre?—what was her name?—maybe if you talked
with her—

I did talk with her, Isabel says, more calmly, and I was impressed with her good sense—she's intelligent and well spoken and not
an alarmist like Pritchard—the first thing *that* bastard thought of was
suicide, remember?—and the bad publicity *he'd* get—but Dr. Haslet is
intelligent and sympathetic and she actually seems to like Kirsten. We
talked for nearly an hour on the telephone. She says that Kirsten is an
extremely sensitive girl, she has an I.Q. in the upper 140s—but we
knew that, didn't we—and she's simply exaggerating the sort of grief
any child would feel, under the circumstances—or, I should say, under

even the ordinary circumstances of losing a parent so suddenly—but—anyway—you must know what I mean, Owen—and the essence of it was, Dr. Haslet advised me not to force myself upon my daughter right now—to wait a while, to give her time, to give her time to want *me*.

But maybe she won't see me either, Owen says. He has become distinctly nervous now. The memory of the manila envelope and its outrageous message, the memory of his having thought, as he stared at it, astonished, sickened, that his sister might very well be drifting into insanity—and the cruel little nudge in the ribs that Isabel dealt him, with her incidental reference to Kirsten's I.Q.—for naturally sister and brother are rivals, deadly rivals, naturally Owen is aware of Kirsten's I.Q. and painfully aware of his own, which tested out, once, three points below hers, and on another terrifying occasion, a full ten points below hers—and the simple blunt force of Isabel's personality, to which he is never equal: the strain is becoming too much: his mouth is so dry he can barely swallow. —Mother? he says. Maybe she won't want to see me either, how do you know? At Christmas she treated me like shit—

One of her games, Isabel says flatly. She wasn't serious.

But—

Her games, her pranks. And she could have been such a beautiful girl, Isabel says in a rush of queer choked emotion.

Could have been! Owen says, oh hey, it isn't too late, is it—I mean —the poor kid is only seventeen—

Owen, Isabel says, her voice rising, I don't have time to argue with you—I don't have time for your games too, your malicious tricks — your sister might be emotionally ill—she *might* be suicidal—and my own nerves are shot—I haven't been able to sleep a full night since last June—

All right, Mother, Owen says quickly, so upset now he has begun to shiver, and is panicked that his teeth are about to start chattering, all right, good Christ, I'm sorry, I'm *sorry*, I'll do any fucking thing you want me to do, I'll fit Kirsten into a straitjacket and commit her to the nearest hospital—I'll drive the poor cunt into the city if you want me to —to Bellevue—

He has lost control; he is speaking in a high breathless reedy voice; his teeth *have* begun to chatter—but, fortunately—a matter of extraordinary good luck (for Isabel would have been furious at his use of "obscenity"; she detests obscene words not her own)—fortunately something seems to be going on at the other end of the line, in Nassau, there is a voice or voices in the background, Isabel has company suddenly, her attention is drawn away from her telephone conversation with her son and her son sits trembling at his desk, the receiver gripped so hard in his hand that his fingers have gone numb. . . .

Voices, muffled laughter.

Owen feels a stab of murderous jealousy.

Mother—? he says. Are you still on the line?

Isabel is speaking but her voice is muffled. He cannot make out the words. And is the other voice a woman's voice, or a man's—

Mother! Owen shouts.

She laughs, not troubling to cup her hand over the receiver. Owen waits, every pulse in his body pounding. . . . You will pay for this, he thinks. You will pay for this. Along with the rest of it. Oh yes oh yes oh yes.

But in a calm voice he manages to say: Hey, Mother? What's wrong? Is someone there? Can't you talk?

She returns to the line, to the conversation. She says: Owen, dear, I feel so much better for having talked with you, you *will* go see her? —and will you telephone her right away?—not tonight, maybe, my God, it's so late, but early tomorrow morning—

Someone is certainly in the room with her. A man. Certainly. Isabel's voice has that musical Spanish intonation, that grave seductiveness, Owen so detests. But he hides his despair, he stalls, he says: But why will she see me if she refuses to see *you?*

You and your sister have always been close, Isabel says.

Oh hey—not that again—

Yes, *very* close, Isabel says, her voice lifting with a sort of distracted coquetry, it's so touching—your father and I were always so pleased—we felt that you were actually protective of her—Nick commented on it too— And— Well— Now I must hang up, dear, this call will have cost Claudia a fortune—

But, Mother, wait, Owen says, I don't think I—

Call Kirsten in the morning, why don't you, she'll be delighted to hear from you, Isabel says, above a murmur in the background—voices? —radio music?—in fact I'd be delighted to hear from you myself sometime, she says flirtatiously, you *never* telephone, dear!—you're breaking my heart. Now. I have to hang up. You *will* call her?—and then call me, immediately—

Owen, his face and sides slick with perspiration, cannot answer for a moment. He sits with his eyes shut tight. Mother, he thinks, you will pay for this. I won't forgive you this.

Isabel is chattering in an airy guileless voice. Of course there is someone in the room with her: her current lover.

Which one of them? Kirsten will inquire.

How should I know? Owen will say rudely. *Nick Martens or Tony Di Piero or some new party, some very new party we have yet to be introduced to.*

Were you jealous? Kirsten will say slyly.

I have to hang up, dear, Isabel says, and thank you so much, I think things will work out, she probably *is* just going through a phase, Maurie always took that attitude—it's so philosophical, so Olympian—is that the right word?—so wise. While I was always too emotional.

Yes, Owen says quietly. Yes. All right. Goodnight.

And you *will* telephone me, immediately afterward?

Yes. I will. Goodnight.

Remember, dear—you're the man of the family now.

The man of the family now.

A felicitous expression Owen does not, for some reason, share with his sister. Though when he hears it the words cut through him like a knife. And he thinks, not for the first time, that Isabel and not Maurie should have died. Isabel, and not Maurie.

If there were justice in the world.

Great-Great-Great-Great-Grandfather: Notes on John Brown

Awaiting execution in Charlestown, Virginia (now West Virginia), December 1859. After the disaster of Harpers Ferry: I have enjoyed *remarkable cheerfulness* and *composure of mind* ever since my confinement, and it is great comfort to feel assured that *I am permitted* to die for a cause and not merely to pay the debt of nature as all must.

Bloody Kansas and the Pottawatomie massacre of 1856, five of the enemy (that is, pro-slavers) killed. No time for remorse or pity. The Lord God directs Old Osawatomie's hand and his wrath. How can there be hesitation when "all things are divinely predestined"? Shotguns, rifles, bowie knives hidden in boots. Captain Brown, he was called. There were twenty-one young men, including blacks, in his guerrilla army. One must suppose they were very brave. They were certainly willing to die. And to kill.

God directs man in all things—all actions. His wrath cannot be denied. Or the searing face of His mercy.

There is such a thing, Old Osawatomie taught, as the Higher Law. Which will bring about—*is* bringing about—the Second American Revolution (that is, Free States vs. Pro-Slave States). One must imagine the screams at Pottawatomie in the mud, one must imagine the terrible mercy of the Lord. *For whosoever shall keep the whole law, and yet offend in one point, he is guilty of all.*

After Captain John Brown was hanged at Charlestown on December 2, 1859, he was mourned by many hundreds of followers as a martyr and a saint. (For, after all, he could have escaped from Charlestown—he and his little band of soldiers might have broken free before Col. Robert E. Lee attacked.) But John Brown taught: *Thou believest there is one God, thou doest well: the devils also believe, and tremble. But wilt thou know, O vain man, that faith without works is dead?*

All things are divinely predestined. Justice is a necessity on earth. *Consequently* the enemy (the slaveholding class) will be destroyed in the Second American Revolution. God does not jest.

No remorse? None. Not even in the body's most secret terror.

John Brown: I felt for a number of years in earlier life a steady strong desire to die, but since I saw any prospect of becoming a "reaper" in the great harvest, I have not only felt quite willing to live, but have *enjoyed* life much.

The friendship of the world is enmity with God. Whosoever therefore will be a friend of the world is the enemy of God.

John Brown and his guerrillas begged food, weapons, money, and horses. They dodged federal marshals who were empowered to shoot them down on sight, as public enemies. Yet Brown was immensely courageous: he spoke in the very places where posters offering money for his capture were displayed: and it was said that he spoke clearly and bravely and with great dramatic force. *The slaveholding class must be crushed. A New Dispensation is at hand. God will not be mocked. His wrath will not be appeased. "I am he that liveth, and was dead; and, behold, I am alive for evermore, and have the keys of hell and of death."*

Not revenge but justice will be enacted on earth—by *earthly agents.*

The Secret Six, militant abolitionists and upstanding citizens, humanitarians, comfortably middle-class. Dedicated to the overthrow of slavery—the cold war between North and South. They raised money for old John Brown. For the ailing old man. Money and sympathy and support and young soldiers for his army. Young men willing to die with him, by the sword. *Ye know not what shall be on the morrow. For what is*

*your life? It is even a vapor, that appeareth for a little time, and then
vanisheth away.*

Old Osawatomie was a martyr, a madman, a murderer, a saint, a demon,
a brave fearless heroic man, the Wrath of God, the Devil's tool. As
General George Washington was to the First American Revolution so
John Brown was to the Second American Revolution. He was hanged,
but his cause triumphed. Still, he *was* hanged; he died an ignoble death.
(However, he sired twenty surviving children, seven by his first wife and
thirteen by his second. The genealogy of the Hallecks of Washington,
D.C., traces a direct line back to one "Judith Brown," daughter of
Brown's first wife, the unhappy Dianthe Lusk. Which makes Old
Osawatomie the great-great-great-great-grandfather of Kirsten and
Owen Halleck, themselves the children of the late disgraced Maurice J.
Halleck. Who was a martyr also. And a deeply courageous man.)

Here is Brown's formal statement, after the capture at Harpers Ferry:
My name is John Brown; I have been well known as Old John Brown of
Kansas. Two of my sons were killed here today, and I am dying too. I
came here to liberate slaves, and was to receive no reward. I have acted
from a sense of duty, and am content to await my fate; but I think the
crowd have treated me badly. I am an old man. Yesterday I could have
killed whom I chose; but I had no desire to kill any person, and would
not have killed a man had they not tried to kill me and my men. I could
have sacked and burned the town, but did not; I have treated the persons
whom I took as hostages kindly, and I appeal to them for the truth of
what I say. If I had succeeded in running off slaves this time, I could have
raised twenty times as many men as I have now, for a similar expedition.
But I have failed.

Tried. Found guilty. Condemned to death. Hanged before a crowd on
December 2, 1859.

No Quarter! was his battlecry. *No Quarter to our enemies!*

Henry David Thoreau said of John Brown: *He is an Angel of Light.* And
Thoreau said: *I do not wish to kill or be killed but I can foresee circumstances in which both of these things would be by me unavoidable.*

Cholera, fever, ague, near-starvation. Pneumonia. Walls splattered
with blood and hair. *I will give my life for a slave,* Brown declared.
The Battle of Black Jack. The burning of houses. Butchery. God's

wrath is butchery of man. Osawatomie. *No Quarter* is God's battlecry. One must imagine pikes, scythes, muskets, shotguns, rifles, bowie knives. Attacks at dawn on sleeping people. History written in blood. Redeemed by blood. Are you afraid? Terrified. Will you give your life? If I must.

The death of John Brown was, in the words of a man named Boyers, "the happy release of a man who had small aptitude for private life."

Genealogy. John Brown, born 1800. Married one Dianthe Lusk whom (it is speculated) numerous pregnancies weakened both physically and men- tally. A daughter Judith was born in 1828 (?) in Boiling Springs, Ohio. And Judith married Elias Trubee, a local farmer, and a son William was born in 1845. William Trubee married Hagar Quinn in Rhinelander, Wisconsin, and their first child was a daughter Elizabeth, born in 1879. Elizabeth married a young Rhinelander merchant named Wesley Hal- leck (destined to become wealthy, and to leave Rhinelander) and their only child was a son, Joseph, born in 1909. Joseph married the daughter of a Chicago paint manufacturer, Abigail Rowlandson, and their first child was a son, Maurice, born in 1930 in Washington, D.C. And Maurice married Isabel de Benavente of Washington, New York City, and Palm Beach, and three children were born to them: Owen Jay (January 14, 1959); an unnamed female infant who lived only a few days (sometime in 1961—Kirsten isn't certain of the date and cannot of course make inquiries since the subject is too intimate, too "serious," and in any case she has always had the terrified idea that the death of the unnamed baby girl is the sole reason for her own birth); Kirsten Anne (October 8, 1962). The three babies were delivered in the same hospital, Mount St. Mary's, Washington, D.C.

John Brown on the eve of his death: . . . It is great comfort to feel assured that *I am permitted* to die for a cause and not merely to pay the debt of nature as all must.

Twins

Gravely, silently, she speaks. Her skin is stretched tight across her narrow once-beautiful face and her eyes are larger than Owen has ever seen them, deep-set, and brightly glacial: a queer hard sheen to the eyeball he finds repulsive. Her red-blond hair is windblown and clearly has not been washed for a very long time. Her skin is sallow, prematurely weary, there are sardonic lines about her mouth that look as if they have been traced into the flesh with deliberate cruelty, an adult's cynicism, rage devouring itself. His sister Kirsten? *His* sister? He stares at her for some minutes before he realizes precisely what is wrong—the idiot has plucked most of her eyebrows out.

Don't pretend, she is saying, silently. *Don't lie. You know what I want. You know what we're going to do. Both of us—both of them. You know.*

I don't know, Owen protests. *I know nothing about it.*

She is waiting for him, Saturday morning. But not in her dormitory as he had assumed. He finds her three blocks from the campus of the Eyre Academy for Girls, sitting on the dirty steps of a diner with a *Closed* sign hanging crooked in its window. She is wearing jeans and a sheepskin jacket with stained cuffs and jogging shoes (blue with yellow trim) that appear to be stiff with dried mud. She is smoking a cigarette in a somnambulist's calm. Aware of him approaching from across the street, aware of his urgency, his anger, or unaware, indifferent, oblivious, an unattractive slouched figure that might be a boy or a girl, possibly fourteen years of age or younger; Isabel de Benavente's daughter. *I make myself ugly,* she proclaims to all witnesses. *You know why.*

Owen is going to demand to know what the hell Kirsten thinks she is doing, dressed like that, scruffy and half-starved and ridiculous, and why hadn't she the minimal courtesy to leave a message for him at the reception desk?—after he'd driven all the way up here to see her. But then he thinks *I am the man of the family now.* He thinks, cautiously, *I'd better not antagonize her.*

He greets her, they shake hands, Owen forces upon her a certain half-bemused preppie style, *his* style, of which he is both self-conscious and proud: it is a role like any other, and one which has always suited him well. Owen Halleck in his handsome camel's-hair blazer, in his dark turtleneck sweater. Strong blunt bones, strong face. Broad shoulders, an easy loping gait, an athlete's grace—or nearly. (No one can guess at Owen's soft belly, his wattled thighs, the band of lardy flesh around his waist.) Perhaps he is not a handsome young man but by judicious and well-practiced smiles and other facial mannerisms, and by the use of his husky voice, he has always been able to radiate a certain aura of intelligence, reliability, good-natured equanimity, calm. In any case he is not visibly a mourner.

You're not getting enough sleep, he says with a brother's quick familiarity, you're not getting enough to eat—they say your hair falls out if you starve yourself. So what the hell—?

Kirsten stares at him. Unable to reply. Her cracked lips are moving just perceptibly; her pale eyelids flutter. It is an old trick of Isabel's —Owen has in fact noted, and been angered by, her repeated use of it with Kirsten—this quick blunt rude irrefutable reference to a physical defect of some kind (pimples, greasy hair, unwashed neck, odor of perspiration) in order to seize control. In order to deflect possible accusations.

She murmurs an apology. Withdraws a step or two. Drops the cigarette to the sidewalk—filthy habit—and crushes it rather slowly, rather too ponderously, with her foot.

You've done something bizarre with your eyebrows, he says. He takes hold of her shoulders and gives her a little shake. Not hard. Perhaps a little impatiently. But with affection—certainly with affection. —Look, sweetheart, are you doped up? This early in the day? Because if you are I think I'll say goodbye. Your games don't interest me and this is an extremely busy time in my life.

Kirsten begins at once to speak: apologizing again, vaguely explaining, this, that, a girl named Binkie, her roommate Hannah, a "heavy" atmosphere in the dorm, until her words trail off and she is staring at him with those deathly nacreous-gray eyes, *You know what I want,* she is saying, *you know what we're going to do, don't deny me,* she is saying, she is pleading, *don't deny him.*

I haven't come here because of that letter, Owen tells her, casually. Very casually. —I mean that thing you sent in the mail.

That thing: I ripped it into pieces and threw it away, he says.

Your games, your jokes. They aren't very amusing.

One of my suitemates—Rob—brought the mail up. He tossed it on my bed and laughed and said, It's either from a girl who really has the hots for you, or from a nut—let me know.

I did no more than glance at it. I ripped it into pieces and threw them away, flushed them down the toilet in fact.

Afterward I told Rob: Just a nut.

The Taste of Death

Why do I think of it so obsessively, you may ask.

The taste is dark, mud-dark, clotted, hideous. It gathers at the back of the mouth. A puddle. Bitter and brackish, like stagnant water. Something metallic about it too.

Water in which sewage has been dumped. Water in which organic life is decaying . . . plant life, algae, tiny fish, insects, worms . . . so that it might blossom again into other life, other organic life.

Should we take hope from that? consolation?

No.

The taste is stale and stagnant and black. Tarry mucous. Collecting at the back of the mouth. The tongue begins to go numb, from the poison. Panic courses through the body. The body goes limp with fright. It's terror that death is approaching—but more than that: life will be extinguished. You'll disappear like water down a drain. Gurgling dirty water down a drain. Neat. Direct. So simple.

Is the event reversible?

Never.

But *why* do I think of it so obsessively, you want to know, with some impatience. Why do I imagine that my anger, my grief, my plans for revenge, my hope for justice will make any difference? After all— the dead stay dead a long time.

Yes, I have driven out to Brean Down County, Virginia. More

19

precisely, I have been driven out by a friend. Yes, I insisted upon getting out of the car. To walk along the roadway, to examine the guard rail which has recently been repaired (it's only thirty inches high—I measured it), to climb down the hill, my sandals slipping on the grass so that I nearly fell. I contemplated the area—no one could mistake it—where his car had crashed and sunk to a depth of five feet. Reeds and cattails and tree stumps had been damaged. The swamp had filled in, of course, the soft rich black mud had filled in, but you could see that something had been there.

I waded out into the water, inhaling the brackish swamp odor, not minding its sudden stink, or the mosquitoes and gnats. The mud was soft underfoot. Very soft. I sank five or six inches. The water was nearly to my knees and I kept sinking but I wasn't afraid. I stooped to splash water on my legs. I tasted it: closed my eyes and tasted it: yes, it was what I had imagined: I had known it all along.

I was going to scoop up a handful of mud to taste that. But I began to gag. Then I began to laugh.

My friend, standing up on the road, called down to me.

I began to laugh because I was comfortably high, and because nothing was exactly real. At the moment. It didn't require that I take it seriously at the moment because he had died a long time ago—weeks, months ago—and his death was accomplished, and that was that. The car had been hauled out, the body extricated. All that was over. I couldn't do anything about it. It was over. I laughed for a while and then I stopped laughing but I wasn't upset.

Brean Down swamp. Eighteen miles from the town of Meckleberg, thirty-five miles north of Waynesboro, about twenty miles northwest of Charlottesville. Not quite one hundred miles from Washington.

The taste of death: exactly what I had imagined. But for him there was the taste of blood as well. His own blood. The surprise of it. His warm salty blood. He *must* have tasted it—he didn't die at once. He probably didn't lose consciousness at once.

Trees without names. I must learn their names. Tall, slender, leaning to one side; with a peeling silvery bark; crisscrossed with sinewy vines. The vines were healthy enough but the trees seemed to be dying. They were dying from the top down. There were many gutted trunks, many stumps. Some looked very old—prehistoric. But I imagined that. I am accused of imagining a great deal. With my "unconventional" and even "disturbing" imagination. With my I.Q. of which my mother has been, intermittently, proud.

A psychopath, she once called me. But not seriously—in conversation, more or less. I think she meant psychotic.

In any case it wasn't important, it was just poolside chat with friends, or a mother-daughter chat while driving, or shopping for winter clothes, or spring clothes, or a new "adolescent" psychiatrist since Dr. Pritchard performed so poorly. I told Father, however. I told Father: She's persecuting me, does that mean I'm guilty of something? He picked up the humor. The joke. Perhaps he failed to pick up the desperation. (Kirsten is always joking, Kirsten has such a wild sense of humor, isn't she inventive, isn't she droll. . . .) Nevertheless he spoke to Isabel about it and Isabel came to me, she rapped on the door which was closed, and I allowed her to enter though I barely looked up from my desk, and she said she was sorry, she was really very sorry, of course she hadn't meant to insult me or hurt me, she couldn't even remember having said whatever she had said—psychopathic, psychotic—she wanted to apologize, she wanted to tell me that she would never say anything like that again, especially before other people. Your father was quite disturbed, she told me, not quite smiling, but with the icy gracious control of the professional diplomat, the professional Foreign Service officer, though of course Isabel Halleck is only an amateur. —Your father takes things very seriously, she said. Her soft voice nudged, her beautiful blond-lashed eyes stared, it was so perfect a performance I believe I burst into applause.

A swamp, a dying forest. Immense. Miles. Most of the trees were leafless. I saw a hawk—my friend saw it—but maybe it wasn't a hawk but a buzzard, a vulture. And, back in a marsh, a beautiful white bird balanced on one leg. A cranelike bird, absolutely white. What kind of bird is that, I asked, but he didn't know, he made a joke or something, kept on talking, I didn't answer and didn't listen because it wasn't the right time, this was only between my father and me, no one else could intrude.

(Later I would tell him that we'd "better not"—not today—there's this itchy little pimple running pus—and the inside of my mouth too—yeah—*yes*—we hadn't better.)

Isabel does not know of this visit, Owen does not know, I was surprised at the rich black stink of decay—a nice druggy smell. You could wade out in the mud. Sink into it, sink deep. Something was sucking my feet as if it was alive. . . . Cool soft black mud. Nice.

I splashed water on my arms and legs; I scooped it up in both hands and cooled my forehead with it. My throat was dry so I tried to drink but most of the water dribbled down my chin. The back of my mouth, the back of my tongue, parched, numb, the panic taste . . . I tried to drink but the water dribbled down my chin. It was tepid. It tasted of algae, rot, death. My throat closed against it.

Why am I so morbid, you ask.

Why so mistrustful.

I leaned over and picked up Dr. Pritchard's jade-handled letter-opener, one of his corny exotic touches—and drew it out of its sheath—and terrified the poor bastard. Why am I so mistrustful, I said, licking my lips, staring at the knife, why do I imagine that certain people are conspiring against my father, that a certain person lies to him frequently by not exactly telling the truth—why do I imagine that things are happening we don't know about—I mean my father and I—and my brother —why am I so mistrustful, why am I so morbid—

Dr. Pritchard did not dare take the letter-opener away. A fact I recalled afterward with amusement.

Why am I so morbid, you ask.
After all—fathers die. Eventually. In the course of things.
Fathers *all* die.

June 11, 1979. The date of his irreversible death.
Why he died seems obvious: he left so many messages, so many scribbled notes, insisting upon his guilt, *his* guilt and no one else's. Yes, he did accept bribe money. In installments. Yes, he did use his position to delay litigation, to destroy records, tapes, documents, memos, transcripts. . . . He confessed "everything," one might say. Including the error of marriage. Including the error of children.

My purpose is to clarify, he wrote, *my purpose is to put an end to rumor and speculation and . . . With deliberation and premeditation I violated the sanctity of . . . the duties entrusted to me . . . the oath I swore to uphold . . . the trust of my associates . . . the faith of my . . .*

Incoherent scrawls. Illegible words. The police were understandably baffled for even Father's associates at the Commission (Nick Martens, for one) could not decipher certain words; even his secretary, who had worked for him for eighteen years; even his wife Isabel. Even his children.

Tumbling falling drunk-crazy-babbling words. He gave up on them, himself, several times in the confession, and simply wrote *I am guilty.*

Unless of course he wrote none of it. Or wrote it under coercion, before he was taken out to be killed.

But how can we know, terrified Owen asks. *If the police . . . If the F.B.I. . . . If . . .*
We know, I say, leaning to whisper in his ear, *the two of us know,*

don't lie to me, don't pretend, not to me of all people: we know. And we know what we must do.

Brean Down isn't the place we would have chosen for you, Father. That swamp. That bog. Muddy water in your lungs, alcohol in your blood, we would have chosen better for you, Father, you were well loved, you will not be forgotten.

I sent Owen a message. Unfortunately it took me a long time to construct. Maybe I wasn't well. There were wild loony nights. Very very long days. *You know what to do,* I told him.

I splashed water on my arms and legs to baptize myself. The kiss on the mouth—the corpse's kiss that smelled of talcum powder—wasn't quite *it,* I preferred the swamp water, I was already high but I got higher still guzzling algae and rot and death.

Swamp birds were calling to one another. I must have disturbed them. There were frogs too. And insects. A small cloud of mosquitoes gathered around my head and shoulders. Began to bite. Greedily, ravenously, you can't blame them, it is only nature. Mosquitoes and gnats whining in my ears.

But you know all this, Father.

You know, you have gone first. You inhaled it, the teeming life. Breathed it in. Teeming life, pullulating life, I love that word I first used in ninth grade, pullulating, you were proud of me, you loved me, I disappointed you in the end but you loved me, you were the only one—the only one.

Is the event reversible?

We will see.

Pranks

Coward, Kirsten says silently. *Liar.*

Owen is talking about many things, swinging his arms in a brotherly manner, tramping through the woods as if it doesn't trouble him in the least that his costly new shoes are getting wet. In the past several years, since graduating at the top of his class from Exeter, and being invited to join his college's most prestigious eating club, Owen has become marvelously social: which means he knows how to talk, and how to talk at length. He is resolutely good-natured though his good nature is sometimes lightly tinged with irony, as it is now.

He thinks it rather foolish, for instance, that he and Kirsten are headed out of town, toward the river, away from a reasonable lunch at the "quaint" old Molly Pitcher Inn where girls from the Academy are usually taken by visitors. He thinks it foolish that they are going to tramp along the river, in the precarious sunshine of a bright harsh March midday. Foolish too that Kirsten should be behaving so oddly. As if it will have any effect upon him. As if it can intimidate him.

Still, he is going to indulge her. In a matter of a few hours he will be free.

Their breaths are steaming faintly as they approach the river: souls expelled in little vapor clouds. Owen resents the cold. He resents having to talk so much, and so cheerfully. (News about mutual friends and acquaintances. Chatter about college—his courses, his professors, his examinations, his papers, his honors seminar, his senior thesis; the wonderful busyness of his life; the defiant normality of his life. Why doesn't Kirsten comment? Has she nothing to say? He drifts onto other subjects, more dangerous perhaps, but mildly stated: news about Nick Martens and his most recent problem at the Commission—a threat on his life evidently connected with an investigation into the misuse of pension funds in a national union; news, or perhaps it is only rumor, that Anthony Di Piero is planning to marry the young wife of the chairman of the board of the Midatlantic National Bank and Trust—when her divorce comes through, that is.)

He mentions, deliberately, because it is time, the important fact that everyone at school has been so cordial to him—so sympathetic— warm and concerned and courteous and discreet—respecting his privacy and his grief and yet not backing away from the situation either. He and Rob, for instance, went out drinking one night, and talked quite frankly, Owen about his father and how he had loved him, Rob about his father and how he loved, but frequently hated, *him.* . . . People have been very kind, Owen says, glancing at Kirsten, if you give them a chance they can be very generous, of course I suppose they talk behind my back and maybe if I were an underclassman now I wouldn't be invited to join the same club, I really don't know, people are only human after all, the case received so much shitty publicity, I suppose we're just going to have to live with it for a few more years, right?—and not break down or make asses of ourselves—after all, we aren't exactly invisible now.

Kirsten stares at the muddy woodchip path at her feet, as if unhearing. As if she were alone. Thinking her own private thoughts.

She does not glance at him and she certainly does not speak but Owen, shivering suddenly, can feel her contempt. *You coward,* she is thinking. *You phony loudmouth son of a bitch.*

Brother and sister, sister and brother. Almost four years between them. One is six feet two inches tall and weighs 200 pounds, the other is five feet seven inches tall and weighs 105 pounds, or perhaps less— the poor anemic mutt *is* skinny, Owen sees—yet it should probably be acknowledged that they are twins. In a manner of speaking.

Children of the late disgraced Maurice J. Halleck. Criminal, suicide. Director of the Federal Commission for the Ministry of Justice from 1971 to February 1979 when he was encouraged to take a leave of absence from his post. Which, after all, is one of the most "sensitive" posts in the federal government and not quite the thing for a deeply troubled and emotionally unstable man.

When precisely did Mother ask him to move out?—Owen cannot recall. Naturally he and Kirsten were away at school at the time. They were almost always away at school, or at camp. Their lives rivaled their parents' lives in wholesome busyness.

Washington children, after all. "Cliffhangers" is the not entirely appropriate word: for the Hallecks have money. A great deal of money.

(But is he a criminal, strictly speaking, Owen wants to ask. I mean if he was never convicted of a single crime, if he was never indicted and brought to trial and found guilty.... *Criminal,* people say, why not as easily say *victim*?)

Sister and brother, brother and sister. Hateful. Loving. Feuding. Twins. One is a prankster with a queer sense of humor; the other is gentlemanly and easily embarrassed and reliable and intelligent and ambitious and canny, the very best (so he fears) of second-best. One is slender and nervous as an eel, and possibly crazy. The other is solid meat, a popular kid, a handshaker, on his way to Harvard Law and a career as a Washington attorney, level-headed, slow to rage, sane. Very sane. In fact he cannot, except in the very early hours of the morning when he wakes too soon and his mind races frantically and he sees again —and again—again—his father's stiffened body on that aluminum table in that dim refrigerated room behind the office of the coroner of Brean Down County, Virginia—except for such moments he cannot imagine a time when he will not continue to be sane. His mind is a naked light bulb burning fiercely in a small whitewashed room. No shadows, no nuances. No place to hide.

So he chatters, shouting against the wind. Sometimes he interrupts himself with laughter. Kirsten does no more than glance at him, her eyes narrowed. *I know you,* she is thinking. *I know precisely who you are.*

But must Kirsten Halleck be taken seriously? Isabel once referred to her, half-admiringly, as that "devious little buffoon." And her penchant for unfunny jokes is well known. (Owen recalls suddenly an occasion, many years ago, at the Martenses' pool in Chevy Chase. When Nick and June were still married, and even "happily"—so far as anyone knew. A minor episode, really: Owen had been about to dive from the side of the pool and Kirsten had popped up out of nowhere and pinched the soft flesh at his waist and wouldn't let go, squealing *Fatty! Fatty! Everybody look here at Fatty!* and Owen had lost his temper and pinched *her*—yes, he'd pinched her right on the breast—her tiny breast —she was wearing a bright yellow halter, she couldn't have been more than eleven or twelve years old. You vicious little brat, Owen had muttered. How do you like it.)

They are very close, the Halleck children. The survivors.

Owen has been reading in the university library about the children of suicides. There is an entire pathology, evidently. Does Kirsten know? Has Kirsten too been doing research? He didn't commit suicide, Kirsten says. You know that. You know.

The claustrophilia of childhood! Peering at her through a doorway, a mirror mirroring a full-length steamy bathroom mirror, gleaming white tile, dazzling flesh: the breasts with their honey-colored nipples, the small red-blond bush of pubic hair.

Can she remember the wild crazy splashing baths in the big bathtub?—the sunken bathtub fluted like a flower, laid with blue tile?—Mother's and Daddy's own bathtub in their own bathroom—Mother and Daddy were out for the evening and one of the girls, it must have been Nellie, gave them a treat. And must have regretted it bitterly afterward, mopping up the mess—water, soapsuds, Mother's champagne-colored bath oil, a jar of green shampoo. You nasty filthy pigs, just look at you, Nellie shouted, aren't you two something!—the *devil!*

Poking in the laundry. In the wicker hamper. Kirsten's white cotton panties with their yellow-stained crotch. Rather like his own, wasn't it? He stared. He sniffed. Yes. Ugly. *Her.* Later there were bloodstains, brownish stains. And he overheard (he couldn't help overhearing) Isabel accuse Kirsten of being unclean, of having dirty slovenly habits, not bathing frequently enough, not wearing a sanitary pad, for Christ's sake what was wrong with her?—soaking her panties, staining her slacks, her skirt, the sheets on her bed, even the mattress. Are you doing this to upset me? Isabel asked. Are you doing this to mock me?

(One evening Owen overheard Isabel and her friends—Claudia and Tony Di Piero and a young Swedish beauty with a charming accent —talking about children, children who grew up too quickly or children who would not grow up at all. Isabel complained in her slumberous astonished voice that she was now eligible to be a grandmother. . . . Isabel Halleck, a *grandmother.* Poor unhappy Kirsten had just had her first period.

Naturally there were exclamations and sympathetic murmurs and an amused query or two. But then Claudia Lleyn pointed out that Isabel was misstating the situation, wasn't she?—since her son Owen could father a child, after all he must be fourteen or fifteen years old at the youngest. You seem to have overlooked your son, Claudia said. Why?

Isabel laughed in surprise. And said: I don't know. I really don't know. I never thought of it—of him. It was just Kirsten's bleeding that made me realize . . .)

Did I ever tell you, Owen asks her, impulsively, about a conversation I once overheard? Mother and Mrs. Lleyn and Tony Di Piero . . . a few years ago . . . you must have been about twelve years old. Did I ever tell you?

Pranks, jokes, obsessions. Kirsten Halleck at the age of four, her small pretty face encrusted with makeup from Isabel's dressing table: what a sight! A darling little clown! Golden-beige putty, pink rouge, lurid scarlet lipstick smeared so thickly on her lips it looked like a Halloween get-up. And how her eyes glowed with mischief! She had smeared silvery-green eyeshadow on her eyelids, unevenly, and messed about with Isabel's mascara brush too—so *precocious.* The room of adults opened to receive her, she ran boldly and blindly into their midst, one strap of her white nightgown slipping from her shoulder. A tall dusky-skinned man in a turban stooped to peer into her heated little face and pronounce her a beauty: Just like her mother. And General Kempe, not such a notorious drunk in those days, but rumored to be one of the President's most valuable unofficial advisers, dear General Kempe tried to take feverish little Kirsten onto his lap—but she squealed and squirmed free. (For someone from another part of the house was in pursuit of her. It might have been Nellie, or Sara, Sara from Barbados who believed in voodoo, and vampires and zombies, and who threatened both Kirsten and Owen with "secret" ways of punishing bad children.) Look at this-here! Look at the little beauty! What is *this*—Miss Baby America? Esther Jackson, the columnist for the *Journal,* Madame LaPorte, the French Ambassador's young wife, Anthony Di Piero in a white linen suit and a pale blue near-transparent shirt, Senator Parr showing his gums as he chuckled with drunken delight: What a darling little monkey! But isn't it past bedtime? Someone tried to pull up Kirsten's shoulder strap, someone else tried to stop her (for she was running wild, giggling, colliding with legs, upsetting drinks and hors d'oeuvres trays), someone said irritably: What the *hell*—as Kirsten knocked a cigar out of puffy fingers, crying *'Scusa! 'Scusa me!* which always made everyone laugh. She had not only smeared several layers of honey-colored mud on her face, and broken the tip of Isabel's scarlet lipstick on her mouth, and done something atrocious with her eyes: she had also doused herself with perfume from that heavy crystal jar someone had brought back from Marrakesh as a gift for Isabel, and she had looped several of Isabel's necklaces around her neck. What a lark! What an imaginative child! *Isn't* she charming! —But the unsmiling wife of Chief Justice Frazer pushed Kirsten away from her fat stockinged legs, seeing nothing charming, perhaps, about the child; in fact she may even have given her a secret little pinch, hard. And Jack Fair the architect drawled unconvincingly: A bold little beauty, isn't she? Quite an actress. Long-haired mustachioed Mr. Max the clothing designer, a bronzed young beauty from one of the Mideast embassies, Mrs. Degler in claret-colored velveteen pants and heavy Indian jewelry—Isn't she darling!—that's Kirsten!—but don't

let her hurt herself, the poor child is overheated—catch her—Where's
Mother? Where's Daddy? Maurie is out of town, in fact he is out of the
country, on official business, but Isabel is in close pursuit of her child,
Isabel laughing with what appears to be only faintly exasperated delight
—Kirsten, Kirsten dear—*Kirsten*—stop—come here—what on earth
have you done to yourself—Isabel in a billowing Moroccan kaftan that
looks as if it has been threaded with gold, yes, surely it *has* been
threaded with gold, and gold earrings swing from her ears, and gold
chains from her neck, beautiful Isabel Halleck who looks far too young
to be a mother of even so young a child, laughing, crying—Oh, please
stop her, she's supposed to be in bed, I can't imagine how this was
allowed to happen upstairs— Kirsten is caught, Kirsten wrenches free,
knowing slyly that her mother's guests don't want a hysterical child to
pummel and kick at them, knowing that no real adult strength will be
used against her—until later, until tomorrow, when Mother will punish:
but that has nothing to do with tonight. So Kirsten squirms free and
runs, shrieking with laughter, she is feverish, she is bold, unpredictable
in her swervings and duckings as a hornet, the nightgown almost falling
off her shoulder—and in the drawing room, by the fireplace, several men
turn to stare at her in astonishment, unsmiling, *not* evidently charmed
—but suddenly there is Nick, Nick Martens, Uncle Nick, striding toward
her, stooping and clapping his hands, smiling, grinning, Nick who
sweeps her up in his arms and holds her kicking and screaming—Who
have we *here*, who is this *naughty girl*, downstairs after her bedtime,
isn't she?—but now the game is over—

She squirms and kicks and shrieks with laughter as Uncle Nick
carries her out of the room, and upstairs, scolding, kissing her forehead,
Bedtime now, sweetheart, bedtime, game's over, playtime's over—*stop*
that kicking—bedtime and night and teddy bear and sleep and all's well
— At the top of the stairs he pretends to be angry—little Kirsten has
kicked him in the stomach, little Kirsten has smeared some of the scarlet
lipstick on his white shirt front—he gives her an impatient shake and
sets her down and is evidently talking to someone else—Isabel—Isabel
who has run noiselessly up the stairs behind them: Jesus Almighty
Christ, can't you control your children, can't you control *anything*—

Of course he isn't serious, he isn't really angry. Nick with his
teeth set hard, his face flushed brick-red, his brown eyes narrowed so
that the irises wink like tiny fish—he cannot really be angry at Kirsten,
whom he adores. —Look at my shirt, Nick is saying, God damn it, Isabel,
how did she get downstairs? She's been running wild, she might have
injured herself—

Isabel slaps and scolds, Isabel is nearly sobbing, but then Sara
with her black fist of a face comes up behind them, panting, What a bad

little girl, what a little devil, I'll take her now, Mrs. Halleck, I don't know *how* she got away, she was asleep when I looked, I swear she was asleep when I looked, Mrs. Halleck—

Suddenly Kirsten is too exhausted to resist; she goes limp; big perspiring muttering Sara picks her up in her arms; the night is over; everything is over. All the wonderful makeup will be cleaned off, the necklaces will be taken from her, she will have to endure the second bath of the evening, and more scolding, always more scolding, and then bed —while downstairs, throughout the house, the party continues.

Kirsten looks over Sara's shoulder as she is being hauled away. Mother and Uncle Nick are standing at the head of the stairs, they have already forgotten her, Nick is saying something to Mother as Mother adjusts one of her gold pendulum earrings, her beautiful bronze-pink mouth thick with resentment, and then Mother interrupts to say: Go in Maurie's closet and take one of Maurie's shirts, please, I'm sure you can find something decent, I'm *sure* you won't be humiliated downstairs—

Suddenly Kirsten cries out: I don't want to go to bed! Come say goodnight! Kiss goodnight! *Kiss goodnight!*

But Nick and Isabel do not hear. Sara carries Kirsten into the nursery, shaking her hard, grunting, saying: Stop that bawling—shut your goddam mouth! *Aren't* you a hot little devil! We all had more'n enough of you for one night!

Pranks and tricks and games. Your little girl is just unusually energetic and imaginative, Isabel is counseled, in fact I think you should be rather pleased, you might enroll her in a modern dance class for preschoolers; but then again she is counseled: Your little girl is immature and aggressive and perhaps even potentially disturbed, she has no patience with children slower than herself, she's restless when attention isn't focused specifically on her, if she can't be first she doesn't want to play the game, she even bullies older children until they turn on her and hurt *her* . . . it's been a pattern all this year.

Showing off, clowning, high spirits, monkeyshines. Unusual in a girl? Silly faces. Silly postures. Reckless on the playground swings, on the slide, the teeter-totter. Pretending to know how to swim—and swimming toward the deep end of the pool.

Fourth grade, fifth grade, seventh grade, ninth . . .

An introvert, a loner, passive-aggressive, bright, quick, inventive, unsocial, remarkable facility for language, troublemaker, ringleader, sarcastic, naturally good-humored, witty, funny, comedian, clown, in fact voted class clown at Hays, her second and final year at that prestigious school, depressive personality, manic interludes, prone to fantasizing, high I.Q., wide range of interests, unusual maturity, sympathy for overseas orphans, project on Vietnamese children, project on John Brown, perfectionist, impatient, immature, sloppy work habits, inability to listen to instructions, hostile to authority, unfunny in fact potentially dangerous sense of humor (telephoning school from a pay phone, reporting a time bomb on the premises set to go off in an hour; describing in detail a man who tried to force her into a car with him who turned out to resemble, very closely, the President of the United States; breaking a plastic vial filled with red vegetable dye over the head of the most disliked—and best—player on a rival hockey team, so that it looked for a few terrible minutes as if the girl might be bleeding to death from a head wound; telling visiting alums at Hays School, and then Miss Pickett's, that lesbian relations were common among girls and faculty members and if a girl chose not to participate, like Kirsten, she was cruelly "ostracized").

She prowls through the other girls' rooms, pokes through drawers and closets and trunks, appropriating items occasionally (fountain pens, bottles of nail polish, love letters, snapshots, cigarettes, candy, pills, dope) as if seeking, in others' untidy but resolutely normal lives, signs or messages or consolations, *things*, to instruct her. Sometimes she is caught, more often not: if caught, she never confesses. Never explain, never apologize, she says airily, it is an expression she first heard at a family dinner, from Nick Martens, her father's schoolboy friend Nick, Nick her mother's dear friend, Nick her brother Owen's godfather, her own Uncle Nick for many years until, abruptly, she stopped calling him that absurd name: He wasn't an uncle of hers, was he? She had her own uncles. She once sent a glamorous photograph of Isabel Halleck found in a drawer to the Midatlantic Photo-Journalists' Beauty Contest where it placed second, to Isabel's horror, and to the delight of the Washington media, the feature pages, the "human interest-funny story" slot of the day, Isabel de Benavente Halleck the hostess, the society woman, the wife of the Director of the Federal Commission for the Ministry of Justice, debutante, daughter of, partygoer, Mrs. Halleck in a black bikini posing with an absurd flower-bedecked straw hat slanting over one eye, lips far too dark for this decade, eyes too owlishly madeup: but beautiful enough, evidently, to have scored with the Midatlantic Photo-Journalists' judges.

She cheats on examinations but then—doesn't everyone? Sometimes she is too lazy to study, or becomes obsessively involved in a single project (the project on that distant "Halleck" John Brown, for instance, done in ninth grade, thirty-five pages long, thoroughly researched and carefully organized and even carefully typed: earning her an A+ from her delighted history teacher but certainly contributing to that term's failure in French and C— in geometry), or becomes what she calls "disillusioned" with a subject or with a teacher or with an entire class of students. . . . She is militantly idealistic: everyone she knows is "selfish" and "spoiled" and "corrupted by affluence." But she wants her allowance increased. She wants a new pair of calfskin leather boots, $210 at the Hyde Shoppe. She wants her own horse, she knows exactly the horse her parents can buy for her (a friend has inexplicably tired of it—the most beautiful chestnut mare with three white stockings and a white star on her forehead), she wants one of those wonderful big coarse Guatemalan macramé shoulder bags—the real thing, and not a stupid American (or Taiwan) imitation. Once she tricked someone into giving her a key to Tony Di Piero's apartment, and she let herself in, and prowled through the rooms, and though she did not steal a thing, she did *not* steal a thing, she did something rather naughty and messy and has always wondered, with a thrill of apprehension, when her mother's friend Tony will *really* demand retribution. . . . But it has been some years now. Three or four. A small lifetime.

Her latest prank, her latest game, springs out of her obsessive sense of herself as a *grieving unforgiving daughter.*

Playing it for all it's worth, Owen thinks sullenly. Daddy's girl. Hanging on his arm, clamoring for attention. Love me love me love me see how unhappy I am see the authentic tears in my big gray eyes.

Insomniac, anorexic, gay and chattering nonstop, mute for days, not showering, not changing clothes, rude to her roommate, weeping in her roommate's arms, sending Owen that repulsive message.

It would serve you right, Owen considers telling her, if I reported to Isabel that you really *are* sick—the "ambulatory pneumonia" has infected your frontal lobes and they might have to be removed.

It's worse than we thought, Mother, Owen says over the phone, his voice tense, you'd better fly up to New York and take the kid out of school immediately.

Yes? Owen? She's sick—?

She's sick, Mother. As you suspected. Very sick.

Kirsten is sick?

Very sick, Mother.

What are you saying, Owen—

He begins to shout: The kid is sick is what I'm saying, Isabel, in monosyllabic words, the kid had better be shot up with Thorazine, strapped in a straitjacket for her own good, I wouldn't bullshit you, Isabel, it's serious, it's the real thing at last, you don't want more publicity, do you, for Christ's sake, too much dope, too many uppers, she's turning into an A-head, Quaaludes too, splashing around in Brean Down swamp, shall I put her on the line, Mother, and you can hear for yourself her babbling and keening and whimpering—her absurd outrageous accusations—

Accusations? Isabel would interrupt. Accusations? But of whom—?

Herewith, the most inventive of her pranks, a prize-winning prank in Owen's judgment: one Saturday morning she signed out of Eyre with an elaborate tale of an appointment with a Manhattan orthodontist, and she took a cab not to the train station but to the Thruway entrance a few miles outside town, where, being young, and attractive, and clearly alone, she was forced to wait no more than five minutes before an accommodating motorist (a male) picked her up. He let her off at Purchase, so that, armed secretly with a razor, she could spend some hours prowling through the stacks of the library of the State University of New York, in search of newspaper photographs of her father's *betrayers* and *murderers*, which she would later tape to a sheet of stiff white construction paper, to be sent to her brother Owen, with an appropriate message. (Did Owen half-know, did Owen guess—? No. Yes. Not really. But as he tore open the gaudily inked manila envelope his hands shook, for it was never the case that his sister troubled to write to him, oh very rarely, a postcard maybe, a comic valentine maybe, and once for his birthday a card with a teddy bear on front, Happy Birthday Cuddly One, and since Maurie's death nothing.)

Newspaper photographs and captions: *Isabel de Benavente Halleck the wife of . . . daughter of . . . financier and philanthropist . . . Photographed here in a Dior gown of fuchsia silk . . . Cream rose pearls, matching earrings . . . One of Washington's most popular hostesses . . . Cochairwoman of the board of the Women's Auxiliary of the Smithsonian. . . .* The occasion was a charity ball for the Smithsonian. A big celebrity night in Washington. Politicians, television performers, high-ranking bureaucrats, a few "statesmen," White House people including the President and the First Lady, liaison people, party hacks, go-betweens, film stars, public relations specialists, foreign ambassadors and their wives, elderly Washington widows . . . the usual crowd. And Isabel Halleck photographed for the society pages of the *Washington Post* in her elegant Dior gown. (The photograph did her justice, in a sense, since it showed a beautiful masklike face, lightly smiling, triumphant. Yet it could not suggest her porcelain skin, so tirelessly creamed and oiled and prepared for the eye; her aquiline nose;

her perfect teeth; her terrifying composure. The crepey skin beneath her eyes had been expertly snipped away a few years ago—a rather premature stratagem, her friends thought. Owen had not really noticed the crepey skin, nor had he noticed its absence. For some years he had had a certain difficulty in simply "seeing" his mother—looking directly at her.)

Adulteress-pig. Bitch. Murderer. So Kirsten had scrawled in purple Magic Marker ink, around the photograph. *She is yours,* she had scrawled with a swooping arrow aimed at Isabel, *you know what to do.*

And bloodstains. Were there bloodstains, or were those smears just ink . . . Owen stared, repulsed. Fascinated. This was to be one of the memorable events of his life: not because the message from his sister surprised him but because it did not surprise him very much.

The other photograph, also a newspaper photograph, was of Nick Martens. Of course. Nick was shaking hands with the President of the United States. The occasion must have been last fall's swearing-in ceremony, both men looked older than their ages, with something querulous and puffy about their smiling mouths. Owen studied the photograph and wondered whether he would have recognized his handsome godfather— the likeness was so poor. Nick shaking hands with the President. At last. It was said about Nick in the circle to which he and the Hallecks belonged that he was "luridly ambitious"—but the expression was always uttered with a sort of amused awe, and covertly; and in any case Owen had thought that ambition—lurid or otherwise—was hardly disfiguring in one so boldly equipped for success. Owen's father had helped Nick immeasurably in his career, by bringing him to Washington, to the Commission, but it was also true that Nick had helped Mr. Halleck immeasurably—surely that was no secret. But it was no secret, either, that Nick had more or less shoved Mr. Halleck out and, after his death, stepped over his body to claim his position. *Nicholas Martens at last Tuesday's swearing-in ceremony . . . Director of the Commission for the Ministry of Justice . . . A former associate of . . .* Bloodstains, purple ink, *The murderer is MINE,* arrows pointing at Nick's head, *I KNOW WHAT TO DO & WILL DO IT.*

Of course Owen ripped it up. Immediately.

And afterward he told his friend, managing to smile normally: Just a nut.

But what do you know, what can you prove, Owen is asking, Owen is begging, Kirsten, please . . . They are walking on a narrow path, single-file, high above the pocked, heaving, beautiful Hudson River, miles from town. Kirsten goes ahead. Kirsten walks quickly, not minding the mud that sucks at her shoes. Not minding the glaring late-winter sky, the wind, nearby woods alive with dark flapping shapes: grackles, starlings, flocking birds, calling to one another, their cries forlorn and angry in tone but, so Owen reasons, so Owen must reason, no more than simple bird calls, the necessary sounds of communication.

A high furious chattering din. But Kirsten is oblivious, Kirsten walks swiftly ahead, seeing nothing, not listening to Owen, hardly aware of Owen.

You aren't well, he says, you're drawing me into something that's sick and crazy and absurd and hopeless, there were no witnesses to the accident, the official cause of death was heart failure, do you think someone forced him off the road, do you think someone forced him to kill himself . . . Forced him to get drunk every night . . . ! Owen wants to grab hold of Kirsten's shoulder and stop her but a hand seems to be pressing hard and flat against his own chest and his breath comes with difficulty. *Hypocrite, coward, liar,* in your camel's-hair blazer with the university insignia, in your turtleneck sweater, Owen Halleck the very best of second-best, Owen Halleck the man of the family, *liar, hypocrite, big phony shit,* his wallet is stuffed with bills of all denominations sent in apricot-tinted envelopes from his mother's pretty little Queen Anne desk, usually without an accompanying note—though of course this is "loose" or "extra" cash in addition to his monthly checks. (One of those checks comes from Isabel's accountant, the other comes directly from the bank, from a trust established by his grandfather Halleck.) Owen with his secret lardy thighs, his petty academic triumphs, papers to write and examinations to take and contacts—that is, "friends"—to make, to be of aid to him in later—that is, "adult"—life. Owen who loved his father, in a manner of speaking, but is terribly embarrassed by all the . . . all the unwanted attention.

No one knows where they are, Owen thinks. The two of them. Miles from town. High above the river. No one near, no witnesses.

I don't know you, he shouts. *I don't know you and I don't give a damn about you and I reject everything—everything—about you.*

By the River

The water-soaked body, the nearly submerged car. Night. Soft black mud. A tangle of trees, vines, bushes. The moon would quiver in the surface of the water and in the shattered windshield. Was there a moon?

She broods, she invents. The imagination her teachers have called "remarkable" and sometimes even "disturbing" has now turned itself upon the fact of her father's death. The *fact* and its consequences. Its hypothetical antecedents.

Wandering across the campus green, prowling the woods, the hiking trail, the thorny path above the river. Brooding, inventing, talking to herself. And sometimes to Owen who is her twin—her twin in a manner of speaking.

Owen who will not be able to resist, finally. Owen who will be her salvation.

For they *must* be punished—the two of them—the adulterous couple.

For of course their father had been murdered.

Could anything be more obvious!

She broods, she invents, she recalls with alarming clarity certain scenes from her girlhood, half-glimpsed visions of Isabel and Nick, half-overheard conversations. (For a while there was Tony Di Piero. Another of Maurie's "friends." A boyhood friend, in fact, just like Nick. And there have been other men, Kirsten supposes, after all her mother is a beautiful woman, a beautiful energetic restless ambitious woman, after all she grew up in Washington and knows everyone, and everyone knows her. . . . But Nicholas Martens is the one.)

Poor Kirsten Halleck whom none of the girls likes, poor Kirsten Halleck with only her roommate to tolerate her (and everyone in the school knows how *nice* Hannah is—how kind, how sweet, how patient, how long-suffering), wandering around like a wraith, skinny and anemic: is she sick? is she a little crazy? does she want us to feel sorry for her? does she want us to feel guilty? is it just another of her acts? Last year she was sarcastic and talked constantly, interrupted other people, knew all the answers, curt and bored and maddening with her drawl which was intended to be mock-Southern; this year she's mute—won't even speak in class when her teachers call on her. (Yes, everyone is being very kind. Yes, everyone is sympathetic. Of course there is talk behind her back, particularly last fall there was a great deal of talk, but nothing very malicious, nothing extraordinarily cruel. Jokes now and then. Innuendos. Allusions. But never to her face—only behind her back or out of earshot. A note or two in her mailbox, maybe. Nothing extraordinarily cruel.)

Poor Kirsten in her soiled windbreaker and jogger's shoes. Staring for fifteen solid minutes at the classy Maillol nude in front of Eyre Hall. One January morning in the snow. Big-eyed, skinny-faced, a profile like a hungry bird's. Friendless except for Hannah—and Hannah is notorious at the Academy for being exceptionally nice. (But then Hannah lost her mother a few years ago. "Lost her mother"—as the saying goes. So they probably have a lot in common, a lot to talk about.) Circling the statue, her hands in her pockets. Brooding. Chewing at her lower lip. Then walking slowly across the hockey field . . . bareheaded despite the wind. Sitting alone in the dining hall, pretending to read a book. That small white prim insufferable face. Starving herself. Fainting in gym class and on the stairs. Silent in class, her arms folded tight across her breasts. Staring. Smirking. Faint lines in her forehead. An odor of inconsolable grief, stale as unwashed clothes. Alone and stubborn and lightheaded. Wouldn't come to the telephone when Mrs. Halleck called. Four or five times—and everyone was wondering: What's wrong with Kirsten *now?* Running a temperature of 103 degrees when they finally persuaded her to check into the infirmary. Her lips parched and cracked, her eyes rolling in her head, half-carried out of the dorm by Han and Phyllis Dorsey, the young athletics instructor.

Hey look, Kirsten, Phyllis Dorsey said, you're trying to get expelled, is that it? Or just trying to kill yourself?

One of the school wits—in fact, a former crony—made the remark that if anyone's father had to kill himself, who's a better candidate than smart-ass Kirsten Halleck?—and the wicked jest (which did arouse a few startled giggles) may or may not have found its way to Kirsten.

She ignores her enemies. Doesn't see them. Hello Kirsten, good morning Kirsten, how's it going Kirsten—but she doesn't hear.

Hurrying headlong down the stairs.

Excusing herself from history class, the pains in her stomach so intense she had to walk doubled over: No I'm all right no please I said *please* I'll be all right I don't need any help thank you. (*So I did eat breakfast & seemed to enjoy it,* she noted with satisfaction in her journal, *but my stomach rejected it & I had to go to the bathroom & vomit,* underscoring the word *vomit* several times.)

Thinking. Brooding. Inventing. Dreaming. Populating her head with fantasy figures that are, in fact, "real" figures. Isabel and Maurie and Nick Martens. Isabel and Maurie and Nick Martens. Or is it Isabel and Nick—and Maurice Halleck. Or (since they were boyhood friends) Maurice Halleck and Nicholas Martens—and Isabel.

Brooding, staring sightlessly, chewing at her lower lip, running her hands brutally through her hair. (And what has she done with her eyebrows? Plucked most of them out? But why? Not even Hannah can say.) She recoils from her French teacher's sympathetic touch—actually flinches (with somewhat exaggerated disdain) when the woman rests a hand on her shoulder. Trudging alone across the bleak hockey field, sitting alone in the glass cube of a library, hunched over her cooling food in the dining hall, alone, very much alone, though there are a number of "other" sad cases this year, girls in and out of the infirmary, girls whose fathers come unexpected to visit them and take them out to breakfast at the Molly Pitcher or the Holiday Inn on the Thruway, and maybe don't bring them back: girls who spend a great deal of time crying, or resolutely not crying, and, if they smoke pot, smoke it to be caught and expelled and sent back home, to more tears, or whatever: once they disappear, it is always some weeks before their roommates learn what has happened.

But Kirsten avoids these girls, and they give every impression of avoiding her. Though, perhaps, none of them exactly "sees" the others.

Kirsten spends most of her time alone. But today—as everyone has noticed, with surprise, and approval, and interest—her good-looking brother has come to visit her, up from Princeton, is it?—or maybe he's at Yale. Yes—*quite* good-looking.

Kirsten remembers not the fastidiously prepared corpse in the satin-lined brass-trimmed mahogany casket—the "man" with the subtly rouged cheeks, the resolutely unsurprised eyes, the stitched and placid mouth—but the living person: she "remembers" with hallucinatory clarity the warm, still-living, still-struggling, panicked body in the car, jammed up behind the steering wheel, trapped, as the swamp water rushes in, as the windshield explodes backward in transparent slivers. The pain in the chest, she has been told, the pain of angina pectoris, is like the kick of a horse's hoof—that sudden, that terrible, that overwhelming. Choking and gasping for breath. His second attack, or might it have been, secretly, his third. . . . And the high alcoholic content of the blood. . . .

(Since when was Maurie Halleck a drinker, people asked, astonished. Maurie Halleck a *drinker* . . . ?)

The terror of it. The helplessness.

And one might imagine a car behind him, a car that had been following closely, for hours, for days and even weeks, in pursuit of him; now speeding past the broken guard rail, the curve in the road, heading up the road to Meckleberg—utterly blameless.

(For there was talk that his life might be in danger. Not for the first time, of course, in his career. Rumors, gossip, vaporous speculations: no one willing to talk openly, for obvious reasons. *So they got Halleck,* someone probably said, reading about the "suicide" in the morning paper, *it was only a matter of time,* Kirsten can hear the words, Kirsten can imagine the facial expression, the mixture of pity and alarm and concern, all ephemeral, held in suspension for perhaps a full minute. Before the page is turned.)

I don't believe it, Isabel says quietly, no it can't be, it can't be, her voice starting to rise, her face draining white, your father wouldn't do anything like that, your father isn't the kind of man who . . .

Later comes the angry weeping, the hysteria. Her eyeballs roll back in her skull, her skin goes a true dead-white, suddenly hideous. I can't believe it, I won't believe it, she cries, he loved me and he loved his children, he would never do a thing like that intentionally, she screams, her "Spanish" blood rising, something furious and wasplike in her sorrow, so that her children turn away, frightened. *He loved me—he would never do a thing like that.*

(Her surprise is quite convincing, Kirsten must admit. Her consternation, her grief. Even the anger. *Quite* convincing. . . . But then her father, the infamous Luis de Benavente, was so gifted a liar he had withstood the interrogations of three high-powered committees—two from the Securities and Exchange Commission, another from the Senate, on highly complicated matters involving foreign investments.)

The weeks pass, Isabel's emotion narrows, but also deepens, until it becomes a swift steady stream of bitterness neither Kirsten nor Owen can bear: your father has ruined our lives, she weeps, your father has betrayed me, he should never have become involved in that ugly business, he should never have stepped in over his head. . . . It is always *your father*, Kirsten notes. *Your father* was a very sick man . . . *your father* was a fool . . . *your father* has done this deliberately to injure me . . . to punish me. . . . *Your father* should never have accepted money from anyone: what could he have been thinking of!

Your father, your father. Kirsten flinches at the words. She and Owen are to blame too, somehow: the disgraced man is, after all, *your father.*

Did you love him, Mother? Kirsten wants to ask.

But she will not. She cannot. Years ago she overheard Isabel on the telephone, talking to a friend, male or female Kirsten did not know. What good did love ever do *me?* she inquired in a droll flat charmless voice.

Father in his green plaid bathrobe, an old birthday or Christmas gift from Kirsten. Stained cuffs, twisted sash. His bedroom slippers loose on his pale bony feet. Sad sallow-skinned Maurie Halleck with his inflamed eyes (from weeping? drinking? sleepless nights reading his Bible?), monkeyish face, thinning hair. Father in his bachelor apartment on the fifth floor of the Potomac Tower, out noisy Wisconsin Avenue, miles from the beautiful house at 18 Röcken. Estranged, temporarily separated, Isabel has asked him courteously to pack his things and leave, he is gentleman enough to obey, kindly, baffled, defeated, doomed.

Kirsten is to visit him six times. She counts them: six. And each an ordeal.

Father living alone in that apartment smelling of whiskey and slept-in unlaundered clothes. He is dying, she notes that immediately, she has always been a perceptive child, quick to feel the stake through the heart. But her primary emotion is resentment: How could Father let Isabel do this to him?—how could he allow a woman *like that* to affect him so powerfully?

The weakness of men. Contemptible weakness. *Love,* they call it. But perhaps there are other words.

Pacing through the living room, the tiny kitchen, the bedroom. Making his way amid the bargain-basement furniture. (Kirsten has never seen a floor lamp—brass!—crook-necked!—so blatantly ugly.) He drinks black coffee, he pours whiskey into the cup, does he imagine he is deceiving his daughter? She sees, she smells, she knows everything. And is deeply ashamed. And will never forgive him.

From the living room window there is a view of the tower of a Holiday Inn Motor Hotel just across the street. Maurie never thinks to pull the blinds.

He lies awake much of the night, reading the Bible, trying to read Sophocles, Aeschylus, Euripides . . . at first in Greek (for he studied Greek once, long ago at the Bauer School, and had acquired a modest reading facility) and then in translation; but it is very difficult to concentrate. The Greeks sound at times too contemporary, he wonders if he is misreading the text. So he drinks himself into a stupor, into "sleep," which he tries to prolong well into midmorning. For after all (as he explains to his daughter who is stricken with embarrassment) he *is* on a leave of absence from the Commission. In a week or two, when he is settled, when he is better organized, he will begin work on interests of his own—old ongoing interests like the reform of American legal proceedings on the most basic levels—city and county; human rights legislation on a worldwide scale; and other things—other very important things he has had to set aside for many years.

He does not use his daughter to seek out information on his wife —for which she is grateful. Nor does he ask about Nick Martens. (About whom Kirsten knows nothing. Isn't Nick, Uncle Nick, rather conspicuously absent from the Halleck household these days?) He asks about her new school, he asks about her friends, her roommate, is she going to visit colleges, is she happy, what does she plan to study. . . . A dying man, Kirsten thinks, frightened and angry.

Small broken veins in the eyes. Puckered yellowish skin. Talking nervously of the Potomac Tower and its waiting list and how fortunate he was to get an apartment though the separation is only temporary and something should be worked out in another month or two; Isabel may even want him to sell the house and buy something smaller, a townhouse, maybe, a condominium.

My God, Kirsten wants to laugh, Isabel will never sell her prestige home! Don't you know Isabel?

His words trail off into silence.

Kirsten's eyes fill with tears. *Why the hell don't you fight back,* she wants to shout.

She visits him six times, dutifully, reluctantly, out of love, and each visit is more difficult, he is drinking heavily, he repeats his questions (her new school in upstate New York, which colleges is she applying to), he speaks incoherently of matters she doesn't understand or has yet to learn about (confidential information that is being leaked to the press, unkind speculations about the future of Maurice Halleck and his closest associates in Washington), he drifts onto the subject of God, prayer, sin, "salvation." . . .

He asks Kirsten if she will join him in prayer. For a few minutes. Prayer. Speaking to God. For what is "speaking to God" but absolute stillness of mind, the mind and the heart united . . . at rest. No yearning, no struggle, no desire.

Excuse me, Kirsten murmurs, her skin warm. I don't understand.

Maurie half-closes his eyes and recites: *You have been told, man, what is good, and what does the Lord demand of you but to do justice and love kindness and to walk humbly with your God. . . .*

He asks her again to join him in prayer. She cannot answer. Father. Doomed man. I love you but . . . I love you. . . .

Will you join me in prayer, Kirsten? For a few minutes? We can pray silently.

She manages to murmur, her face burning: No.

That's what I told him, she says. I told him no.

Owen inclines his head near. His expression is neutral; one might almost call it professional.

He asked me to pray with him, he needed me and I said no, Kirsten says carefully, I told him I had a tennis date.

A tennis date, Owen repeats slowly. Well. That's all right.

No it isn't.

You couldn't have known . . .

No it isn't all right. It isn't.

You couldn't have known what would happen.

I knew.

You didn't *know*.

I said I had a tennis date.

Did you have a tennis date?

I couldn't breathe in that place.

Of course not.

He was drinking. It was just past noon and he'd been drinking for a long time already.

It wasn't your fault.

I told him—no. I just said no. Like that. *No.*

He couldn't have blamed you.

He *didn't* blame me.

He didn't blame *me*—when I said I couldn't meet him in New York.

I didn't have a tennis date, I was just headed for the club. I didn't know who the hell would be there.

He wouldn't have known that.

He didn't care, he wasn't judging me. Or anyone. He was drunk.

It wasn't your fault, what happened—it had nothing to do with you.

Or with you.

Nothing to do with us.

I could have stopped it, though. So could you.

We couldn't have saved him. I mean—we didn't know.

I knew. I could have done something.

No.

Yes.

No. Don't be childish.

I said *yes.*

I said *no.* He wanted to go to Africa once, didn't he, as a kid, he wanted to be a missionary or something like Albert Schweitzer.

What has that got to do with it?

The prayer, the God-business.

What has *that* got to do with it?

You're a greedy little pig, Owen says suddenly, smiling, grinning, gobbling it all down, aren't you—a nympho—always Daddy's special child, Daddy's sweetheart—

What?

Sucking up all the grief for yourself, aren't you?—*look at me, look at me,* big-deal Kirsten, Daddy's little girl, taking it all so fucking hard—

What—what are you saying?

You know what I'm saying.

I don't—   .

You know exactly what I'm saying.

I *don't.*

Owen lays his hands on her shoulders, rather heavily. As if to keep her in place. He says: You're sick, you really *are* sick, I'm going to take you back to the dormitory and see about a doctor. A real doctor —a private doctor—someone in town.

Get your hands off me, Kirsten murmurs.

You shouldn't be out in the wind, in this ridiculous place, Owen says.

It isn't ridiculous—it's beautiful. I come here all the time.

I bet you do.

I do.

I agree, I agree, yes, I'm not contesting the fact.

Let me go, take your hands off me, Kirsten says, her eyes bright with tears, you big phony shit, you liar, you hypocrite—

You see?—you're not well, you're sick. I'm going to take you back.

Go back yourself.

I'm not leaving you here.

—coward, preppie-asshole—

You're crazy, you exaggerate everything.

You don't exaggerate, do you!—not you. Not Owen Jay.

You couldn't have saved him and I couldn't have saved him and that's a fact we'll have to live with—

Oh, you pompous shit, you should hear yourself!—talking before the court—you should be on tape—

—like the fact of his death and how he died and what has been said about him and will continue to be said—

He called *you*, you said—he called you at school—

Yes, all right, fine, I'll talk about it, Owen says, still gripping her shoulders hard, raising his voice against the din of the nearby birds, I'm not particularly proud of it but anyway: father was in New York early in May and he telephoned and asked if I could come up, take a train up, we could have lunch or dinner together, talk about some important things, we'd been out of communication lately for which he apologized —and he *did* apologize, at agonizing length; and I told him no. I said a lot more than that, as I always do, it isn't my style simply to say no, but it evaporated away to no, no thank you, *no* thank you, Father I can't handle this right now. I can't handle you.

Yes, says Kirsten, smiling queerly. Go on.

There's nothing more to say.

There is. What did you tell him, exactly?—I'm assuming this was your last conversation with him.

Yes, it was my last conversation with him. I told him I was in the midst of studying for an exam.

Which exam?

Economics 331. The Economics of Public Policy.

And how did you do?

A minus.

Not bad.

I'd hoped for an A. I'd been sucking up to the bastard all semester. It might have been lower.

It *would* have been lower, if I'd gone to New York.

So you saved yourself that at least. A B plus or even a B on your transcript.

Which might have kept me out of Harvard Law.

Yes, right. Where Father went.

And Nick. And virtually everyone.

But what exactly did you say?

I fumbled around and said I wasn't sleeping well these days, the pressure of exams and papers and grades, the usual thing, undergraduate crises, he probably went through it himself, and of course I was concerned about matters at home—

Of course.

—since Mother never called and he never called and I was so goddam busy *I* never called—that sort of thing. I was having anxiety bouts.

And you're so large: *that* must be something to see.

Large people succumb to anxiety as readily as small people. Prick an ox and he bleeds—you know the thinking.

I know the reference.

You know the drift of my thought.

Yes. I do. You told him no.

I told him no. In five thousand words or more. Just as you did.

Actually I didn't require five thousand words. I stammered and looked at the floor and couldn't think of anything except that I had a tennis date. I'm not very articulate. Did I tell you, I went up there in my tennis outfit? I prepped the act up beforehand.

But I *did* get into H.L.S.

Father would be proud if he knew.

You think he doesn't—somehow—know?

I think maybe he doesn't. I think that's what we are talking about. I mean—I think that's the basic text here.

The basic text is very much along those lines.

But you're going to ask how.

How—?

How we are supposed to maneuver.

Maneuver—?

Weapons, strategy. That sort of thing.

I don't think I'll ask. I think I'll tromp back through the mud to my car and drive up to Conn College for my weekend. My "real" weekend.

Go fuck yourself, then.

I don't have to. That's a point too.

All right—go. I'll stay here awhile.

I don't think so.

Yes, the hell with it. Go on. And tell Mother anything you want.

I'm not going to leave you here, that might not be prudent.

Oh—for Christ's sake.

Let's tromp back together through the mud and have a sandwich in town and then I'll drive off and you can go back to your dorm and rest. Calm down. All right? Or maybe I'll take you to the infirmary. Have your temperature checked.

He never drank before, did he. Wine at dinner. Grapefruit juice, V-8 vegetable juice in those little cans, in a row on the inside of the refrigerator door.

I could hear the ice cubes tinkling, over the phone. Maybe his hand shook.

He didn't actually drink in front of me. I think he even brushed his teeth before I arrived.

He was always so considerate of others. . . .

He was very considerate.

That remark about weapons—

And strategy. Strategy comes first.

—I think I'll strike that remark.

Yes. I know.

If it's agreeable with you.

How well documented must the report to Mother be?

A general outline, maybe a sort of impressionist garbled paragraph.

Do you want to strike it?

I think so. Yes. Your forehead is burning, after all. I can practically taste the inside of your mouth.

Which is—?

Dry. Very dry. In fact parched.

Yes. Parched. And yours?

It hurts to swallow, I must admit.

And so this all negates my—?

Your prepping-up your act? Yes. Maybe.

I don't think it does.

I don't know. But I'll say no.

Just no?

No.

Because I'm running a temperature?—because you aren't?

I didn't say I wasn't, in fact I seem to have said the reverse, but let it go. No.

That simple, that clear?—no?

No.

Kirsten loosens his fingers, pushes his hands away, not hard, not angrily, but with a queer slowed thoughtfulness. Her face is white and knotted, her eyes are brimming with moisture, possibly from the wind.

It is a late-winter wind, blowing in fitful gusts across the great river.

No meaning—?

No meaning *no.*

She pushes his hands and walks away and says over her shoulder, All right then, goodbye, I'm not going back immediately, I'll be fine, I just want to walk awhile. I walk out here every day.

Owen follows.

Kirsten glances back at him, annoyed.

It's dangerous out here, Owen says.

Oh shit. Go on back.

I don't think I can leave you. I mean—like this.

You can, though. You will.

I don't know.

You will.

I don't think this is settled yet.

Yes. It's over. Go on back.

No. I'm not sure.

Your shoes are getting wet.

My shoes *are* wet.

For Christ's sake, you said no, we both agree no, we both agree you're an asshole liar and a coward and—all right?—we both agree. So it's no. And anyway isn't she waiting?

Isn't who waiting? Owen asks.

Go to hell. Go to *her.*

This isn't settled yet.

It's settled. You told me no.

I told you—*I don't know.*

It's over, it's settled. Go make your report.

No.

I can do it myself. I know what has to be done.

No. You can't.

I will.

Not alone.

Alone.

No—not alone. You can't.

Try me.

You *can't.*

Make your report: tell her everything.

No.

Weapons, strategy—

You can't do it alone.

I will.

We have to—
"We"—?
We can't—
"We"—?

A long time has passed, and still Owen stands, blank, dazed, struck, benumbed: and, when Kirsten says softly, It's all right, you can leave me, you'll be late, isn't she waiting for you?—it is with a look of childlike befuddlement, too simple, in a way too pure, to admit of terror, that he asks: *Isn't who waiting—?*

II. Wild Loughrea

Loughrea, Ontario,

August 1947

The Accident

The accident will finally happen, the canoe will capsize, no one's fault exactly. Why speak of fault, of blame? One of the boys will be thrown against a rock, dragged forward by the current, his body tumbled over and over, light and unresisting as a canvas sack. In fact his skin will become a kind of sack in which bones and flesh and blood are contained —bones, flesh, blood, spirit, life, *being.*

Help me! Save me!

But no: no words. The accident will happen so quickly, the body will be thrown from the canoe so abruptly, no words are possible. Not even terror. Not even surprise.

(What did you feel when it happened? Did you think you were going to die? Did you think you had already died?)

The drizzle of three days has lightened, reluctantly. Streaks of china-blue sky appear, too bright. The canoers' eyes ache. Something is wrong. Maurie, Nick, Tony, Kim. Something is going to happen. Is it Nick's fault for pressing forward, when they had agreed to stop after six hours? Nick the bully, Nick the impatient. Come *on,* murmurs Nick, jabbing his friend Maurie in the ribs, I'm sick of your ugly face, I'm sick of this fucking river, come *on.* Spruce, pine, balsam, piercing shards of sunlight on the water, the spirited rush and hiss of white water, the sudden terror of rocks that are too large, too close together. Where is the passage through?—isn't there a passage through? The map issued by the provincial park promises a channel, common sense promises a channel, it is unthinkable that they won't be able to make it. They have been on the Loughrea for three and a half days and they have another two days ahead and they are exhausted by the beauty of the river, the forest, the massive sky.

Nearing the three-mile stretch of rapids—the long white rapids—about which they had been jocularly warned (you'll get your feet wet, you might have to do some fancy maneuvering), some thirty miles east of Lac Seule, the boys hear the low murmurous white-water sound, the warning sound, a distant avalanche. They should paddle over to one of the banks, they should study the rapids. They should study their map more closely. But Nick wants to keep going. Inertia carries him forward; he is so exhausted he doesn't want to stop. The day has been long, it's past six o'clock, their clothing is soaked, they are edgy and impatient. Tony wipes his face and indicates with an apathetic shrug of his shoulders that he doesn't care: he's ready. Kim laughs and shouts what the hell, making a sucking kissing noise in Nick's direction. What the hell! —come on! We'll be out the other side in two minutes.

Maurie alone sits staring, unable to respond. Nick queries him a second time. He doesn't hear, he is staring ahead, at the swift-running current, at the moist turbulent air. He is struck with the paralyzing conviction that he has been here before and that this is a dangerous place.

Here, on a narrow twisting river between high stands of forest, in the desolate and beautiful wilderness of western Ontario, in the prow of a smart green Presalex canoe, with Nick Martens impatient in the stern. Nick saying, Maurie? Maurie? All right? (Perhaps he shares this eerie sense of déjà vu, for he and Maurie commonly share feelings—it is a source of puzzled vexation in Nick. Does he have a presentiment that something will go wrong? That in another minute they will be screaming like terrified children as both canoes capsize? But after all the boys have spent the past three nights in their damp tents, listening to the rain and talking about such things as courage, grace under pressure, and the willingness to die at the right time—they might have imagined that such bold, somber adult topics would protect them from actual harm.)

Maurie? All right? Let's go.

Kim and Tony have started forward, Kim in the stern. Maurie sits inert, his thin shoulders hunched. His weak eyes ache behind his green-tinted glasses: the sun strikes and shatters and reflects savagely from all sides, from thousands of angles, like slivers of glass: and this too is familiar. Come *on*, God damn you, Nick is murmuring, Nick his closest friend, Nick the impetuous, admired and disliked by most of the boys at the Dauer School, and loved by Maurie Halleck. I'm sick of your ugly face, the back of your ugly *head*, for Christ's sake, come on, what are you waiting for?—Nick's normally low and pleasant voice is hoarse with fatigue.

Has Maurie any choice? His shoulders and upper spine are throbbing with pain, he knows he should insist that they paddle over to the bank, but Kim and Tony have plunged ahead, Nick is about ready to jab him from behind, he really hasn't any choice. He nods, he acquiesces. The canoe moves forward. He is being hurtled suddenly toward a place where an irrevocable event, a suspension of physical law, might occur —has already occurred.

A single anarchic moment and everything he knows, everything that can be known, will dissolve.

Watch out! Nick shouts.

Rocks of all sizes, all shapes—boulders—ledges—white foaming water—churning—delirious—deafening. The air has turned to water, to be inhaled in quick panicked gasps. Black water, bluish-green water, white froth, bubbling and roaring. A rock flies by, another rock flies by, to the left, to the right, Nick is shouting, frightened and elated, the canoe is bucking, Maurie's bowels feel loose, he has a sudden painful need to urinate which a moment later he forgets. They are plunging—flying— racing, it seems, on the very surface of the water—and nothing can touch them: nothing can hurt them. Maurie Halleck and Nick Martens: seventeen years old: hurtled past steep banks and walls of pine forest they can no longer see.

They will live forever! *Nothing* can touch them!

And now to the left, that eddy just below the next drop—

A fallen pine, rotted—an enormous white boulder with ghostly indentations for eyes, nose, mouth—rocks piled upon rocks—chutes slick as playground slides—the taste of panic in the mouth—a shout of boastful joy—Maurie thinking clearly only seconds before the canoe is to slam into a hidden rock—*It isn't true that we live and die alone, look how we are together, look how we are always together—*

The deafening roar. The near-invisible rainbows dancing overhead. The thrill of terror deep in the guts. A hundred yards ahead, two crouched figures in an aluminum canoe, about to disappear from sight in a bank of mist. The canoe is shipping water badly, Maurie tries to breathe but sucks in spray, his body has gone numb, angry veins throb in both his eyes. He obeys his friend's shouted instructions. He obeys without thinking. *It isn't true that we live and die alone, look how we are together, at this moment, at this terrible moment, look how we are together, how we are always together—*

Friends

Maurie Halleck with his gnomish monkeyish face: the features under-sized and squeezed together: pale blue watery eyes, snub nose, puffy lips, narrow jaw. His skin was blotched and battered. Pimples like tiny purple berries erupted not only on his face but on his neck as well; and everywhere on his back. Poor Maurie! So homely. So hopeful. With his spidery arms and legs, his myopic eyes, his slight stammer, his earnest heart-piercing smile. Maurie the son of Joseph Halleck. Five feet eight at the age of seventeen, in his senior year at the Bauer School, weighing 125 pounds, poor Maurie, good-hearted Maurie, embarrassing his friends with talk of "God" and "Christ" and the "privilege of being alive."

Maurie declared himself a Christian without denomination. To honor Christ in one's fellow man—to seek a means by which Christ might come alive in *oneself*—this seemed to him the great challenge. He spoke freely, earnestly, sometimes stammering in his excitement, not noticing if others rolled their eyes or grimaced with boredom. He was bright, he was quick, despite his physical size he was a fair athlete—at tennis, gymnastics, track—and much of the time he was perfectly rea-sonable: so he got along well enough at the Bauer School, after the misery of his first term. It did not escape his classmates that he was Maurie Halleck and that his father was Joseph Halleck (of Halleck Copper & Aluminum), but this was the Bauer School of Krampton, Massachusetts, and possibly one-third of Maurie's class of two hundred boys came from families as wealthy as the Hallecks, or nearly; and there were, in every class, a half-dozen "famous" names. At Bauer it did not greatly matter—it was not supposed to greatly matter—who one's family was, with whom one's family consorted, how much a boy might whimsically estimate he was worth.

Maurie Halleck who charmed and impressed and exasperated Nick Martens. Maurie the baby (who was not ashamed at the age of seventeen of bursting into tears), Maurie the stoic, the enigma, the butt of innumerable crude jokes, humming to himself, waking at six in the morning, cheerful, quick to smile, quick to forgive. (And he did have a great deal to forgive. For—sorry to say—even his friends at Bauer sometimes mistreated him.) He was annoying, he was sunny and generous, he was liked well enough, or merely tolerated; or laughed at; or admired for his rather quixotic courage in challenging the school's most dogmatic and authoritarian teachers in front of an entire class. There were days when he knew all the answers and was a match—*almost* a match—for the smartest boys. There were other days when he couldn't get anything right, when he failed tests, blushed and gnawed at his knuckles, slipped away to be alone. (What does he do, alone? Pray? Go down on his knees and pray?) He simply didn't fit into his skin as other people did. With his short spidery legs, his frequent lack of coordination, his weak eyes. (The left eye was particularly bad. Once Maurie clapped his hand over the right eye and, gazing at Nick, blinking, announced that he was all but blind in that eye—he was probably "legally" blind. Which embarrassed and annoyed Nick, for what in hell was Nick supposed to say to *that?* His own vision was near perfect.)

Sometimes he did quite well at sports, fired with an almost desperate energy: he was not one of those clever undersized bespectacled boys who pretend *pride* in their lack of physical skill. He swam, he ran, he was precise and graceful in gymnastics; he tried crew; he tried basketball; he even tried, for a brief farcical month, boxing with Nick. (The school placed a curious emphasis on boxing.) He could play three sets of decent tennis and then a fourth in which he made one blunder after another, suddenly clumsy, ill-coordinated, tripping over his own feet, his face and neck flushed crimson. He muttered to himself, he apologized, he "didn't know what was wrong." At such times Nick felt no triumph, for what did winning at tennis matter with an opponent like Maurie Halleck? That fool, that clown. It was absurd for Nick to waste time with him. The more contrite Maurie became, the angrier Nick became, so that it always seemed that Nick was angry with Maurie for making mistakes. Stop. Shut up. *Don't.* (Even as a boy Nick had made it a maxim never to explain and never to apologize—except of course to adults—to important adults.)

Enough, Nick would shout suddenly, walking off the court. Enough. Fuck off. Forget it.

But they were friends. Intermittently. They *were* friends—Nick once admitted to Maurie that he was the closest friend he'd ever had, and maybe the only one: the reason being that Nick could trust him.

Nick who was so popular, Nick who had so many friends. President of his class for three years running. (Though each year he won by a narrower margin—which secretly infuriated him—for didn't that mean that former supporters were betraying him?) Handsome Nick Martens with his wit, his sarcasm, his zest for competition, his plotting, his calculating, his restless mannerisms (clicking his pen, winding his watch, shifting about in his seat), his tireless self-promotion. Courteous to adults—to those *important* adults—he was hilarious as he mimicked them behind their backs. As a scholarship student at Bauer it was indiscreet of him to be less than grateful, and certainly he was grateful, at least so far as anyone knew. His darkish blond hair was thick and springy, his nose was straight, his lips well-defined, he spoke glibly and forcefully, he was liked by all, or nearly all: though it should be said that he had his enemies: and he made it a point to know exactly who they were.

What do you see in Halleck, Nick was frequently asked, that asshole—?

Of course Maurie *was* the son of Joseph Halleck. And Mr. Halleck quickly grew fond of his son's energetic friend from Philadelphia.

But it was more than that; it was certainly more than that. Though often Maurie simply tagged along with Nick and his friends, benignly tolerated by them, it was still true that Nick *liked* Maurie, and something of a mystery. Nick who was so relentlessly popular, Nick who had so many friends. . . . (Though his sarcasm alienated a few. And his edgy ebullience. His habit of playing one boy off against another. His nervous gloating sense of himself.)

What do you see in Halleck? Tony Di Piero asked, out of curiosity rather than rancor. Doesn't his *goodness* wear you out?

Poor Maurie: tirelessly faithful, not injured by the rudest of dismissals, willing to lend Nick money and emphatic upon insisting, afterward, that he didn't want it back, he didn't *need* it back.

Which angered Nick, of course. Who said, Do you think I can't pay you back?—I can't afford to pay you back?

So that Maurie ended up apologizing, his pale eyes welling with tears.

You know I didn't mean that, Nick, he stammered.

I'd like to know what in hell you *did* mean, Nick said

Hey, Nick—come on. You know I didn't mean that, Maurie said.

Pleading, begging, apologizing. His mottled face and neck flushed a bright painful red.

Nick the boxer (150 pounds, nearly six feet tall), light and graceful and shrewd on his feet, with slim hips and strong sinewy hairy legs. Nick the swimmer, the track star, the basketball player (co-captain of the varsity team), Nick the straight-A student, the scholarship student, Harvard-bound. Nick the school tennis champion. Nick the actor: he played Mark Antony in *Julius Caesar,* and Jack in a farcical production of *The Importance of Being Earnest.* He had, he confided in Maurie, even studied piano for a considerable period of time, though at Bauer he professed a dislike for music. (Maurie discovered very interesting—very beautiful—doodlings of Nick's, strewn about his desk top. Musical notations, bars, treble and clef signs in elaborate calligraphy, done with a fountain pen and yet quite playful. Maurie examined the doodlings but could not read them and did not know whether this was really music, whether his friend was trying to compose, or simply doodling; and he knew better than to ask—not because Nick would sneer at his ignorance but because Nick might be embarrassed that Maurie had seen the notations. But the musical notes *were* beautiful and Maurie could not resist stealing one of the sheets of paper . . . which Nick, evidently, never missed.)

And there was Nick the president of the debating club. And Nick the third- or fourth-best chess player in the school. Nick the school politician. Tireless, confident. Sometimes a little vindictive—but that was understandable since he put so much of himself in school politics: he really seemed to *care* about how votes went, what committees decided.

Nick, Nick. Sometimes the air rang with his name—or so it seemed to Maurie Halleck.

(Maurie Halleck with his silly "self-disciplines" and his pimples and his chatter about Christ. Maurie whom Nick evidently pitied, as if he were a weak younger brother; to whom he tried to give boxing lessons, and actually did teach to play a respectable game of tennis.)

What *do* you see in Halleck? Tony asked. He's always hanging around.

I like him, said Nick. He's all right.

Of course he's all right, Tony said, yawning. He's too good to be true. But what do *you* see in him?

Nick thought a moment. He was not accustomed to being questioned so closely and would not have troubled to answer anyone else. Finally he said, making a face: What do I see in him? I don't know. I haven't a clue.

(Tony Di Piero was a tall, slender, lazily morose boy, with an olive-dark skin and very dark eyes. His smile was fleeting and sly; his black hair oily. In the school pool, surfacing after a dive, he resembled a seal—sleek and dark and muscularly graceful. He had been born in Brussels and brought to the States at the age of three. His father was dead—there was a school rumor that he'd been killed, years ago, in Rome: but whether the murder had been a political assassination, or simply the consequence of a disorderly private life, no one exactly knew, and of course no one could ask. His mother was American, the heiress to a fortune—in tobacco?—liquor?—petroleum?—the stories varied. It was rumored that she had committed suicide . . . or was hospitalized for alcoholism . . . or drugs . . . or mental illness. Of course no one could ask. In any case Tony seemed never to lack money, though he was not particularly generous with it. He dressed in expensive clothes with a stylish European cut, he owned a Jaguar—forbidden, of course, at Bauer —he had a number of girl friends, primarily in New York City; he was intelligent in his laconic way; his grades were always high. No one ever came to Bauer to visit him, though he sometimes received telephone calls, about which he never spoke. During holidays he either stayed at the school or went to New York City (his hotel was the Pierre) or accepted invitations to friends' homes. He and Nick Martens were friends because they sensed themselves equals and because Tony was the one boy Nick understood he could not manipulate.)

You're just going to hurt him, Tony once said, with an uncharacteristic impulsiveness. You *want* to hurt him.

You're full of shit, Nick said. You don't know a thing about me.

Maurie was his good conscience, perhaps. His younger brother. (Though in fact Maurie was several months older than Nick.) He was someone to talk with late at night in the common room, or after a game of tennis, or on a long hike to town. Plans for the future, was there a God, should he go into law, or politics, what should he do about his father (though there was very little a sixteen-year-old boy could do about Bernard Martens); how seriously should life be taken; what did loyalty and friendship mean; could you really *trust* anyone; was the world shit, or did it . . . did it have possibilities . . . ?

Undersized Maurie Halleck with his stammer, his disfiguring acne, his boyish giggle: his exasperating *hope*. He was no fool though he sometimes behaved like a fool, trapped in querulous arguments with boys who challenged his religious preoccupations, or his maidenly primness (obscene jokes and tales actually made him blush), or the phases of "self-discipline" he went through. (For a while, junior year, he rose at dawn every morning and went running in the woods in order to meditate. He was a vegetarian for several months, and would not even eat bouillon or eggs; he went through a period of a semester or more during which he fasted one day a week. He practiced silence, he practiced Christian humility. It seemed at times—so Nick sarcastically observed—that he "practiced" being human.)

And the anxious zeal with which he made certain he did *not* consider himself a better person than his classmates particularly annoyed them.

Poor Maurie!—that asshole Maurie.

Trying to read Wittgenstein, of whom no one had ever heard. Trying to read Cassirer. Arguing in class about the "pagan roots" of Nazism. Reading in a trembling voice a theme for English class on the "immortality of the soul." Defending the administration of "King Andrew the First"—Andrew Jackson. Debating the feasibility of world government, euthanasia, travel to and colonization of other planets. Taking flute lessons. (He turned out to have no natural aptitude at all —Nick cruelly tested him and declared him a musical illiterate.) Reading Dostoevsky, Tolstoy, Kierkegaard, Nietzsche. Arguing passionately, late at night, about religion and what it means to be religious: to *be* a form of Christ. Not minding how the other boys mocked him, or dismissed him rudely; not even noticing their amused indifference. (Nick, who took his family's nominal Lutheranism very lightly, as his father did, was uneasily impressed with Maurie's singular passion. How to assess it?—how to deal with it? When he came to Bauer at the age of fourteen Maurie had already read St. Augustine and Tolstoy's *Resurrection,* he had already studied, on his own, the recent papal encyclicals, Barth's *The Resurrection of the Dead,* James's *The Varieties of Religious Experience.* He was familiar with Morris Cohen's "The Dark Side of Religion" and he could quote from William Clifford's "The Ethics of Belief." He professed to adore Albert Schweitzer above all men. He had memorized much of Tolstoy's "My Religion" and he was given to quoting, with his eyes shut, certain lines from William James: *The intellect, even with truth directly in its grasp, may have no infallible signal for knowing whether it be truth or no.* But when Nick asked him bluntly whether he had had any real religious experience of his own he smiled sadly and said, No. I haven't. I'm waiting.)

How long do you intend to wait? Nick wanted to inquire.

Poor Maurie Halleck, who wore his detractors down with his sheer guileless optimism . . . !

They met the first week of September 1944.

Nick was always to recall, with peculiar vividness, the circumstances of that meeting. As if he had known at once that he and that monkeyish smiling boy with the wire-rimmed glasses and the short legs were fated to be brothers.

That is—to be friends.

Very close friends.

Bound together by blood?—by violence?

There was Maurie shelving books, in khaki pants and an undershirt, scrawny and perspiring, muttering to himself. (Though possibly he was singing to himself. He was to try his suitemates' patience with his eerily inappropriate songs that term: "White Christmas," "It's Only a Paper Moon," "Stormy Weather.") Turning to see Nick and Mrs. Martens in the doorway he stared for a long moment, then darted forward, putting out his hand, stammering a greeting: Oh I'm sorry—oh I didn't expect—I—I'm Maurie Halleck—I'm assigned to this room—

Before Mrs. Martens could shake his hand he withdrew it and wiped it on his pants.

His blemished face reddened coarsely; his small anxious eyes blinked behind the lenses of his glasses.

Nick managed to smile and introduce himself. And his mother, who stood a little apart. Maurie repeated his name, blushing more deeply and apologizing. He hadn't expected anyone today, he said, he had been told his suitemates were all coming the next morning. Then he excused himself and hurried into one of the bedrooms. Nick and his mother exchanged a glance. This boy? This odd little boy? Assigned to Nick's suite? Surely he could not be fourteen years old . . . ? When he reappeared a moment later, thrusting his arms into a white shirt, he was still apologizing.

They told me you were all coming tomorrow, he said.

Nick looked at him calmly. And did not speak.

Maurie apologized for the state of the room. His books, his suitcases, the dust, the debris in the fireplace (which the former tenants of the room must have left), the dirty windows. He had intended to do a little cleaning before anyone arrived. He explained that he had taken the bedroom on the left because it faced the courtyard and might get the most noise in the morning. He had taken the smallest bookshelf. (But if the other bookshelves weren't completely filled, he hoped he might be able to use them. He'd brought several cartons of books, as Nick could see.)

A ticlike smile distorted Maurie's face. He licked his lips nervously. It was necessary now for Nick to speak, it was time for him to say something jocular, or consoling, or witty, or enthusiastic: to ask where "Maurie Halleck" was from and if his parents were on campus: to volunteer where he was from. But he simply gazed at the agitated boy as if he'd never seen anyone so idiotic.

Mrs. Martens stood apart, dabbing at her face with a handkerchief. She wore a handsome silk suit, a very pale beige, and her face was
blandly pretty, a little puffy about the eyes. Nick's father had taken a
train early that day to see a cellist friend, at Juilliard for a concert that
evening: Nick guessed that his parents had quarreled, though of course
he had not asked. (He would not have inquired about his parents' emotional life together any more than he would have inquired about their
sexual life. He feared that, if he questioned his mother, she would probably tell him everything.) Now Mrs. Martens peered at herself in a tiny
compact mirror and ignored Nick and this odd little boy. If she pitied
either of them she gave no indication.

Nick said finally: That room facing the courtyard—you took it
because it has the best light, didn't you?

Maurie gaped at him. At first he was too startled to speak.

It faces the south—the windows are big—that's why you took it,
didn't you? Nick asked.

Maurie said, blinking: I—I—no, I thought—I mean, I—

Nick strode into the room, examining it. It's the largest room, isn't
it, he said.

Maurie hovered in the doorway. They're all the same size, he said.
I'm sure they're all the same size.

No, this one is bigger. These windows are nice, Nick said. He
swung one of them open farther and leaned out, inhaling deeply. You
have a good view too.

But I didn't mean—

You got here first: you have first choice.

But I *didn't* mean—

It's all right, Maurie. That's your name?—Maurie? It's all right,
Nick said with a cheerful smirk, you got here first.

But I don't care which room I have, Maurie said anxiously. Look
—you take it.

No, it's yours. You have first choice.

I haven't unpacked much of anything—I can take this stuff back
out—

No, the hell with it. Calm down.

But I took it because I thought—the courtyard there, you know
—there was a lot of noise before—some guys were shouting to one
another—I didn't mean—I didn't think—look, please: I'll take my things
back out and you can have it.

Nick was leaning out the casement window, breathing deeply. His
eye took in the steep slate roofs of the Bauer School, the tall chimneys,
the bell tower, the hills in the distance. The Martenses could not afford
to send their son here but Bernard had insisted: Lawrenceville or Exeter

or Andover or Bauer: or the hell with it altogether. The Philadelphia
Academy of Music Arts (of which he was the director) was not doing
badly, but his investments evidently were, though of course he refused
to discuss such things with his wife and son. I don't belong here, Nick
thought with a curious gloating elation. Down in the flagstone courtyard
a boy and his parents and their black chauffeur appeared, carrying
luggage and boxes of books. At Nick's elbow "Maurie Halleck" was
pleading with him to take this bedroom—to *please* take this bedroom.
I don't belong here, Nick thought in triumph, but here I am.

Though everything had happened quickly Nick had had time to
absorb his suitemate's name. Halleck—? Copper—? And hadn't he been
a friend or an aide of F.D.R.'s?

Maurie begged and explained and apologized. He came close to
touching Nick's arm. Nick would resist for another minute or two, then
give in suddenly, a boyish smile raying across his face. All right. All
right, then, if Maurie didn't mind, if he *really* didn't mind giving up the
room. . . .

They were to shake hands again, as if settling a deal. Maurie's
grimy little paw was cold with perspiration and Nick—fastidious Nick
—had to resist the instinct to shudder with revulsion.

Wild Loughrea

It isn't the first river they have canoed on together—Mr. Halleck invited his son's friends up to Bitterfeld Lake in the Adirondacks, the summer before—but it is the most distant, the most challenging. The most dangerous.

Expensive? But expense is no problem. Not for Mr. Halleck.

The week in Loughrea provincial park is a graduation present for the four of them—Maurie and his friends Nick, Tony, and Kim. They were flown in by float plane to Whiteclay Lake, from Sault Ste. Marie. Rental arrangements—the canoes, the tents, the pack baskets, most of the fishing gear, the cooking equipment, etc.—were made ahead of time by Mr. Halleck's secretary. The boys brought along their own rain gear, woollen socks and sweaters, gloves, rubber boots, sleeping bags, toiletries, steel knives, paperback books, playing cards, and other miscellaneous items; they bought, at the Whiteclay Lake supply outlet, plastic forks and spoons, paper plates and cups, insect repellent, a First-Aid kit, and a considerable quantity of food (canned, dehydrated, cellophane-wrapped: chicken, tunafish, Spam, eggs, peanut butter, raspberry jam, grape jelly, bacon, bread, crackers, chocolate spread, powdered soup, instant coffee, raisins, prunes, dried apricots, biscuit and pancake mix, chocolate bars, Lifesavers, and several varieties of gum). Tony bought three cartons of Camels. And though the boys were too young to buy beer or wine both beer and wine were bought for them, and slipped into their pack baskets.

Thirty years ago Mr. Halleck and five of his friends went on a canoeing trip down the Loughrea, and it was one of the most extraordinary experiences of his life. He remembers the week vividly and speaks of it often with great emotion. The millions of acres of untouched wilderness; the immense silence; the fresh clear air; the great river itself, undammed, absolutely natural. Three canoes, six young men. Close friends. One of the high points of their lives. Yes, it did rain. Yes, they did quarrel. There were blackflies, there were woodlice. They had one or two minor accidents, nothing serious. A few scratches. A sprained ankle. Yes, they were exhausted after the first several days, their bodies ached, their clothes were damp, they were grateful for the last five or six miles of wide flat placid river emptying into Lac Seule . . . grateful to be free of one another's company. Yet the trip was one of the memorable experiences of their lives.

Mr. Halleck with his sad pouched eyes, his opaque gaze, fixed in space. Rubbing his nose thoughtfully. Frowning. Smiling. He'd had his first heart attack the spring of Maurie's freshman year at Bauer and in the months following he had lost more than twenty pounds of surplus weight. So he looked fairly trim. He looked, from a distance, fairly young.

One of the high points of our lives, he repeated, smiling.

The eerie calm of the days: pelting rain, an opaque gray drizzle, the sudden assault of the August sun. The river widens, becoming broad and flat and benign; then it narrows again; rocks surface, the water splashes white, pines rise tall and steep on both banks. Maurie and Nick and Tony and Kim traverse the first of the rapids—Whiteclay Rapids—without much difficulty. Maurie spies a red-tailed hawk overhead, dipping and soaring as if it were following them. Flushed, excited, he takes notes in a small red-covered book. *Never so happy in my life*, he writes.

Whiteclay Rapids, Little Rapids, Long White Rapids, Whistling Swan Rapids, Lower Loughrea Rapids—it is the Lower Loughrea in which the boys will have their accident on the fourth day of the trip; and the Lower Loughrea in which (so they will be told, flown back to Whiteclay to the First-Aid station) a canoer died that spring. A twenty-five-year-old biologist from the University of Western Ontario, a skilled canoer, no naïve amateur. He and a friend made the mistake of underestimating the river—running the rapids at near-flood time in early May. The young man was thrown from his capsized canoe and washed along for more than a mile, broken against the rocks. His face was badly mutilated. The other canoer was fortunate. he was washed against a bank and suffered only a few cracked ribs.

The eerie calm. The seamlessness of the days. Dark water. Swift-flowing water. A light feathery rain, a sudden sunburst in which the sky cracks open: and the boys, sweating, miserable with heat, tear off their rubber rain gear.

Maurie and Kim note surface-feeding ducks: mallards, black ducks, pintails. (Kim's eyes are sharper than Maurie's. But he sees birds he can't identify, birds they can't find in their book. Widgeon? With a curved white crown? They can't draw close enough to see.)

They turn a bend and the view is breathtaking: miles of river, broad, rippling blue, wide as a great boulevard.

Never so happy, Maurie whispers.

Beauty. Monotony. The aggrieved hurt of the arms, the shoulders, the back, the thighs. A flush of sunburn. A peeling nose. Gnats, mosquitoes, small flies. (Not blackflies, fortunately. Their season was last month.) Paddling, they eat Milky Ways, Tootsie Rolls, O. Henry bars, Mars bars. And raisins, peanuts, saltine crackers. Nick and Kim disagree about something, across the expanse of water. Nick is funny, bright, sharp, perhaps a little too dogmatic. (They are speculating on the probable cost of a Presalex canoe of this size, which Nick has decided he will buy once he gets home.) Kim says bluntly that Nick can't afford the canoe, he's just shooting off his mouth. Nick denies it at once. Maurie, in the prow of their canoe, can feel his agitation—the tension of his legs and thighs. Don't argue, Maurie begs softly. Don't spoil everything.

Sunlight, heat, monotony, beauty. The boys' idle voices. Laughter. Their moody silence. Tributaries flow into the Loughrea constantly, making it wider, dense with islands. (The boys stop to explore one of the larger islands. Find the usual remnants of campsites. Maurie discovers a half-burned paperback book and pages through it, curious. Is this a sign? Isn't everything, in the paradise, a sign? But the book is evidently a detective novel; Maurie finds himself reading a passage in which a man named Rolk, armed with a machine gun, mows down several men as they flee in terror from an abandoned Cadillac. One, crawling on his hands and knees, manages to escape into a marshy field . . . a swamp . . . but the murderer with the machine gun follows him. . . .)

The sun moves swiftly and effortlessly overhead, yet the days are long. Nothing happens. Everything happens. It begins to seem faintly preposterous to Maurie (tanned, competent with his oar, stronger than he has ever been in his life) that he was a schoolboy a few months earlier; and that he will enter college in another four weeks. That his name is *Halleck,* that he is burdened with a certain face, a certain personality. (But can't he alter himself? Isn't anything possible? Out here—on the Loughrea—isn't any miracle possible? He's so lightheaded from the exercise and fresh oxygen and the mesmerizing sweep of the water that he begins to wonder if he couldn't trade places with Nick Martens. Insinuate himself into Nick's charmed life—into Nick's handsome body.)

Happiness, Maurie thinks, his eyes welling foolishly with tears, *and pain*.

Conversations falter, laughter dwindles, words drift away. A small flock of Canada geese flies overhead. In the midst of a long jocular story about a world-famous violinist with a penchant for very young girls, a friend of his father's, Nick grows silent, as if he has suddenly lost interest in his own words, or has become ashamed of them.

Maurie wears a canvas hat to protect his face from the sun. He finds the dull ache of his shoulder muscles consoling.

He is not thinking of home: the townhouse on East Seventy-fifth Street, the summer house in the Adirondacks. He is not thinking of college. (His father wants him to go to law school eventually. But he is considering, in secret, theology school. He hasn't yet given up his hope for—his absurd hope for—a "religious" career.) The years at Bauer, his boyhood, are retreating swiftly behind him, and he is able to surrender them without a flicker of emotion. Even if it means giving up Nick.

Half-dozing. The sunlight, the rocking waves.

Then, without warning, an attack of hunger.

A suddenly ferocious hunger: and they all begin eating again: stuffing their mouths with peanuts, raisins, chocolate.

Starving. Their fingers trembling, eyes watering. Mouths flooded with saliva.

(Maurie did not know if it was shameful, or funny—being reduced to an animal, an appetite, so frequently. They all ate like pigs. Each meal, with the possible exception of breakfast, when they were too groggy to be really hungry. Gobbling down food, anxious that there might not be enough, reduced to a mechanism that burned calories in order to keep paddling, to keep existing. The first night, building a fire, Nick said, It's like this—we're like this—someone has to keep supplying us with food or we burn down. Maurie saw the grim merry twist of his friend's mouth but he was too exhausted to think of a reply. His shoulders and arms throbbed with pain, his head felt queer. A bleak truth, a terrible truth. They were mechanisms that devoured calories, heat, life. Protoplasm gobbling down protoplasm. Ravenous until they stuffed their bellies— at which point they became faintly nauseated. Or diarrhetic. It crossed Maurie's mind for the first time that there might not be enough food for the four of them, for six more long days.)

They fish for trout, they drink warm beer until their bellies bloat. They are really quite proud of themselves for having come so far: each of the boys thanks Maurie again for his father's generosity. Kim is bitten by a yellow jacket, on his beefy forearm, and the sting immediately turns red and begins to swell—dead-white at the center. Maurie dabs salve on it, thick as putty. The swelling is the size of a grape, then a plum, then a small apple. The boys examine it, they've never seen a bee sting quite so large.

They fish, explore islands, take their time choosing campsites, wander off alone. On a bluff overlooking the river, in a stand of stark white birch, Maurie watches as the sun, at the horizon, bleeds into the sky like a broken egg yolk. He stares and stares, forgetting himself. Down below one of his friends is shouting to another. The voice is bodiless, insignificant. Mere noise. Someone replies, someone laughs. A cigarette has the uncanny power of fouling great stretches of space but this too is insignificant: the wind finally eases the smoke away, the wilderness closes in again. A loon is calling, the sun blows itself up into peculiar and alarming shades of amber-red, Maurie is alone, shivering, unable to remember why he has agreed to this trip—why he greeted his father's proposal with enthusiasm. He knows very well that Nick and Tony and Kim don't really like him: they jeer at him behind his back, exchange ironic glances in his presence. Nick and Tony and Kim. . . .

Their bodiless voices, their insignificant lives. The silence of the immense wilderness is so vast, surrounding them, Maurie wonders with a touch of panic how they will survive even the night.

The Prayerful Witness

There is the example of Albert Schweitzer. The example of Cardinal de Monnier. St. Francis of Assisi—whom Maurie secretly prefers, as a companion of the soul, to Christ Himself. And George Whitefield who wrote: *Everything I meet with seems to carry this voice with it—"Go thou and preach the Gospel; be a pilgrim on earth; have no party or certain dwelling place." My heart echoes back, "Lord Jesus, help me to do or suffer thy will. When thou seest me in danger of nestling— in pity—in tender pity—put a thorn in my nest to prevent me from it."*

Pity!—Maurie thinks, astonished and disturbed. How can one resist pity? It is an impulse, an instinct, more powerful in him than sexual desire.

Schweitzer, de Monnier, St. Francis, George Whitefield. And others, legendary, mythical. But what of John Brown? Captain John Brown? Old Osawatomie who helped bloody Kansas in the 1850s, and led his deluded little army at Harpers Ferry?

Nick Martens thought it fascinating, that little Maurie Halleck was a descendant of Brown's. Perhaps it was an error in judgment for Maurie to have ever mentioned it—they must have been discussing their families, their backgrounds, very late one night—for from time to time Nick would allude to Brown, speaking of Maurie's "great-great-great-great-grandfather." Which disconcerted Maurie, who felt no connection at all; none in the slightest. Nick teased, You've got his blood in your veins, your heart is pumping *his* blood, but Maurie couldn't see that at all—he laughed, embarrassed, and tried to change the subject. (Nick, like several others at Bauer, was inordinately curious about family backgrounds. As a shorthand means of explaining and "fixing" the present. It was also a fact—he dared make no secret of it, at Bauer—that his own family, his parents' families, were "historically undistinguished.")

He quizzed Maurie about documents, letters, other artifacts of Brown's—weren't they in the family somewhere?—hidden away?

I don't think so, Maurie said. I've never heard of them.

He found his friend's queer smiling interest disturbing.

Those things are worth money, Nick said. But also . . . Well, they're worth money.

Brown had twenty children, Maurie said vaguely, and dozens of grandchildren . . . great-grandchildren. . . . He's nothing to us, my father never mentions him.

A friend of Roosevelt's, a pal of Ambassador Kennedy's, your father *wouldn't*, Nick said sagely. He knows his way around.

Maurie's skin prickled; his face and throat reddened unevenly. My father isn't—it isn't like that, he protested. I mean—he wasn't a close friend of Roosevelt's, they didn't always get along, and he never sees Kennedy any longer—

Moving up in the world, Nick said cheerfully. Aren't we all.

But you're exaggerating, Maurie said.

Nick laughed, poking him in the ribs. *Aren't we all,* he said.

Maurie Halleck, asthmatic, weak-chested, hopeful. Maurie who never seems to fit into his skin. (As others do? His classmates, his friends? Easy in their skins like cats, fish, lizards.) He envies them all. Adores them. Feels no bitterness. Only an intense sympathy, a mesmerizing *interest.*

Yet he frequently studies the photographs of athletes and male models, covering their legs with his hand, judging whether one could assess the probable length of the legs on the basis of the torsos. (Maurie has short legs. Not merely thin but short—*almost* stunted.) Like other adolescent habits it will gradually die away as a consequence of its futility.

Nick Martens, Kim Ryan, Harry Anders, Tony Di Piero: and others, several others: he *doesn't* envy them, not exactly. It's true that he watches them covertly in the pool, on the basketball court, on the playing field, even in the dining hall and in class. He admires them, approves of them. Even as he disapproves of their frequent churlishness. (Their habit of punctuating quite ordinary conversations with profanity and obscenity. *Fuck, tit, suck, bugger. Shit. Jerk-off. Son of a bitch, bastard, prick, fag.* Maurie writes the forbidden words in his little notebook with the red leather cover, hides them with his hand, broods, muses, shrugs his shoulders. Forbidden? Magic? A boy's code? But he can't and won't say them, his throat would simply close up. And *why* should he utter them since in fact—in secret—he knows himself superior to Nick and Kim and Harry and Tony and all the others?)

Maurie the butt of jokes. Maurie about whom it was said—quite truthfully—that he developed a sallow sickly skin that resembled a symptom of jaundice because he had been eating too many carrots. (His family physician discovered the problem, informed his parents, scolded him. What has eating carrots got to do with anything? *Not* eating meat? "Disciplining" himself in odd conspicuous ways?) Maurie with his curious hope of being a "prayerful witness" like Cardinal de Monnier.

A witness of what? Nick Martens asked.

A witness of . . . of suffering. Of the world, Maurie said.

Yes, said Nick impatiently, but a witness of *what? Where?*

Maurie's lips barely move. He is confused and ashamed. He doesn't really want Nick to hear. . . . Of the world, he says.

Nick considers this. And finally says, slowly, as if he were just realizing for the first time: But—isn't that all of us?

Maurie who can be relied upon to invite his friends, and sometimes the friends of his friends, home for the holidays. To the townhouse in Manhattan, or to the "camp" at Bitterfeld Lake, in the mountains.

He soon understood that in order to entice X into accepting an invitation, it was pragmatic to invite Y first, or at least to speak of (to promise?) an invitation to Y.

But the boys at Bauer *do* like him. He will be voted outstanding citizen of the senior class.

Nick apologizes for not inviting him to *his* home, in Philadelphia.

Maybe next fall, Nick says. Thanksgiving.

All right, says Maurie. Good.

Things are sort of busy right now, Nick says.

I understand, says Maurie.

Bitterfeld Lake, the Hallecks' lodge, the mountains, the trout streams: which impress the wealthiest of boys. (Skiing at Christmas and over January break and, if there's snow, over spring break in March. In the summer, virtually everything: swimming, boating, canoeing, tennis, fishing, hiking, mountain-climbing. Poor Maurie has no brothers, his parents say, but he does have a number of close friends.)

There is the example, the living example, of Cardinal de Monnier of Africa.

He was archbishop of Quebec. A beloved prelate, as "liberal" as one might be in that context. At the age of fifty-seven he left his residence in Quebec City and went to work with the sick, the handicapped, and the dying in Cameroon, West Africa. Suddenly left—resigned—stirred a veritable blizzard of rumors.

But why did he leave Quebec, and his power? His worldly glory?

A voice.

Just as he obeyed a voice forty-five years earlier when, as a boy of twelve, he was meditating alone, after communion, in the small parish church of St. Gabriel De Valacritier. The voice said simply, *You will become a priest.*

Only that: *You will become a priest.*

Now Father de Monnier is seventy-eight years old and is reflecting on the end of his life, which he feels to be imminent. He speaks of the unmistakable calling, the simplicity of the claim for his vocation, the curious impersonal nature of his subsequent life. Until the age of twelve he was sickly—in fact, consumptive—but after that his health improved; and as an adult man he was never sick at all. Not even in Africa, where he was surrounded with sickness of the most hideous kind, not just in white men like himself (Europeans, mainly) but in black Africans. How to account for it? How is it possible that he was spared for more than twenty years, even of dysentery and common fevers?—of the most common parasites?

Maurie reads of Cardinal de Monnier, saves clippings, interviews, the long story in *Life.* Maurie reads and rereads as if puzzling out a riddle. The seventy-eight-year-old priest who is director of the Centre for the Rehabilitation of the Handicapped at Yaoundé. The elderly man who, though content to be dying "within a few years," looks so vigorous—so youthful. De Monnier is quoted as speaking of the vocation of fidelity to suffering; the vocation of the active pursuit of pain and horror; the vocation of being a "prayerful witness" even if one is unable, finally, to alleviate the most extreme forms of suffering. The imitation of Christ. Christ-in-the-world. An observer who will be a witness to the dying as they assert themselves, or to the dreadfully handicapped (lepers, primarily) of all ages.

Nick Martens stares at the glossy color photographs in *Life.*

I don't think I'd be . . . equal to this, he says uneasily.

Studying with barely concealed distaste the lepers with their stumps, their expressionless rotted faces. The oily sheen of their black skin. Their lustrous eyes.

Cardinal de Monnier himself, his skin a peculiar grayish-white, lined and creased and pouched. His hair is starkly white and lifts in curt surprised tufts from his head. An elderly man. Dying. But regal. A saint?

Maurie reads the cardinal's words about the mystery of the "biological joy" the Africans seem to possess; a tranquillity, a power, white men don't have. Europeans, North Americans. . . . He says the black Africans know how to die, Maurie says, trying to conceal his excitement. He's been there twenty years and has worked in the hospital with them, and in their villages, but he says he doesn't understand them: it isn't given to him, to understand *them*.

Nick rubs his eyes. It is late, past two in the morning; they will have to get up by seven. He says slowly, Well—it's good for him, I mean it's good that he can take it. That someone can.

You couldn't? Maurie asks.

Nick shrugs his shoulders. He is wearing soiled khaki pants and a white undershirt that gives off a dry sharp odor of perspiration. His skin is grainy with fatigue. Darkish, flushed, as if permanently windburnt. Sly almond-shaped eyes in which (so Maurie imagines, covertly gazing) the dark brown-black irises wriggle like tiny fish. Nick, with his reputation for cruelty. For being sardonic, sarcastic. At midnight that night Maurie was nearly asleep when Nick—pale with anger and grief, his eyes red-rimmed—rapped softly on his door. Maurie? You awake? Can you talk? Maurie?

Maurie turns the magazine pages, disguising his nervousness. He does not want the precious subject of Cardinal de Monnier to fade.

You couldn't, Nick? You wouldn't be strong enough?

Would you?

Maurie sucks in his breath, laughing. *Me!* Never.

He closes the magazine. Studies the photograph of the cardinal on the cover—a stark close-up of the old man's head.

Perhaps that is all he is: an old man?

Maurie too wants to be a prayerful witness. He *knows* it is his "vocation"—yet what, precisely, is it? But he is reluctant to display much excitement in Nick's presence. Emotions offend and embarrass Nick; eccentric enthusiasms are apt to be—at a later time, in the presence of others—recalled and ridiculed. (So, fondly and yet mockingly, Nick once alluded to Maurie's interest in the flute; laughed over his month-long but intense interest in ants; jocularly reviewed his "progress" as a boxer.)

Not me. Never. I'm not strong enough, Maurie says. He hesitates, licks his lips. I'm not strong enough yet.

Well, says Nick, sighing, yawning. Well. It's good that there are people like—what is his name?—Monnier?—in the world.

Nick stretches; his small compact muscles become prominent.

Another of their talks—their late-night, secret talks—in which they discuss with schoolboy intensity such marvelous subjects—is evidently coming to an end. Maurie cannot prolong it. Nick is restless to leave; he *is* exhausted. (Nick with his undisclosed problems, his prickly grief, that appear to have something to do with his family. His father? Bernard Martens whom Maurie has never met? The man is director of the Philadelphia Academy of Music Arts, a privately endowed institution, not large, not—so Maurie gathers—very prosperous at the present time. He is a former concert pianist though he can't have been successful because no one Maurie asks remembers his career. Nick's mother too is something of a mystery. Maurie gathers from half-overheard telephone conversations that she is having difficulties of some sort—the marriage is probably disintegrating—but Maurie can't, of course, ask. He wouldn't dare. He must wait patiently to snatch up hints and allusions Nick drops like crumbs, or gems, careless and regal even in his misery.)

Maurie cannot shake his mind free of Cardinal de Monnier and the mission hospital at Yaoundé. Though he has no hope of making his friend understand; and is clearly boring him. (Late at night, during their three years at Bauer, Maurie and Nick discuss, frequently in great detail, with all the ephemeral passion of adolescence, such topics as the meaning of death, is there an immortal spirit, is there only biological and mechanical existence, what is love, why is it so difficult to tell the truth to one's parents, is the honor code an excellent idea or a quixotic ideal, nothing less than an *enticement* to dishonesty?—and such subjects as their teachers, their friends, the rector of the school, the quality of Bauer itself, which college to attend, and which law school—as if there were any choice about *that.* They discuss God: whether He exists or not: whether He is merely an It, a force. They discuss free will and determinism; dualism (whether mind and matter are separate substances); what does "insanity" mean; is suicide ever justified—for instance, if one is going to be tortured and might betray one's friends or comrades. And the problem—for it is truly a problem—of how to live. How to apply one's strength. Law, politics, education, art?—business?—medicine? What does it mean, precisely, to choose a *vocation?* If not in the sacred sense of the word, then in the secular?)

Maurie is talking about the cardinal's pursuit of pain and suffering, his choice to be a prayerful witness even when he can't—and often he can't—bring about much change. The priest carries within himself the form of Christ, His spirit, through charity and humility and love and work and unflagging consciousness—*witnessing:* but what a riddle, what a puzzle! Maurie knows but cannot understand. He *knows* but cannot explain.

Nick has appeared not to be listening. He is picking at a scab on his ankle. But he says, in a suddenly startled voice, glancing up at Maurie: Look—to have the power to do good, how can you *be* good? I mean with all this—he makes a vague disgusted gesture, presumably taking in not only Bauer and the countryside but the nation itself—all this shit.

To have the power to do good, how can you *be* good?

So Maurie ponders, broods, picks at his own scabs (the pimples on his face and back), wonders if there really is a distinction, or whether Nick simply spoke, as he often does, without thinking. To be good, to do good. To *be* good, and yet to possess power. For without the power what value has one's goodness? Yet if one manages to attain power, how can goodness be possible?

Adolescent passion.

Painful. But ephemeral.

It *must* be ephemeral—otherwise we couldn't survive!

God and love and the immortality of the soul; life and death; where to go to college; whether to report —— who constantly cheats on his French tests.

Maurie finds himself thinking of Cardinal de Monnier, as the months pass, not as a person—a man—an elderly man, dying—but as an essence, a spirit. On the Loughrea River, as the hours pass in a turbulent dream; in his damp and somewhat clammy sleeping bag; at the edge of the campsite on a high bluff where he stands, at night, staring at the extraordinary sky: the piercing clarity of the multitudes of stars, the three-quarter moon so bright it makes the eye uneasy. It is dismayingly cold for August. Maurie, wearing two sweaters and heavy woollen socks, is shivering. (The other boys, Kim in particular, don't appear to feel the cold. Stocky suntanned Kim, his upper lip darkening with a mustache, strides about in shorts and a thin cotton pullover sweater, whistling, setting up camp.) Maurie wanders off, grateful to be alone. He is thinking . . . he is waiting. . . .

Rain most of the day, clearing just at dusk, and now a wonderful freshness, a green fragrance, the odor of swift-flowing water, wet grass, pine woods, cold that rises in breaths from the earth. Maurie inhales deeply. His teeth begin to chatter with cold, or excitement, or hunger.

A hundred yards away Kim is frying a dozen small trout the boys caught earlier that day. Maurie is ashamed and frightened of his appetite: his mouth is watering violently.

He is thinking of, he is waiting for . . . ? Cardinal de Monnier understood the terms of his contract at the extraordinary age of twelve.

But Maurie is still waiting. Maurie, soon to be eighteen years old. Which means adulthood, which means manhood. The future. He hasn't, at this moment, his muscles aching from the river and his stomach knotted with hunger, saliva flooding his mouth, any idea what he is waiting for.

Maurie? Where the hell is Maurie? someone calls.

The voice is raw and youthful and impatient. It might belong to anyone, but Maurie hears it as Nick's.

The Sacred Vow

On the third night of the canoeing trip Nick Martens, mildly and happily drunk, tells his friends a Swedish folktale.

(Maurie learns for the first time that Nick has a Swedish grandmother. On his mother's side. She died only a few years ago. She used to insist that Nick, as a very small child—two, three years old—have coffee at breakfast, coffee greatly diluted with cream and sugar. And was it good? Oh delicious.)

Once upon a time two friends exchanged a sacred vow. They were young men in their twenties. Each promised he would attend the other's wedding, wherever he might be at the time: even if he was on the high seas, or at the very ends of the earth. One of the young men left the village to seek his fortune and disappeared—no one knew where he went. The other stayed close to home.

Where was it? Oh some village in Sweden, Nick doesn't know.

So the young man who stayed in his own village became engaged to a girl, and married her, and he felt very sad—he was very disappointed—that his friend didn't come to the wedding after all. But years had gone by, and no one knew where he was.

But then—

But then, late at night, on the wedding night, the friend *did* come to the bridal house. The guests had left, only the bride and the bridegroom remained. They offered him food and drink but he refused. He took nothing but a mugful of water, and a handful of earth.

A handful of—?

A handful of earth, Nick says impatiently. *Earth.*

He claws at the ground, to gather up earth, but manages only to pull out blades of grass. Which he lets drop into the fire.

So the friend returned, and came to the bridal house, and danced three times with the bride. And before he left the house he said: Now you have to come with me, and keep your promise, because I'm celebrating my wedding tonight too.

So the bridegroom went with him. Though he didn't want to go.

It was his wedding night—after all!

But he went with his friend because of their vow. They walked a long distance. It was very dark, and the way was strange; but finally they got to a house of some kind; and there were wedding guests there too, and a bride in a long white gown, with a veil, and lilies of the valley in her hair. So the bridegroom danced with his friend's bride—he danced three times—and excused himself and said farewell. Because it was late, and he wanted to return home to his own bride.

He wasn't certain of the way back. It took him most of the night.

It took him a long time.

When he returned to his own house something was wrong: the house was changed: it was really another house, standing where the first one had been. It was much larger, with red shutters. There was a woman with a baby in the garden—a woman he had never seen before.

It turned out that the people who lived in this house were strangers. He didn't know them, they didn't know him. They had never heard of his name.

Everyone in the village was a stranger.

Everything had changed.

He was very frightened. He thought he had lost his mind. So he went to the village priest, who was also a stranger, but the priest looked through the parish register—and discovered that the man had celebrated his wedding three hundred years before.

So three hundred years had passed during the night! While he was dancing with his friend's bride. On account of their sacred vow, which he couldn't break. Three hundred years, and his wife and everyone he knew were gone, and he hadn't anywhere to go except back to his friend in the Land of the Dead.

So he went back? That's the end of the story?

He went back, that's the end of the story.

To the Land of the Dead?

To the Land of the Dead.

Tony Di Piero says softly, lighting a cigarette, that he knows a number of Italian folktales, himself. Told to him by *his* grandmother, a long time ago. (A very long time ago. Tony has no family now.) But he wouldn't dream of boring people with such shit.

The boys laugh, startled. Even Nick laughs. Even Maurie.

After all, says Tony, gratified by the laughter but remaining expressionless, exhaling a cloud of smoke, the Land of the Dead—where's *that?*

Schweppenheiser

To the Bauer School there came, in the early forties, an instructor of history by the name of Hans Klaus Schweppenheiser: German-born, an emphatic anti-Nazi (and sometimes, with explosive exuberance, he declared himself anti-German as well), the son of immigrants who had farmed, with meager success, in the Halberstadt region of Germany. Hans Klaus's accent was strongly German, but when teaching, particularly when giving one of his lengthy, convoluted lectures, he made every attempt to pronounce significant words in an "English" manner. His students could not judge what was serious and what was prankish. His mispronunciations and wrongly accented words and phrases gave off a swaggering cynical energy: the Gettysburg Address, Woodrow Wilson's pleas for the League of Nations, Winston Churchill's speeches to the British people, passages taken from the assigned text and read aloud with tireless merriment: all became marvelously *Schweppenheiser.*

He was in his mid-thirties when Maurie and Nick were at Bauer, though, with his pale bald head and his near-hairless face, and his stocky barrel-chested body, he looked a decade older. There were rumors that he had suffered "minor" acts of persecution during the war years—swastikas on the door of his apartment in Cambridge, occasional rocks thrown at him in the street, insults in stores and restaurants—and there was the puzzling matter of his failure to receive a Ph.D. at Harvard though he had (so stories went) revised his seven-hundred-page dissertation two or three times to satisfy the whims of his advisor. It was commonly understood that Schweppenheiser, despite his clownish appearance and his droll teaching methods, which verged at times upon outright burlesque, was the most brilliant, and certainly the most stimulating, teacher at Bauer. A genius, most likely. With a "tragic" heart condition. (Which exempted him from service during the war, of course —to his own embarrassed disappointment.) The rector and the board of trustees saw shrewdly that they had a bargain in Schweppenheiser who should have been teaching at a university; he was a genuine scholar, eccentric of course but that was to be expected, energetic, devoted to his students and his research, quite witty at teas and luncheons and receptions, gallantly flirtatious with even the least attractive of the wives (which of course did not sabotage his career at the school), warm, entertaining, an "original," a "character," never exactly offensive in public (though some of the reports from boys in his classes *were* a bit disturbing), without any hobbies or diversions or vices, unmarried, quite alone, oddly conservative beneath his satirical stance (he always sided with the rector and the older faculty members at Bauer, dismissing notions of reform as "ill-advised at this time"), in a way "charming," "touching," "gentlemanly," anxious to please, to entertain, a veritable parody of Teutonic egotism—and willing to work for a modest salary, without complaint. I am eternally grateful for your kindness, Schweppenheiser was said to have announced, with a click of his heels and a curt but deferential bow of his head, when the rector hired him; and he must have been telling the truth.

Schweppenheiser with his perennial maroon plaid shirt, his tweed jacket worn at the elbow and stained at the cuffs, his tight brown gabardine trousers. A yellow bow tie carelessly clipped in place. He wore rain hats, rubber-soled leather boots, carried a water-repellent knapsack, all from L. L. Bean's. In the classroom he was literally a mesmerizing presence: even the least studious boys, even the most systematically indifferent boys, could not look away from him. He bristled, he preened, he paced, he scribbled on the blackboard, erased chalk marks with his sleeve, made jokes and puns that went over most heads (it was several years before Nick, then an undergraduate at Harvard, was to recall and at last grasp the meaning of one of Schweppenheiser's muttered jests —he had been mercilessly reading to the class a boy's paper on the Civil War, interrupting himself with wheezing laughter, shaking his fist, at last arriving at what was, in his words, the *turd force* of the attempt). He was tyrannical, he was a clown, he was ribald, cynical, jeering, and then quite suddenly kind: he listened to tales of family sorrows or personal anxieties with immense sympathy in the privacy of his office: Schweppenheiser alone, the boys quickly saw, was another man altogether from Schweppenheiser in public.

Certainly he was an "original." And no doubt a genius. It was Bauer's pride that Bauer tolerated him, and anticipated the day when his immense study—"The Madness of Greatness" was its working title— would be published to scholarly and perhaps even popular acclaim. A dynamo in the classroom, people said. So good for the boys. Shake them up. Make them think. Startle them a little. And he *is*—beneath all that hammy bluster—really quite sweet.

Schweppenheiser divided the six-day week (for at Bauer classes met six days) into three lectures, a "colloquium," a "question-and-answer" session, and a debate. The lectures were alarmingly formal, delivered in a quick high voice, with few interruptions for jokes, puns, or other amusing asides. At such times he paced importantly about, turning a piece of chalk in his fingers, staring at the ceiling, squinting, rolling his eyes, inhaling deeply, sighing, scratching himself under his arms, pausing to repeat his words with a minor but significant variation in tone or accent. (His lectures were his most "English" sessions. Even the jokes—and there were jokes, subtle and ironic and buried—had an English and not a Teutonic flavor.) Students took notes as if they were undergraduates, grimly and feverishly. Though Schweppenheiser boasted that no boy would pass *his* course by simply "regurgitating" lessons, it was nevertheless true that one had to know every fact he mentioned, every name and date, every event, as a minimum requirement. Bauer students afterward claimed—even those who loathed Schweppenheiser—*especially* those who loathed Schweppenheiser— that he had prepared them for the most difficult of their college professors: he gave them a touch of the "real" academic contest.

The colloquium, however, was less formal. The question-and-answer session was less formal still. Noisiest of all, and by far the most disturbing, was the Saturday debate in which Schweppenheiser selected boys to sit on a sort of panel at the front of the room and debate subjects he gave them, interrupting them at whim, contradicting them, telling them to shut up if they couldn't speak with more intelligence, force, or character. He barked out questions, he strode to the front of the room and grabbed a shoulder and shook, hard, he ridiculed, he made gestures of incredulity and disgust, he stirred the class to near-hysterical laughter. To be bested by Schweppenheiser was no grave insult, for even the most brilliant students, even Schweppenheiser's pets, were ground under by his merciless wit and his infinite knowledge; the test was whether one burst into tears and hurried from the room.

Schweppenheiser in his glory: mocking the pretensions of Bauer, the upper-middle class, the United States, the West, the "civilized world," all of history. He fairly salivated as he tore into the pomposity and vanity of so-called great men. No illustrious personage escaped his corrosive tongue. With dizzying speed and an arsenal of detail that must have been the consequence of a photographic memory, he sketched in political squabbles, party loyalties and betrayals, ignoble rivalries, secret arrangements, deals, bribes, and occasional blackmail, and outright threats, to show *why* certain men were nominated by their parties to run for the presidency. "You think it is on the basis of merit! Moral and intellectual superiority! Old Jefferson's ideals!" Schweppenheiser brayed. "In grade school perhaps you are taught such twaddle—but no longer, not here, not in *my* class."

Schweppenheiser grandly demonstrated that there was nothing divine about history, and particularly not American political history. The crudest sort of scrambling and opportunism held sway. Or sheer luck: one man's misfortune was another man's fortune. And the pack of men who presumably "rose" to public distinction! Like Jonathan Swift (whom Schweppenheiser proudly acknowledged as one of his mentors) he divided most of humanity into fools and knaves. He was hilarious on the subject of the fools, scathing on the subject of the knaves. Quite often, of course, the fool and the knave were one—consider the hypocrite incompetent James A. Garfield who almost (*almost:* Schweppenheiser winked conspiratorially at his pets) deserved the ten weeks of unrelieved agony he endured after having been shot in the back by a typically loony American assassin. And Ulysses—"Useless"—S. Grant, with his astounding ineptitude (and his homely cross-eyed wife), administering the highest office in the land out of a veritable sink of corruption. What of the shameless alcoholic Franklin Pierce, whose election to the presidency (after his own party, the Democratic Party, required nearly fifty ballots simply to nominate him as their candidate) was stellar proof, in Schweppenheiser's merry eyes, of the "tragic folly" of democracy?

He pranced, he crowed, he pummeled the air. His bald head glistened with a film of perspiration that took on a queer gray-green cast. Even the shyest boys—even the nicest boys—were reduced to tears of laughter as he impersonated, with florid gestures, bizarre facial tics, and an oratorical rotundity enhanced by his own gallimaufry of accents, the fools, knaves, and hapless victims of the American electoral process. Here is William Henry Harrison, the forgotten ninth President of the United States, who insisted upon delivering the longest inaugural address on record (one hour and forty-five minutes) outdoors on a bitterly cold day in Washington: with the result that he took sick immediately, went to bed, and died exactly one month later of pneumonia. Was ever human vanity so richly rewarded? Here is the tough old buzzard General Zachary Taylor—the twelfth President—who insisted upon standing bareheaded in the pitiless Washington sun during Fourth of July ceremonies, took sick immediately, and died on July 9. So much for "Old Rough and Ready"!

Schweppenheiser knew how to shock and titillate his adolescent audience by speaking quite bluntly of the private lives—the sex lives—of certain Presidents. Grover Cleveland, infamous for having sired a bastard whom he dared not deny; funny Rutherford Hayes with his incestuous love for his sister, which Schweppenheiser speculated, in a witty aside, was probably no more rewarding than any love for any sister, physical or otherwise. Most comic of all was Warren G. Harding with his stable of mistresses, courtesans, and prostitutes. He suffered from a most amusing disorder called satyriasis (which with Olympian disdain Schweppenheiser declined to explain: the curious could rush for dictionaries as soon as class was over) that *rather* exhausted him and that, along with numerous other maladies, mental as well as physical, killed him off, in Schweppenheiser's words, not a minute too soon.

"Old Hickory"—Andrew Jackson—was the most physically wretched man ever elected to the presidency, despite his popular image of courage and tenacity: he suffered from so many ailments that simply their litany (delivered in Schweppenheiser's most comically "English" voice) evoked gales of laughter. Fevers and agues—dysentery—respiratory ailments—chest pains—abscesses in the lungs—hemorrhaging—infection—chronic exhaustion—depression—wild swings of mood—a condition called bronchiectasis which brought forth disgusting quantities of puslike mucous—rotted teeth—violent headaches—partial blindness—and, most humbling of all, an old-fashioned malady called "the Big Itch" which caused the unhappy man to itch almost constantly from head to toe. (Yet this was the very President, Schweppenheiser marveled, who consolidated the power of the office as it had never been consolidated before!) One might have imagined that George Washington, whom Schweppenheiser grudgingly admired, might be immune to his merrymaking: but one of Schweppenheiser's most hilarious comic routines dramatized this extraordinary hypochondriac's self-administering (he was adroit at "bleeding" himself, without the aid of doctors; he was reported to be taking his pulse as he died). Another cruelly funny comic interlude involved President William McKinley and his half-mad epileptic wife Ida. It seems that the President, far from being ashamed of his wife and sympathetic to the distress she evoked in guests and visitors, insisted that she accompany him on ceremonial occasions and even help him officiate at state banquets. How wildly ludicrous barrel-chested Schweppenheiser was, acting the roles of both McKinley and Ida at the dinner table! McKinley knew the symptoms presaging his wife's petit mal attacks and was adroit at quickly throwing a napkin over her head, while his guests—some of them kings and emperors—stared in astonishment. The poor woman went into convulsions at the table, grunting, moaning, whistling, shrieking, wetly smacking her lips, beneath the heaving napkin; and when the attack was over, McKinley whisked the napkin away and the dinner continued as if nothing had happened.

That didn't happen!—that *couldn't* have happened! So the well-bred Bauer students cried aloud.

Ah but it did, it did, Schweppenheiser assured them, winking and sweating, clawing at his bow tie. (In later years, encountering one another at meetings, conferences, parties, in judges' chambers, in board rooms, in Congress, in private dining rooms on Wall Street, virtually everywhere, Bauer graduates who had passed through Schweppenheiser's glorious reign vied with one another to reenact his "Mr. and Mrs. McKinley" routine. Schweppenheiser was, of course, inimitable; but even crude attempts were hilarious. Grown men bent double with laughter as if in violent pain, their cheeks streaming with tears. The napkin, Ida dearest! Time for the napkin! Ah yes!)

Jefferson, whom Schweppenheiser had no choice but to admire, escaped his wit, but Lincoln, poor Lincoln, whom Schweppenheiser also admired, to a degree, drew forth some of his most ingenious impersonations. Lincoln's terror and flight on his wedding day—his depressions and manic seizures—his frequent bouts with what must be called outright insanity: all were grist for Schweppenheiser's mill. (It was not commonly known that Lincoln had been kicked in the head by a horse, as a young boy, and had certainly suffered brain damage.) But most surprising was the behavior of Lincoln's wife Mary, who was insane beyond any doubt, hysterical, obsessive, and frequently violent, most likely (so Schweppenheiser believed) as a consequence of syphilis. (The word hung oddly in the schoolroom, sibilant and mysterious, made all the more remarkable by Schweppenheiser's possibly deliberate mispronunciation: *sif-e-LISS.*) The poor man had even fathered a mad child, the "whirlwind" Tad, who ran wild in the White House, broke china and furniture, defiled the walls, refused to be completely toilet-trained, screamed and shrieked with idiot laughter: he fired guns from the windows of the mansion, he drove a team of goats through the downstairs rooms. A mischievous little demon!—but his Daddy doted on him, and refused to rein him in.

And it wasn't known by the masses, Schweppenheiser told them (his mouth twisting comically about the word "masses") that Abraham Lincoln, far from being universally beloved by Northerners, was in fact generally despised—and many a citzen rejoiced in his assassination! For the tyrannical president had suspended civil rights during the war, he had not greatly cared about the emancipation of the slaves *except as a political issue* (the esteemed Proclamation affecting, after all, only the seceding states—and not the border states, whose allegiance he shamelessly courted), he was ruthless, and often out of his mind, and, in any case, he was a dying man (afflicted with the incurable Marfan's syndrome) when that fool John Wilkes Booth so histrionically martyred him on April 14, 1865.

A fool, and not a serious criminal, Schweppenheiser said, for Booth made the error, like all assassins, of imagining that his victim was worth killing . . . !

There was Teddy Roosevelt who boasted that his Rough Riders suffered seven times as many casualties as other volunteer regiments in the War against Spain, and who told reporters, after his well-publicized charge up one or another Cuban hill: "I waved my hat and we went up the hill with a rush. The charge was great fun. I've had a bully time and a bully fight! I feel as big and as strong as a bull moose!" (This being read by Schweppenheiser in so grotesque a falsetto voice, that even the boys who ordinarily resisted his humor roared with laughter.) Beloved Teddy! He hated and feared the Indians, but for his inaugural of 1904 he released the aging Geronimo from a military prison, so that the old Apache might ride in an open car up Pennsylvania Avenue, wearing, among other things, a black silk top hat. He made claim to other men's conservation reforms, while he slaughtered so many buffalo, grizzlies, antelopes, and deer, that no museum could contain the countless "trophies" he donated. When he left office in 1908, Mark Twain said of him —this also uttered in a Schweppenheiser voice, low and twangy—"He's still only fourteen years old."

On the subject of the much-venerated Woodrow Wilson whose doomed League of Nations, Schweppenheiser allowed, *was* a fairly good idea, though unworkable, he was wonderfully bold as well: and it was a measure of his comic genius that boys whose families revered Wilson, and even boys (in Maurie's and Nick's class) who were distantly related to the Wilson family, could not resist dissolving in laughter as Schweppenheiser sweatily imitated the twenty-eighth President of the United States in his secret manic-paranoid states: for the madman had imagined spies everywhere, he had imagined that God had chosen him as His special servant on earth, he was ranting and incoherent and infantile and megalomanic—! Schweppenheiser was even more hilarious imitating Wilson's second wife, the "rhino-shaped" Edith Bolling Galt, who ran the country for eighteen infamous months while the President "recovered" from a stroke—that eventually killed him.

So the boys were convulsed with laughter. For it was very funny —*very* amusing. The "intellectual" Woodrow Wilson, of all people! As mad as most of the others.

Well, Schweppenheiser said carelessly, not *continually* mad. The old fool had his moments of lucidity, and ostensible sanity, as we all do.

On the subject of F.D.R., Schweppenheiser was considerably more reticent, for there were a number of boys in the school whose fathers had worked with him, in one capacity or another: the son of Roosevelt's second Secretary of the Treasury was in Maurie's class, an honor student, and one of Bauer's most popular boys. And, too, there was an undeniable mystique about the man, that Schweppenheiser's humor could not *quite* overcome. (Still, he could not resist, after class, hinting to a few interested boys that he knew of a "fascinating psycho-pathological incident" in Roosevelt's life, which would one day be exposed by "objective" biographers in the later years of the century.) As for the present day—the *present* President—why, it was too risky to rattle the skeletons, and haul them out into merciless daylight. One could get into trouble, Schweppenheiser said knowingly, one could raise a considerable squawk from the roosters as well as the hens—so, in his reiterated words, *he had best observe a judicious silence.*

Of course boys protested now and then. They had favorites among the Presidents and other "great men" of history. Robert E. Lee was a hero, Captain John Brown was (sometimes) a hero, Alexander Hamilton, Washington and Jackson and Lincoln, and a few others. But Schweppenheiser might have been debunking greatness itself as he mopped his broad bald forehead and tugged at his yellow tie, always sloppily askew. *Aut Caesar, aut nihil!* he sometimes bellowed. (He once alarmed a Saturday class, to which both Maurie and Nick belonged, by giving them a surprise assignment on this topic: they were to write an "impassioned" essay within the hour. And boys who could not decipher the Latin were not aided.) Folly . . . futility . . . egotism . . . vanity: history itself.

Nick Martens with his hard handsome profile and his sly winking eyes and the well-modulated disingenuousness of his voice was an early favorite of Schweppenheiser's, naturally. It was rare that a pun or a quip or a muttered aside sailed over *his* head. He took notes, dutiful as any undergraduate at college, frowning as if he were already (as indeed he was) swimming fiercely upriver, elbowing his classmates aside for a place in Harvard Law. (Which is to say, H.L.S., as it was already known to Bauer students.) His laughter was sometimes shocked, but it was often explosive; and intensely gratifying to Schweppenheiser who closely observed his audience. He had the kind of mind into which dates

and names and unrelated facts might be tossed, as into a lightweight
wicker basket to be carried easily about; at the same time he could draw
together motifs and themes his teacher had been stressing over a period
of weeks or even months, and write extraordinarily perceptive essays of
an abstract nature. If he disagreed with Schweppenheiser—if he was, in
fact, one of the boys who most loathed the toad-ugly perspiring creature
—his alert manner and his perpetual frowning half-smile gave no indication of his feelings; nor did his industry (his extra-credit assignments, his
hunger for "outside reading"); nor his consistently high grades. Like
many Bauer boys Nick readily did Schweppenheiser imitations for his
friends and classmates, when no adults were near. He could screw his
face up and puff out his cheeks, he could roll his eyes, prance about with
an imaginary potbelly straining against his belt, he could bellow and
bray and roar, mispronouncing words, simpering, preening, visibly sali-
vating: but the curious thing was, he couldn't really *mock* Schweppenheiser: Schweppenheiser in his essence couldn't be touched.

Maurie Halleck dared question Schweppenheiser from time to
time. He defended Presidents as varied as Martin Van Buren, Andrew
Jackson, and Lincoln himself; and of course Woodrow Wilson, whom Mr.
Halleck admired. Schweppenheiser was delighted with Maurie's stubborn yet weak-voiced protestations and simply ran right over them, with
the grace of a bulldozer, sometimes pinching the boy's cheek or patting
him fondly on the head. Yes! Yes! Is that so! But the facts argue otherwise! When Maurie, blushing painfully, stammering, insisted that Woodrow Wilson was not being judged fairly, Schweppenheiser murmured a
sudden assent: he even volunteered the fact that he had, for no fee,
translated some of the President's writings into German, simply because
he considered them considerable accomplishments.

Which doesn't alter the fact, my sentimental little friend, that
Wilson was, like most of the others, *quite* mad.

And he beamed at Maurie, and rubbed his hands briskly together.
While the rest of the class obligingly laughed.

The Handclasp

They were not to speak of it, afterward. At any time.

Except in the most abstract of terms.

Thank you for saving my life. Thank you. The most abstract of terms.

For to speak of something so profound in their lives—so violent, so sudden—so intimate and yet impersonal—would have been a desecration. Nor could others speak of it, except in the most abstract terms: for of course no one else knew.

Thank you for saving my son's life. How can I ever repay you?

No witnesses. No one who knew.

A boy's arm flailing wildly, his fingers stretched wide in terror—in helplessness—the deafening roar of the water—spray stinging like ice—another boy clambering to him, slipping, almost falling—on his hands and knees hauling himself across the rocks. *Help me* the drowning boy cannot cry. Blood streams across his forehead, very red, very bright, and is washed immediately away. *Help me* he shouts. But the roar of the water is thunderous. The mad frothing merry white water wants only to carry everything away and smash it against the rocks.

The terrified fingers pluck at the air.

The body's wise panic. The body's irrevocable knowledge, to be held in secret for a lifetime.

Here I am. Here. Here. The desperate clasping of hands, fingers closing hard about fingers.

Yes. Here. Here. I have you.

Lower Loughrea Rapids

Thirty miles east of their destination at Lac Seule, on the fourth day of the trip, they enter the Lower Loughrea Rapids: a three-mile stretch of frothy white water plunging amid rocks, boulders, fallen trees, and scrub willow. At this point the river suddenly narrows. It bends, it twists. Visibility is poor. The air has turned to vapor. One can feel not only the violent thrust of the water and its many currents but the drop, the weight, of gravity itself. The river is falling—one's bowels register the shock.

Someone shouts. But the roar of the water is thunderous, drumming, a din so loud the ears can no longer gauge it. Adrenaline floods the body—the heart races in a panic. A boulder flies by, a rock flies by, a ledge, a stunted birch clump, on one side, on the other, the canoe is heavy with water, air has turned to water, inhaled in panicked gasps. Flying, plunging, racing, skimming the surface of the river, then sinking too low, shipping water—a mistake—the bowels constrict, knowing the mistake—but already the canoe has plunged forward. Bucking and heaving and bouncing. Like children tempted by a wicked amusement ride. Kim and Tony in the lead, then Maurie and Nick. Fatigued and euphoric, their pulses a clamor. Someone shouts and the shout turns into a scream.

It is late in the day though the sun is still fairly high: past six o'clock. They have been on the river for five hours. The inertia of exhaustion draws them forward: to be nearing the mouth of the Loughrea!—to be coming to the end of their trip!

Their eyes dazzled by too much beauty. A mute inexplicable beauty. Balsam, pine, spruce, grassy islands, the bright quick mesmerizing river, the night sky, the profound discomforting silence in which their chatter—their jokes—even their self-consciously serious conversations are swallowed up and lost. They sleep at night as if they had been clubbed into unconsciousness. Never less than eight hours, sometimes nine; and even then they wake groggily, hardly able to recall their names. They devour their food with the appetite of starving beasts: not always waiting for the trout to be completely cooked, or the pancake batter completely crisp. The hours are measured out in sweaty handfuls of raisins, peanuts, salty crackers, chocolate bars. Tanned faces and arms, hardening muscles, a new competence with the canoes, the hands calloused and strong. Each of the boys has lost weight and has had to make new notches in his belt. Kim estimates, marveling, a little nervous, that he might have lost as much as fifteen pounds—is that possible? He is drunk on oxygen, gay and exhilarated and eager to press forward. How good and simple and clear everything is, on the Loughrea! The rest of the world, even the little village at Whiteclay Lake, is remote as a dream, and as inconsequential. How clear, how wonderful! Nothing can touch them—they will live forever. How beautiful! The silence, the secrecy. Maurie's mind drifts free of his body. He is hypnotized by the motion of the oar, by the mechanical movement of his arms, by the water's swift current. Good, clear, simple, direct, to know what one must do, minute after minute, without having to think about it, the mind easing free of the body, airy as the mist. If he attends to his thoughts he discovers, to his surprise, that they are disturbing thoughts: a conviction both that he has been in this place before, and that it is no place—nowhere—an emptiness not even his friends' shouted conversations can disrupt. The immense Loughrea region has no pattern, no order, no center. Its streams and hiking trails—its charted pathways—really lead nowhere. They are accidents, mistakes. One can push forward into the woods and discover a new trail, *force* a new trail, but this too leads nowhere, had not existed a moment earlier, will cease to exist after one moves on. The silence is not quite mocking but it is distinctive, with its own tone, its peculiar texture—its voice. A vast seamless ocean into which Maurie and his friends make their way like intruders who are also victims. If the great mouth opens—! If they suddenly slip inside—! In his sleep he must have moaned aloud because Nick said irritably: Maurie? He believed he was awake because he could see—he could see through his eyelids—but then he was grinding his teeth and Nick said again: Maurie, wake up, cut it out. And afterward at breakfast Nick was irascible and impatient, lapsing into his Schweppenheiser voice, mocking things Maurie said, mocking even Kim and Tony. Unshaven, coarse, childish, with his canvas hat pulled low over his forehead, the colorful feather flies stuck in its band. Squatting at the camp fire, his thighs hard with muscle, straining at his khaki shorts. He wore a sweat- and beer-stained T-shirt. Grime showed in uneven patches, like shadow, through the glistening curls of hair on his legs. He swore at the fire, at the frying pan, at the bacon. Picked his nose. Snorted contemptuously at a remark of Kim's. In Schweppenheiser's very voice he commented on the "delicious" drizzly air and Maurie, still groggy from sleep, turned to him and said in that brave bold pouty defiant voice he sometimes managed: *You* —why don't *you* shut up?

Now Nick prods him, pokes at him, sneers. Come on, what the hell are you waiting for, come *on*. I'm sick of your ugly pimply face, I'm sick of this fucking river, I've had enough of all of you, come *on*.

Tony has been withdrawn and moody and apathetic. He eats with his fingers, wipes his greasy mouth on his shoulder. His beard is the darkest of all: his face looks soiled. Fastidious Tony with his continental table manners, his nightly inspection of the linen napkin at his place in the dining hall. (Sometimes the napkins are faintly scorched. Or folded incorrectly. Once a boy shook his napkin open and the desiccated coin-sized remains of a black beetle flew out onto the table—to everyone's amusement.) On the first two nights of the trip Tony told stories the others could not *quite* believe about his sexual adventures in Italy, Greece, Spain, Germany, and Sweden; and about a precocious "dirty-minded" girl of thirteen who had not only been willing to do certain things with Tony and to Tony, one sleepy August day on a yacht moored off Crete, while the adults played bridge and drank, but had actually made the suggestion herself. Tony with his hooded eyes, his olive-dark skin, his head sleek and graceful as a seal's—Maurie detested him and chose not to believe his stories; Kim hooted with surprised appreciative laughter; Nick grunted and looked away. But as the days passed Tony spoke less and less, withdrawing into a silence somehow different from his usual arrogant silence. (Though afterward—of course—like the others—Tony will testify, and not only to Mr. Halleck who had paid for everything, that the canoeing trip was one of the most important experiences in his life.)

Come on! shouts Nick. What are you waiting for!

Tony wipes his damp face on his shoulder and shrugs indifferently. Kim makes a sucking gesture at the handle of his oar, waving it in Nick's direction. What the hell!—let's go!—we'll be out the other side in two minutes!

Maurie's bowels constrict, sensing danger. He has been here before—has stared at that configuration of tree, cloud, and china-blue sky before—but the inertia of the river has mesmerized him.

All right. Yes. Good. What the hell.

Right? What the hell.

They move forward. Maurie in the prow, Nick in the stern. Pehaps Maurie wants to escape from Nick—to get free of his needling, his bullying, his Schweppenheiser voice. (But it is more than simply a voice. Uncannily, handsome seventeen-year-old Nick Martens can almost transform his face into Hans Klaus Schweppenheiser's puffy grayish face—if his audience is sharp enough to appreciate his wit, he can almost transform his slender body into Schweppenheiser's barrel-body. What an inspired mimic Martens can be! There's genius of a kind in his very malice.) All right, Maurie whispers, I'm ready, what the hell, have your way. At Bitterfeld Lake two winters ago, during Christmas break, the boys went skiing on Mount Kisthene (a moderate slope, not very tricky: both Maurie and Nick are no more than fair skiers) and Nick wore Maurie's heavy beige cable-knit sweater and afterward it smelled of perspiration and Nick said embarrassed that he would have it dry-cleaned and Maurie said not to bother, taking it from him and stuffing it carelessly in a drawer, and that was all right, but a day or two later at breakfast in the lodge with Mr. Halleck and his friends (up from Washington for a few days) Maurie happened to be wearing the sweater —it *was* the beige sweater—and he saw that Nick stared at him oddly; stared at him. And said not a word. Of course it was the case (as Maurie argues endlessly to himself) that (1) he had forgotten entirely about the sweater and simply yanked it out of a drawer, and (2) the sweater hadn't really been soiled.

Don't you believe me?

I'll make you believe me!

One hundred yards into the Lower Loughrea Rapids the aluminum canoe carrying Tony and Kim capsizes. Neither boy can say, afterward, how it happened—a submerged rock, a protruding log, clumsy oaring in a canoe almost sinking with shipped water? They are overturned, they find themselves in the water, gasping and choking, profoundly startled, grabbing by instinct at the canoe's sides. In their desperation, and quite by accident, they do the right thing: place themselves on either side of the canoe, on the upstream end. Battered by rocks, bruised and bleeding, stunned, they are too astonished to feel pain and are simply carried on downstream with the canoe.

But the handsome green Presalex is thrown sideways, smashing broadside against a rock. Maurie is pitched forward at once, screaming. Nick tries to clutch at the canoe but his fingers slip. He falls, swallows a mouthful of water, surfaces to find himself somehow on the downstream side of the canoe; and without thinking ducks to let it pass over his head. Despite the confusion of the moment he realizes that he has come very close to being killed.

If he had been trapped between the canoe and the rocks—

If the canoe had slammed into him, with the weight of thousands of pounds—

He is clutching at a partly submerged log. He is able to breathe in short ragged gasps: he isn't drowning.

Maurie?

The water is shallow, probably no more than four feet deep. But wild, thunderous, and very cold. It keeps knocking his feet out from under him. He can't figure out what has happened, he can't get his bearings, he is too surprised even to feel pain though he has badly banged his right shoulder. Isn't someone calling him? Calling for help?

Maurie—?

He steadies himself against the log. Tries to stand upright. He isn't drowning, he won't drown, he can breathe, he can hold his own against the current.

Maurie? Where are you—?

Then he sees someone ahead, washed along, tumbled about, over and over, in the churning white water, light and limp as a strip of cloth —is *that* Maurie?—is that a human being?

He shouts in disbelief. Almost in anger.

Maurie—

He follows downstream, slipping and scrambling, his fingers scraped, bleeding. His shout is hoarse and incredulous.

Maurie disappears. And surfaces again, farther downstream. A strip of cloth or canvas. Nothing human. Helpless, drowning, without any apparent weight, the envelope of his skin suddenly a frail membrane in which flesh and blood and bones are contained.

Maurie—

Nick scrambles after him, staring, blinking in disbelief. His legs have gone numb from the cold. He is going to collapse—the rapids will sweep him away.

He *can't* believe what is happening.

Then Maurie is dashed against a ledge. And Nick makes his way toward him. Slowly, painstakingly. He is very much alone. No one can help him. Maurie? No one can help him. Only a few yards away. Only a few feet. Churning white water between, a roaring frothy channel, great danger. Maurie? An arm waves helplessly. Flails in terror. Blood streams across Maurie's forehead, bright red blood, washed away at once in the water, then springing out again, bright dizzying sickening red. Maurie's eyes have rolled back into his head. He is dying. Drowning.

His arm flails wildly. The fingers stretched wide. Panic. Sheer terror. Oh God.

Nick reaches out and manages to grab Maurie's hand.

Here. Here I am.

Maurie— Grab hold—he cries.

Fingers close hard about fingers. The handclasp is solid, desperate, permanent.

III. The Tryst

New York City,

April 1980

Central Park

They might be lovers who have bitterly quarreled, or who have done some irrevocable injury to each other: Kirsten approaches him so slowly, so shyly. He hasn't yet seen her. Or recognized her. Her heart has begun its humiliating acceleration though she is certain that she isn't afraid of him. Not of *him.*

But of something he will tell her?

Over the telephone she said softly: I just want to talk with you, Mr. Di Piero. About my father. I won't cry—I won't get upset.

He said lightly: *Mr. Di Piero?*

His question was meant to convey surprise; it sounded merely mocking.

Kirsten's voice was low and reluctant and embarrassed: Tony. *Tony.*

I just want to talk with you. I won't take up much of your time. I know you are busy. I know you don't want to see me. I know you are loyal to Isabel—you're her friend.

I'm not sure I understand, Di Piero said, could you speak louder—?

Whatever you can tell me about it—

Yes? What? I can't hear you, Kirsten.

I just want to talk with you about him. About what happened. You don't even have to say whether you think he's innocent or not—I know he's innocent—I know you're loyal to them and don't want to talk to me

—but anything you could tell me—anything—I would be grateful—I would be grateful—grateful—

Her nails were digging into the palms of her hands. Her forehead was beaded with sweat. She hadn't recalled that she had hated Di Piero so much.

I know you're on their side—I know you're loyal to them—but if I could see you for an hour—if I could talk to you—

Please, Mr. Di Piero—

I would be so grateful. Grateful.

He was reluctant to see her, naturally. She couldn't blame him: it wasn't simply that she was Maurie Halleck's daughter, and everything about Maurie Halleck was an embarrassment, but they—Kirsten and Di Piero—actually shared a secret together. They had had a brief adventure together, several years ago, of which Kirsten thinks from time to time without much emotion. (Her emotion—her loathing—she must keep pure for her father's murderers. She hasn't time to brood over Anthony Di Piero, she resents any emotion she might feel for him. A pig, she has heard women call him, a beautiful pig, she has overheard laughter at 18 Röcken, in the drawing room, on the terrace, Isabel herself once said airily that he used women like Kleenex but perhaps they considered the experience an honor. . . . After all, Isabel said, her accent lightly Spanish, her expression probably disdainful, Tony isn't an ordinary man: even his enemies will tell you that.)

I would be so grateful. . . .

So now he is waiting for her on this windy April afternoon, in Central Park. Not far north of the children's zoo. He checks his watch, he walks in slow measured paces, he pauses to light a cigarette, he stands with one foot up on a bench and his elbow on his knee in an attitude of patient waiting—but his waiting is self-absorbed, he doesn't look around, doesn't scan the faces of people who pass by. (He is using a cigarette holder now, Kirsten notes. A new affectation. She hasn't seen him in two or three years.)

Anthony Di Piero, olive-skinned, slender, with his sleek dark hair combed close to his head, his sunglasses tinted a very dark green. Dressed as always with impeccable taste: he is wearing a tweed sports jacket with slightly exaggerated proportions (shoulders, lapels) in the newest European style, a pale chamois color; and a mauve-gray necktie that is probably made of silk; and a white cotton voile shirt with gold cuff links; and gleaming black shoes, extremely slender in the toes. His jaw is somewhat narrow, his skin somewhat pale, but surely he is a handsome man—a beautiful man, even—though Kirsten would never call him that. A pig, perhaps. Dear Tony, as Isabel would say. Greeting him with a stately handshake, then rising to kiss him on one cheek, and then on the other. On the lips too, no doubt, if they were alone. Dear Tony. How good you are looking.

Kirsten has stopped on the path, some yards away. A young father is taking photographs of his wife and little girl, who are sitting on a park bench; Kirsten pauses, not exactly hiding behind them. She is smiling, blinking rapidly, her hair blows into her face, she feels suddenly very queer. In jeans and a shaggy red sweater, wearing sunglasses of her own, amber-tinted; Kirsten, reckless and frightened and out of breath from running. (The train was delayed, coming down the Hudson to Grand Central Station.) That childish sense of euphoria that comes from being truant from school. Mr. Di Piero? Anthony? Tony? Do you remember me?

Of course I remember you. The Halleck girl.

(*Isabel's daughter,* he might have said. Doubtful that he would have said *Maurie's daughter.*)

Nervously she had joked with him on the telephone: You're a very difficult man to track down. Your answering services aren't friendly and you don't seem to be in the habit of returning your calls and at your office (on Wall Street, this is: Kirsten got the number from rifling through her mother's desk back in December) the receptionist was as protective of you as if you were royalty. (Who shall I say is calling Mr. Di Piero? "Kirsten Halleck"? Could you identify yourself further, please?)

A week of her life was given over to contacting him. Making telephone calls, leaving messages, rehearsing conversations. Mr. Di Piero was her father's friend originally. (Prep school together. The Bauer School. Harvard for a while.) But then he was her mother's friend —one of her mother's most intimate friends—for a while. A friend too of Nick Martens's: but Kirsten doesn't know how close.

Mr. Di Piero? I only want to ask you a few questions.

I won't break down. I won't get upset. I won't even need to use your handkerchief.

I *won't* ask about you and Isabel—that would be in poor taste, at the present time. And it doesn't bear upon the immediate problem.

(Odd that she hadn't thought of Di Piero, when Owen was with her. That Saturday. Hiking along the river. The wind, the high scudding clouds, the shrieking birds, Owen's disbelief, Owen's anger. And their embrace—finally. Weeping together. Finally. For he knew, of course; he knew; he knew who the murderers were and what must be done. But Kirsten hadn't thought of Di Piero until later that day, after Owen had gone. He might be the one, he might know all their secrets, she realized, suddenly. The thought pierced her like a marvelous razor-sharp blade. Anthony Di Piero! Of course. *Dear Tony,* her mother's friend. Her mother's ex-friend.)

Was he royalty, Di Piero? He had once been engaged to marry a *principessa,* the daughter of a descendant of the Longobard kings. But something had gone amiss: perhaps the girl turned out to be, finally, not rich enough. Or Di Piero hadn't been beautiful enough.

I would be so grateful, Kirsten whispered. Digging her nails into the palms of both her hands. So very grateful.

You bastard. You pig.

(He hadn't returned any of her calls. Eight or ten calls. And she knew—she supposed—exactly why.)

But he agreed, finally. Not troubling to disguise the reluctance in his voice. For of course—of course—he is a very busy man: in fact he is flying to Frankfurt day after tomorrow. Nevertheless he agreed to meet her for an hour or so. A kind of tryst. A secret meeting.

You promise you won't tell Isabel? Kirsten begged. I mean—you won't telephone her as soon as we hang up?

He was silent a moment. She feared she had lost him.

Kirsten Halleck with her reckless mouth!

Kirsten the idiotic little bitch who spoils everything!

Softly Di Piero said: But why should I telephone Isabel, what is Isabel to me? What has Isabel to do with any of this?

Kirsten laughed wildly. Oh yes yes yes. No.

Now in jeans and a soiled red sweater, her heavy leather bag slung over her shoulder, Kirsten stands on the path, staring, licking her lips, blinking as if dazed by the sunshine. Even the most indifferent passerby, glancing at her, might guess that something is wrong with her, something gravely wrong: for why otherwise would a girl of her age hold herself so queerly upright? Her young back is arched, taut as a bow. Indeed she is a bow that has been drawn *very* taut. (What is she carrying in the leather bag? What weighs it down? A weapon? A gun?) Her forehead would be blank and smooth, except that it is creased; her mouth would be pretty, except that it is frozen in an expression of bizarre coquetry—part gaiety, part terror.

Mr. Di Piero—

Tony.

The cherry trees lining the path are heavy with white blossoms. Overhead feathery branches move in a slight breeze: the small green buds, shot with sunlight, appear golden. And the child standing on the park bench in her mother's embrace, babbling happily as if this were the first day of creation . . . But Kirsten is innocent of these sights. She is blind, staring at the man in the chamois tweed jacket a short distance away.

Her heart is pounding absurdly. Though he is not one of the murderers—he is not that important in her life.

(But where will you get a gun, Owen asked shrewdly. Even in his agitation, in his revulsion for her, he knew the right questions. *You—a gun!* And how could you get Nick alone? He isn't our "Uncle Nick" any longer. . . . Drawing back from Kirsten, staring, beginning to laugh. His eyes swam with tears. He swayed as if drunk. It must have been the wind, the noise of the choppy gray water, the shriek of the birds. You can't do it, he said. We can't. It's impossible.)

On the telephone Anthony Di Piero had murmured, as if in embarrassment: Your father—it was a pity. He should not have despaired over such a thing.

Kirsten, gripping the phone, had to imagine his hooded eyes, his guarded expression. Though his words were sincere enough. (Di Piero was a man who might reasonably fear that his telephone conversations were being taped.)

He should not have despaired over such a trivial thing.

Despaired—! Kirsten whispered.

Significant, wasn't it, that Di Piero declined to invite her to his apartment or to his office on Wall Street; he hadn't even arranged to meet her in a hotel lobby or a restaurant. Instead they were meeting in the park, in neutral territory. A tryst, Kirsten thought cynically. A secret rendezvous. . . . But then she couldn't blame the poor man: it was three years since he had seen her last. (He had been overseas last June and hadn't attended Maurie's funeral in Washington.) No doubt there were rumors about the Hallecks, how well was Isabel taking it, the shock of the death, the ugly publicity, the humiliating disclosures, and what about the children . . . the boy Owen, and the girl, what is her name . . . ! The strange one, the unstable one, Kirsten.

I want to see you, Kirsten said.

Do you, Di Piero said.

Whatever you can tell me, anything you can tell me, Kirsten whispered, I would be so grateful. . . . I promise not to cry.

Now he is waiting for her a short distance away. His foot on a park bench, his elbow on his knee. Waiting. Behind him an enormous outcropping of rock has been defaced with white spray paint. The man and woman with the little girl are walking away. Kirsten hesitates, staring. She *is* sad and gawky; she hasn't any faith in her appearance. Over the months her body has grown flat, her small breasts have nearly disappeared, she no longer menstruates, she lies awake seeing again and yet again the car settling into the swamp, the swamp water rising, her father's pale lank hair beginning to float; so captivated, she cannot attend to being female.

Please see me, she begged. For an hour.

All right, said Di Piero carefully. But I don't understand what you want.

Now she approaches him, her manner as casual as possible. She is not hurrying, nor is she holding back. He may notice her exceptionally straight posture. The tension in her slender neck. The way she grips the strap of her shoulder bag. (What *is* she carrying inside? The bag appears to be so heavy.)

I don't understand what you want, Di Piero said, and now she could sense his irritation. Her eyes were shut tight; the telephone receiver was jammed against her face. Over Christmas she had gone through her mother's desk, in a bright airy alcove of her mother's bedroom, and she had discovered three telephone numbers for Di Piero: so she had copied each down. So she had tracked him to his lair. He could not avoid her. An imminent trip to Frankfurt, another to Tokyo in mid-May. . . . He could not avoid her, he could not *really* say no. I promise I won't cry, Kirsten whispered, I won't ask you questions you don't want to answer, it's just that—it's just that—I think of him all the time—I—I want to stop him from dying—drowning—if someone had seen the car go off the road and helped him—if they had called an ambulance—after he had the heart attack—maybe he could have been saved—I don't think he would have died—if someone had seen him—he would be alive now—he could explain everything—don't you think so? Mr. Di Piero? Don't you think so? The things he left behind—the notes, the documents—maybe they weren't even his—they might be forged—no one has proven they weren't forged—he was all alone—he might have been trying to get away from them—I mean the people who were his enemies—his killers—I think there was a hired killer who followed him that night—but I won't ask you about that—even if you know, even if you know who arranged for it—I won't ask you—I won't get upset—I know you are loyal to your friends—even if you don't see Isabel any longer I know you are loyal—you and she respect each other—maybe you're afraid of each other—and you're a friend of Nick's too—you all respect one another—I won't ask you to tell me anything that would violate your friendship—I promise I won't cry—I would be so grateful, Mr. Di Piero—so grateful—you remember me, don't you?—Kirsten Halleck?

The words had tumbled from her, of course he hadn't heard. Only the very last. So he said, embarrassed, irritated, and now clearly in a hurry to hang up: Of course I remember you, Kirsten. With the pink and white bathing suit. Little seahorses, weren't they?—in white, embroidered, on the fabric.

April 17, 1980. A Thursday.

Yesterday—Christ, was it only yesterday!—Kirsten telephoned Owen, to tell him about Di Piero. The proposed meeting with Di Piero. But Owen was hiding: she called four times, and he was never in, and she called his club, and she could hear the name being shouted *Halleck! Halleck!*—and a wave of faintness rose in her, a wave of exhilaration, certainty, *Halleck* was the name, *Halleck* was his name, he had agreed to help, he had agreed "to take care of *her*," he could not escape, he could not betray her, *Halleck* was the name, just hear how it was being shouted—

But Owen wasn't at his club. In any case he didn't come to the phone.

So Kirsten telephoned his room again and one of his suitemates picked up the receiver and was perfectly courteous in promising to take a message, but Kirsten interrupted, it was an emergency, a family emergency, she had to talk with her brother *at once*, he had to return her call *at once*, and then suddenly, she didn't know how, she was very angry, and sobbing, she was shouting things she didn't mean, coward, liar, fucker, she was saying, I know he's there, I know he's standing right there, the coward, the asshole, tell him his sister knows all about him, tell him she'll do it by herself, tell him it's started, everything is started, it can't be stopped, it won't be stopped, tell him—

And then someone was shouting at her, and it was Owen: and she went silent at once, in utter panic.

He shouted at her for some time. It was a very long time—she couldn't gauge its passage. An hour, a minute, a wild *long* minute, during which she had the opportunity to think, with surprising lucidity, *Halleck, he's Halleck, he can't escape.*

When Owen quieted, she said, meekly, slyly, smiling an invisible provoking smile, I thought maybe you'd changed your mind, that's all. I thought maybe you were going to give me both of them.

If you call me again like this, Owen said, calmly now, I'll take care of you too. I'll wring your neck.

If you call me again like this, Owen said, calmly, I'll take care of you too.

Di Piero! Di Piero.

A honey of a name, to wrap her tongue around.

She does not notice the bright-dazzling sky, she does not notice the blossoms, so lovely, so perfect, Isabel would exclaim over them, but are they real?—nor does she take careful note of who is close by, who might be observing, as she approaches Anthony Di Piero, forcing herself not to hurry, not to betray signs of haste, yet exhibiting no girlish *shyness* either: for certainly that would bore him.

Hello, Kirsten says.

A tall slender man in a sportsjacket with fashionably exaggerated proportions—the shoulders *slightly* too wide, the lapels *slightly* too pronounced. (There is something subtly erotic in the very cut of his costume, Kirsten thinks. Because, for all its ephemeral perfection, and despite the excellent quality of the fabric, it will be discarded within the calendar year: it has been fashioned, and purchased, with that in mind.)

She says, Hello, again—for he hasn't heard.

He turns to look at her, with no sign of recognition.

(But *is* this man Anthony Di Piero? My God, Kirsten thinks, he is older, much older. There are lines bracketing his mouth. Faint white creases about his eyes. Stay out of the bright sunshine, Isabel has warned, once it's too late you'll know why: you won't be a pretty little girl forever, with that smooth skin.)

Very odd, very interesting. The alterations in Di Piero.

Hello, Kirsten says another time, smiling, raising her voice. Mr. Di Piero—

It's a holiday, after all. She is a truant. Cutting her Thursday classes—telling Hannah that she "has an appointment in the city"— dental X-rays—wisdom teeth, courteous enough for once to lie: for the school, pitying her, is making every effort *not* to expel her.

The daughter of the late disgraced Maurice Halleck.

Hello, Kirsten, Di Piero says.

He has not risen from the bench, he has waited for her to approach *him:* a gesture not lost on Kirsten. So she begins to chatter, nervous blushing word-tumbling chatter, the delayed train, the taxi, traffic backed up at Fifty-seventh Street . . . .

Di Piero's sunglasses are black-rimmed and stylish. The lenses are so dark a green that Kirsten can see only the lithe movement of his eyes, not their focus.

They shake hands formally, like guests at 18 Röcken. Strangers who have just been introduced but have every reason to suspect they know each other.

Thank you so much, Kirsten says, chattering nervously, I know how busy you are—I know that—on a weekday—an afternoon— It's so nice of you to—

His smile is measured; he isn't a generous man. He allows her to rattle away—an idiot, an ass, why is she so breathless, why this gawky coquetry!—while he stares at her, cigarette holder in hand. Then, with a gesture both careless and deliberate, he brushes her hair off her forehead.

That's a little better, he says.

The Suicide Club

After the death in December 1977—by barbiturate overdose—of the fourteen-year-old daughter of a prominent member of the President's Council of Economic Advisers, it was suggested in the public press that a secret suicide club was in existence at the Hays School.

The club was said to have an elaborate initiation ceremony, secret passwords, a secret handshake. It was known simply as The Club. One columnist who claimed to have interviewed a member, anonymously, stated in print that there were as many as twenty or twenty-five girls involved.

The girls had in common not the experience of having tried to commit suicide once or twice or several times (the uncontested champion was the overweight red-haired daughter of a Washington attorney whose name was frequently in the papers), and not even the intention of committing suicide someday: they had in common (so the story went) simply an intense, obsessive, and all-absorbing *interest* in suicide.

They collected clippings and magazine articles. They compared methods. (Drug overdose was by far the favorite method. Though carbon monoxide poisoning had its appeal. Slashing one's wrists, blowing one's brains out with a revolver, jumping out a high window—and, of course, hanging—were considered far too violent and disfiguring.) They spent hours and hours in one another's rooms, recounting stories of suicides in their families, deaths reported as "natural" in the press, accidents which were in fact not accidental. They read biographical essays of famous suicides, to discover precisely *how* it was accomplished. Simone Weil interested the two or three ascetics in the group, Hemingway interested those who fancied themselves literary, and of course there was Sylvia Plath, and there was Marilyn Monroe: in her case both *how* and *why* were particularly significant. (In general, *why* was not significant. Divorce—alcoholism—professional failure—financial embarrassment—loss of reputation—loss of health—chronic depression—drug-taking—mental instability: these causes were interchangeable, the girls reasoned, and not very important.)

That Marilyn Monroe should choose to kill herself struck the "ugly" girls as wonderfully consoling. It also struck the beautiful girls as consoling.

Naturally the Hays School denied the rumors. And issued courteous and inflexible statements of "no comment" on further questions.

So publicized, so gossipped about, The Club dissolved: only the least popular girls, the girls who had *not* belonged, made claim to know anything about it, uttering certain buzz words meant to provoke and tantalize.

But then, in early spring of 1978, a girl in Kirsten's form—a boarder at the school—slashed her wrists very late at night, in a storage room off the gym, and almost died, and, a week later, another girl, a graduating senior, named to the court of the Cherry Blossom Queen, and *very* pretty, slashed her wrists and did die.

These were, on the whole, termed "senseless" deaths. And whether the girls had belonged to The Club—no one seemed to know.

Consequently the Hallecks withdrew Kirsten from the Hays School, despite Isabel's fond memories of it. (Some of the happiest—the very happiest—days of my life were spent there, Isabel claimed, her eyes bright with tears of sorrow, or anger, or simple vexation, and now even my memories are ruined!) They would try St. Timothy's, perhaps, or the Potomac School, or Miss Pickett's, or Exeter: whichever was accommodating enough, and willing to accept Kirsten Halleck.

Miss Pickett's it was—the other schools declining her application, with sincere regrets.

Before these pragmatic arrangements were made, Maurie thought it both politic and wise to take his daughter to lunch at the Shoreham: just father and daughter. Without mother. For, after all, it had been a very long time since they had talked.

When he asked Kirsten, gently enough, if she knew anything about the suicide club (which he called "that club," being unable to bring himself to say the words), Kirsten's response was disconcerting: she continued to pick at her crabmeat salad, showing no surprise, and said carelessly, *Those* assholes?—I don't know a thing.

Maurie may have winced slightly at his daughter's language. But he drew closer to the table, he reached over to squeeze her hand.

Kirsten looked at their hands.

You don't know anything about it, the club, the group of girls . . . ? Maurie asked.

No, said Kirsten at once.

Since early childhood Kirsten's eating habits had been eccentric, and obsessive. She occupied herself with dividing the food on her plate into sections, working quickly and deftly and, it seemed, with her eyes half-shut: some things were to be eaten, some not. In a crabmeat salad there were suspicious ingredients—sliced black olives, minced pimiento —that could not be eaten. Now she brooded over her plate, picking and sorting. Her fork moved swiftly.

At this time Maurie was experienceing certain difficulties at the Commission. Some were not surprising because they were woven into the texture of such proceedings: the law moves by baby steps in order to take a giant step but it is usually necessary that the baby steps be done in secret. Other difficulties, other blockages and snags, were more mysterious. They had to do with the assemblage of evidence against two corporations—one entirely American-owned, the other American and Japanese—that had been involved in illegal activities in South America during the 1970s. Political "donations," bribes of various kinds, interference in campaigns and elections: Bolivia, Honduras, and Chile. Particularly Chile. Six-count felony charges were about to be brought against three men, one of them a director of public relations for the South American division of GBT Copper, for "clandestine efforts to prevent the 1970 election of Allende" as president of Chile. The investigations had taken years—had involved a team of eight men and innumerable assistants—and evidence and witnesses were hard to come by and Maurie and his associates grimly anticipated pleas of nolo contendere and the usual fine ($50,000 was the statutory ceiling under the Sherman Act), perhaps suspended sentences—six months, thirty days.

Conspiracy to commit murder was a possibility too. But an increasingly distant one. After the nationalization of Chilean copper in 1971 there were—quite naturally—a number of unexplained deaths; there were a sizable number of unexplained deaths. But evidence and witnesses were extremely hard to come by.

Maurie was able to take the afternoon off, however. He had arrived at his office at six-thirty, and by twelve-thirty things had gone well enough, routinely enough, to allow him to leave for luncheon with his daughter.

They were alone together so rarely.

They spoke together so rarely.

The Shoreham for lunch, for an elegant lunch? How does that sound?

Kirsten crinkled her eyes at her father but did not say no.

Perrier water with a twist of lime, in a handsome crystal glass. Onion soup with crusty cheese. The crabmeat salad: on an enormous gold-rimmed plate. French bread, butter. And salt. (Why did she salt everything? So lavishly?)

Kirsten, Maurie said in his soft puzzled voice, why don't you look up at me? Is something wrong? I had hoped we might—

She raised her eyes to his slowly. A gray hazy stare, revealing nothing.

I'm not one of your witnesses, to be interrogated, she said.

It was clumsily done, so she tried again: now the remark was cute.

Maurie said gently that he wasn't interrogating her. He had hoped only— He had wanted—

Kirsten shrugged her shoulders. She was wearing what appeared to be a cotton T-shirt—bright yellow, with a manic grinning face on its front—though Maurie supposed it was a "real" shirt, from an expensive shop on the avenue. Of course she was wearing her usual tight faded jeans. But for the Shoreham, for the occasion, she had combed her hair nicely—it was *very* beautiful red-blond hair—and put on lipstick: she looked pretty despite her odd mannerisms and her habit of staring and frowning at her plate.

Pretty Kirsten. Fifteen years old. Bad-tempered, unreliable, shrewd, bright, funny. Her sense of humor, her tricks—! Maurie had no idea where she got that strain from, that diabolical energy: telephoning friends of Isabel's very late one night to say that Isabel had been injured in a car crash and needed blood at once and would they come down to the hospital and donate a pint: *not* a very funny joke in anyone's judgment.

If there was really a suicide club at your school, Maurie said, I want you to tell me about it.

Kirsten wiped her mouth on her linen napkin and looked her father full in the face and said no. No I won't.

You won't—?

I don't *know* anything about it.

You don't know anything about it?—really?

Only what I've read in the papers. Isabel's friend Bobbie Tern— or maybe they aren't friends now.

But you don't know? There wasn't a club, your friends weren't in it, you don't know anyone who was in it—*you* weren't in it? Maurie asked.

Kirsten stared coldly over his head. Scratched her throat, sighed, sniffed, used her napkin as a handkerchief. Decided she wanted a chocolate mousse for dessert—but it had better be good. She was something of an expert on chocolate mousse.

You weren't in it—? Maurie persisted.

Of course not, Father, Kirsten said airily.

And you don't know anyone who was? Not a single girl?

Not a single girl. I don't have many friends—you know that.

You have friends, Maurie said.

I don't have many friends, Kirsten said, giggling. They get mad at me. They can't take a joke.

No one in your class? No one you know?

No one, Father. Do you want me to take the oath? Swear before your committee?

This is a very serious matter, Kirsten. Your mother and I—

Oh, everything is serious, Kirsten said bluntly. She waved to their waiter.—Chocolate mousse is serious.

If you know anything about it I wish you would tell me, Maurie said. His low courteous voice pleased her: he was begging. In another moment he would reach across the table again and squeeze her hand. Her limp cold thin indifferent hand. She would like that: she prepared herself. Kirsten?—you *would* tell me?—if you knew? he said.

He was blinking rapidly. Poor man, poor Daddy, monkeyish and homely, but now *almost* handsome in his grief: and he was wearing the dove-gray seersucker suit Isabel had insisted he buy, tailor-made. An ugly striped tie but that hardly mattered. (Isabel was in New York for the weekend. Had she been home, she would never have allowed Maurie out the door with that tie.) Kirsten might take pity on him, she might hint that of course she knew—knew just a little—but the senior girls kept to themselves—and The Club was mainly senior girls—only three or four or five younger girls—*not* Kirsten Halleck of course: she wouldn't be a candidate for any secret club no matter how she yearned to be asked.

Maurie reached over, nearly upset her water goblet, squeezed her hand. It startled her that his own hand was cold and unpleasantly damp.

You *would* tell me, honey?—Kirsten? You *would* talk to me if—?

Of course, Father, Kirsten said, not troubling to withdraw her hand; but not returning the pressure of his fingers either.—You or Mother. Don't Owen and I tell you everything?

After the Funeral

When he died I went down into the grave with him, Kirsten wrote in her journal, *but it wasn't in Georgetown Memorial Cemetery, it was a swamp in Brean Down, Virginia: mosquitoes and stagnant stinking water and black mud thick as shit.*

She considered sending another telegram to Audrey Martens. But had she ever sent the first . . . ? She couldn't remember but it must be written down somewhere. This time the telegram would be anonymous: *So difficult to breathe here but I am waiting patiently, where is Nick?*

She turned up the phonograph and loved it that her heartbeat accelerated in time with the hard heavy music: so loud it blasted through her, ran delirious along her veins, made her laugh softly to herself. In such a cascade of sheer noise no one could hear her secret thoughts, *no one would know.*

But they made her turn the music down.

Han—poor frightened Han—weeks and weeks of it—Kirsten "dancing" barefoot around the room, humming to herself, murmuring to herself, remarkably heavy for a girl who now weighs only ninety-seven pounds: Kirsten suddenly frank and lucid and very much her former self, and not even sarcastic: Look, I think I need to be alone, why don't you move out, there's that vacancy with Marnie and Barbara, you *know* you'd rather be with them, look Han I won't be hurt I really *won't* be hurt if you move out—

She couldn't sit at her desk for more than five minutes, she was up, she was pacing about, humming, singing under her breath a song no one at school knew, *Frankie and Johnny were sweethearts, O how those two could love,* dancing about the room because she was high without smoking anything and her heart pounded like a fist pounding knocking at her chest and she could feel her elastic veins all along the length of her amazing pulsing body, *Frankie was loyal to Johnny, just as true as stars above,* the Hallecks had a record of the song, an old Negro blues singer, New Orleans maybe, Kirsten didn't know, it had once been sung by Isabel in a musical revue at school, *she shot her man 'cause he done her wrong,* but it didn't say what happened afterward: whether Frankie was arrested and sent away or whether what she did was all right, because Johnny had deserved to die.

The telegram to Audrey Martens would read: *Mr. Halleck did not deserve to die but Mr. Martens does.*

No, Kirsten cried aloud, vexed, no, that's a mistake, put nothing in writing, nothing that isn't in code.

Isabel's highly successful and highly visible girlhood was pre-served in scrapbooks and bureau drawers and framed photographs in her boudoir at 18 Röcken, there were souvenirs of old conquests, love letters, dried and flattened corsages, snapshots, newspaper photographs of "Isabel de Benavente, daughter of the financier Luis de Benavente" looking beautiful and radiant and surely—surely!—marked for extraor-dinary success: amid all this Kirsten had found (had often found: for in fact it was a childhood preoccupation of hers, sorting through her mother's things, reverently, with awe, not yet with resentment, on rainy Washington days when she couldn't play outside, or on those wonderful days when, slightly feverish, or reporting a sore throat or a "funny feeling in her head," she was allowed to stay home from school—the only child in the house)—had often found evidence of Isabel's girlhood tri-umphs; formidable evidence. Not Mrs. Maurice Halleck but Miss Isabel de Benavente, a Washington debutante.

She decided against the second telegram. For it might call atten-tion to her plans for Nick. And would Western Union accept the word *shit?*—Kirsten doubted it. *S——* would not have quite the same dra-matic effect.

You can move out if you want, Kirsten said, not looking at Han-nah. I don't give a damn. I don't need you poking and spying and feeling goddam fucking *sorry.*

She scribbled in her journal notes in a secret code. For, after all, the magnitude of her plans called for strict secrecy.

Owen will exact justice from Mother, I am assigned to Nick Martens. The choice of weapons must soon be made. (Mother has a gun

—doesn't she? Somewhere in her bedroom? Or locked in the safe? I
have never seen it and Owen says the idea is absurd—Father wouldn't
allow a gun in the house. But I seem to know that she has one. I seem
to know. I know.)

Pretty Hannah Weil who will major in archeology and Spanish at
Stanford; Hannah who will graduate second in Eyre's Class of 1980;
Hannah whose father has been in the diplomatic service since 1955
(Athens, Rome, Damascus) and whose mother died of cancer when Hannah was twelve (after six operations, two years): a solemn dark-haired
girl with a high forehead and slightly prominent teeth and a low quizzical
voice: Kirsten's only friend at Eyre.

I don't give a fuck what you do, Kirsten muttered. She was sitting
Indian-style on her rumpled smelly bed, barefoot, bare-legged, in her
white cotton panties (stained at the crotch: she hadn't troubled to change
them for a week) and a flannel shirt missing a button.

I know everyone hates me, Kirsten said.

She steeled herself, waiting to be contradicted.

And if she was not contradicted—?

Don't be silly, Kirsten, Hannah said at once. You know that isn't
true.

But I don't give a fuck if it *is* true, Kirsten said.

She sat very still and stared at her toes. Grimy toes, grimy toenails. She would have to fix herself up for the trip to New York City. For
Anthony Di Piero.

Idly she sniffed under her arms. Not very pleasant. No. And he'd
notice—*he* would—from a distance of several feet. She would have to
shave too. Under her arms, and her legs. It had been a while.

Night after night they had talked, in the autumn. Hannah in her
bed across the room, Kirsten in hers, grateful for the dark and for the
fact that Hannah whom she loved could not see how ugly she was—her
face contorted with the effort not to cry. (It was the mouth that became
particularly ugly, she had noted. Twisted and queer. Like Grandfather
Benavente after his stroke. But the eyes too—suddenly crinkled—small
and red-veined and helpless—terrified. Surrounded by fine white wrin-
kles of the kind Isabel had had removed from *her* face.) I just don't know
what to do, she whispered, I don't know how to live now, I have to think
about putting one foot down in front of the other or how to brush my
teeth or how to eat . . . why I should eat . . . why some things are
important. Everything is just a dream. It isn't real. I can't connect. I
don't remember how. He shouldn't be dead. If it was a heart attack and
there was someone behind him on the road they could have called an
ambulance, they could have pulled him out of the car maybe and kept

him from drowning and now he wouldn't be dead, he would be alive, I don't know what that means, *to be dead,* I don't know where he is, I keep seeing him in the swamp, in the car, I keep tasting the water and the mud, I dream about pulling him out . . . I can see his hair so clearly . . . floating in the water . . . I can *see* it . . . I must have been there.

Hannah spoke of her mother's death. The prolonged suffering. The operations, the hope, the dread. Kirsten listened closely. She bit her lower lip, listening. The first diagnosis . . . the X-rays . . . the biopsy . . . the operation . . . the chemotherapy . . . the second operation . . . the third operation. . . . Hannah spoke softly, evenly. You had to imagine her eyes open wide, unblinking, staring at a corner of the ceiling. (Where the shadow was darkest. Kirsten too stared at that corner, for comfort.) The thing about death, Hannah said, beginning now to falter, is that you can't say anything about it that sounds right. You can't say any words that are appropriate. Just that I loved her and I miss her all the time, I miss her every day, I even talk to her, but I can't explain it and I don't know how to talk to you—I'm so ashamed.

He had wanted her to kneel with him, to pray. His breath stinking of whiskey. As fetid, as sad, as General Kempe. *Ye know not what shall be on the morrow. For what is your life? It is even a vapour, that appeareth for a little time, and then vanisheth away.*

She began to think, to brood, on John Brown again. An enthusiasm—as it had been Owen's before her—of a few years previously: which is to say, in adolescence, half a lifetime. But she said nothing to Hannah, who would not have understood.

Hannah clutching her hand, blinking back tears. Kirsten—any time you want to talk—any time you want to talk about *it*—

I can't talk about anything else, Kirsten said, trying to laugh. I mean—no matter what I say—even in class—even when I answer a question—I'm talking about *it.*

John Brown, Old Osawatomie. He had not hesitated to kill in obedience to a higher law. *I have pledged my life.* Justice. The exacting of justice. *I will give my life,* he said. A quiet stern fearless man.

No Quarter his battlecry.

No Quarter—!

(She began to laugh. Pressing her knuckles against her mouth. It *was* absurd, it *was* sheer fancy. Neither she nor her brother could as much as lift a finger against their father's enemies: they were preppie kids, after all, possibly more spoiled than most, with a genuine distaste for vulgarity and bad manners not their own. Even flabby-waisted, Owen Halleck had style. he was Ivy League, he was the real thing; no doubt about it. And Kirsten for all her bitching, her unlaundered clothes and greasy hair and plucked-out eyebrows—she had plucked them out in a rage one night because they had been growing in queerly, across the bridge of her nose, and she foresaw decades of trimming her face, cultivating her "beauty"—even Kirsten with her mother's classic profile, that long elegant nose and slightly square, defiant chin, was the real thing. To lift a finger? To raise her voice? Impossible.)

No Quarter, Kirsten wrote in her secret journal. The words sprawled lazily as if questioning themselves.

Owen thought she was crazy. But then, blinking back tears, his big face tight as a clenched fist, he had acknowledged that she was right: of course she was right. Even before he received the message from her he knew she was right. . . .

His murderers deserve to be punished. Yes. But who is going to do it? So Owen asked, turned slightly away from her.

She had poked him in the arm, hard. No not hard, just in play. Baby sister, big brother. Daring. Mischievous. Reckless. And then she was screaming at him—You big phony bastard, you preppie shit, why have you come here?—why the hell have you come here?—you know who has to do it!

It was funny, it was a little crazy. They wiped tears from their eyes and grinned at each other. The air was wild with birds.

In any case John Brown, their great-great-great-great-grandfather, *was* a little crazy. And yet Henry David Thoreau (born David Henry Thoreau, a detail Kirsten thought significant) said passionately of Brown: *He is an Angel of Light.*

Kirsten inscribed this in her journal too, in the same lazy questioning hand. The acceleration of her heartbeat was palpable.

I will give my life, she whispered aloud. To Owen, silently, she said: Will I give my life?—will *we?*

On the way back to town, plodding along the muddy path, they had said very little to each other. Kirsten's head swam with fatigue, Owen walked heavily, his hands stuffed in his pockets. The expensive material of his sports coat was being stretched but he did not notice. Have we decided? Kirsten wanted to ask. Is it going to happen—?

But it was play, of course. Play-acting. Preening in front of mirrors, sticking out her tongue, examining her breasts in profile, scowling at her face. Pretty Kirsten? Her father's daughter? Ugly Kirsten? Plain Kirsten? It seemed to matter so much—her future was bound up with it—but as she stared at herself, examining and assessing, she could form no real judgment.

Isabel found fault with her, of course: bad posture, hair in her eyes, pimples on her forehead. Stop making faces, Isabel said, genuinely shocked. Do you want to *injure* your face—!

Isabel found fault with Kirsten's appearance, as Maurie never did. That was because (so Kirsten reasoned) Isabel *saw* her and Maurie did not.

The panic I feel, the sick-feeling, Kirsten tried to explain to Hannah, late at night. I know it's selfish: my father was the only person in the world who really loved me . . . and I can't be Kirsten for anyone else, in that way . . . it's like I died too, with him . . . drowned with him . . . someone he knew . . . but no one else knows . . . do you understand? . . . it's so selfish! . . . I hate myself!

Don't say that, Kirsten, Hannah whispered. Try to sleep.

Try to sleep, try to sleep, Kirsten repeated. Her eyes were open wide. The clarity of her self-loathing was bright as a beacon. It was the one *correct* sentiment of the night.

After a while she said: I wish I could be like you, Hannah. I wish I could be you. You're so strong. You don't make other people miserable.

My mother died five years ago, Hannah said. That makes a difference.

But that's *worse*, Kirsten said, shocked. I mean—that so much time can go by. That you might start to forget. Other things—other people—they will start to matter—next year you're going away to college—it will become confused—your love for her—

She was silent for several minutes. Then she said evenly: And of course your mother wasn't disgraced, at her death. She didn't confess to taking bribes, she didn't get drunk and drive off into the country and kill herself.

Gradually she stopped talking. Even to Hannah. Her ceaseless conversation with herself—her curt knowing and occasionally ribald queries to her enemies (Nick Martens and others at the Commission; and of course Isabel; and frequently Owen) drew all her energy, her fiercest concentration.

Where the shadow is darkest—it had something to do with that corner of the room. Beside the casement window, above the pine bookshelf. You could stare and stare at it, through the night.

In French class one November morning the instructor briskly erased a panel of the blackboard—chatting in French as she did so, smart and cheery, their almost-chic Mademoiselle Shefner. A half-dozen irregular verbs Kirsten had meant to copy down; but she hadn't been able to do so; she was groggy from a near-sleepless night. *And the blackboard was erased. Every word erased.*

Every word erased. As simple as that.

She found herself recalling with painful clarity, as if it had occurred only the previous week, a casual dinner at home . . . years ago . . . Nick Martens just back from the Mideast with a frightening tale to tell. . . . Owen was away at school, June Martens must have been gone as well, there were just Isabel and Maurie and Kirsten, ten years old at the time. An intimate dinner. Something secretive about it. Unforgettable.

Less than a week before, Nick had been one of a dozen Americans attending a disastrous diplomatic reception at the Saudi Arabian Embassy in Khartoum, Sudan. He had come close to death. Hadn't he? It was in all the papers, on the television news. . . . He had escaped a terrorist attack. Arabs, Palestinians. That hellish part of the world.

Now he was back home. Safe in Washington, safe with his friends Isabel and Maurie, in the smaller of the two dining rooms at 18 Röcken where the eye wasn't needlessly distracted by the dream-peacocks in the Lévy-Dhurmer panels, or the interior balustrades Chinese-style, visible through the arched doorway to the living room. Safe at home. Luxury. Civilization. Washington, D.C.

An intimate dinner, just the four of them. Isabel had spent the afternoon cooking, in a breathless half-panicked ecstasy, not altogether familiar with her own kitchen (Oh Jesus has she let the saffron run out, Isabel cried, what the hell has she done with that whisk—) and Kirsten had volunteered her help. It was a "tradition" that Isabel prepare for Nick, for special occasions, a paella heaped with all the delicacies children might find repulsive: lobster, clams, squid. But of course the meal was not intended to please a child.

Did he almost get killed, Mother? Kirsten asked repeatedly, did they shoot him?—is he all right?

You know he's all right! Isabel said in exasperation. You talked to him on the phone, didn't you?

Is he—is he different? Kirsten asked. Did they do something to him?

He'll be here in an hour, Isabel said, distracted, blinking, please don't bother me. . . .

Did they do something to him? Kirsten insisted.

How Nick Martens had come to be in the Sudan—whether he was just passing through that part of the world or had flown to Khartoum directly to spend a few days as a guest of the American *chargé d'affaires* Curt Moore—whether he was speaking on American politics and law for the United States Information Agency, or was a private traveler, a tourist—Kirsten could not recall seven years later. Certainly it was simple bad luck that had brought him to Khartoum, and had drawn him into a farewell party: bad luck uncharacteristic of Nick Martens's professional career.

Which might, of course, have been cut short in March 1973.

Kirsten knew very little about what had really happened, and of course she did not care. It was enough that Nick was back in Washington, and alive; it was enough that he was seated beside her, giving her a wink from time to time. And a surreptitious squeeze of her fingers if, in clowning around, she kicked his ankle or his knee.

The Nick she adored. The Nick they all adored. But changed—subtly changed. For one thing, he looked older.

Eight Black September terrorists had taken over the Saudi Embassy. They broke into the garden reception in honor of Curt Moore and the new American Ambassador Cleo Noel. There was no warning: one minute Nick was deep in conversation with a journalist assigned by *Le Monde* to investigate the political and financial network that supported transnational terrorist groups, the next minute there were rifles, shouts and screams—and the terrorists had broken in. As in a dream it all happened so quickly, with such horrific inevitability, that Nick had no clear idea afterward of what *had* happened: within a few minutes he had been herded out of the embassy at gunpoint, along with most of the guests, through the palatial Saudi headquarters and through the walled front yard and into the street where a small crowd was already gathered.

My God, Isabel said softly. And we didn't even know you were in the Sudan until we read about it in the paper. . . .

But Nick hadn't been important enough for the Palestinians to keep as a hostage; Nick had been forced out with the others; Nick was safe. Shaken but safe. Aged a few years in the space of those few minutes—but safe. He spoke slowly, looking from Maurie to Isabel to Maurie, trying to smile, trying to explain . . . the sickening surprise of the rifle shots and the shouts and screams; the commands in a language he couldn't understand, given by Arabs who gave every impression—he wasn't exaggerating—of being simply insane. He had stood in the garden paralyzed when the shooting began. I can't die, he had thought, I can't die yet, I have so much to do back home.

But he wasn't important enough to keep. A high-ranking Commission man, but unknown to the Palestinians, who wanted only five hostages: Curt Moore and Cleo Noel and the Belgian *chargé d'affaires* and the Saudi Ambassador and the Jordanian *chargé*. Like all Black September raids it had taken place with such precision it might have been rehearsed. And no one had resisted. It's true about complicity, Nick said, rubbing his hand hard over his face, a kind of spiritual complicity, I mean you simply want . . . you simply want to live.

The terrorists' demands were presented as nonnegotiable, and defiant in their absurdity: Jordan must immediately release seventeen Black September men who were imprisoned there; the United States must immediately release Sirhan Sirhan; the detested Israelis must release all Arab women *fedayeen* prisoners; the West Germans must release their Baader-Meinhof prisoners.

None of the governments gave in. Nixon made a brave statement that the United States would not be "blackmailed." And three of the hostages were summarily murdered: Moore, Noel, and the Belgian officer. Like that. And then the raiders surrendered. And were taken into custody by the Sudanese police.

It was a scenario, it went as planned, Nick said slowly. There were no surprises. I mean—for people who knew what was going on.

Kirsten is to remember Nick's air of befuddlement, which wasn't characteristic of him—it frightened her more than his story. She is to remember the queer way he blinked and squinted at Maurie and Isabel as if he were having difficulty seeing them. The way he lost his voice, or the logic of his own words . . . the way his disjointed tale trailed off into silence. Why his wife was not with him for this evening at the Hallecks' would not have been a question appropriate for a ten-year-old.

What I can't grasp is—the way they were killed, Nick said slowly. The way their lives ended. I heard the gunshots myself, I knew what they meant. Curt Moore erased like that. Like that.

Years later Kirsten is to remember her father's prolonged silence; the way in which Isabel leaned forward on her elbows, not minding how clumsily her loose sleeves fell back, or the indentations her fingernails made in her cheeks. Kirsten is to remember Nick's sudden fury. *The way their lives ended. Erased like that. The filthy maniac Palestinians. "Revolutionaries." Animals. I could see them all dead—we should start a policy of retaliation ourselves, like Israel.*

Maurie was startled, Maurie disagreed, you can't mean that, he said, you're still very upset.

I mean it, Nick said.

The Palestinians are desperate people—

You weren't there, you didn't see their faces, Nick said.

There is terrorism on both sides, Maurie said, but—

You weren't there, Nick said flatly, with a sudden bored contempt.

He went on to predict—correctly, as it turned out, though both Maurie and Isabel protested he was being too cynical—that the Sudanese wouldn't really punish the terrorists; they were too cowardly. One day we'll hear they flew them out of the country and released them . . . and that will be that. Until the next raid, the next murders.

Everyone liked Curt Moore, he said. His mouth twisted. And then to hear those gunshots . . .

No. It was going to be necessary to forget.

Jesus, there's so much to forget, Nick said, looking across the table at Maurie. Have you ever . . . realized? I mean . . . as we get older. . . .

Kirsten is to remember: the Hallecks united in love of Nick Martens. Shocked frightened love. For hadn't they almost lost him, their Nick?—Maurie and Isabel and dry-mouthed Kirsten. And the godson Owen who loved him too.

Erased like that. What I can't grasp is. The way they were killed. The way their lives ended.

She took careful note of the blackboard episode, and to prevent it from turning into one of her nightmares—she had quick blurry not-quite-unconscious nightmares—she entered it into her secret journal. Which was destined as she halfway anticipated not to remain forever secret but to be shared with Nick Martens's godson.

Owen's scrutiny, Owen's critical judgment: the thought of it was salutary, made her style enigmatic and compact and less self-indulgent.

Erased like that. What I can't grasp. The way they were killed. The way their lives ended.

Kirsten, what's wrong? Hannah asked. Why don't you talk to me? Why don't you look at me?

Kirsten?

Grunts, shoulder shrugs, indifference. She didn't always need Hannah. Go to hell, Hannah. Mind your own business.

Sometimes she wrote in her secret journal in code. The most secret secret plans.

Kirsten, is it something I said?—are you mad at me?—what's wrong? Won't you even *look* at me?

Hannah, her closest friend. Her only friend in fact. But Hannah would always be there—she could return to Hannah whenever she wished. When things were sorted out in her life. When things were clear.

Isabel telephoned. Hannah answered. Kirsten lay propped up on her rumpled bed, writing in her journal. She appeared not to have heard the telephone's ringing; she dismissed Hannah's announcement, and then her astonished appeal, with an impatient shrug of her shoulder.

It amused her to overhear an actual conversation between Hannah and Isabel. A *conversation* about a very peculiar subject. Kirsten herself.

(Mrs. Halleck—I'm afraid I can't find Kirsten right at the moment —she's probably in the library—yes—fine—oh no, it's no trouble—yes, she's fine—I mean all right—she's *fine*—yes I'll tell her—no, I don't think she's planning on going home for the weekend—she hasn't said anything—no—she hasn't said anything—well, I don't know—I mean, she doesn't tell me *everything*—oh no, no—no—no, Mrs. Halleck—no— really—it's no trouble—of course I'll tell her—tonight or tomorrow morning—yes—fine—yes—I'll tell her—yes I'm fine—things are busy but going pretty well—yes I'll tell her—well I could try but I think she's out of the dorm—probably in the library—yes—we both have a big history exam on Monday—well, I don't know: Kirsten doesn't always tell me—I'm sure she's doing all right—I mean I don't think she's failing anything—of course I'll tell her—she should telephone you later tonight, or tomorrow morning—I'll tell her it's important—yes—good—fine, Mrs. Halleck—*fine*.)

In her journal Kirsten noted *He hath a daily beauty in his life that makes me ugly.* And again, from another of Iago's speeches, *What then? How then? What shall I say? Where's satisfaction?*

One day she nearly fainted, hurrying down a flight of stairs. The strength in her legs vanished, her brain seemed to black out. She saw the steps rushing up to meet her. The tiled floor below. The blackboard from which the chalked words had been erased, unfairly.

Several girls screamed, seeing her fall. Someone caught her.

She rehearsed a telephone conversation with Audrey Martens. Tell me everything you know about your father and my mother. Everything. From the very beginning. Mount Dunvegan Island, Bitterfeld Lake, Washington, Chevy Chase, the parties, the dinners, the boat rides, the outings, the softball games, the tennis games, the swimming, the visits in New York, the telephone calls. Don't lie. Don't pretend. You must know. We all know.

Though perhaps she should visit Audrey at Exeter. Next weekend. Very soon. Audrey would invite her to stay in her room, probably —Audrey had always liked her—admired her, maybe—was afraid of her —shied away from her quick funny razor tongue—her good-natured bullying. At first Audrey was the daughter of the man Kirsten's father was helping to make his way in Washington, the man Kirsten's father had brought to Washington to the Commission; then Audrey—a year younger than Kirsten—was the daughter of the man who had gone beyond Kirsten's father. *Gone beyond* was a curious expression. Even before the trouble started (Maurie's drinking, Maurie's bouts of lethargy and depression) it was commonly understood that Nick Martens had *gone beyond* his friend Maurie Halleck and might be in fact helping *him* with his work. All this was idle speculation, of course, since the nature of the work was classified. But there was a great deal of idle speculation just the same, some of it in print.

Gone beyond.

Gossip columns, Owen said contemptuously. Shitty columnists. Father should sue.

Maurie *should* sue. Though of course that would only call attention to—to the situation.

Nick telephoned, greatly upset. He had already telephoned the paper, and had written an angry letter. (Which was never printed. But Maurie received the carbon and no doubt it is among "his things" at the present time. Boxes and files, folders, manila envelopes, stuffed with letters, papers, documents, scraps of paper, left in quite a mess in the apartment in the Potomac Tower.)

Just when do you think your father *went beyond* my father, Kirsten would inquire of Audrey, perhaps taking the girl's hand in her own, or circling the girl's wrist with her strong fingers. (Kirsten's fingers *were* strong, despite her present appearance.) Did you discuss it at the dinner table? Did you gloat over it? Tell me everything you know, and don't lie.

Your father and my mother. Fucking. In secret. Gloating over that too. In secret. Years and years of it.

Don't lie.

She changed her mind and prepared a declaration, a document, to send to Owen. Days passed as it took shape in the corner of her room above the bookcase, in the corner of her head, where the shadows overlapped and were consequently very dark. A sheet of stiff white paper; Isabel's and Nick's photographs (they had to be newspaper photographs, of course, ripped out of back copies of the *Washington Post* Kirsten tracked down in the library of the State University of New York at Purchase: otherwise the gesture wouldn't have the right style); a smear of blood (not easy to come by since she'd lost so much weight she had stopped menstruating, and had to cut her fingertip with a razor); a cryptic message. Magic Marker pen. Purple ink. Gaily and girlishly she addressed the envelope to Owen, pleased that the Magic Marker pen brought out curlicues and flourishes in her handwriting she had not known existed.

She is yours, Kirsten wrote. You know what to do.

Afterward she regretted sending it. Almost. Considered calling Owen to explain. Oh, just rip it up, I don't know what the hell got into me, please ignore it, forget it, she would say. You know me—shooting my mouth off. Forget it, okay?

The telephone rang but it was never Owen, it was Isabel. Calling from Washington, then from New York. Then from Nassau.

Kirsten isn't here, Kirsten can't come to the phone, Kirsten is in the library, in the infirmary, tramping out along the river, wandering aimlessly through town. Kirsten has a fever, a temperature of 103 degrees. Kirsten is starving herself. Kirsten is mute. (Her latest prank! She's indefatigable.)

I'm sorry, Mrs. Halleck, poor Hannah said, fighting back tears, I really *don't* know, I don't understand, she doesn't talk to me anymore, no, I don't know, I think you'd better talk to our dorm advisor, maybe she can help you, no, I don't, no, I'm sorry, no, I just don't know what to say, Mrs. Halleck, no, yes, that's right, yes, well, I don't know—she doesn't talk to me now. Well—I'd rather not. I mean, she has a bad temper. She gets—you know—awfully angry sometimes.

Poor Hannah. Sweet-tempered long-suffering boring Hannah.

I despise "good" people, Kirsten scribbled in her journal.

(It was a joke, after all, Maurie Halleck's generosity. His even temper, good nature, reluctance to believe evil of anyone, even his conniving associates. Maurie Halleck who wanted to win all the prizes just for being *good.*)

She never got around to calling Owen, to explain. She changed her mind about going up to Exeter. Maybe a telegram instead? *Black mud thick as shit. Difficult to breathe. I am waiting. Love & kisses M.J.H.*

But then it occurred to her: why send a telegram, why announce her plans? Warn her enemies?

Please talk to me, Kirsten, Hannah begged. Tell me what's wrong. Was it something I said. . . .

She hummed, she snapped her fingers, danced about the room with a cigarette in her mouth. Snatching up her things to make her escape. The sheepskin jacket, the boots. Calfskin. Bonwit's. Expensive but Isabel had thought they were worth it: so slender, so beautiful: as beautiful as her own. (It "broke her heart" to see how salt-stained they were now, scuffed, ruined. So far as Kirsten was concerned they were last year's boots and what the hell.) She fled the room, avoided the other girls, stayed away from the dining hall as much as possible. Breakfast was no problem: she always skipped breakfast. Lunch she might eat at the diner on Main Street where they made surprisingly good chili; and she could crumple four or five saltine crackers into her bowl. (Sometimes she got into conversations with people who lived in town. High school boys, frequently. Eyre Consolidated Junior-Senior High School. There were older boys too, from time to time. A contact from White Plains who sold Kirsten dope at a much more reasonable rate than she had paid in Baltimore.)

Kirsten, what's wrong? Please—what's wrong?

Kirsten, are you sick?

Can't you talk?

Oh, for Christ's sake look at me!

And, one day: I'm not answering the phone for you again, I'm not talking to your mother again, I've had enough! God damn you!

Go fuck yourself, Kirsten drawled.

Slamming the door to the room. Stomping downstairs in her two-inch-heeled boots.

Across the snowy playing field, along the hiking trail, along the river. Bareheaded. No gloves. *What then? How then? What shall I say? Where's satisfaction?* She knew who the murderers were but she had no proof. She had no proof. Owen's clumsy sobbing embrace, a few weeks later, was a confirmation of her knowledge: but still she had no proof.

One night she woke from a suffocating dream, a dream of mud, and the thought came to her at once: Anthony Di Piero.

Di Piero. The pig. Him. Of course he would know.

Anatomical Studies

One sunny weekday afternoon in June of 1977 Kirsten took a taxi to the Fox Run Apartments where Anthony Di Piero was living at the time. The manager's wife, an olive-skinned Greek woman who spoke a shy, tentative English, was on her knees weeding a bed of zinnias and snapdragons when Kirsten appeared. Kirsten said at once, Mr. Di Piero locked himself out of his apartment, he'll have to borrow your key to get back in. The woman squinted at Kirsten, smiling, clearly confused. We'll have to borrow your key. We're waiting, Kirsten said. In her white tennis outfit she must have looked forthright and assured, another rich kid, perhaps older than her age. She was only fourteen but already she was taller than her mother.

Kirsten cleared her throat and said loudly, Mr. Di Piero—you know him, don't you?—apartment 11E?—he's in a hurry—he doesn't have time to waste—he locked himself out of his apartment and there are a number of his friends coming over—we need the key—all right? —*the key.*

The woman got to her feet, brushing at her knees. She was still smiling, and saying something about her husband, something apologetic, but Kirsten couldn't understand her—she had no patience with foreigners—and so she interrupted: Mr. Di Piero is waiting. He needs his key. He locked himself out. Do you understand? We're in a hurry—we need the key. Apartment 11E. Mr. Di Piero.

Kirsten's voice was clear and bell-like and peremptory. She might have felt no agitation at all, her manner was so calm. The key. Understand?

125

So the manager's wife relented, and gave Kirsten the key. Fox Run Apartments, 11E; a brass key attached to a plastic oval. Thank you, Kirsten said curtly, as if tipping the woman.

Without glancing back she set out for Di Piero's apartment, which was on the far side of the courtyard, beyond the shimmering turquoise pool.

A prestige apartment-and-condominium complex, Fox Run. Bounded on the north by Little Falls Park. A half-hour drive from Röcken Place, forty-five minutes from the White House itself. Di Piero had moved in only the year before and Kirsten had seen the apartment twice, in the company of her mother. She suspected, however, that her mother had seen the apartment more than twice.

No children were allowed in Fox Run. No pets. There were stands of blue spruce in picturesque arrangements, there were rock-and-pebble-and-gravel gardens, Japanese style. On the Spanish terra-cotta tile beside the enormous pool attractive women were sunning themselves as Kirsten passed, their tanned bodies oiled and their eyes closed. Kirsten tried not to stare. She hated it—strangers staring at *her*. But the women were oblivious of her. Their bodies had the heavy perfection of statues, there was something profoundly disturbing about them. Thighs, hips, gleaming legs, painted toenails, bellies, swelling breasts. . . . They might have been any age. Several were more beautiful, even, than Isabel Halleck: or so it struck Kirsten's quick eye. But then they were younger.

Kirsten wondered if Di Piero knew any of them. He knew so many women.

(Tony, you mean? Isabel had said over the telephone once, when Kirsten hadn't quite meant to overhear. But he can't help it. He isn't like Nick. I mean he can't *help* it—it's part of his charm.)

Brick and stucco. Leaded windows. An ornate and almost convincing "colonial" look. Apple-green doors with smart black knockers. Very nice, very expensive. Di Piero also owned a summer home on Nantucket and a villa near Grasse which Kirsten, of course, had never seen.

In her white tennis outfit, her long hair loose down her back, Kirsten bounded up the steps to 11E and fitted the key into the lock. She didn't try the doorbell or the knocker, she didn't glance back over her shoulder to see if anyone was watching. (The Greek woman? One of the women by the pool?) She opened the door and stepped inside without hurrying and then immediately closed the door and bolted it. There. Safe.

Her heart was pounding erratically but she did not believe she was frightened. She was rarely frightened—she and Owen had discussed the matter at length. (Am I normal? Is something wrong with me? Instead of getting scared I want to laugh, Kirsten said. Owen said,

Oh you're normal enough—for this time and place.) In the taxi it had crossed her mind that a cleaning woman might be in the apartment; and though it was a weekday, and Di Piero should have been downtown at the bank, it *was* possible he would be at home. (He wasn't at 18 Röcken. Isabel was gone for the day—the annual Cystic Fibrosis Charity Ball was being planned and Isabel was on the central committee: she had been picked up by the wife of the Undersecretary of State, a new but warm acquaintance, and driven to the Metropolitan Club for a luncheon meeting.) Di Piero traveled frequently on bank business, to Tokyo and Hong Kong in particular, and in preparation for one of these sudden trips he might very well be in the apartment packing. . . . It's Kirsten, she called out gaily, just in case. Hey. Hello. Tony. Anybody home?

No one answered. She felt the apartment's solitude—an odor of something both harsh and melancholy—but did not, for a long moment, wish to trust it.

A trickle of perspiration ran down her left side. Her bright smile was fixed. Though she knew that Isabel was downtown at the Metropolitan Club, that she was surrounded by her women friends and acquaintances and "contacts," she had the idea too that Isabel might be here, in the apartment. In the bedroom, with Di Piero.

Once she had blundered into them. Isabel in her white French bikini, her kimonolike robe untied; Di Piero in a green jersey shirt and white linen trousers. By the pool. By the white wrought-iron table on the terrace, where the telephone was frequently brought. They were not kissing or even touching—they were simply talking in low earnest amused voices—Isabel had the telephone receiver in hand, Di Piero was either dialing or had sabotaged Isabel's call. They were standing quite close together in the half-light, as Isabel and Maurie never did. . . . Or had Kirsten, jealous Kirsten, imagined it? She blinked and they drew apart and their conversation was quite ordinary. Whether they should call the Silbers and ask them to pick up Claudia Lleyn or whether it would be easier for Charles Clayton to swing around and get her. Or were Claudia and Charles still quarreling?

It's just Kirsten, Kirsten called out.

The living room surprised her, she might not have recognized it. Long, airy, white, with white walls and white furnishings, tables made of a gleaming synthetic material, a kind of plastic, sloped and curved and sculpted, flawlessly white. Everything in its place, everything exquisite. Chinese scrolls on two walls, a stylized Oriental figure made of jade, cut-glass vases and decanters, a lacquered and gilt table, immense lamps with long tubular shades. A showroom: glass and chrome and white, white on white, innumerable textures of white.

On the long low glass-topped table, with its gleaming chrome legs, there was a copy of *Architecture in America*, neatly placed. And a large jade ashtray. The ashtray was clean, the glass of the table glared.

Everything in order, exquisite and dazzling. In such perfection the eye flies helpless from place to place, ricocheting from one color, one shape, one texture, to another.

Kirsten quickly closed the Venetian blinds. It was a relief, that the sun-flooded room should divide suddenly into slats of hazy light; and that the slats, controlled by her fingers on the cord, should darken or lighten according to her wish.

She had seen this apartment only when it was crowded. There had been a Sunday brunch the previous spring, when Di Piero had just moved in; and a cocktail party around Christmas to which Kirsten had been invited, under the assumption that she and the thirteen-year-old daughter of Di Piero's current "fiancée" would enjoy each other's company. (They did not. The girl was overweight, with a chunky sullen face; she hoped to impress Kirsten with talk of her friends—the daughters of famous Washingtonians; and Saudi and Syrian "dates" who drove recklessly about Georgetown in their Italian sportscars.) It was not really probable at these times—though of course it was possible—that Di Piero and Isabel were lovers.

Was it significant, Kirsten later wondered, that neither her father nor Nick Martens managed to attend these parties—?

Di Piero had had domestic help, of course. A black couple, light-skinned, much in demand for their catering and bartending talents, passed about from friend to friend, competent and even-tempered and not very visible. But Isabel had insisted upon preparing her own avocado dip; she had brought over a bottle of French champagne—Di Piero's favorite, evidently—as a housewarming gift from the Hallecks. She was vivacious, cheerful, flushed with pleasure, and very beautiful: Kirsten remembered a bronze silk dress with a very low neckline, and the strands of pink-toned pearls Grandfather Halleck had given her as a wedding gift. Di Piero's fiancée had not been in evidence at the Sunday brunch—it was likely that they hadn't yet become acquainted—and so Isabel had played hostess with her usual energy. And her legendary charm.

Kirsten poked her head into the kitchen. All very chaste and clean: the top of the stove, the linoleum tile, the aluminum sink. There weren't even toast crumbs on the counter. No smeared fingerprints on the refrigerator door. On the long windowsill were bell shaped glass jars filled with spices and nuts and peppercorns and pasta in various shapes—and the jars were a uniform distance apart.

Kirsten opened the dishwasher to see that Di Piero—or someone —had placed his breakfast dishes neatly inside. A small plate, a cup, a single knife. So chaste.

He sat at the breakfast nook, probably. With a view of the blue spruce on their artificial hillock, screening the asphalt parking lot beyond. Anthony Di Piero, alone. Reading the newspaper. The newspapers: the *Post,* the *New York Times,* the *Wall Street Journal.* Sipping black coffee, eating a single piece of toast. Butter? Jam? Di Piero turned the pages impatiently. Very little interested him except the financial sections; but even then his expression rarely changed.

Alone. A bachelor. "One of Washington's most eligible." About whom tales were told—rumors, scandalous stories. At school more than one girl had approached Kirsten to ask about him: Di Piero who had drifted into their lives, who had become suddenly important in their lives (that is, in the lives of their mothers or older sisters), and who had then disappeared. Where is he now, what is he doing now? they inquired, usually without rancor. Kirsten resisted boasting but it *was* a fact that Di Piero had been a friend of the Hallecks for a very long time—a school friend of her father's, actually. He had helped save her father's life a long time ago. Well—he had done something to help save it. Up in Canada, in Ontario, on a canoeing trip. Long ago.)

At the Christmas party, amid the laughter and raised voices, Kirsten had drawn near enough to Di Piero to overhear him say to his fiancée's daughter: You've been eating like a pig. Watch yourself.

Once in Kirsten's presence he told Isabel that a strand of her hair —her lovely silver-blond hair—had fallen across her forehead in an "unbecoming" way. Isabel had brushed it back at once. And tilted her head gracefully, coolly, to show that the gesture—and Di Piero's remark —had cost her very little.

Do you think there's anything between Mother and Tony, Kirsten had asked her brother Owen. But Owen refused to listen. I don't *think* anything at all about any of them, he said contemptuously.

He was away at school most of the year, in New Hampshire. Over vacations he often visited friends—a ranch in Montana, a "compound" of some sort in the Dominican Republic, where a friend's uncle owned a great deal of property. He refused to comment on his sister's speculations, he refused to eavesdrop on his parents' quarrels, or what appeared to be quarrels. (Only Isabel raised her voice. Maurie's voice, when it was at all audible, was low and earnest and pleading.) As for Washington gossip—as far as Owen was concerned it was beneath contempt.

In Di Piero's study the white louver shutters were partly closed. No curtains, very few pieces of furniture. A brown-and-black Turkish rug on the hardwood floor, a desk made of a gray synthetic material, thicker and evidently harder than ordinary plastic; a drawing board covered with a sheet of stiff white paper; transparent bookshelves in which books were sparsely and neatly arranged. (It was said of Di Piero that he discarded most books after he read them, even hardcover books. He had once shocked a colleague at the bank by ripping in two an expensive brochure issued by the Bank of Tokyo—its pages of meticulous print interrupted by elegant glossy photographs of mountains, Buddhist temples, and ancient Japanese art—because the man had expressed an interest in reading it after Di Piero had finished; so Di Piero simply ripped out the pages he had already read and handed them over.)

Kirsten glanced through the bookshelves. The titles meant very little to her. *Bouvard et Pécuchet. Gargantua.* Churchill's volumes on Marlborough. Studies of Le Corbusier and Gropius. An economic history of the Orient. Paperbacks on archeology, mountain-climbing, German grammar and vocabulary. She knew that Di Piero had studied architecture for a while, and that he had a degree in international finance from the University of London. He could speak several languages fluently, including Japanese. At one time he had been a classmate of Maurie's and Nick's at Harvard Law. The three of them had been at the Bauer School together, long ago, but precisely how close they had been was a mystery. (Maurie and Nick were close, of course. Very close. Like blood brothers, Isabel had said, with a curious little smirk.) Di Piero's father, a banker, had been killed in Rome when Di Piero was a boy—but whether it was an accident, or murder, Kirsten did not know. As for Di Piero's mother: Isabel had the idea that the woman, an American, was hospitalized somewhere in the States.

Di Piero's legend was that he stood to inherit, or had already inherited, a great deal of money. But there was a malicious counter-legend, that he was nearly penniless (except of course for his salary at the bank, which must have been respectable), and had made a career out of being a guest in the homes of the wealthy. And of bringing certain people together. He was such a social success that he had no need, even, to marry money—yet. He would not be forced to so severely limit himself for years.

He had no friends—he was everyone's friend. One might suppose him Isabel's companion—her closest companion—but months might pass when he wouldn't telephone, though he was in the city. And then he would reappear suddenly to attend three or four of Isabel's elegant dinner parties in a row. . . . The latest escort of Senator ——'s bitterly estranged wife. The only man in Washington on comfortable terms with ——, ——, and ——, who had never sat at the same table together—until Di Piero insisted. A friend of —— of the oil and gas lobby, and —— of the Department of the Interior; a poker-playing companion of —— of Health, Education, and Welfare, and —— of the House Appropriations Committee; a friend of the attractive young women—some of them "assistants," "receptionists," "research aides"—who were in turn friendly with Senators, influential Congressmen, presidential aides. Not a guest at the White House—not during this administration—but a guest at the homes of people who scorned the White House. At times it appeared to be Di Piero's real vocation—precarious, possibly dangerous, and no doubt financially rewarding—simply to bring certain men together, in the same drawing room. With the assistance of Washington hostesses like Isabel Halleck, of course. (Di Piero's handicap—or was it a virtue?—was his failure to marry, and to be provided with a hostess for all seasons.) One of the President's attorneys, Japanese business executives, a member of the Federal Commerce Commission, lobbyists, campaign organizers, experts on money, public health, excise taxes, narcotics; men like Nick Martens, Reid Silber, Charles Clayton; Vice Admiral William Watkins; Tom Gast; Phillip Moulton of the State Department; Hal Seawright, Claudia Lleyn, Morton Kempe, Chief Justice Hamilton Frazer; Eve Neilson, the companion of Senator Parr; Esther Jackson the columnist; Bobbie Tern the columnist; Jack Fair the architect and the dear friend of Martha Degler, the admiral's widow. Newspaper editors, television producers, embassy people, bright young models who really hoped to be writers; political analysts; society doctors; high-ranking bureaucrats who had held onto their jobs through a change of administration, or two, or three; military men; Medicare people; Pentagon officials; the new Deputy Special Representative for Trade Negotiations (who turned out to have been a classmate of Di Piero's at the Bauer School). The Hallecks' beautiful stone house at 18 Röcken—a block off Connecticut Avenue—was thrown open to garden parties, afternoon teas, dinner parties, late-night suppers after the opera or theater, long elegant luncheons that broke up past four in the afternoon, to accommodate certain of Di Piero's friends. Or the network of people known casually as his friends. And joined with them, usually with propitious consequences, were the countless Washingtonians and important visitors and embassy people Isabel Halleck knew—which is to say, nearly everyone in Washington of some significance.

Kirsten was not jealous of Isabel: she was not jealous of Isabel's friends, or the men who appeared and disappeared and reappeared in her life. Isabel was one of the three or four highest-ranking Washington hostesses of the era, after all—what could her daughter expect? What could her son expect? The attention and fidelity of an ordinary American mother—?

Kirsten analyzed her feelings, and sometimes discussed them, though obliquely, with her brother, or one or two girls at Hays who might reasonably be expected (being the daughters of similar mothers) to understand. She was not jealous, nor was she bitter. Certainly not "competitive" as Dr. Pritchard had charged. She wished Isabel no harm, in fact she wished her mother continued success, for Isabel's happiness was warm and generous as sunshine in a public garden, and spilled over always onto her children, and onto her husband, and might possibly be the means—might possibly have been the means for years—of preserving the Halleck family as a family. So Kirsten wished her mother happiness and was fairly certain that she had gone beyond infantile impulses of envy. Wasn't she proud, after all, when at school girls remarked upon Isabel's beauty (a photograph on the first page of the Sunday society section of the *Post,* a television interview on WWBT with Jamie Inger in connection with the spring fund-raising activities of the Multiple Sclerosis National Society Central Organization) and expressed the desire to meet her someday; didn't it please her that the telephone was always ringing at home, that Nellie was always saying in her chocolate-warm voice, "Halleck residence," with a special lift to her words that expressed both her mistress's gratification at the call and her necessary caution— for of course Isabel could not accept *too* many invitations, she had to be judicious. Kirsten wasn't jealous or spiteful and even her wildest pranks couldn't be said to be malicious. She simply felt a certain *interest* in her mother's affairs. That was it—a certain unobsessive *interest.*

She was a fact-finder, an interpreter. A kind of translator. She listened, she watched, she took note, she observed. But did not judge.

Now she found herself staring sightlessly at drawings arranged in rows on the study's white walls. Anatomical studies: highly detailed representations of shoulders, torsos, legs, arms, even the interior of a throat. The bodies were in parts; only one showed a complete human figure, but that was a corpse.

Ugly, thought Kirsten.

Yet there was something fascinating about the drawings. Despite the exactitude of the details, the fidelity to tissue, bone, textures of skin, minute hairs, the drawings were dreamlike: in a way quite beautiful.

Leonardo da Vinci. From the notebooks. Yet Kirsten had the curious idea that Di Piero himself had done them.

She examined the drawings closely, tapping her fingernail against the glass. The partly dissected corpse (a man's corpse) . . . the graceful curve of a disembodied leg, its muscle and tissue carefully laid open . . . the remarkably intricate interior of the thorax.

Very strange. But beautiful, really.

She wondered why Di Piero had bought the prints. What they

meant to him—what he saw when he looked at them. Of course it would have been impossible for her to ask; Di Piero did not answer "personal" questions.

(She had heard him speak candidly and amusingly of his life, but always in the form of anecdotes; always in the form of little stories with ironic conclusions. So the "personal" became with him—and with other adults of Kirsten's acquaintance—deftly impersonal, and fit for social discourse. The Loughrea River canoeing trip, for instance, and the accident in the rapids that had almost killed Maurie: this was the subject of several anecdotes, told by Di Piero, Nick Martens, and Maurie himself, but in each version it was a separate story, and neither Kirsten nor Owen was altogether certain of what had happened. Their father had almost drowned as a boy of seventeen—that much was certain. But exactly how his canoe had capsized, what happened to him, and how Nick managed to haul him to safety (aided by Di Piero?—or by another boy?—or alone?) the children did not know. Di Piero alluded to the canoeing trip as one of the "profound" experiences of his life but it was impossible to guess what he meant by this, or whether in fact he really meant anything. His first visit to Japan as a young man of twenty-three had also been "profound," and so was his experience in attempting to climb a mountain in France called the Dru (he and a young Frenchman were trapped for three days by a sudden blizzard before a rescue team arrived). Yet he spoke laconically, as if recounting an event from a past not his own. Yes, he too had capsized on the Loughrea and might have drowned; yes, he had been frightened of freezing to death on the Dru —his companion, in fact, had lost all the toes on his right foot. But these events were obscure. These events were impersonal.

One day, Kirsten asked Di Piero if he planned on returning to France to climb again. He turned to stare at her. Climb? In what sense? he asked.

It was a most unpleasant moment. Di Piero shook cigarette ashes into a little pewter tray, looking at Kirsten. His high-bridged nose gave his face a calm, sculpted look; his dark eyes touched Kirsten without absorbing her. He was not mean, not even unkind.

I mean—you know— Didn't you say once— Mountain-climbing—? Kirsten stammered, greatly embarrassed.

Isabel interceded. Mountain-climbing, Tony. In the Alps. She's asking if you are going back this summer.

Di Piero appeared to think for a moment before saying, No. Of course not. I haven't climbed for years. With an air of regretful satisfaction he said, Those days are over.

The next morning Isabel entered Kirsten's room without knocking and said, He doesn't like anyone to be personal with him—anyone at all. Don't you know better?

Rock music blared from Kirsten's radio. Isabel turned it down and repeated what she had said.

He? said Kirsten, reddening. Who the hell is *he?*

She tried the drawers to the gray plastic desk. Locked. And again locked. (Did he anticipate prowlers? What was he hiding?) One of the lower drawers was unlocked but it contained only stationery supplies. Paper, stamps, rubber bands, pencils. . . . Shit, said Kirsten. She tried the drawers again, tugging at them. Letters, snapshots, scrawled notes, perhaps a diary, the evidence of Di Piero's secret life: they *must* be kept in this desk.

A voice, somewhere near. Voices.

Kirsten froze, bent over the desk.

Noisy heels on pavement; a woman's strident laughter. A man's voice, the words inaudible.

A great hot pulse beat at the base of Kirsten's skull. But she was safe: they were only passing by outside the window, down on the sidewalk.

She had grown very warm.

Damn him, she murmured.

She entered the bedroom. His scent, here. Suddenly recognizable. Hair lotion or cologne. She knew it immediately though she could not have described it.

The bedroom was large, and as orderly as the other rooms. But Di Piero did keep, on the lacquered table beside the bed, a pile of books and magazines. Evidently he read at night? A pillow behind his head?

For an instant she saw him. Clearly. His sleepy hooded eyes, his mouth pulled slightly downward at the corners. . . . He was alone in the oversized bed and that both pleased and disappointed Kirsten.

Her eye darted from place to place. White walls . . . a lacquered Japanese table . . . a black leather chair with chrome-plated legs . . . framed photographs of mountain scenes: dazzling whites and deep crevices of black that seemed, from a distance of a few yards, purely abstract designs.

Things Isabel would know intimately.

Though he must bring other women here too. The realization made Kirsten feel slightly faint. If she had time to carefully search she would find evidence of strangers: a tube of lipstick rolled beneath a bureau, a stray earring, beads from a broken necklace, perhaps even clothes. Hairs on his pillows. In his bed . She felt slightly faint, her face grew hot.

Her mother's lover. One of her mother's lovers.

And there was one of his telephones, on the bedside table. White plastic. Small and stylish. A stack of newspapers and magazines; an old-fashioned fountain pen, ebony trimmed with silver; another spotlessly clean ashtray; a digital clock that brainlessly flashed the time. Second after second, heartbeat upon heartbeat.

Kirsten picked up a magazine and saw that someone had marked a number of pages. Columns of print were set off by asterisks; there were careful underlinings. The strange thing was, the magazine was a well-known women's fashion magazine.

One of the magazines Isabel routinely bought. But then she bought so many magazines. (Which she had no time to read. She leafed through them idly while sipping coffee, then set them aside; and they found their way up to Kirsten's room eventually where, sometimes late at night, she studied them with greedy scorn.)

An article with a title in two-inch red caps. On sexual techniques.

Kirsten found herself skimming it. One column had been especially marked: . . . *during sexual intercourse, there is the possibility that the penis will push bacteria into the urethra. Women using a diaphragm should urinate after having sex in order to expel any bacteria trapped there.* And again: *If intercourse is repeated more than once during a six-hour period additional jelly or foam must be inserted without removing the diaphragm. Although a well-fitting diaphragm should not slip it can be dislodged, especially in certain positions; it should consequently be checked by the woman or her partner during intercourse. Two fingers should be inserted into the vagina to feel that the cervix is covered by the dome of the . . .* Kirsten blinked dizzily. She felt extremely warm. Di Piero had marked such peculiar things with his fine-tipped fountain pen. *Quick check . . . Very important . . . If it has been dislodged . . . Securely positioned over the cervix . . . Should not buckle as the penis thrusts into the . . . Side effect: possible cystitis or bladder infection. . . .*

The magazine slipped from Kirsten's fingers and fell to the floor.

She felt peculiar. A sensation in the very pit of her stomach, as if her period had begun. A sense of nausea, panic. An alarm so deep, so profound, it could have no object.

Pigs, she whispered.

Angrily she struck a pile of magazines and newspapers, knocking them to the floor. Seized the digital clock and threw it down. Pigs. All of them. All of you, she said aloud. Half-blinded, she opened a drawer in the bedside table and pawed through its contents—a memo pad, snapshots, a nearly empty tube of Vaseline. Pigs. I hate you. *Pigs*, she said.

She scattered the things—kicked at them—yanked a pillow from the bed and threw it down.

Panting, she paused to retrieve the snapshots. She thrust them into the pocket of her blouse, to examine another time.

Bastard, she said. I know all about you.

She yanked the heavy satin bedspread off the bed and tore at the sheets. (Pale green linen. Unwrinkled.) She tossed the other pillow away. Despite her great anger—the terrible pulse beating in her head—she believed herself remarkably calm. She took time to examine the sheets —yes, they were clean—fresh—or very nearly fresh. No discernible odor except that of Di Piero: his aftershave lotion, his cologne, whatever.

The next several minutes passed in a kind of delirium. Though she still remained, in a sense, defiantly calm. She ransacked a closet and found a can of toilet cleanser, and brought it back into the bedroom, and shook the tiny blue crystals into the bed. (Poison, were they? Burning to the touch?) She yanked open the bureau drawers and pulled things out —socks, underwear, pajamas. Then went through the closet. Suits, sport jackets, trousers hanging neatly from presses . . . shirts still in cellophane wrappers . . . neckties . . . shoes. . . . Kirsten ripped, she tore, she threw things down, and finally she began to sob, her hair in her face and her heart beating painfully.

Pig, she whispered.

Pigs.

She kicked Di Piero's things into a heap. A blue linen necktie, a single shoe, a silk seersucker shirt which might have cost $150. A gray tweed sports jacket, a ribbed cardigan sweater. She held her breath, listening. Was the front door being unlocked? Had he come home?

Nothing. Silence.

No one.

Gradually her heartbeat slowed. She emptied the can of toilet cleanser on the clothes and threw it down and prepared to leave. The pressure was slightly relieved, in her head and in her loins; the great heaving pulse in her chest still beat.

I know all about you, she said in triumph.

She was looking through the snapshots, sitting at a bus stop, when someone said, . . . time it is, miss? and she realized the woman was repeating the question and that, until that moment, she had no idea what time it might be. She stared at her watch. It was only three-fifteen. She had entered Di Piero's apartment at two-ten and only a little more than an hour had passed. But now she was exhausted, as if she'd played an entire day of tennis.

I said—d'you know what time it is, miss?

A woman in a bright floral dress, carrying an oversized straw purse. A quick glance might have suggested that she was well-to-do—she was "all right"—but Kirsten's eye was sharp. She saw the stubble beneath the woman's arms, the iridescent green on her eyelids. She said, curtly, hiding the snapshots: I'm sorry. I don't talk to strangers.

One of the snapshots showed Di Piero in sunglasses and bathing trunks, on a beach. Possibly in a foreign country. (Palm trees, white sunshine.) Another showed Di Piero with a small narrow mustache, standing beside a swarthy-skinned man in white. Both were squinting into the camera; both were quite handsome. Di Piero in a camel's-hair coat, Di Piero with a tennis racket, Di Piero standing close beside a slender woman with long straight blond hair. . . . (Not Isabel, of course. A much younger woman.) One of the snapshots had been neatly scissored in half, and only Di Piero—in a stylish three-piece suit—remained, smiling calmly at the camera. (A minaret in the background? The silhouettes of exotic trees?) There was a darkly tanned Di Piero sitting at a table with two women—both Japanese—and another man, presumably an American. (Nick Martens? Kirsten studied the snapshot but could not be certain. The man sat in profile, his hair resembled Nick's, but his shoulders were slightly rounded as Nick's were not.) The last snapshot showed Di Piero with his "fiancée" and her daughter, against a background of dazzling crimson azaleas. Di Piero was expressionless, both the woman and her daughter were smiling broadly. Without thinking Kirsten ripped this snapshot in half.

Though why had she bothered? According to gossip this "fiancée" —a wealthy Washington divorcée with cultural pretensions—had already been dropped. *She* had not even lasted a year.

It was not until two days later, and then late in the afternoon, that Di Piero tracked her down.

A Friday, hazily warm. Isabel's friend Claudia Lleyn dropped by around four and the two women sat by the pool sipping bloody marys and talking of mutual acquaintances: crises, reversals, surprises, neurotic behavior, good fortune, rotten luck, developments that were amazing, or alarming, or hilarious. The President and his aides had unwisely granted a press conference the day before over network television, and the women dissected it in detail. As they talked they watched Kirsten swimming in the pool. She swam forty lengths without pausing and though she certainly made no attempt to overhear the women's conversation she did hear fragments from time to time. The name *Di Piero* was frequent.

. . . yes?

Well I *think* so.

I haven't heard.

I *think* so.

Kirsten climbed out of the pool, ungainly and self-conscious. She was lithe and slippery as a fish in water—she'd had fantasies, for a time, of being an Olympic swimmer—but climbing out, water streaming down her body, attracting the casual glances of others, she felt suddenly graceless. Don't look, she begged. I am invisible.

Tall and thin, her breasts the size of plums, her collar bone prominent. In the pretty two-piece bathing suit Isabel had picked out for her: pink, with small white seahorses. She did not want to attract the women's attention but she had to ask: Is he coming over today?

Isabel's expression was both critical and affectionate. She was gazing at Kirsten without seeing her.

—Tony, I mean. Mr. Di Piero.

But Isabel did not know. Nor did Mrs. Lleyn.

I *think* he wants to drop by, said Isabel. I haven't talked with him for a few days. Then she smiled. Why do you ask, Kirsten?

Kirsten murmured a reply and ran into the house. She dreaded to hear—but did not actually hear—the women laughing behind her.

Upstairs she threw herself on her bed, in the wet suit. She undid her hair roughly.

Later that afternoon, when she went back down to practice diving, Claudia Lleyn had gone. But now Eve Neilson was visiting, and Charlotte Moulton, and a French couple who were associated in some way—the man was a novelist? a poet?—with a cultural exchange program run out of the State Department; and a new woman acquaintance of Isabel's with stringy tanned legs and a gregarious laugh. The woman was so homely and at the same time so confident, Kirsten understood that she had money.

A little after six o'clock, Di Piero himself arrived.

He greeted everyone, shaking hands formally. His sports jacket was cream-colored, his trousers were a pale gray. Despite the afternoon heat he did not look warm. Since Kirsten was in the pool they couldn't greet each other—Di Piero waved at her, perfunctorily, as he usually did. ("Children" did not interest him.) Kirsten felt the pit of her belly drop away.

She had been going to dive. But now she could not. She paused, frightened. No one was looking toward her—no one gave her the slightest notice—but she stood on the end of the diving board, paralyzed. Was he looking at her, covertly? Did he know? Isabel was asking him if he wanted to swim, or a drink first. Kirsten could not hear his reply.

Di Piero's swimming things were kept in the Hallecks' bathhouse. He came by whenever he wanted; it was Isabel's command that he not bother to telephone beforehand. He was a close friend, an old friend, a "friend of the family." In fact Di Piero came to 18 Röcken less frequently than Isabel wished, and when he was there his manner was formal. Or so Kirsten had observed.

But he did like to swim. So he took a drink with him into the bathhouse, and changed, and reappeared five minutes later; and dived from the board with his usual spare, undemonstrative dive, which always made Kirsten think of an animal—a seal, an otter—plunging artlessly into the water. At the far end of the pool he emerged, his dark face streaming.

Kirsten hoped that none of the guests, or Isabel herself, would make an inane comment, or applaud.

She was in the pool, treading water. She swam to the edge to steady herself. He did not appear to notice her: he did not trouble to glance her way. But this detachment, this coldness, was not uncharacteristic. Did he know?

Di Piero swam without haste, ignoring her. His expression was inward. He looked contemplative, even peaceful. Despite the raised voices at the poolside—and now several more guests had arrived—he swam effortlessly as if he were alone. His body cut through the water with an evident delight in its own motion, its own instinctive skill.

Kirsten shied away. But he swam past her and hauled himself out of the pool. Dripping water, shaking his head. A tall solidly built man with thick dark hair on his chest, arms, thighs, legs. In his stylish clothes Di Piero gave the impression of being slender; like this, in his bathing trunks, he looked as if he might someday get heavy. Kirsten could imagine a roll of fat at his waist, his lean face thickening.

He returned to the diving board. Dived again, deftly and without self-consciousness.

He knows, Kirsten thought. She felt weak and suddenly exhausted. Does he know?

The manager's wife must have described Kirsten to him. Unless —and this *was* possible—her story was that she knew nothing, nothing, at all.

The chlorine made Kirsten's eyes ache, as if she had been crying.

Nellie had brought out an enormous party tray. Scotch, bourbon, white wine, imported beer. Caviar. Bowls of salted nuts. Thick Danish crackers that broke dryly when snapped in two.

. . . Tony? Isabel called. Scotch, was it? A little water?

Di Piero swam past Kirsten and, as he climbed out of the pool, he accidentally brushed against her—his elbow caught her in the chest.

But not hard. Not really hard. She winced more out of alarm than pain.

Isabel wore a pale orange shift, and her silver-blond hair had been fashioned into a braided chignon. She looked very beautiful. But perhaps too animated. Her ivory and jade bracelets rattled a great deal, her laughter was as loud as anyone's. She called to Kirsten—You've been in there all day, you'd better come out—but Kirsten ignored her and swam slowly back, the length of the pool.

Di Piero had struck her—accidentally. It really did seem to have been an accident.

Nellie returned with a cheeseboard. Kirsten's mouth watered: she was hungry suddenly. But she would not approach the food.

Kirsten, did you hear me? Isabel called.

She was affectionate, she was vexed, it was because she loved her daughter so much (as Maurie explained) that she bullied her before others, upon occasion.

Nellie set the long cheeseboard down on one of the wrought-iron tables. Cheeses, a silver-handled knife, slices of chewy French bread. Kirsten would not eat. Her stomach felt quite strange.

She climbed up and Nellie brought her a thick towel and she folded it about herself, shivering. Isabel patted Kirsten's shoulder as she "explained" Kirsten to the Frenchwoman—age, school, plans for the summer—and Kirsten stood motionless. All very dreamlike, very strange. He had struck her by accident but not really hard; but still it hurt; just above her left breast.

Her chest was so bony, her bones stood out. So ugly.

The Frenchwoman wore a pretty straw hat with a scarlet ribbon that tied beneath the chin. She was much younger than her husband, and very beautiful: the kind of face Kirsten saw too often. But Isabel did not appear to mind. She seemed much taken with the young woman, whom she had evidently met a few nights before.

So many people. So much to talk about. Chatter, news, delighted laughter.

Isabel asked Kirsten to hunt up that copy of *Newsweek*. The one with the interview with Nick Martens in it.

(The interview was a "masterpiece of diplomacy," someone had said. Martens had managed to say a great deal, he had managed to speak with obvious sincerity, yet nothing significant—nothing troublesome—had been said at all.)

Look in the bathhouse, Isabel said. Go *on*.

The bathhouse was made of stucco, painted white, with a green roof and green shutters. It was a charming little building but a certain odor pervaded it—damp bathing suits, damp towels, chlorine, tobacco smoke. Kirsten poked her head inside. There was a stack of magazines on a stool and she went to look through them, and as she turned she saw someone follow her. He was going into one of the changing rooms. No, he was approaching her.

She looked up, frightened. It was Di Piero.

She stammered a greeting. She said "hello" as if he had just arrived.

He said nothing. His expression was neutral; his lips were almost slack.

I'm looking for that *Newsweek*, you know, that interview, Kirsten said faintly, with Nick—

He said nothing. He touched her arm with his forefinger. Just touched it. Kirsten winced. She drew back, bumping her head against something.

I— I'm— she said. Please, I—

His manner was grave, even courtly. He ran his finger down her arm as lightly as possible.

Kirsten dropped the magazine. She heard herself giggle.

He was in no hurry. It did not concern him that someone might intrude. He stood above her, breathing evenly, contemplating her, his mouth still expressionless. He showed no anger, he did not even show a great deal of interest.

Then he took hold of her left wrist. His fingers were dry and strong. As he began to twist her arm Kirsten's knees weakened and she sank clumsily toward the floor. Her murmur was surprised and apologetic. She did not cry out. The bone is going to snap, oh my God the bone is going to snap, she thought; but she did not cry out.

Her face creased with pain. Her eyes narrowed. She prepared for the snap of the bone—for the hideous sound—but then Di Piero released her.

She was kneeling on the damp concrete floor. She rubbed her wrist, sobbing. I didn't mean— she whispered. Mr. Di Piero—I—

No urgency to his movements, no sense even of curiosity. He hurt her, he was going to hurt her further, but his breathing was even, his manner was controlled; the faint creases about his mouth deepened as if he were going to smile. But of course he did not smile.

Now he gripped the back of her neck. She winced, she sobbed, she stammered for him to let go: he was hurting her.

He said nothing.

His eyes were very dark, the whites were unusually clear. For the first time he looked foreign.

Mr. Di Piero— Please— she said.

He did look *foreign*, from another part of the world. Not American. She saw that suddenly. She began to laugh.

I didn't mean— I wasn't— she said, laughing.

He squeezed her neck beneath her damp hair. Holding her at arm's length; standing clear. She was frightened she would scream. And then everyone would come rushing. Everyone would know.

Then, quickly, his breathing less controlled now, he ran both hands over her: her shoulders, her breasts, her stomach, her hips, her thighs. There was no anger, no careless haste. No emotion she could discern. He might have been stroking an animal, not to give it pleasure but simply to keep it in place: to assert his own mastery.

It was a measure of her terror—she would remember this afterward—that she did not try to break free.

Now he squeezed her, hard. A shoulder, a breast. Hard. As if to wring, to destroy. And it hurt very much. It hurt very much. But she did not cry out. She cowered beneath him, staring. A look of rage, of satisfaction? A look of recognition?

Nothing.

His slightly more rapid breathing. His narrowing eyes.

And then it was over—he released her and walked away.

Afterward, during the days that followed, Kirsten might have thought it had never happened: except for the bruises.

She would have thought—No, that's silly, not him, not like that, with people around; not *me*.

Except for the bruises. Which were very real. Blotches of dull purple, eerie streaks of yellow. Her skin? Her pain? How had he done it? And in such silence—!

She stayed away from the pool, naturally. If Isabel had asked her what was wrong she planned to say that she was bored with swimming. But Isabel didn't notice, Isabel didn't ask.

Neither Maurie nor Owen was home. Maurie and several of his assistants had flown to Mexico City, to interview witnesses for the government's case against an American corporation. (Secret in detail, the Commission's activities were generally public in outline. Mexico City? Kirsten asked. Who's there? Is Father in danger?) Owen was spending the last two weeks of June at the home of a friend from Exeter. (The boy's family owned a large horse ranch in Kentucky. Kirsten gathered from the melodious way in which Isabel pronounced the family name—Tidwell—that they were both wealthy and eminently respectable.)

And if Nellie wondered why Kirsten was avoiding the pool—if

Nellie even happened to notice a bruise or two on Kirsten's arm—she was prudent enough to say nothing.

Rapt with fascination she contemplated herself in her bedroom mirror, with the door safely locked.

Bruises, welts. Blurred flowers. Like the flesh of fruit mashed against her flesh.

A bruise on her left shoulder was especially striking. Were bruises opaque maps of blood—blue and purple and unsightly orange-yellow—trapped beneath the skin? Kirsten pondered, brooded, drew in her breath slowly. It was awkward, craning her neck to study one triangular bruise on her upper back which she particularly admired.

Hours, days. Gradually they faded.

When Di Piero released her he simply walked away without a word. Went into one of the changing rooms and closed the louvered door behind him.

Kirsten, panting, snatched up the copy of *Newsweek* and ran outside with it. She had taken so long—Isabel would be impatient—Isabel might be about to come after her.

But they hardly noticed her approach.

She crossed the hot concrete with the caution of a drunk or a convalescent. Only Isabel glanced around. Oh thanks, Kirsten—I wasn't sure if it was in there, she said. She took the magazine from Kirsten's fingers without noticing Kirsten's flushed face or the unnatural brightness of her eyes.

Isabel's guests gathered around. They were interested in the magazine, in Nick Martens's interview; they were certainly not interested in Kirsten. Isabel began to read some of Nick's replies in her high clear voice, giving her words a slight Spanish intonation, as she always did when she was being dramatic or sly. Kirsten would have escaped, but her knees were still trembling.

In a short while Di Piero came out of the bathhouse, lighting a cigarette. Though Isabel was reading from the magazine she noticed him at once and said, laughing, waving, Oh, Tony—come see.

The Witness

Don't speak from now on. Don't say a word.

She opens her mouth to protest—or to comply.

Don't say a word, he says. The faintest irritation in his voice.

He undresses her systematically. Without haste. Without urgency. His manner is subdued, even clinical. She is spared shame and even embarrassment. Not being Kirsten right now: not needing to answer to that name.

His thick black hair, combed neatly back from his forehead, threaded with gray. But very lightly. Hair lotion, hair oil. Sleek quills that shake gradually loose.

A vertical crease between his eyebrows which she has not noticed before. Sharp, attractive. "Distinctive." As he undresses her and studies her the vertical crease is penetrated by one or two horizontal lines. So he is having second thoughts. Too skinny. Too waxen-pale. Her grief too obvious. . . .

But he doesn't hesitate. The bath water has been running, the moist air is fragrant with bath crystals, mist and steam and harmless delirium, hasn't he promised her—informed her—that if she tells him to stop he *will* stop?—at once.

Otherwise be still. Don't say a word.

I warn you: *Don't say a word.*

I want to see you, Kirsten had begged over the phone. I want to talk with you. About it. About him. I promise not to cry.

Do you promise not to cry? Di Piero asked.

I've cried too much. I'm empty. I mean I'm tired. —Then, with a derisory little giggle: Maybe I'm bored with crying.

April 17, 1980, and he has been dead ten months and nothing has been resolved and she *has* cried too much, another strategy is required. She swings her leather bag and walks jauntily at the side of the handsome man in the stylish sports jacket and the dark-tinted sunglasses. One might imagine a sensual droop to the lips, an amused appraising habit about the eyes: but in fact Anthony Di Piero looks tidy and prim and reflective. A Nazi, Owen once said (on what evidence? any at all?) but the kind of Nazi who believes in discipline and restraint. Up to a point.

I have a present for you, Kirsten says coyly, brushing her hair out of her eyes as girls do. Presents.

She hands over the snapshots.

Ah, the snapshots! After so long— But he says not a word.

She studies Di Piero's expression covertly and sees that he is surprised—yes she's managed to surprise him—and though he simply takes the snapshots and riffles through them and puts them in an inside pocket without another word she can see that he *is* surprised: and she feels as reckless and gleeful as a very young child.

You never thought you'd get them back, did you, she says boldly.

Di Piero murmurs a half-audible reply.

You *never* thought you'd get them back, she says.

They are walking around the boat basin, they are not distracted by the cries and shouts of children; they are not distracted by the frequent glances of passersby who must be tourists. (A man of that age with a young girl? And the girl so desperately flirtatious, leaning toward him, brushing her arm against his? Peering up into his face? One cannot even pretend to imagine that they are father and daughter, there isn't the slightest resemblance between them.)

Tell me about your fiancée, Kirsten insists. Mother says she's very pretty. The wife of the chairman of the board of . . .

Di Piero cuts her off with an amused snort: Ask Isabel if you're curious.

Kirsten says lightly, smiling a sly smile: She seems to be taking it very well—Isabel, I mean. No jealous rages that I know of. No melancholy.

Di Piero will not be baited.

He extends his arm and glances at his watch in a gesture whose elegance has nothing to do with courtesy.

Kirsten flushes. In a peevish little girl's voice she says: Are you in a hurry? Late for an appointment?—I'm hungry, I haven't had anything to eat today. Take me to Rumpelmayer's.

Guarded and doubtful and yet amused, beginning to be amused. Beginning to be interested.

(Hadn't she seen the swelling of his groin, in the bathhouse that afternoon? Seen and imagined she felt it—though in fact he hadn't pressed near her. Mr. Di Piero, don't hurt me, Mr. Di Piero I didn't mean, oh please . . . Seeing nothing at the time. Her eyes hazed with tears of pain, after all. Her terror having much to do with the possibility of her bowels running loose: and what humiliation that would be! She saw nothing at the time and was too frightened to imagine anything but afterward, certainly afterward, oh yes afterward, she saw and imagined a great deal. And heard again the quiet ferocity of his breathing, which never slipped out of control.)

In the cool wood-polished dark of a French restaurant on East Seventy-first Street Di Piero takes off his sunglasses and puts them carefully away. Kirsten swallows—in eagerness, in hope—at the way in which, like anyone else, Di Piero rubs the bridge of his nose.

There isn't anything to say, he tells her bluntly. Your father was a good man—a very generous man—but he fell into misfortune—he despaired—he lost perspective.

That's an expression that has always interested me, Kirsten says in a bright mocking voice. "Lost perspective."

Di Piero is fitting a fresh cigarette into his cigarette holder. He does not look at her but his smile is brief and rakish.

It means having no fixed point of view, no center. From which you can look outward. From which you can measure the world and put it in scale, Di Piero says. It is his strategy to ignore both her mockery and the desperation beneath it. He says, as if tutoring her: All the old figures of speech, in all the languages, have their truth. "Losing perspective," "losing faith," "falling into despair."

"Falling in love," says Kirsten.

They have much in common, yes, says Di Piero.

She's in love with—Nick? Kirsten asks, lifting her chin. She and Di Piero are facing each other in the dark, across a small circular marble-topped table. They're in love with each other?

Di Piero shrugs his shoulders.

Are they going to get married? Kirsten asks.

Has anyone said they are going to get married? Di Piero asks neutrally.

Isabel wouldn't discuss such a thing, Isabel is in mourning. She's a grief-stricken widow, says Kirsten. Her friends are helping her convalesce. They drag her out in the evenings and make her wear colorful clothing and buy her trinkets, take her to nightclubs, discos . . .

She's back from Nassau, isn't she, Di Piero asks.

Don't you keep in touch? She's in Mexico until May 1, with Mrs. Degler and Jack Fair and a few others.

In Acapulco?

Guadalajara. Mrs. Degler has a big place there.

Kirsten has begun fussing nervously with a tiny box of matches. She watches Di Piero through her lowered lashes and says, as if shyly: I thought you and Isabel kept in close touch. I thought you spoke every day on the phone.

Not quite, says Di Piero.

But you did at one time.

No.

A few years ago.

No.

Didn't you?—a few years ago. When you lived in Washington.

Hardly every day, says Di Piero.

But you're out of touch now?—you don't talk every day on the phone now?

Di Piero signals a waiter and orders two glasses of white wine.

The waiter hesitates, and inquires about Kirsten's age. He is in his mid-thirties, as dark as Di Piero, with a thick drooping mustache. But Di Piero says curtly: She's old enough.

Tell me about them, Kirsten says.

Them?

My mother. And Nick.

Di Piero rubs the bridge of his nose again. But this time the gesture strikes Kirsten as deliberate: he is pretending to be troubled, to be thoughtful.

My mother and Nick and Maurie, Kirsten says softly.

He stares at the tabletop. His expression is no longer neutral—there is a stubborn thickening about his mouth.

Tell me about them, says Kirsten, and I won't bother you again, I won't ever bother you again.

Di Piero says nothing.

Kirsten says, leaning forward, I know they were having an affair —Isabel and Nick—everyone knew it more or less—but I need to know if Maurie found out. And who told him. And when.

These are very complicated matters, Di Piero says. You can't hope to . . .

His words trail off. Kirsten leans farther forward.

Yes?

You're very young, Di Piero says slowly. You can't understand.

I don't need to understand right now, I need to know.

There are things that go back before you were born. . . .

The "things" I want to know have to do with right now, says Kirsten, last June when he killed himself, and the winter before when he moved out of the house. Did you ever see his apartment? No? It was very sad, the Potomac Towers, out Wisconsin. Quite a way out. You were never there? He moved out in December, I think she asked him to leave. It was supposed to be a mutual decision—a mutual arrangement—an "amicable" separation"—but I think she asked him to leave and I think she asked him for a divorce and I think—I *think*—she must have told him she wanted to marry someone else.

That's possible, Di Piero says. He hesitates, then presses her hand with his own. He stills it, calms it, extricates the matchbox from her nervous fingers. —But you don't really know, if no one told you.

Kirsten's heart is pounding violently. She knows what she is going to say is absurd, wild and crazy and unforgiveable, and indeed irrevocable, but she says it nonetheless. —I need to know, Mr. Di Piero, if they killed him.

He withdraws his hand from hers. The waiter approaches and sets down their glasses.

Di Piero raises his glass and makes a curious sucking noise with his lips. It may be an expression of astonishment, or amusement, or simple derision. Now he is staring quite directly at her. —You should call me Tony, he says.

Yes. I'm sorry. Tony.

Her heartbeat is painful. Blindly she reaches for her glass. Raises it. A toast? A secret toast in the dark of a cavelike restaurant? For this is a tryst, after all.

Well, says Di Piero awkwardly, a toast to—?

To meeting again, says Kirsten, grinning. To your charity. Your forgiveness.

Di Piero raises his eyebrows.

Forgiveness—?

You know.

But it was nothing, he says. High spirits on your part. Misdirected excitement.

You were very kind not to tell my parents, Kirsten says.

Slyly and nervously she observes the effect of the word kind on this man. She has read that people are most susceptible to flattery when told the very opposite of the truth. And she has, from time to time, witnessed skillful flatterers in action. (Isabel de Benavente Halleck is a devoted wife and mother, Nick Martens is a family man, Maurie Halleck has a "head" for logic. Owen Halleck is good at sports. Kirsten Halleck is sweet.)

Misdirected passion, Di Piero says, as if not hearing her compliment.

Kirsten laughs, swallowing a large mouthful of wine. It is very dry, very tart. Oh I don't know, she says. That was three years ago, I was only fourteen. . . .

Three years ago? So long? He appears genuinely surprised.

Three years.

So now you're seventeen?—and a senior, Isabel says, at that place in Baltimore?

A place in Eyre, New York.

Di Piero frowns, sucking at his cigarette. As if such details matter.

But perhaps they *do* matter. An odd pleased gloating expression passes over his face. Yes. Oh yes. The Eyre Academy. Girls. I knew some girls there when I was at Bauer. We weren't far away. There were dances, weekends, that sort of thing.

Yes, says Kirsten, watching him closely, yes—Bauer—it's coed now—but the boys come over—sometimes—we visit back and forth—sometimes. That sort of thing.

You do? You have boy friends?

No, says Kirsten. Not me. Not personally.

Certainly you do.

No.

I think you do. Boy friends, lovers—whatever you call them.

Not really, says Kirsten.

You're lying.

Oh, not really, she says, laughing, almost dropping her wine glass, I mean I don't—I don't have time.

Isn't that rather odd? says Di Piero.

I don't know—*is* it? Kirsten says giddily. I mean—I—I'm not very —I don't really have—I don't have interests along those lines.

I'm not your father, you aren't expected to lie to me, Di Piero says.

I didn't lie to my father, Kirsten whispers.

Children always lie to their fathers.

Kirsten presses the cool glass against her forehead, then against her cheek. She regards Di Piero with a faint smile. She says, You did like him, didn't you? My father? You were friends. . . .

I liked him, Di Piero says slowly, as if unconvinced. But we weren't precisely friends, he adds.

Yes, says Kirsten. I mean no. Not the way he and Nick were friends.

Nick saved his life, you know, Di Piero says. Adroitly he shifts the subject; he is looking past Kirsten's head, into a corner of the room. For a moment his manner is almost expansive. —Of course Nick caused the accident, he was so impatient, and careless, making us go into the rapids without studying it first; we should probably have carried the canoes. It was his fault. He was such a pushy bastard even then. But when the accident happened—the canoe capsized—he went after Maurie and hauled him out. He didn't hesitate for an instant.

I've heard the story so many times, Kirsten says. She feels the need to pretend that she doesn't care to hear it again. —From Maurie, who always said Nick had saved his life; and from Nick, who always said Maurie had exaggerated, he wasn't close to drowning.

But he was, says Di Piero quickly. Maurie was close to dead.

—Even from Isabel, Kirsten says, continuing as if she had not been interrupted. Isabel who wasn't there. Who has to have her version too.

And what does Isabel say? Di Piero asks, curious.

She says—she used to say—when she told Owen and me the story —she said that you were just boys—playing at being in danger—you had to exaggerate. Create legends for yourself.

Really, says Di Piero, that's Isabel's line—?

Well—you know Isabel.

I suppose so, says Di Piero, shrugging.

Her version is close to Nick's. That Maurie wasn't really in danger of drowning, that Nick didn't *really* save his life. . . .

Nick saved his life, Di Piero says curtly.

Oh yes, says Kirsten, how?

He went into the rapids to get him—went downstream—almost lost his footing—got hold of Maurie and pulled him to shore—he was bleeding badly from a cut on his head—and Nick was bleeding too, his hands especially—and Nick—well, Nick pulled him onto the bank—saved his life—

Gave him artificial respiration—

Mouth to mouth, yes. Saved his life.

What did you do?—you and the other boy.

We were half-drowned. We didn't do anything.

Who *was* the other boy?

I don't remember—no one whose name you would know.

He isn't important?

Isn't important?—what do you mean?

No one has kept in contact with him?

Di Piero shakes his head irritably. I don't know, I don't think so. The important thing is . . .

Nick did save my father's life.

Yes, certainly.

You would really swear that?

Why should I swear it? I don't make it a habit to "swear" anything, Di Piero says mildly. Unless I am in court. Or before certain committees with the power to subpoena and hand down indictments and sentences. . . .

You were a witness, Kirsten says slowly.

A witness, yes.

Was it—terrible? Frightening?

That one of us almost died? No—it was too confusing—it happened too quickly. The wound on his head, *that* was frightening—it required ten stitches. But everything happened too quickly. Our canoe was capsized and we were thrown out and almost drowned. . . . Di Piero makes a quick brusque motion, his forefinger beneath his nose. What I remember about it is very clear: Nick hunched over Maurie, sobbing. He thought Maurie was dead at first, he lost control, he was really sobbing —babbling—he was almost hysterical. He *thought* Maurie was dead.

I didn't know that, Kirsten says carefully. No one ever told me that.

Yes, says Di Piero, it was Nick carrying on like that that scared us. Nick almost hysterical.

Is that right, says Kirsten.

Because he thought it was too late, he thought Maurie was dead.

They must have been close friends, says Kirsten. For him to feel that way.

Di Piero hesitates, frowning. I suppose so, he says. I don't know much about friendship. And it was a long time ago.

Kirsten takes another swallow of her wine. She wills herself to get high: to get high immediately. If she had a joint, if she could casually light up, not just for the pleasure of it but for the comfort, the feel of the thing between her fingers. . . .

But Nick caused the accident in the first place, didn't he, she says.

Di Piero dismisses the subject with an abrupt movement of his shoulders. All this happened a very long time ago, he says. I was *seventeen* at the time.

His smile is brief but wide and white. His voice fairly throbs with contempt.

Seventeen—! A hundred years ago.

Walking east on Seventy-fourth Street Kirsten says in a voice that does not tremble: But did they kill him. Are they responsible.

Di Piero, guiding her across the first stretch of Park Avenue, his fingers lightly at her elbow, says in a distracted voice: Responsible—? Which means—?

Did they hire someone.

Di Piero snorts with amusement.

Hire someone—!

Kirsten says in the same even voice: Yes. You all know about these things. Yes. Someone to kill him. To remove him. The way the witnesses were killed in Chile. . . .

Di Piero grips her elbow more firmly. They are standing on the traffic island, waiting for the light to change.

You listen to too much gossip, Di Piero says, amused, you read too many radical journals. Up at Eyre, do they play around with such things?—someone on the faculty, maybe?—playing leftist?—"revolutionary"?

I'm not an idiot, Kirsten says, blushing. I know that my father and Nick were putting together a case against GBT for what they tried to do in Chile, to Allende—

Allende, Di Piero says, correcting her pronunciation. *Salvador Allende.*

Did you know him? Kirsten asks stupidly. Did you—meet him?

Of course not, Di Piero says, what the hell have I to do with Chile?

I'm not an idiot, Kirsten says. Di Piero guides her across the pavement, to the crowded curb. It crosses her mind—swiftly, madly—that the crowds on the street give a certain authority to what she is doing. They are strangers, they are anonymous, but as she and Di Piero move through them they become witnesses.

I know what my father's confession is supposed to be about, I mean the details, I know what he "confessed" to, Kirsten says hotly, even if it's secret—even if it's classified. I know.

But you don't *know*, do you, Di Piero says.

I— I—

You really don't *know* anything, dear.

Now she is truly alarmed: now the word *dear* unnerves her.

But she has no choice, she must accompany him. To an apartment building overlooking the East River.

I won't cry, she has promised, biting her lower lip like a child. I really *won't.*

Aloud she says, pulling her arm free: Salvador Allende. And the other name—the one they gave the money to—was Tomic—the other man, I mean—

Really, says Di Piero, who told you that?

It isn't any secret now, it's out—everybody knows—

Ah do they *really*, Di Piero says, laughing silently.

They are walking without haste along Seventy-fourth Street. Kirsten even takes Di Piero's arm. Two attractive people: a man in his late forties, wearing dark sunglasses; a girl in her late teens, wearing somewhat lighter sunglasses. Stylish people, despite the girl's wild hair. Very much a couple despite the disparity in their ages.

Did they kill him, Kirsten says. Did they hire someone to kill him.

Don't be ridiculous, Di Piero says.

So she would inherit his money. And Grandfather's money. Not just the divorce settlement. . . .

Calm down, Di Piero says.

I'm all right, Kirsten says, fighting the impulse to laugh, I'm not excited, what the hell do you mean?—I just want an answer to my question.

Your question is ridiculous.

He was run off the road, wasn't he. Someone followed him. Maybe he was followed for a long time—for weeks. Tracking him down. Hunting him down. For the money. Because the divorce settlement wouldn't be enough for them. I mean for Isabel and Nick. This other business, this crap about taking bribes, I don't give a damn about that, Kirsten says fiercely, he didn't kill himself for *that*.

Calm down, Di Piero says. People are looking at you.

This shit about taking bribes, this connection with Gast or whoever it was, my father didn't take any bribes, he never accepted a bribe in his life, everyone knows that, the confessions were forged, the police could have forged them, the F.B.I., the C.I.A., maybe Nick himself ransacked the apartment, Nick could have forged his signature, anyone at the Commission could have forged his signature—Isabel could have done it, *you* could have done it, Kirsten says wildly. He didn't kill himself for *that*. Not for anything so small.

Be quiet, Di Piero says. He squeezes her arm and for a shocked moment she is quiet.

Then she says, softly: He didn't kill himself at all. Not my father. He wouldn't have left me. He loved me. He loved *me*. It wasn't just her—there was more than that in his life—he didn't give a shit for her—I know he didn't. He told me so himself. When I went to see him. He had me kneel on the carpet and we prayed. I was embarrassed at first—I wanted to get the hell out—oh anything!—anything—I had a tennis lesson—but then I gave in and got down on my knees and he started praying and it was all right—it was all right. He was serious, he loved God. He would never have killed himself. He loved God and he loved me and Owen—he loved his children. He wouldn't have killed himself for *her*. Once he got started praying it was really all right. When you pray you forget where you are and who is with you. There's no need to be embarrassed. I didn't mind. I stayed on my knees for ten minutes—fifteen minutes—oh I don't know, my knees got sore, she says, laughing, I'm not used to kneeling, it isn't anything I've had much practice in—

Wipe your face, Di Piero says. Do you have a tissue?

She fumbles inside the bag. Draws out a crumpled pink Kleenex.

He didn't kill himself, he wouldn't have done anything like that, Kirsten says. Someone had him killed.

Di Piero guides her along in silence. He does not trouble to refute her.

Someone had him killed—isn't that right? It happens all the time, Kirsten says. I'm not an idiot.

Anthony Di Piero with his sleek, rather oily hair, fastidiously combed back from his forehead; Anthony Di Piero in his beautiful chamois sports jacket, his silky mauve necktie. Not troubling to reply. Hauling her along.

(Of course I remember you. The Halleck girl. Kirsten.)

Just tell me: *did* they? she whispers.

Di Piero walks with her to the steps of an apartment building at the very end of the street. An attractive granite façade, stained glass in the vestibule windows, an ornately carved portico that looks Mediterranean. A doorman in uniform, an elderly white man, lounging inside.

As they leave the street Di Piero glances back over his shoulder, over her head. His gaze is swift and thorough. But unperturbed: evidently he sees nothing that might be out of order.

H'lo, Mr. Di Piero, the doorman says.

Hello, Henry, says Di Piero.

The doorman punches a button in the elevator, then steps outside, holding the doors open for Di Piero and his companion.

Thank you, Henry, says Di Piero. He is panting slightly and there is a faint, a very faint, film of olivish perspiration on his face.

Kirsten digs her nails into the back of his hand. The elevator doors close without a sound.

Tell me: *did* they? she whispers.

Di Piero adjusts his tie, brushes his hair back with a quick practiced motion of both his hands. He has been eying himself in a frosted gold mirror, an antique mirror, at the rear of the little elevator.

It isn't impossible, dear, he says casually.

IV. The Storm

Mount Dunvegan Island,
Maine, July 1955

Turtle Love

Struggling, are they, or mating?—or (with their curious, coldly regal reptile heads averted) actually unaware of each other?

What are they *doing*, Maurie's fiancée says with a little cry, drawing back as if she feared the turtles might snap at her bare toes. She glances at Nick slyly. She is amused, mystified, fastidiously "alarmed" as a young woman might be, suddenly confronted with two such very strange creatures. And if the turtles are mating (in such plain view, right on the beach!) she should be embarrassed as well. A slow warm rosy flush should color her delicate skin.

Box turtles, Nick says.

What—?

Box turtles. A species of turtle.

Like rock or earth come sluggishly to life, their eyes unblinking, their tails rigid. Prehistoric creatures. Monsters. Their shells are somewhat humped, and handsomely colored (streaks of yellow on the dark mud-green shell); their legs are awkwardly extended. Male and female evidently look alike. Unless they are not trying to get into position to copulate—unless they are fighting each other (two males?)—or simply trying to push their way through a pile of rocks, driftwood, and other beach debris, when of course it would be no trouble at all to crawl around the pile.

What *are* they doing? the girl says, trying to hold her whipping hair in place. The poor things, they look so *serious*.

The girl's slight Spanish accent provides a maidenly edge to her boldness. Nick hears himself laughing, a receptive male. The turtles with their tense but expressionless faces—though it is difficult to think of them as having "faces"—the turtles with their small cold pealike eyes that look blind—are precisely the sort of thing, the sort of meaningless social diversion, that young women who look like Isabel de Benavente exclaim over in the presence of young men who look like Nick Martens. So he laughs, willing to present himself as *charmed*.

Part of her pale-golden hair has been braided, and is fastened at the crown of her head by a gold barrette—almost too large—in the shape of a dove. A romantic touch, quite Latin. The rest of her hair flies free in the ocean breeze and she is kept busy trying to hold it in place, or brushing it out of her eyes in quick pretty gestures. She hovers over the turtles, frowning. That they should continue their curious struggle—pushing against the debris and against each other, their ugly heads rigid, their feet slowly pawing the air—that they should scramble forward and fall to the side, or back, nearly on their domed shells, in defiance of her excited interest in them (What kind of turtle did you say they are, Nick?—box, boxer?) strikes her as peculiar indeed, or so her posture indicates.

Their heads are ugly, says Isabel, but their shells are very attractive. For a moment she seems about to touch one of the turtles with her forefinger. It's strange, isn't it, they don't see themselves?—they can't see their own shells? They're really quite beautiful. If you take the time to look.

Yes, Nick murmurs, they're beautiful.

Isabel, bent over the turtles, does not hear. One might guess from her behavior that she is genuinely interested in the turtles—out of a courteous respect, perhaps, for this rather scruffy stretch of beach north of the Martenses' cottage.

Out of a respect for her fiancé's closest friend, about whom she has heard (so Nick suspects, uneasily) rather too much.

Isabel de Benavente with her absurd painted fingernails and toenails, her jeans rolled pertly to the knee, her red shirt tied beneath her breasts to expose her tanned midriff: Isabel with her pouty mouth, her frosted-gray eyes, her Roman nose: an accident of nature that strikes Nick as catastrophic. (He is thinking, of course, of Maurie. Who is hopelessly in love. And desperate to marry.)

Isabel with a Halleck engagement ring (a square-cut diamond edged with small rubies), extending her hand for Nick to shake—or to kiss?—as if she were royalty. Yes, I've heard so much about you, she said shyly. So much about you.

And I've heard so much about *you*.

Isabel de Benavente, the daughter of, the only child of, Luis de Benavente of New York City, Washington, Palm Beach, and Madrid. A financier, an "investor." (Most recently, in oil drilling operations off the coast of Mexico.) There is a mother too, Maurie said, but unfortunately she's estranged from her husband and daughter—Isabel says she lives with relatives in St. Paul and rarely comes east. But I think I'll be seeing her soon.

At the wedding? Nick asked.

Oh—long before the wedding, surely! Maurie said.

(But the wedding is scheduled for the first Saturday in October. Which strikes Nick—who has been hearing about lovely Isabel for only two months—as rather premature.)

Silver-blond hair, the bangs cut straight across her forehead, just at the eyebrows. Perfect skin. Poreless? Pale gray eyes like washed glass. . . . Nick, staring at her when they were introduced, as nervous chattery Maurie urged them together, was struck immediately by those eyes: something hard and knowing and sly in them, exactly like his own. (His jealousy of his best friend's fiancée. Was that it?—an emotion so simple, and so contemptible? Better jealousy than envy, at any rate.)

Hello, Nick, lovely to meet you, I have heard so much about you.

Delighted to meet you, Isabel, I've heard so much about *you.*

Wide handsome dazzling smiles that turn uneasy. A handshake that becomes clumsy in midgrip.

Isabel de Benavente whose beauty hurt Nick's eye, and afterward offended his sense of proportion. She appeared to be only eighteen or nineteen years old. But clearly sophisticated. (She was a graduate of the Hays School, had attended three semesters at Mount Vernon College, and despite her father's "sensitive" reputation in Washington she had been a Junior Cotillion debutante the season before.) Her "Spanish" blood was not immediately evident until one looked more closely, listened more attentively: but there it was: there some measure of exoticism was, intelligently understated, hardly more than a nuance, an echo. For Isabel de Benavente was extremely self-conscious and her self-consciousness had the air of a supreme composure. (You won't find her very "Spanish," Maurie warned Nick, as if warning him against disappointment. She says she hates Spain, she has never really learned Spanish, as a reaction evidently against her father—a difficult man. He's an anti-Communist, a royalist, a McCarthy supporter—that sort of thing. According to Isabel he treated his wife very badly.)

Nick, observing his friend's fiancée, thinks cruelly of a certain *aperçu* of Nietzsche's: . . . Women would not have their genius for adornment if they did not have the instinct for playing a *secondary role.*

You are the two people I love most in the world, Maurie said, his eyes misting over with emotion. How typical of Halleck, to say such things, to blurt out secrets, embarrassing everyone—including himself! Which is why, Nick supposes, we love him. And tolerate him.

Poor Maurie: besotted with love, flummoxed, infatuated.

I have never met anyone like her, Maurie said softly. And raised his eyes to Nick's shyly as if to see: Did Nick guess his lie?

Beautiful Isabel turning her engagement ring around her slender finger, fussing with her pale-golden hair. Small gold loops pierce her ears. Her perfume is cool and faintly astringent, like lilies. Visiting the Martenses' cottage in Maine cannot be this young woman's idea of a good time, Nick shrewdly thinks, but of course she wants to accommodate her fiancé's whims—she is confident he will have very few.

When are you going to invite Maurie up? Mr. Martens kept asking Nick. Telephoning him in Boston. (Nick has a position with the law firm Bell, Janeway, Prescher & Prescher. Maurie is already in Washington, with the newly established Commission on Civil Rights.) —Invite him and his father both up, why don't you? Maine is so beautiful this time of year.

I don't think Mr. Halleck can come, Nick said. He's a very busy man.

Have you tried? Have you spoken with him?

He's a very busy man, Nick said, shutting his eyes. He has to watch his health.

He was so generous to us, Mr. Martens said.

He's a generous man, Nick said.

. . . Helping you out at Harvard like that, Mr. Martens said in his low ambiguous voice. (One could not tell—Nick could never tell—whether he was deeply reverent or mildly mocking, in that tone of voice. On the subject of Joseph Halleck's "generosity" to Nick Martens, as a consequence of Nick's having allegedly saved Maurie's life on the canoeing trip in Ontario, Mr. Martens was still, perhaps, *undecided.* Since he was in financial straits, as he phrased it, and had been so for years, he was certainly grateful for cash aids—loans, that is—but at the same time he had his pride. He was Bernard Martens after all. He had his pride.)

Do you keep in contact? Mr. Martens asked doggedly.

In contact? With Maurie? Or with his father? Nick asked.

With the father, Mr. Martens said. I know you keep in contact with the son.

No, said Nick.

No?

My life is complicated too, Nick said resentfully.

(He had acquired a girl, himself. June Penrick who taught at a Quaker School in Boston. To whom he was almost officially engaged.)

So you and old Joe are out of contact now, Mr. Martens said in a low quizzical voice that shaded into a chuckle. . . . D'you think he expects the money back? Five, six thousand it was, wasn't it?

He wouldn't accept it back, Nick said, his face burning.

You're sure?

He wouldn't *think* of it, Nick said.

Mr. Martens laughed. You sound like a girl who has heard a naughty word, he said. I was only making an innocent inquiry.

Of course, said Nick.

But Maurie, at least: you'll invite him? And his fiancée? You said he has a fiancée? Invite them both, try for Fourth of July weekend. Your mother won't mind. And maybe at the last minute the old man will tag along. He's had a heart attack or two, hasn't he, maybe he'd like to relax up in Maine.

The Hallecks have their place in the mountains, Nick said evenly. It's a long trip up to Maine.

Can't they fly?

I don't *know,* Nick said irritably, but I'll ask Maurie about coming up. Fourth of July. With his fiancée.

Rich girl, eh?

I wouldn't know.

Good-looking?

I wouldn't know, we've never met.

Well, said Mr. Martens, suddenly bored with his son, maybe you'll find out.

And so they drove up, all the way out to Mount Dunvegan Island across the five-mile bridge, Maurie and Isabel in Maurie's new car: a green-plum-colored Alfa Romeo which Nick knew, before making his oblique inquiry, must have been Isabel's idea.

Handsome car, Nick said, stroking the fender. How does it handle?

Maurie is becoming accustomed to it, Isabel said with her wide white smile, aren't you—?

It's all right, Maurie said, blushing. It's fine.

Nick stared at Maurie. It had been some months since they'd seen each other. (A quick lunch in Cambridge, at the German restaurant just off the square. A few days after Maurie's twenty-fifth birthday. They were eager and slightly apprehensive as they compared notes: jobs, associates, new friends, living quarters, plans for the future, girls; and what news from their classmates? Nick dreaded the sudden surprise of an old rival's success. But Maurie was innocent enough not to spare him.)

Maurie looking sunburnt, boyish, vigorous. In a beige sportshirt with stylish button-down collar and khaki shorts that matched his fiancée's skirt. The red-blond hairs glistening on his forearms and legs. His droll wise monkeyish face puckered with smiling. (Nick wondered if Maurie thought, as he did, when they met after a considerable absence —*Has he forgotten?*)

How beautiful it is here—
That lovely long bridge—
The smell of the ocean, the breeze—
Those birds, are they gulls?—their wings are so white—

The girl, the fiancée at last, about whom Nick has heard so very, very much: bold and confident in her beauty as she strides to Nick and extends her hand: to be clasped, to be kissed?—like royalty.

The girl Isabel, Maurie's bride-to-be. Descended in fact from a "noble" Spanish house. Or so it is said. Barcelona? Royalists? The father left Spain at the age of seventeen and made his way eventually to the New World (arriving in Montreal, moving southward to Boston and then to New York where he worked for an import firm); the mother was, or is, a Midwesterner whose family did not approve of Luis de Benavente. (Have you met him yourself? Nick asked Maurie, and Maurie said, surprised, Of course I've met him—three or four times: he's a very busy man. Do they expect you to turn Catholic? Nick asked. The subject has been brought up, Maurie said, and I know Isabel would like me to take instructions . . . but of course I can't do it, I can't even consider it. Belief to me isn't a social gesture.)

Isabel de Benavente, smiling at Nick in the moist quivering sunshine. Hello. *Hello.*

Nick was too practiced, too skilled a player to give the girl the satisfaction of guessing his surprise. He shook her hand readily enough. With a sort of clumsy zeal, in fact. And smiled as one might smile in greeting anyone at all, welcoming any guest to the Martenses' summer place. The fog has been burning off all morning, how was the drive, can I help you with your things . . . ? Nick with his brick-dark skin flushing darker, his white cotton pullover snug against his shoulders and upper arms, trying not to stare at his friend's fiancée. (Though he is thinking —and despises himself for the thought—that Isabel is far more attractive than June.)

They stand in the gravel drive by the low-slung little car, talking excitedly. The wind off the ocean is festive, Isabel's hair whips about her face, her skirt shows the elegant curve of her thighs. She is wearing a satiny red shirt (which has not yet been pulled up and tied beneath her breasts: that will come later this afternoon) and a khaki skirt slit to the knee. Golden earrings, golden chains looped about her neck, a wrist-watch with a tiny face, rings on both hands, the dove-barrette on her head which manages to be both absurd and glamorous at the same time. Nick feels the continued shock of her eyes—her calm level amused stare —her arrogant smile. Ah yes. Nick Martens. Yes. I know you: you are the boy Maurie used to adore before he met me. You are the boy who almost caused his death, and almost saved his life. Yes? I've heard all about you, I know Maurie's secrets, I know there is an "understanding" —a "sacred bond"—between you of which you never speak. How very *good* that I am meeting you at last. . . . So her stare fixes him, the silence beneath her chatter.

The wedding will be a fairly large one after all. Since Isabel has so many friends, and the Hallecks know so many people. St. Anthony of Padua Church, Georgetown. There will be a special arrangement . . . since the groom of course isn't Catholic . . . the details have not yet been worked out . . . but both Maurie and Isabel are delighted that Nick will be best man.

It's my honor, Nick says awkwardly.

They are a couple, Maurie and Isabel. How surprising—how very *unexpected.* For Nick has seen his friend in the company of other girls, of course, over the years; girls to whom he may have introduced Maurie; girls who (it might be discreetly said) were rather inclined toward Nick. But Isabel is a stranger, prettily exotic, a Washington debutante, stand-ing easily at Maurie's side and not at all intimidated by Nick's assessing stare.

It is 2:50 P.M. when he and Isabel come upon the turtles.

They have drifted off together, hiking along the beach, in the direction of "Tower Rock"—though the promontory is probably too far for them to go. (Nick would enjoy the walk—luncheon lasted for a very long time—but he doubts that Isabel de Benavente is equal to the dis-tance.) Maurie wants them to become acquainted, Maurie has conspicu-ously stayed behind with Mr. Martens, but their attempts at conversa-tion have come to very little and Nick supposes they should turn back. They have been walking fifteen or twenty minutes.

The box turtles are a welcome diversion. Something to exclaim over, make inquiries about, observe.

And it seems that they *are* trying to mate after all. Slow stupid stubborn things, pawing half-consciously at each other, still trying to climb the pile of debris. (One charges forward abruptly, loses his balance, falls back; the other gropes and blunders across his head.) Poor things, says Isabel, brushing her hair from her warm face, I wonder if we should help them . . . !

Nick laughs obligingly.

Though it isn't amusing, for turtle love is as unfocused and pitiless and without affection—without *attention*—as the great waves dashing upon the beach.

The reptile heads protrude rigidly from the humped shells, the eyes are beady, lusterless, and unblinking. Rock or earth come sluggishly to life, dream-creatures, persistent in their struggle, blind, blundering. . . . As he and Isabel walk on Nick hears himself telling her about an incident from his childhood he hadn't remembered until now—some boys smashing a turtle against a rock—and his stricken horror—his mute disgust—though (and he doesn't tell Isabel this, of course) perhaps he was one of the boys who smashed the turtle, hooting and jeering at the creature's inept struggle to escape: perhaps it was only afterward he imagined horror and disgust.

Well—boys are cruel, Isabel says.

They continue walking though the noise of the surf obscures half their words. Maurie this and Maurie that, plans for next year, a book Maurie wants to write on the history of the human-rights lobby in Congress, an application he has made for a Fulbright year abroad (Norway? —Nick can't quite hear and doesn't want to ask Isabel to repeat herself) though someone-or-other (evidently his boss) is reputed to be "unhappy" about these plans. . . . Nick is covertly watching Isabel's bare feet. Narrow, pale, pretty toes sinking in the sand, toenails painted coral pink; slender ankles. Nick is wearing shoes and can stride along without any difficulty.

Do you think you'll be happy with him, Nick doesn't ask, do you think he's the kind of man who would make *you* happy?

Sand flies and screaming gulls and the need to keep up their conversation because of course Maurie is so eager, so hopeful; so well-intentioned. Isabel won't tell him that his friend Nick is an arrogant bullying bastard, Nick won't tell him that his fiancée is vain and shallow, and her charming accent is probably an affectation. —It's lovely along here, Isabel says, raising her voice to be heard over the wind. The mist by those rocks—it is mist, isn't it?—look, there's a rainbow—*almost* a rainbow—

Nick squints and shades his eyes. Though he sees nothing but a great pile of boulders beneath the sea cliff he makes a grunting assent.

Isabel walks, with difficulty, at the edge of the surf; in the collapsing sand. She wriggles her arms like a gay drunken sleepwalker.

Five to three, Nick notes. They should probably be turning back.

Tower Rock—one of Nick's secret boyhood places—is another mile or more; the Martenses' cottage is at least a mile back. Though Isabel seems cheerful and energetic enough Nick knows how suddenly a young woman of her type can become exhausted.

The sun is bright, the air is chilly. Seaweed, kelp, small dead fish, driftwood, forth leaping up and falling back. The sea's rocking motion. Wind and surf and spray. A pulsing urgency that isn't Nick's heart but the great ocean itself, dissolving into cloud at its horizon. Are you getting tired, Nick asks, should we turn back . . . ? But Isabel, a few yards ahead, now exclaiming over something at her feet (a starfish, a conch) does not hear.

They walk on. Far ahead something is trotting along the beach: a dog: but it turns away with the curve of the land and when Nick points it out Isabel sees nothing. It's usually deserted along here, Nick says, you can walk and walk for miles without meeting anyone; and Isabel says, It *is* deserted.

Gulls rise from the carcass of a large fish, their wings flapping. Isabel pointedly looks away. Nick, glancing back, sees with a curious trip of his heart their footprints in the wet packed sand—his enormous, hers small, the toes clearly defined. Wavering footsteps, trailing in and out of the surf. Leading back along the beach and out of sight—the curve of the land is such that the Martenses' property can't be seen from this point.

Isabel is speaking. Nick turns back, apologetically, cupping his ear. He hasn't heard. Hasn't been listening.

I know you disapprove of me, she says. You and the rest of Maurie's friends.

Nick is too startled to speak. He feels his face grown warm; he is guilty as if she has read his thoughts.

Isabel's voice is defiantly steady, perhaps she has rehearsed her brave little speech. I know you don't like me, she says. I know, I understand. Because he really is an exceptional person. You think—everyone thinks—he's worth a dozen of me—and I don't contest it—I understand —I know how everyone loves him. But I love him too.

When Nick begins to protest Isabel silences him with an assured gesture—she takes hold of his wrist. She says quickly: No. I understand. I don't blame you. You've known him for ten years. But I want to explain —please let me explain. Maurie addresses a woman who stands in my place and is superior to me. He loves her, he adores her. I think I love him because of that woman—I want to grow into her. Do you understand? I love him because of that woman. . . .

Nick is terribly embarrassed, he can't even draw away from her.

I do love him, Isabel says, passionate as if she has been challenged. I love Maurie as much . . . as much as I can love anyone.

A Lover's Complaint

A beautiful girl, Mr. Martens says, beautiful shining eyes and teeth, I
noted the teeth, pearly and luminous and wet—a carnivore. I congratulate you.

Three-thirty. In fact three-thirty-two. Maurie, dry-mouthed,
breathing with difficulty, sees the time without at first registering it.

Raised voices, laughter. Firecrackers. Children who are nieces
and nephews of the Martenses', or friends of the nieces and nephews,
running about. Down to the beach, up from the beach. Shouts. Screams.
The adults sit on a weedy flagstone terrace sipping drinks and talking
of the county board of supervisors (which is corrupt, Maurie gathers)
and the need to enforce zoning restrictions. An imminent turnover at
Socony Oil. The illness—presumably cancer—of a mutual acquaintance
whose name Maurie has never heard before.

Maurie strolls down to the beach, drink in hand. The ice cubes
have nearly melted.

A beautifully plumed bird, its feathers golden, but so fair, so
light, they resemble silver. Flying to him. To *his* arm. . . . A dream-
creature. Those eyes. So penetrating he grows weak.

Carnivore, Mr. Martens said with his husky jolly laugh. Clapping
poor Maurie on the shoulder.

Mr. Martens has gained twenty pounds since Maurie saw him last.
He drinks too much, eats too much, radiates a queer dissatisfied heat
when he speaks—one can almost see the sweat beading on his pale
flaccid face.

169

A lovely girl, seriously, Mr. Martens says. When is the wedding again? I congratulate you.

A wink that manages to be both shy and risqué. As if beauty were slightly obscene and must be joked about, man to man.

Now if Nick could only . . . But he flies off in all directions at once. . . . Amanda, did you meet her?—on Saltonstall's staff, in Boston. Then there was the Sherman girl, my wife and I liked her, and felt sorry for her—you know Nick. And now there's June. . . . Has he introduced you to June?

Yes, says Maurie.

Teaching at a Quaker school, a fine girl, good family too, Mr. Martens says frankly, popping a handful of cashews into his mouth. But I don't think, you know, that she's strong enough for Nick. I mean strong enough to direct him. To stand up to him. He needs someone . . .

Layers of cloud at the horizon, growing thicker. Dense and bruise-like. The sun has a wintry glower; someone on the terrace exclaims over a drop of rain.

No, it can't be.

It *isn't* going to rain.

The radio said . . .

Rain, thundershowers? Small-craft warning?

Mr. Martens draws Maurie along, evidently to show him something. Maurie doesn't resist. He feels lightheaded, weak. The lovely silver-gold bird, the iridescent feathers, the graceful undulating flight. . . . And on her finger *his* ring: which is to say, Grandmother Halleck's. (It's very beautiful, Isabel said softly. She leaned forward to kiss him. Her hair swung, yes her hair swung and brushed his face, the moment was subdued and melodic and not very real, though in fact it happened: and Isabel de Benavente became Maurie Halleck's *fiancée*. His eyes filled with tears, his fingers trembled. He was going to be married. He was in love, and his love was returned, and he was going to be married. Not very real to him though in fact it seems to have happened—some months ago.)

He needs someone who's a match for him, Mr. Martens says.

Maurie, who likes June Penrick very much, protests: But I think June is quite strong. . . . I think Nick and June are well matched.

Do you, says Mr. Martens.

Leading him away to show him renovation work being done at the rear of the cottage. (Maurie shades his eyes against a sudden sunny glare and looks down to the beach. Children, a few sunbathers. A trotting dog. No sign of them. And the time?—ten to four.)

He swallows painfully. The back of his mouth tastes of sand, of grit. Where is his drink? He must have set it down somewhere. . . .

Has Nick confided in you, about June? Mr. Martens asks.

What do you mean, confided in? says Maurie.

I mean—you know—has he talked frankly—about his plans, or hers—whether they intend to—whether they're serious? Mr. Martens says. I don't mean simply whether they—well—you know—

And his voice trails off. Perhaps he is slightly embarrassed.

Nick respects June very much, Maurie says. A final glance over his shoulder. The beach, the sea cliff, the crashing gray-green waves, a thousand knife-flashes of light that hurt his eyes. They had strolled off to the left, to the north, after lunch. At Maurie's suggestion. His tacit suggestion. (He had said to Isabel, driving up, Please don't let Nick's manner put you off: sometimes he's a little assertive, a little outspoken. He made a number of enemies at school. But he has friends too—he has loyal friends. And you know what a friend he's been to me. Just ignore his sarcasm if he's sarcastic, don't mind his humor, and try to get a chance to talk with him alone. . . . He's different when he's alone. When he's not trying to impress an audience.)

"Respects" her, Mr. Martens says stiffly, well, I should think so. The Penricks, after all. . . . And June herself. . . . She's coming up later this afternoon, did Nick tell you? The four of you should . . . It will be nice to . . .

Mr. Martens falls silent. He draws his bare arm roughly across his perspiring face, as if the thought has suddenly struck him—or does poor Maurie imagine it?—that his son and Maurie's fiancée have been gone a very long time on their walk.

Fortunately there is a diversion: a string of firecrackers explodes near Mr. Martens' sandaled feet, and children scramble away through the scrubby grass, noisy with laughter, and Mr. Martens shouts furiously at them. Get the hell out of here! You little brats! How dare you! What d'you think you're doing!

To Maurie he says with an angry resigned smile, They're spoiled rotten, these days. My sister's kids. Worse than Nick ever thought of being at that age. And there's a small gang of them, that house over there, the Cape Cod, see?—the beach is getting worse every year.

Yes, Maurie says vaguely.

About Nick and June, now, Mr. Martens says, he hasn't said anything?—I mean to you? I mean—you know—has Mr. Penrick talked to him at all? I'd think they would be grateful to get someone like Nick on at Western Electric—of course it isn't his specialty exactly—corporate law—and I know he's ambitious for other things—or imagines he is—but certain facts of life should have a calming effect on him—what do you think, Maurie?

Maurie glances up, startled. What does he think . . . ?

One month it's politics and he's got Saltonstall interested in promoting him; then it's civil rights and he wants to go down to Washington to join you; then it's criminal justice . . . he's got some ideas of his own, I'm sure he's told you, about reforming the courts. Then again he wants to take a year off—at his age!—at this crucial point in his life—to do some U.N. work in Geneva and elsewhere, maybe Africa. Southeast Asia. Teach English. Learn languages, local religions, customs, that sort of thing. As if the world would wait for him to return and resume his career. . . . And of course Nick has a shrewd eye for business too: he might surprise us all someday.

Business? says Maurie doubtfully. I don't think so.

Business, real estate, the stock market. You can't tell. He likes to fool around with money, other people's money, he likes the idea of speculation, investments . . . but of course that isn't his line of work right now. That's why I thought June's father might have approached him. But you haven't heard? No?

I haven't heard, says Maurie.

He peers at the sky. Sees nothing. Does not glance again at his watch.

The only thing Nick isn't interested in at all is his old man's business, Mr. Martens says with a rough unconvincing laugh. Not music to perform or to peddle.

Maurie murmurs an inaudible reply. His skin itches in a dozen places but he does not dare start to scratch: once he begins he won't be able to stop.

The trouble with my son, Mr. Martens says, clapping a warm hand on Maurie's shoulder, exhaling his whiskey-sweet breath into Maurie's face, is that his mind works too fast. It's a demon, it's worse than a computer. He runs through people and possibilities without ever—you know—without ever exactly comprehending them. At college and then again in law school there was one professor after another he idolized, and then something went wrong and he detested them, and still he needed them, you know—of course *you* know—Nick's a born protégé, isn't he?—he should be clerking at the Supreme Court—so I gave up trying to keep them clear. But of course you know all this, you know Nick better than I do.

I don't think that's entirely true, Mr. Martens, Maurie says.

Call me Bernard, for Christ's sake!—I'm not an old codger yet. Call me Bernard, eh?

All right, yes—I'm sorry—

Nick calls me Bernard, you've heard him?—not always with the most transparent respect. Started when he went away to school, age of fourteen.

Yes, Maurie says faintly.

Always was an outspoken little shit. I *knew* he'd go into law, and I *knew* he'd do well. . . .

Maurie wants to run away sobbing from this garrulous old fool. A gross soft flaccid version of Nick. His belly sprawls over his handsome leather belt, his forearms are ham-sized, and hairy. Nearly as tall as Nick, with the same sly winking intelligent eyes, and the well-defined lips; formerly a handsome man—which Maurie would know even if he hadn't seen Bernard Martens in old photographs. (Posed at the piano, his expression both angelic and self-absorbed. His chin slightly uplifted. His profile "noble.") Even the voice is Nick's—almost. It rises and sinks, swerves from a well-modulated baritone to a raspy grating querulous bass. Where Nick's shoulders and arms are muscular Mr. Martens's are slack and drooping. He is an aristocrat gone to fat, but uncomfortably so: a hedonist deprived of pleasure, an intellectual turned sour. An "artist" whose failure at art (and at business) has made him clumsily cynical.

Look, kid: don't let him take advantage of you, Mr. Martens is saying in a low conspiratorial voice. I mean—I know you're grateful to him for certain things—that business up in Ontario for one—I know you're very close—you trust him—but—

Maurie draws away, startled as if his friend's father had struck him; or caressed him.

I have no real reason for saying this—I don't know what I *am* saying, Mr. Martens laughs, but—but, well—you see—

In his thick face those almond-shaped eyes with their curly intelligent wink are alarming: Nick's eyes, aren't they?

Maurie blushes and turns away. His skin burns with itching—forehead, throat, the small of his back, buttocks. He feels faint: for an instant he sees, lying in the grass of a hidden cove, their bodies spangled with damp sand, Nick and Isabel clutching at each other. . . . Grasping and panicked with the need to hurry. For of course there isn't much time.

Mr. Martens leads him on as if nothing were wrong. A chattery aging man carrying his drink, wearing thonged sandals, showing a guest the "new wing." It is a long room overlooking the sea cliff, glass doors at the far end, a stone fireplace partly built. The flooring will be of pine but Mr. Martens is already dissatisfied. It seems that someone—the architect or the contractor—has lied to him.

Don't ever work with an architect, he says, you and what's-her-name—Isabel—yes, Isabel—you and Isabel, you just drive around Washington and look at the for sale signs and pick out the house you want, buy it already built and after people have lived in it, in fact the older the better—but I don't need to tell you that, or her. Never mind your dream house, to hell with that business. You can't trust anyone. . . .

Maurie stumbles about, pretending to examine the room. There is very little to see: unfinished walls, flapping strips of insulation, debris underfoot. Someone has left a wadded-up lunch bag, a banana peel, a Coke bottle, cigarette butts. What can he say? What can he find to admire? The fireplace *is* attractive . . . and the glass doors, the view. . . .

What am I doing here? Maurie thinks wildly. Where is Isabel—?

Mr. Martens points something out, a flaw evidently, and launches into a querulous monologue. The self-importance of architects . . . the escalating prices of building materials . . . the hourly wages of carpenters, electricians, plumbers, and mere laborers. He is so angry he begins to laugh, sputtering.

The room will be very beautiful, Maurie says feebly. The view . . .

Mr. Martens continues his complaint. Maurie walks carefully about, touching exposed timbers, rapping his knuckles against a windowpane. He cannot stop himself from staring toward the beach though he knows perfectly well that Nick and Isabel strolled off in the other direction.

Lost, are they lost, but that's a joke of course—one can hardly get lost on a beach. And Nick has been coming to Mount Dunvegan Island all his life.

A raindrop, star-splotched. On the grimy plate-glass window.

The sky is clouding up, the horizon is obscured in mist, the air smells damp and slightly cold. An imminent storm. New wind, winds. From the east. Blowing off the ocean, whining, in a way exhilarating. But of course Maurie's mind is on other things.

(Does everyone know? Are they talking about it?—feeling sorry for *him?*)

(Laughing at him. Poor boy. Not even married yet and look: what audacity!)

The time? A few minutes after four.

Isabel had not really wanted to drive up to Mount Dunvegan Island. Though of course—as she said—she was anxious to meet Nick But she and Maurie were invited to a party at the Mazurs' horse ranch in Brean Down, Virginia, and a number of Isabel's friends from school were going to be there, including the daughter of the French Ambassador who was so very fond of Isabel. And it wouldn't be politic to miss the party, as Isabel said, with her charming accent and the half-embarrassed little twitch of her nose which meant that she detested herself for knowing such things, let alone speaking of them: it wouldn't be at all politic because one of Maurie's associates (one of his rivals, that is) had been invited too and would certainly attend. And . . .

Nevertheless they declined the party. And drove up to Mount Dunvegan Island to spend Fourth of July with the Martenses and their guests.

And if Isabel was more than momentarily disappointed she gave no indication.

For of course, as she said, she *did* want to meet Nick Martens. She wanted to meet all Maurie's friends.

Mr. Martens sighs and knocks rather too hard for Maurie's comfort at a single beam that is holding up part of the ceiling. He has caught sight of his reflection in a pane of glass, he says pontifically: The challenge of increasing age, my boy, is to be able to tend to the ugly brute in the mirror, without succumbing to pity or disgust. It helps to be able to think of him in the third person. It *helps*.

Maurie, not knowing what response is expected, manages to laugh. His throat constricts suddenly and he hears a sob.

But no, no. Impossible.

They have only gone for a walk, they have only strolled up the beach. And wasn't it his wish?—that they become acquainted.

You mean more to me than anyone in the world, he has whispered shyly. The two of you.

The two of you.

O love.

He blinks and squints and sees them suddenly, a couple, a slender young woman and a tall young man, hurrying back to the cottage. Not holding hands of course. Not touching. Hurrying back because the sky is so threatening and the first raindrops have fallen.

He squints, he sees them. Making their way past the children's abandoned sand castles and trenches. A girl in a scarlet shift, a young man in white shorts. . . .

But of course they aren't Isabel and Nick.

Maurie's mouth has gone dry. Brutally dry. He tries to swallow but cannot. Pulses beat in both his temples. He hears, at a distance, Nick's father talking. Words and words and words, a skein of words, a lover's lament, ceaseless. What is life's sorrow but that of love, expressed in so many different words?

The architect, the contractor, a bit of trickery, but what can you expect these days. . . .

Mr. Martens's complaint trails off. He stares at Maurie and his expression for once is not jocular and cynical.

Suddenly he is saying: What I think has happened, Maurie, is that Nick—you know Nick—wanting to show her around—Isabel—I think that Nick probably set off for Tower Rock—d'you know where that is? —two miles up the beach—maybe a little farther—I think he probably wanted to show Isabel the rock, it's a sort of landmark on the island, he played there as a boy—and it's farther away than he anticipated— and they lost track of the time—and now the weather is changing, and maybe—

Maurie cannot face Mr. Martens. He runs his forefinger along a board, wincing at its splintery surface.

D'you know what Tower Rock is? Mr. Martens asks. His manner is suddenly enthusiastic, as if he were speaking to an unwell child. It's quite a landmark on the island, a real freak of nature. . . . An enormous rock high up on the sea cliff, egg-shaped, off the North Shore Road, about eight miles from the bridge. . . .

Maurie half-shuts his eyes. For a moment he feels faint; but the moment, of course, passes. He swallows, and turns to Mr. Martens, and manages to say politely that he knows about Tower Rock—he's seen it —Nick took him there once, hiking along the beach.

Ah yes, says Mr. Martens uneasily, though smiling, then you know where it is—I mean, you know it's quite a walk. Quite a distance.

Quite a distance, yes, says Maurie.

Four-fifteen. But he isn't going to look at his watch again.

Schoolboys

Always, when they meet after a considerable period of time, they look anxiously at each other—even as they are shaking hands vigorously, like gentlemen—to see if anything has changed between them.

To see if the other has forgotten.

Or has decided to become indifferent to sentiment.

Or has found someone more important, more central, to his life.

Maurie is generally shy when they first meet, blushing with pleasure, stammering his greetings; Nick is ebullient and energetic and even somewhat bullying. (It is his playful schoolboy manner, with its ingenious echoes of Hans Schweppenheiser.)

If Nick succumbs to an old habit of boasting, even when he and Maurie are alone together, meeting for a drink or a quick lunch, it is nevertheless the case (as Maurie tells himself) that Nick has a great deal to boast about; his life is wonderfully complicated. And Maurie is always eager, even anxious, to hear.

The months with Senator Saltonstall's staff, from whom he learned a great deal—a great deal more than the Senator might have wished; an odd interview with the Attorney General of the State of Massachusetts, who had taken a liking to Nick but who couldn't afford him at the present time; an intense but short-lived affair with a woman attorney in her thirties; an obsessional interest in tennis; a projected trip around the world; and most recently the high-paying position at Bell, Janeway, Prescher & Prescher. Of course Nick still wants to come to Washington eventually. But on his own terms. He admires Maurie for accepting a job at the Civil Rights Commission; but the salary . . . ah yes, the salary! . . . Nick murmurs with a sardonic smile that he can't yet afford such conspicuous idealism.

And cannot—being Nick, and inclined to saying the almost-abrasive, the almost-insulting—resist adding that his family background did not quite equip him for idealism: he would have to earn it himself.

Yes, Maurie hears himself acquiesce, blushing more deeply for his own guilty good fortune as an heir to Halleck Copper & Aluminum, yes of course, though Nick should know that Maurie has accepted very little money from his father since the age of eighteen. . . . Nick in fact does know but finds the knowledge irrelevant.

Yes, Maurie acquiesces, yes of course you are right. Idealism shouldn't be acquired too cheaply.

Schoolboys, adolescent boys. Sharing certain memories. Anxious and not inclined to forget. When they shake hands the dry strong energetic handclasp indicates nothing of the emotion each brings to it. — Have I been replaced? Have you forgotten? Am I no longer central to your life?

There is another possibility, a very ugly possibility. That one of them will have decided to dismiss not only the sentimentality of their bond but the fact of the bond itself. For perhaps nothing significant *had* happened that August afternoon on the Loughrea River. . . .

(As Isabel is going to suggest one day. With that shrewd common sense that underlies even the prettiest and most "feminine" of her mannerisms. After all, anyone could have pulled Maurie out of the river. Who were the other boys—someone named Kim, someone named Tony?—but surely any observer who happened to be near would have done as much. And maybe Maurie wouldn't have drowned. Maybe he wasn't that seriously injured and might have been capable of saving himself.)

Another possibility is that one of them will fall in love. Not as Nick is inclined to fall in love—quickly, over a weekend—not as he falls in love, at any rate, at the present time. But seriously in love, profoundly in love. The schoolboys are growing up after all. They are not boys any longer, they are not in school any longer.

It was shortly after Maurie's twenty-fifth birthday, when he and Nick met for a quick lunch in Cambridge, that he told Nick about Isabel de Benavente.

Sandwiches and steins of beer in the popular German restaurant they had patronized frequently as undergraduates. The elation of their meeting, the usual pumping handshake, a nervous exchange of smiles and greetings. Maurie and Nick, Nick and Maurie, and very little changed. *Very* little changed that meets the eye.

Gossip about former classmates, which always intrigues them both, Nick in particular. The good fortune of others, the bad fortune, surprises, reversals, mysteries—who would have guessed that Kim Ryan would be working for CBS in Hollywood, as a director of advertising and publicity; who would have guessed that a skinny mousy boy just a year ahead of them at Bauer would be an Air Force test pilot; and Tony Di Piero—the latest news about Tony is simply that he has disappeared, no one has heard from him in months, he had returned from London and saw a few friends but then disappeared without a word leaving behind an extremely distressed girl Nick knows slightly. . . . A New York debutante, a father on the stock exchange. One assumes that she can take care of herself.

The most shocking news, however, is Hans Schweppenheiser's suicide.

Nick knows very few of the details. The story is jumbled and possibly unreliable. It seems that Bauer acquired a new headmaster, a youngish but conservative man who was not pleased with Schweppenheiser's classroom performances, and expressed his displeasure not only in private but at faculty meetings. Schweppenheiser in retaliation became even more sarcastic and eccentric; he cultivated an increasingly offensive public manner which involved slovenly attire (a soiled woollen stocking-cap, bedroom slippers, stained vests, socks stiff with dirt) and shocking table manners (he inquired of others at lunch or dinner at what age they began the practice of "so-called self-abuse"), and the telling of elaborate but totally fictitious tales about the headmaster and certain anti-Schweppenheiserean members of the board of trustees. He was outrageous, he was reckless, he was perhaps terribly distressed, and fearful of being dismissed from Bauer—for where could he go, who would have him, he had never completed his Ph.D. at Harvard and his massive book, rumored to have grown to over a thousand pages, was years from publication! The most surprising news of all, in Nick's opinion, was that poor Schweppenheiser was no longer amusing. His classroom jokes fell flat, the boys stared in silence and refused even to smile. Other members of the faculty wisely avoided him. The wives of his colleagues ceased to be charmed. Schweppenheiser ran for public office in the township—as a prank, no doubt—he ran for the position of "dead deer pickup" coordinator—and of course he lost; and at graduation ceremonies, sloppily resplendent in his academic cap and gown, he rose from his seat on the platform to correct the headmaster's pronunciation of a Latin phrase. His audacity was greeted with shocked silence. He took advantage of the dramatic situation to leave the gathering with as much dignity as he could manage, granted his bulk, and the beads of sweat rolling down his porcine face. *And was never again seen at Bauer.*

He returned to his boardinghouse, packed some of his things, and left without giving his landlady a forwarding address. The school sent his last paycheck to his family home in Boston, but it was never cashed: by then (so it was said) the poor man had killed himself. He had hanged himself, or blown out his brains; he had drunk a quart of vodka straight down and fallen over dead of heart failure on the spot. Or had he slashed his throat with a bread knife. . . . Rumors varied but all agreed that Hans Schweppenheiser had died "by his own hand."

When Bauer graduates telephone the school, however, they are told by a curt administrative assistant only that Schweppenheiser is no longer on the staff. And that no one at Bauer has any idea of how to contact him.

Maurie absorbs the news in silence. It does not surprise him, it certainly does not alarm him as it alarms Nick.

Isn't that a hell of a thing, Nick says repeatedly. Schweppenheiser with his crazy sense of humor . . . his wit, his intelligence. . . . *Isn't* that a shame!

After a moment Maurie says quietly, without a great deal of conviction, that it *is* a considerable surprise; it *is* a shame.

Schweppenheiser of all people, says Nick.

Well—he was a terribly unhappy man, Maurie adds.

Unhappy? Was he? *Was* he? Nick says, staring.

Maurie cannot think of a suitable reply. He looks away from his friend's incredulous frown.

Was he—! Nick marvels. I never noticed.

Schoolboy rivalry, adolescent emotions. Certain painful memories. Is there a bond between them, is it "sacred," or perhaps the consequence of a profound fright—a fear of physical annihilation—that can be simply explained? Or does the understanding between Nick Martens and Maurie Halleck go much more deeply *even* than the experience of such fright?

Nick tries not to think of it. Doesn't think of it, really; he hasn't time.

Maurie thinks of it often. Odd, that his love for Isabel de Benavente should awaken certain old memories rather than replace them.

It isn't true that we live and die alone, look how we are together, look how we are always together. . . . He tries to explain his friendship for Nick to Isabel, quite apart from the near-drowning, but fails. Not because Isabel isn't attentive—she is wonderfully and prettily "attentive"—but because the correct words don't come; Maurie hears himself stammering banalities.

Friendships between men are extremely important, Isabel assures him. I always judge a man by his friends. Whereas with women —it's different with women—I really don't *trust* women.

It is equally difficult to explain his feelings for Isabel to Nick, though Nick, subordinate for once, gives every sign—or nearly every sign—of being sympathetic.

How funny, how sweet and touching!—and of course it's wonderful too—Maurie Halleck in love for the first time in his life.

Blushing and inarticulate and proud and frightened—for isn't he still a boy, a schoolboy? How can he imagine at the age of twenty-four that any young woman at all, let alone Isabel de Benavente, will care enough for him to marry him?

Don't be ridiculous, Nick says impatiently. It's one of your bad habits—undervaluing yourself.

Love, marriage, children, family life.

And she hopes (she expects, she will insist) for a handsome house in Washington. And a "place"—a more resplendent place, even, than she has had as the de Benavente girl—in Washington's social world.

I have never met anyone like her, Maurie says softly. With the same air of sobriety with which Nick spoke of Schweppenheiser's unfortunate death.

Tower Rock

There it is, at last. A natural stone "tower" high above the beach, perhaps seventy-five feet from the ground. Egg-shaped, monstrous, with a disquieting look (so Nick always thought, as a boy) of being enchanted.

Quite something, isn't it? Shall we climb up—?

But it's going to rain, it's already started to rain.

A dense clotted sky. A faint flash of lightning, a tree root illuminated for an instant against the heavy banked clouds. How beautiful!

Beautiful.

But what time is it—?

Not late. A little after three.

Beautiful. . . .

Isabel in her tight faded jeans rolled to the knee and her shirt tied up beneath her breasts; her slender midriff exposed as if . . . as if her naked skin meant nothing more than anyone's naked skin.

Brushing her pale golden hair out of her eyes. A strand caught, for a brief instant, in the corner of her mouth.

The milky pearly damp luminous teeth. Bared in a grimace that might be mistaken as a smile.

(Does Maurie make love to her, Nick wonders. Does she allow him near. Burrowing into her, sobbing into her shoulder, my love, my love, I will do anything for you, I have never known anyone like you. Does she open her embrace to him, Nick wonders, his heart contracting with pain and envy.)

182

Lustful Nick, studying the footsteps that lead away behind them. Out of sight. Into the mist. No one near. No one to know.

What time is it? Isabel murmurs, daring to take hold of Nick's arm casually, to examine his watch. —Oh, I thought it might be later.

Five minutes after three. Shall we climb the tower?

Another fork of lightning, far away inland. So distant the thunder is a graceful near-inaudible rumble.

How beautiful, the sky. Banks of clouds above the heaving Atlantic.

The rock *is* like a tower, Isabel says, marveling. It looks as if someone set it down like that. A giant set it down centuries ago.

Shall we climb up, or are you too tired? Just let me know.

Tired? Isabel says with a catch in her throat.

(Isabel de Benavente who can dance all night. Who has danced all night many times, in the years before her official engagement.)

Isabel and Nick, striding along the beach, breathless, a little giddy, oblivious of the changing air. The damp chill wind has intoxicated them, they cannot remember how far they have walked, whom they have left behind on the terrace of the Martenses' cottage.

Is Maine always so cold in July, Isabel asks, shivering. You couldn't go swimming in *that!*

The stink of seaweed, lovely brackish briny odor. Nick draws in his breath deeply, and more deeply still.

Intoxicated.

Shall we climb? Here's the path—no, here—over here.

Taking her hand. It must always be a surprise for Maurie, Nick thinks, himself surprised, to discover this hand so slender, the bones so light. Delicate as a sparrow! And her manner subdued for the moment as she wonders—almost audibly—whether the climb might be dangerous; whether her bare feet might slip or be cut on the rocks.

If you're afraid of falling, Nick says gallantly, we won't try it. Not today.

Another time? Tomorrow? If the weather clears? Maurie can join us . . . Nick says insincerely.

He takes her hand, gripping it tight. How droll, how amusing, a young woman who has polished both her fingernails and her toenails, in preparation for a long windblown spray-splattered hike on the northeastern beach of Mount Dunvegan Island—! Her stylish braided hair, the silly gold dove-barrette, the five or six thin chains around her neck. But she is smiling. Smiling. Slowly her lips part and her magnificent wet teeth are exposed.

A carnivore, Nick thinks. But of course not seriously.

I played here as a boy, Nick says aloud, in a hearty cheerful voice innocent of all intrigue. I've climbed up this path hundreds of times and it isn't as tricky as it appears.

Breathless and giddy, her eyes shining. She can match him in the climb—nearly. But of course he is helping her. When her feet slip on the wet rock he holds her tight. No, she *won't* slip.

Watch it—! Nick cautions.

She smiles nervously. Perhaps she is out of breath—perhaps she is a little lightheaded. She did no more than pick at her food, at lunch. (He observed her. So subdued an appetite, one might imagine her in love.) A sudden gust of wind. But there's no danger—you can always flatten yourself against the stone face.

You played here as a boy? Isabel says. You came to the island often?

Twenty feet above them the queer misshapen egg-rock just out over the sea cliff, glistening with damp. Or perhaps it is raining? There are still glowering patches of sunshine, there is a shimmering rainbow-moist iridescence to the air. —So beautiful, Isabel whispers in awe.

Mount Dunvegan Island, less than twenty miles in circumference. Humped and domed like a turtle's shell. Its beauty so harsh, so colorless, as to appear almost repellent.

I can't see anything, Isabel says, staring. Which way is the house? —your family's cottage?

Nick points. But there is nothing: stunted trees, rocks and boulders, wild grasses. Mist easing in from the ocean.

Are we lost? Isabel says, perplexed as a child.

Of course we aren't lost, Nick says impatiently. The cottage is about two miles in that direction.

Isabel cranes her neck. One can feel the strength in her, the resistance. But she says nothing.

I suppose we shouldn't have come so far, Nick says. They might be worried about us.

Isabel is panting. She does not speak, perhaps to save her breath.

The ugly piles of rocks, rockslides. A place no one inhabits. No one explores. Tower Rock which (so Nick says, with an air of pride) was used for several decades in the early 1800s as a lighthouse. Visible for long distances when the air was clear. When the fog was in, of course, it couldn't have been of much aid.

A lighthouse, here? says Isabel. But where?

Up here, says Nick. Can you make it?

Climbing, her right hand in his left hand. Fingers gripping fingers tightly. Damply. An impersonal strength to Nick's gallantry.

Bad judgment, to climb up here with her bare feet. And why the hell did she come on this walk, barefoot?—so Nick would like to ask her. No one else would be so boldly frivolous.

Hey—have you cut yourself? Nick asks.

No, says Isabel faintly. I'm fine.

She is staring at the crumbled foundation of the lighthouse. Not much remains of it in 1955.

Did you cut your foot? Nick says irritably.

There are smashed beer bottles among the rocks. Dark glinting curls of glass. And birdlime. A great deal of birdlime. It has an ornate sculpted look and in this light appears to glow.

I'm all right, Isabel says, shivering. I'm fine.

Several terns circle them, screaming. Nick wonders if the birds have been nearby all along without his having noticed.

Where is your cottage? Isabel asks, craning her lovely strong neck again. I can't see anything. . . .

Nick points. But there is nothing to see: the fog has started to move in.

We've been gone a long time, Isabel says faintly.

But Nick checks his watch. Holds it to his ear: it seems to be working.

Not really, he says. It's only ten after three.

Ten after three, Isabel says slowly. And hesitates. As if she is about to ask, Which day? Which month?

Nick notices that he has scraped his ankle and it's bleeding. But he feels no pain. Shyly, in embarrassment, he tries to wipe the blood away—uses a handful of grass. If Isabel sees she gives no indication. She stands on one foot, suddenly birdlike herself, and cups the other foot in her hand: a lovely gawky girl, her hair in her eyes and her gold dove askew. The sole of her foot is very, very dirty.

Why are the birds so angry? she asks.

They won't hurt us, Nick says at once.

Do they have nests up here? Why are they so angry?

More birds appear, swooping down toward the rock. There are a dozen, two dozen. Very excited. Very noisy. As if they had never seen human beings before. Falcon-sized, their graceful muscular wings flapping, their yellow beaks cruelly hooked. They have slender pinkish legs and clumsy webbed feet. Only terns, says Nick, tossing a rock in their midst. They won't hurt us: they're just a little excited.

Isabel crouches beneath the weight of their furious cries. She presses her hands against her ears like a child.

They're harmless, Nick says. They always do this when someone climbs the rock.

He cannot remember if this is really true.

Are you all right? he asks Isabel.

I'm fine, she says in a hollow voice.

She remains slightly crouched, blinking rapidly as if her eyes were flooding with tears. And indeed her cheeks are damp—but it's rain —raindrops. Nick stares at the sky. When did it start to rain? He hadn't noticed.

And it's cold. The temperature has dropped considerably.

Nick shouts at the terns, and throws another rock. The birds retreat a short distance and hang in midair, screaming. Go away, you silly sons of bitches, Nick cries, go on, get the hell out of here. The anger in his voice does not suggest the elation he feels; his throat is fairly bursting with it.

Get the hell out of here! Nick shouts, waving both his arms.

Isabel turns away. She gropes for a firm footing but does not trust herself to step down.

Watch out, Nick says irritably. Wait for me.

I don't think I can get down from here, Isabel says. It's so steep . . .

It isn't steep, it's an easy climb, Nick says.

Isabel stares down toward the ocean. Miniature mountains, humped and peaked, on either side of the path; rain lashing the beach like machine-gun bullets. The ocean has turned leaden gray and its waves are roiling and greasy and alarmingly tall.

Isabel, hugging herself, takes a hesitant step and nearly falls.

I said watch out, for Christ's sake, Nick shouts.

(After all, isn't he responsible for her?—his closest friend's bride-to-be.)

Now the terns have fallen back and away, and the wind has increased, and Tower Rock is partly obscured by mist. Visibility is limited to less than one hundred yards in all directions.

Nick's face is burning despite the damp wind, and he has to check the impulse to take hold of Isabel's shoulder and give her a hard shake. The fool, the silly bitch, to try to climb down the rock without his assistance—to risk injuring herself, to risk death—

Give me your hand, damn it, Nick says. And why the hell did you wear *that*—you're dressed too lightly—this isn't Washington, this is Maine—come *on*.

I'm sorry, Isabel murmurs. Why are you so angry—?

Though it was summer when they began their pleasant outing, a very long time ago, it is clearly not summer now: the air's texture is autumnal, even wintry, and the wind is viciously strong.

Enormous rain-splotches strike them suddenly, with nearly the ferocity of hail.

Oh Jesus, Nick shouts.

Isabel's long wet hair whips into her eyes. Nick stands close beside her, to steady her. They are both panting; their clothes are soaked; yet there is a curious abrupt beauty to the rock, and the beach, and the storm-pocked ocean.—Well, says Isabel, when she can breathe again, it looks as if I've made my first mistake.

"I"

A babble of voices. Discordant but friendly. Mr. Martens, Mrs. Martens, others to whom he has been introduced but whose names he cannot recall, all very solicitous of him—of his embarrassment, his silence.

Rain striking the windows, hammering on the roof. But firecrackers just the same: are the children setting them off in back?

Maurie does not appear to be waiting for Isabel and Nick to come back. He is smiling and congenial and, despite his profound stricken silence, even talkative in the way holiday people—strangers to one another—can be talkative.

Yes, I think so. Yes, that's right.

No thank you—this is fine.

Yes. Certainly.

Yes.

How simple the matter of performing in the world, in the visible world. One smiles, one nods, one murmurs agreement or courteous disagreement, one says a few words from time to time, managing not to stammer: *that* is a triumph.

Now and then Mrs. Martens glances toward the door, drifts to the window, says unnecessarily: They must be waiting out the storm. Poor Isabel! She'll never want to come back to visit us again!

Maurie does not glance toward the door, does not stand at the window; he sits on a rattan sofa beside an ebullient perspiring Mr. Martens who is discussing—"debating"—the merits of the Warren Court. A silver-haired gentleman from down the beach has an opinion

188

(the nine Justices should be impeached), a buoyant curly-haired woman of indeterminate age, introduced to Maurie as an "actress," has an opinion (the Congress will ram through amendments to restore the power of the House Un-American Activities Committee—don't worry), Mr. Martens himself has what Maurie assumes is an outrageous opinion hereabouts: the *Brown* decision was necessary, and required a great deal of courage on the part of the Court.

Courage—! says the actress. But it doesn't affect *their* lives. . . .

Maurie must speak too, of course, as a representative of his generation (which "sees things differently") and as a young lawyer involved in civil rights litigation. He speaks frankly and quietly and without any hope of convincing his listeners; beneath his words, deep inside them, silence spills like ink and he wonders if he will ever have anything to say to anyone again in his life.

But that's an exaggeration: his fiancée and his closest friend are simply waiting out the storm. There's a flash of lightning, a roll of thunder, and then another, deeper, alarming roll: like a rockslide: jarring and distracting. That poor girl, Mrs. Martens says, I blame Nick—dragging her off like that. Of course he had to take her down to that rock of his. That old lighthouse . . .

"Waiting out the storm." Which sounds plausible.

Four-thirty, twenty-five to five . . .

A sunless day, the air luridly green, the sky settling down upon the earth, suffocating. Maurie finds it difficult to breathe. And his knee, injured long ago in the canoeing accident, has begun to ache as it frequently does in damp weather.

Isabel de Benavente at a country club breakfast, leaning her head against her escort's shoulder, convulsed with laughter. A beautifully plumed bird, Maurie observed—a creature one must be content to admire at a distance. And then again at a debutante party at the Shoreham, to which Maurie went most reluctantly (at his parents' insistence—his father was nearly as adamant as his mother): Isabel in a long silk dress in a pink and green floral pattern, the swelling of her breasts discreetly revealed by its wide scoop neck, her thick pale hair in a chignon, her lovely hands moving animatedly as she talked. Slightly drunk. Charmingly "high"—as the expression went. Dancing with young men whom Maurie knew and half-knew and generally disliked though they were courteous enough to him as a Halleck—smiling her practiced dazzling smile as a young man cut in upon her escort—moving her head in a certain way, speaking and smiling and laughing in a certain way—Isabel whom he stared at rudely without knowing that he was being rude. (Isabel de Benavente was a girl whom Maurie half-knew. And though her father's exact occupation was something of a mystery—he was a financier, he was a "philanthropist," he may have had something to do with loaning money abroad—he was fairly well known as a social presence about town.) Maurie fell irrevocably in love with her at a noisy party in a palatial Chevy Chase house when, with two other pretty girls, she danced atop a long dining room table in her stocking feet, singing "Happy Days Are Here Again," "Frankie and Johnny," and "I Got Rhythm"—a charmingly silly and uncoordinated routine the girls had done, evidently, some years ago at the Hays School. The desperation of his love for such a girl fueled him with a curious gay recklessness: even his stammer, for a time, exuded confidence.

Maurie recalls Wittgenstein whom he has not read in years—he hasn't had time: the "I" is not observable, perhaps does not exist; in the world there are objects—colors and shapes and textures—but no witnessing "I."

(Is it true? Is it a comprehensible thought? Maurie Halleck is for himself the limit of the world—and not a part of the world.)

Dry-mouthed, breathing with difficulty, his glasses misting over. There is Isabel laughing, leaning her head against Nick's shoulder: the rings glittering on her fingers as she protests. She is wearing white silk pants that flare at the ankles, and a brocaded Japanese blouse or jacket with somewhat pronounced shoulders. Why is she laughing, about what is she protesting? A pulse beats in Maurie's throat. He cannot swallow —the back of his mouth tastes of grit.

The gentleman from down the beach—from the handsome dark-shingled Cape Cod called Windy Acres—is asking Maurie about his days at Bauer. He went there, didn't he, along with Nick?—he was a classmate of Nick's?

Mrs. Martens returns from the kitchen, where she has answered the telephone. She exchanges a frightened look with one of the women guests—pulls at Mr. Martens's arm—murmurs something about June on the line, asking for Nick.

What can I tell her? Maurie overhears.

What d'you mean, what can you tell her? Nick isn't here—that's all, Mr. Martens says too loudly.

He rears back to glare at Mrs. Martens as if she had said something extraordinary.

But I mean—I thought—since June is late, you know—she's been delayed—I mean, Nick *would* be here, wouldn't he, if—if—everything had gone as planned

For Christ's sake, just tell her Nick has stepped out—he's driven to town for something—take a message—say he'll call back—what's the problem? Mr. Martens shakes his head. His face is large and brutal and still rather handsome: a crude version of Nick. But he is not so graceless as to glance Maurie's way. —June isn't a hysteric, he says more evenly, she'll understand.

Twenty minutes to five. But of course the wind, the downpour, the flashes of lightning . . . the premature dark. . . . It's surely the case that the two of them have taken shelter somewhere.

June has been delayed because of the rain. The highway is partly flooded, she says.

June Penrick: Nick's girl: she teaches at a Quaker school in Boston.

Yes, I think she *is* driving up alone.

"Taken shelter somewhere"—a plausible theory.

In an antique shop in New York Maurie had come upon the pretty little dove—a "golden" dove—slightly battered. A girl's hair-barrette, English, probably from the 1890s. Silly and charming and not terribly expensive.

How delighted Isabel is with gifts!—expensive or inexpensive.

Greedily licking her lips, smiling her broad white damp smile, exactly like a child. How sweet of you, how thoughtful of you, it's adorable, it's too heavy to wear—oh, maybe it isn't—but anyway thank you, thank you: you're always so kind.

It is a time of methodical romance, a time of marriage between strangers. Maurie and the other young men who are invited to the round of debutante parties needn't even wonder if their brides-to-be are virgins: what, after all, are the alternatives?

Gossip about Mary Anne Forster, and that other girl, the redhead whose family seems to have so much money, just up from Houston. . . . Even Maurie, who hasn't any time for such nonsense, who avoids most of his Harvard classmates whom he encounters all too frequently in Washington, knows certain scandalous suppositions: and knows, without having ever sought the knowledge, that Isabel de Benavente is "all right."

(Is she . . . a nice girl? Maurie's family asks. But always discreetly. Using different words. No one asks, Is she a virgin?—are you sleeping together?—she isn't pregnant, is she?)

She isn't pregnant, she *is* a virgin. That shrewd shrewd girl. The daughter (after all) of Luis de Benavente who is no fool.

I love you, Maurie has whispered, burying his face in her neck, in her hair, against her small hard lovely breasts. I love you, he has whispered, alone in his bed, transfixed by her image, humiliated by his sexual desire. (He has come to think that he hadn't grasped the power of sexual desire, until now. As a boy his physical needs, his physiological needs, were perhaps less violent and less obsessive than those of his schoolmates; but normal enough; or so he assumes. But desire was so immediate, so physical, so without grace or charm or intelligence or direction—as diffuse as thirst, and as romantic. Now Maurie's sexual yearnings are focused upon a single person, a single young woman, and he is alternately dazed with happiness and terrified of losing her—indeed, he cannot comprehend "losing" her. And she assures him, she assures him daily, even as she forbids him to touch her in what might be called an intimate way, she assures him that she loves him in return: preposterous to think of losing her!)

Can we make love, Maurie whispers, I won't hurt you, I won't . . . I won't. . . . He cannot bring himself to say, I won't make you pregnant. He cannot bring himself to say the words, made ugly by being, in popular usage, so familiar: I'll be careful.

Nor can he say the words he barely allows himself to think (for Maurie Halleck is, after all, for all his "superiority" and the depth of his love, very much a child of his era): I won't respect you any less.

Can we make love, Isabel, he whispers, grinding his teeth in an agony as much emotional as visceral, unable to meet his fiancée's gaze (which is sometimes troubled, sometimes sympathetic, sometimes brimming with love and even—can it be possible?—desire for *him;* and sometimes hurt, offended, shocked that he would propose such a thing, knowing the teachings of the Catholic Church and the peculiar Latin sensibility she has inherited): I love you so much.

I love you, I love you so much.

So much.

I love *you.* And only you.

So much I can't bear it. Can't understand it.

Do you sometimes resent an emotion, Nick once asked, I mean an emotion like love, desire, yearning. . . . Do you sometimes feel a violent loathing for the object. . . .

My beautiful girl, my beautiful Isabel, dancing atop a table, silly and careless, showing her legs, innocently showing her breasts, smiling that wide white damp smile as everyone stared. Confident in her flesh, in the contours of her body. I want the two of you to become acquainted, to be able to talk freely, Maurie said, excited, boyish, blushing, you both mean so much to me. . . .

Five minutes to six.

Isabel in a ruffled polka-dot dress, strapless. Big red polka dots. Oversized summer jewelry, white earrings, strands of fake pearls. Flowers—lilies of the valley—braided in her hair. Standing with her back against a railing, arms lazily outspread. A terrace, a cocktail reception.

Speaking a charmingly accented English with a man from one of the embassies. But not much engaged in the conversation. Her eyes moving, roaming, prowling. Maurie's diamond ring on her finger.

Do you sometimes resent it, the way we feel about *them,* Nick once asked. A boy of sixteen. Tapping his fingers on a two-page photograph in a detective magazine.

There is Nick crouched above a woman, his warm face pressed against her stomach, her loins. His tongue piercing her. Until she cries out, thrashing. Until she screams.

Nick kneading her buttocks, hard. The red polka-dot skirts, the white petticoats, wet with sand.

Perspiration in rivulets on Nick's naked back. The rippling of flesh, muscles.

Mr. Martens is talking about the Juilliard School, which is overrated. Its students are fiercely competitive, they know nothing but their instruments, they come to despise their instruments and music altogether, then again they never want to leave Juilliard—as long as someone will pay their tuition. Well, you do always hear about them, a guest says vaguely, and—what is it?—the Curtis. You always seem to hear about those schools.

The Curtis is overrated, Mr. Martens says bluntly.

Maurie tries to think of his office, his desk: paperwork: the early sketches for litigation in certain counties in Georgia: voter registration violations. Year after year and decade after decade and if he might possibly shift the conversation to an important book he is reading on Reconstruction . . . the role of Negroes in Reconstruction . . . four million ex-slaves, think of it! . . . four million human beings. *Negro entered into white man as profoundly as white man entered into Negro.* If he can shift the subject to civil rights, to justice, to something worthy of conversation. . . . But he does not speak. The others' words wash about him. His mouth is dry, there is an ache in his chest, yes in the region of his heart, an ache, but then his heart is weak . . . no his heart isn't "weak" . . . a doctor would have to employ an extremely sensitive instrument to detect anything wrong and perhaps by now there is nothing wrong. Nick taught him to play a decent game of tennis at Bauer. And he ran well too—if he remembered to breathe correctly he ran very well.

The porch screen dotted with rain; the heaving tireless ocean; the desolate beach. Miles of beach. Maurie stands on the porch, hands in his pockets, hunched slightly, aware of the Martenses and their guests watching him. He stands with his nose a few inches from the screen, watching. Waiting. No pretense. Is it shame he should be feeling, or simple embarrassment. Humiliation. Anger. Anger?

Nick's oldest friend. Closest friend. Yes, he's the boy, I mean the young man, his father is Joe Halleck, yes, that one, Halleck, no, I think he's retired now or has an ambassadorship. . . .

I love you so much.

So much I can't bear it, can't understand it.

But there's no emergency here, no cause for alarm or panic. They have not been gone *that* long. They weren't in a boat, they weren't swimming, you can't get lost along a beach. . . .

I'd rather not drive all the way up to Maine, Isabel said, if you don't mind, Maurie, I know you're anxious for me to meet Nick and I want to meet him but there's plenty of time, after all this party is an important one for your career and Agnes is going, Agnes and Mack, why don't we drive out together, Father might lend us the car and Carlos for the day. . . .

A desolate stretch of beach. Rain, mist. Transformed by two figures: a young woman, a young man. The woman is slender and blond, the man is tall, strong-legged, rather abrupt in his movements when he believes he is being watched. . . .

Maurie blinks, staring. But there is no one. Nothing.

What on earth can Nick be thinking of, Mrs. Martens is saying, out of earshot in the kitchen. But not really out of earshot. —How can he behave like this!

Behave like what? Mr. Martens says irritably.

You know.

He isn't *behaving* like anything, they're just slow getting back, why don't you mind your own business?—put some more beer on ice, what did you do with those cheese snaps?—making a mountain out of a molehill.

I'm thinking of Maurie. I don't *know* how Nick can behave like this. . . .

It's perfectly innocent, they'll explain themselves, Mr. Martens says with a sigh, don't worry. Neither one of them is a fool.

I'm thinking of Maurie. I'm thinking of June.

Maurie is taking it all right, he's a gentleman, and as for June— she doesn't know a thing.

Nick has never done anything like this before! Mrs. Martens says, half-sobbing.

What makes you so certain? Mr. Martens asks.

On their third or fourth date Isabel de Benavente was silent for much of the evening. Or responded to Maurie's questions in a subdued voice. Yes, no, yes I've always thought so, yes I suppose you're right, no I don't think I'll try to get a job in journalism, it isn't a field for women, they don't like women, they resent women, my feelings have been hurt more than once, I suppose I'm not strong enough . . . not competitive enough.

And then, shortly before Maurie was to drive her home, she burst into tears; and murmured something incoherent about her father—her father who bullied her—because he resented her mother—because he disliked and distrusted women—because he hoped to use her. Maurie was astonished at Isabel's change of mood: one moment her face was tight-skinned, a clenched muscle: the next, she dissolved into childlike trusting tears. And did not push him away when he tried to comfort her. (He had moved to embrace her, without thinking. As he might have embraced anyone who broke down in his presence.)

Use you? What do you mean—use you?

I hate him—

What do you mean, Isabel? What's wrong?

Oh God I hate him, I wish he was dead—I wish he would let me alone—

Isabel? What is it? What does your father want?

He embraced her, his face burning. He comforted her. Ah, how his heart beat! It was one of the extraordinary moments of his life—he would remember it forever—he would remember it as his car careened along the narrow Virginia road—a girl he had come to love with enormous secret passion and terror—a girl of such esteemed beauty—bursting into tears in his presence, allowing him to touch her, to comfort her; trusting him with her sorrow.

What does your father want? he asked, trembling. Can you tell me—?

She wept. Her words were incoherent. A strong Spanish intonation. Her shoulders shaking, her lovely face wet with tears. Money, her allowance, a Mexican businessman, spying on her, listening when she spoke on the telephone, asking questions about Maurie, jealous of her letters to her mother, insisting upon reading the letters her mother sent *her*. But she was unhappy too about other things. Friends, acquaintances. The shallowness of the Washington crowd. Girls who had betrayed her, young men who were disappointing, interested only in their careers, going out with wealthy girls, or crude in other ways: Maurie could guess how.

Beautiful Isabel de Benavente sobbing in Maurie's arms: I'm so unhappy, she said, I'm so disillusioned. . . .

So Maurie held her, and stroked her hair, and kissed her overheated face. And after a while she grew quiet. And he was wise enough not to upset her—he would ask about Mr. Benavente at another time, he

would surely ask about the "Mexican businessman" at another time—
he had only to hold her, to hold her tight, as one might hold a heartbroken
child.

But he knew even then that he didn't deserve her. He didn't
deserve her beauty, her arms around his neck, her frankness, her distress, her tears. Or the trembling and utterly unsought gift of her
"disillusion."

After the Storm

Twenty to six. The lost couple appears. At last. Hurrying. Their clothes drenched, hair in their faces, noisily apologetic. Nick wanted to take a shortcut back to the bay so they went inland but got mixed up in the marsh . . . had to go around . . . all the way around to the road.

Isabel's shirt is now tucked primly in her jeans. Nick is so astonished at the time that for a long moment he simply stares at Maurie's watch—he has grabbed Maurie's wrist in an awkward clowning gesture. —Twenty to six! That isn't right! What the hell!

Nick sneezes, hasn't a handkerchief, for a fraction of a second there is something wet and green in his left nostril.

Isabel too is astonished. But more subdued. How can it be that late, she says in a faltering voice, we thought . . . we didn't think . . . It *can't* be that late, she says.

My watch stopped, Nick says. Stopped at three-thirty.

He sneezes again. Goes off to change his clothes before June arrives. And Isabel, poor Isabel—she is shivering, her long hair has come undone, she too must hurry away to change into dry clothes. She squeezes Maurie's fingers. Did you worry? Did you think something had happened to us?

Mrs. Martens has brought Isabel a towel for her hair. Maurie takes it and wraps it tenderly around her head, like a turban; he surprises himself, he is so husbandly. He kisses his fiancée's clammy forehead.

I'm so sorry—his watch stopped—I *thought* it must be much later

—it was an idiotic idea, tramping all the way to that rock—it would have been better if you'd come along—*you* have more sense—we wouldn't have been so far away when the storm broke—

She bites her lip, she is vexed, almost tearful. She says suddenly, patting her head, Oh, it's gone—the dove—is it gone?—did I lose it? Or wasn't I wearing it? I can't remember— Oh hell—

Early evening, a glowering chill rises from the sand, the rain has stopped but the air is heavy with moisture. Maurie sniffs and smells autumn. Though everyone is inside now, safely inside, a large plastic bowl at the center of the table heaped with lobster shells, though there is nothing now to see along the beach, no one to await, Maurie slips away unobtrusively (he has a talent for being unobtrusive) and prowls about. Nick and Isabel had come from the direction of the road; they had not come from the beach. But it was the beach, the shoreline, the splashing surf, he had memorized. They would appear *there* . . . when they returned to him. The girl in the red shirt and blue jeans, barefoot; her long lovely blond hair whipping about her face. The young man beside her, taller by a head, his skin brick-dark as if with perpetual embarrassment. Nick, Isabel, love, O love. But they had returned to him just the same.

V. The Convert

Washington, D.C.,
May 1980

The Uruguayan Flying Carpet

Take off your shoes, the sensation is interesting, Owen's new friend says.

Owen is staring at the floor. At the carpet.

The most curious carpet he has ever seen.

It looks like synthetic hair, Owen says, blinking, smiling hazily, braided with—feathers? Are those feathers?

Genuine macaw feathers, says Ulrich May, stooping to ruffle a clump of puffy red-orange feathers. The gesture takes some effort—May winces as if his back hurts. —Jungle-bird feathers, the real thing. And the hair—?

Owen considers the carpet, which nearly covers the floor of Ulrich May's large bedroom. Black hair—crow's-wing black—with a high hard sheen. Braided with feathers of the most extraordinarily beautiful hues: red, red-orange, yellow, green, an iridescent turquoise, a creamy white. I've never seen anything like it, Owen says.

It's from Uruguay. A gift. From a dear friend of mine. Some years ago, unfortunately—I haven't seen him since. Why don't you take off your shoes, my boy, the sensation *is* interesting, I walk barefoot in here all the time. And have you noticed the photographs?—on the walls—

Owen looks about, pleased and dazed. He is feeling mellow—not exactly high—not high enough to violate his sense of propriety. Who are you, haven't we met, Ulrich May asked Owen as Owen wandered about the fringes of the Moultons' noisy party, I think we know each other—?

May extended a hand, Owen stared rudely at it without shaking it, but could not maintain the pose—in Owen good manners are instinctive, have the force of biology—and finally shook hands, surprised at the firmness of May's grip. There are handshakes that are mere greetings, there are handshakes that hint of destiny.

My name is Ulrich May, and your name is—?

You said you knew me, Owen murmured.

Thinning hair combed carefully forward across a slightly mis-shapen but elegant head; crisp cinnamon tendrils that looked dyed. Ulrich May was perhaps in his mid-fifties but dressed in a youthful, rather New Yorkish style: an embroidered silk shirt unbuttoned to reveal frizzy gray chest hair, close-fitting white linen trousers. His manner was languid but attentive, his gaze was warm and chocolate-brown, oddly flattering. Owen thought *fairy* but did not draw away. The man was a friend of Phil Moulton's, perhaps, or a friend of friends—perhaps he was even a friend of Isabel's. So many people were.

Don't be coy, May said, don't be boring. If I say *don't we know each other, haven't we met,* you should be shrewd enough to know that I am speaking in large terms—in archetypal terms. Our types recognize each other, our family histories possibly overlap. You look like old Washington stock and I . . . well, it's hardly a secret . . . our line goes back to Alexander Hamilton, a fact of which I am neither ashamed nor particularly proud. In any case, you are—?

Owen Halleck, Owen said. And swallowed, watching for the man's response.

Ah—Halleck!

Halleck, yes. Halleck, Owen said, flushing with anger. You might know Isabel, my mother. You might have known Maurie.

So you're the son of—Maurice.

The son of Maurice, yes.

Maurice Halleck . . . May says slowly. The son of Maurice Halleck. . . .

Yes, that's right, why are you staring at me, Owen asked, is it really so bizarre? My father isn't exactly the only man to—he's hardly alone—I mean—after all this is—this is 1980.

That isn't what surprises me, May said, leaning close. He brought his face within a few inches of Owen's: he smelled agreeably of alcohol and piney shaving lotion. One might have thought, glancing across the crowded terrace at the two of them—the slightly disheveled college boy with a week's growth of whiskers, the stylishly dressed middle-aged man with the Roman profile and the cinnamon curls—that the gesture was friendly, even affectionate: but in fact Ulrich May's fine-boned face stiffened with contempt. —*This* is what surprises me, he said, and pinched hard at the flab at Owen's waist. *This. In you. Of all people. You.*

We must surprise them together, Kirsten has said. In bed together.

That's going to be difficult, Owen has said prudently.

The two of them—together! Otherwise it's no good. Otherwise it won't work.

Her hot angry tears, her laughter, the raw elation of her childish grin. Owen brings along a half-dozen Quaaludes wrapped in a tissue, stuck in his jokey knapsack—in fact a yellow and red plastic bag used for takeouts at the *That's Some Chicken!*, a college hangout, the logo of which is a smiling chicken with long eyelashes and a peaked carnival hat, smacking her tongue. Owen brings along the Quaaludes to calm his sister down, she gives off a high speedy radiance over miles of telephone wire, it's rather difficult to communicate with someone operating on her frequency. His suitemates have become disapproving of late and rarely poke their heads in his doorway now to ask *How's it going, Owen,* meaning his senior thesis, meaning they grasp the fact that he isn't working on it and he isn't attending classes and he isn't despite his look of perspiring agitation doing very much at all. They have become disapproving: they warn him against certain new acquaintances he has been cultivating. The rumor is a drug raid the first Friday of reading week, they say. There's always a rumor, there's always going to be a drug raid, Owen says, bored.

We must surprise them in bed together, Kirsten says, striking the palm of one hand with a fist. *I have pledged my life.*

Please, no, not that John Brown bit, Owen pleads, holding up his hands, I don't like to think I've inherited *him.*

You don't like to think you've inherited anything, Kirsten says.

What the hell is that supposed to mean?

You know what it means.

What does it mean?

You know, fat boy.

It's amazing, the emotion churned up between them: they are children again, suddenly: Owen is thirteen and Kirsten is ten, Owen is ten and Kirsten is seven, they tease, they taunt, they make faces, they tremble with rage, they would tear each other into pieces if they could, pummel and kick and rake and kill. It happens so suddenly, a switch is flicked, a button pressed. Sister and brother. Childhood. Crowding through a doorway, elbowing each other on the stairs, sticking out their tongues, whispering *asshole, cocksucker, shitface* in the very presence of Mother and Father. Owen's clenched fist of a heart pounds. A delicate blue pulse trembles in Kirsten's forehead. No, let's not succumb, let's *not* allow this to happen, Owen says softly, for he is twenty-one years old—after all. And of course Kirsten agrees, for they have important matters to discuss.

Very important matters.

But their truce, their calm, never lasts. Kirsten will chide him for being a coward—he's finding so many difficulties!—Owen will chide her for being abusive to his suitemates when they answer the telephone and claim (quite truthfully—most of the time) that Owen isn't there.

Screaming names like that, you simply call attention to yourself, Owen says. Don't *ever* do it again.

Don't ever do what?

Run off at the mouth. Call me names so they hear. Don't you know they'll be witnesses?

Oh hell—*witnesses!*

Afterward, says Owen, his voice slightly quavering, you know— you know what I mean.

There isn't going to be any "afterward," neither one of us has the courage, Kirsten says sullenly.

Afterward—if something happens to her—you know who I mean —her and *him*—the police will ask questions, they'll ask questions about us, you can be sure of that, Owen says. And my suitemates—I really don't know what they will say. I don't trust the bastards.

I don't trust Hannah, Kirsten says primly. Which is why I don't tell her anything.

I don't *tell* my suitemates anything either, Owen says. The point is you, babe. You and your hysteria. That time you called last month and I didn't happen to be around and—

I called four or five times, Kirsten says. You were afraid to come to the phone. You wouldn't come—you were hiding.

Oh hell.

You were *hiding,* Kirsten says, her cheeks belling out like an eight-year-old's, triumphant in spite, you wouldn't return my calls, you were exactly what I said you were—a goddam coward, a hypocrite phony asshole—

Shut up! Owen says viciously. And, after a trembling moment: What ever did happen with him—? You've been rather quiet on the subject.

I told you everything, Kirsten says, looking frankly into his face. We met in the park, we walked around the boat basin, he acted very guilty—the son of a bitch—and finally admitted it all. Mother and Nick, the two of them, years and years of it, and everyone knew except Father; which didn't surprise me. I mean, I *knew.* Everyone in Washington knew.

Did you ask him whether—you know?—he and Mother were ever—

Whether they were ever fucking on any sort of regular basis, Kirsten says evenly, yes, I did ask him though not in those precise words, and you can imagine what he said—you know Di Piero—

Actually I don't know him, Owen says. You're the one who knows him.

I don't know him, he's just a friend of Mother's, Kirsten says.

Of course they were lovers too, I think that's obvious, Owen says. He was always hanging around. He stayed overnight, practically. There was a continual party—all Maurie had to do was go out of town on business—in they swarmed—General Kempe was the worst—I mean, Death marching into our living room—!

He's got throat cancer, Kirsten says.

How do you know?

Mother said so, in a letter. She still writes. Her perfumed stationery. Now she's exclaiming to me about *you*—she thinks you've turned against her too—she's getting frightened. I mean, she must know. She must know how we feel.

Oh no no no, Owen says, whistling through his teeth. Oh no, she doesn't.

Anyway he's got throat cancer, he's had an operation and his vocal cords are gone, Kirsten says. He'll never talk again.

Poor old fucker.

Oh the hell with *him,* I don't care about *him,* I don't care about any of them, Kirsten says giggling. Her eyes are large and bright. The pretty little blue vein at her temple beats. —Do you ever think, Owen, that you don't *care?*—I mean about anybody, anything—

I care about him, Owen says stiffly.

Kirsten puffs out her cheeks again. Her eyes grow brighter, tears begin to spill. Of course, she says quickly, quietly, *him.*

I care about the way they fucked him over, the way they wrung him dry and discarded him, Owen says.

Of course, of course, Kirsten says, rocking from side to side. I didn't mean that. I forgot.

I was reading Blake the other night—you know how everything is coming together now?—I mean, Jesus!—everything—a paperback I used in sophomore year, I walked over to the bookshelf and opened it

—I couldn't sleep—some cocksucker was playing rock music across the way—I went and opened the book and told myself that whatever I read, it would mean something—it would mean something very important—so I opened the book, kid, and guess what I read: I opened it to *The Marriage of Heaven and Hell* where he says *A dead body revenges not injuries.*

Oh God, says Kirsten, drawing in her breath sharply. For a moment she stares at Owen: she isn't drugged, not even high: her vision is clear. Then the gaze softens, shifts out of focus. —*A dead body revenges not injuries.* What does that mean?

I can think of at least two meanings, Owen says. It pleases him that his sister has been so affected by his words. But one of them isn't very consoling.

A dead body revenges not injuries, Kirsten says slowly.

We all love Blake, Owen says, he tells us such sly whimsical unforgivable things. . . . *He who desires but acts not, breeds pestilence.* Nice, isn't it? *Sooner murder an infant in its cradle than nurse unacted desires.*

Strangle, isn't it?

What?

Sooner strangle an infant—

What did I say?

You said murder.

Sooner murder an infant in its cradle than—

No, I think it's strangle.

Strangle, murder, what the hell, stop interrupting me, Owen says, suddenly furious. You always have to stick in your two-cents' worth, don't you! Piping up at the dinner table, or in the car—anything to get your daddy's attention—and most of the time you're wrong—

Owen, for God's sake, Kirsten says, in her "reasonable" schoolgirl voice which so maddens him, I'm *sorry.* Look, I'm *sorry.* Let's not quarrel, we don't have much time.

Drive your cart and your plow over the bones of the dead, Owen says. How do you like that sentiment? Do you like it?

No.

That's what *they've* done. To him. What they're trying to do.

Do you think they will get married? I mean—after enough time goes by—

How do I know what they'll do? I'm not their confidant, Owen says. And here's another—I couldn't believe it, the things I read in that book—everything came together in a flash!—here—*What is now proved was once only imagined.*

Oh, I like that, Kirsten says. I like that.

What is now proved—

—was once only imagined.

Yes, says Owen, we'll be able to say that then. Afterward. When it's over with. When they're both dead.

What is now proved was once only imagined. . . .

Her voice trembles with gratitude.

Suddenly her nose is running, she paws her pockets for a handkerchief. Of course she doesn't have one—her brother will have to supply her. Silly Kirsten! When will she grow up! She is laughing uncontrollably, her eyes are streaming tears, her thin shoulders shake. No drug is powerful enough to subdue her.

Owen looms above her, grinning, swaying. He too gives off a marvelous radiant heat. Think of that, babe, he says, when it's all over —when it's a matter of two-inch headlines—when the murderers are punished! *What is now proved* . . . We'll say it together then, won't we? Won't we?

Oh yes, Kirsten whispers.

We'll make them confess. First. We'll make them tell the truth, a written confession, a joint confession, maybe a taped conversation too —at their bedside! Yes? Right? Won't we?

Oh yes, Kirsten whispers, giggling, choking, oh yes yes yes yes yes.

May 13, the second Tuesday of reading week at school, and Owen finds himself not reading for exams or working on his thesis but in warm humid mesmerizing Washington, D.C., the city of his birth, the city he adores. *To Carthage then I came,* he murmurs to himself, giddy, delighted, ready for battle.

He finds himself at a party to which he hasn't been invited— exactly. But of course the Moultons are old, old friends of Isabel's and Maurie's, of course he is welcome: who among the Hallecks' circle would be inhospitable to the Halleck children, wretches though they are . . . ? "Troubled," "troublesome," "unhappy," "disturbed." Washington children, in short.

Though primed for battle Owen finds himself on the northernmost edge of the Moultons' large flagstone terrace, in an intense but civilized discussion with a stranger who both is, and is not, the sort of person one meets at the Moultons' parties. They are not discussing politics, which would be vulgar—they are not even discussing personalities, which might be intriguing—they are instead discussing philosophical principles of a fairly abstract and pedantic nature.

If a friend of Isabel's eases close to overhear . . .

If one of the Moultons' security people brushes past . . .

Owen has of course been indiscreet, despite his methodical plans. Perhaps he has even made a blunder. Of sorts. His visit to Claudia Lleyn the other day somehow went wrong. . . . However, if Charlotte Moulton reports on his behavior to Isabel, later tonight, she will have very little to complain about. Owen is simply talking with one of the Moultons' guests. Talking quietly, intelligently. In an "intellectual" style. Ulrich May professed to be amused by the neon device the Moulton's have installed on their terrace to kill insects, and Owen is amused as well, and so they stand watching the insects fly into the sinuous blue tubing where they are loudly sizzled to death. One after another after another! Remarkable!

Marvelous pop art, May says, laughing, dabbing at his lips. It *is* an intentional work of art, I believe, isn't it?

They talk about bourgeois vulgarity, the "bottomless pit" of American bad taste. They talk about electrocution as a means of state execution: May says quietly that he was terribly impressed, terribly moved and frightened by the execution of the Rosenbergs—before Owen's time, of course. (I read descriptions of it everywhere I could find them, he says. They made me physically ill. I will never—never—forget.) They move onto the philosophical principle of suicide. Aren't the insects, the idiotic insects, committing suicide? Owen handles the subject with remarkable urbanity and restraint, as if he were discussing an entirely impersonal issue. Though he is somewhat piqued that his new friend hasn't the tact to change the subject.

Light is an element that draws the insects to it, he says slowly, as if he were in a seminar, laboring discreetly to impress, because they think it's warmth—they think it's life. But it's death. Their death is an ironic accident.

Not at all, May says, disagreeing politely. The attraction to light —to warmth—to *death*—can't possibly be an accident. It's programmed into them, it's an instinct. By which I mean that suicide is an instinct in them.

That's improbable, Owen says. Suicide can't be "instinctive" in nature.

It's incontestable, May says. Only watch—!

And another insect, a moth with two-inch powdery wings, flies against the neon tubing and is killed: the device makes an ugly sizzling frying sound.

Which proves nothing, Owen mumurs, laughing nervously.

Which proves everything, May says. The fact of the *deed*, triumphant over the hypothesis of the *word*.

They leap to the subject of the Donatists, about whom Owen knows a little (a friend at college once did a long paper on the Donatist heresy) and May appears to know a great deal. He says, It was a natural development—the Christians simply absorbed so many of the noble Roman ideas! But without understanding them. Without any grace, any subtlety. It wasn't genuine death they wanted but their silly Christian Heaven, suicide wasn't an end but a means, they craved martyrdom and made nuisances of themselves begging to be killed—wanting to elude sin and go directly to God. Gibbon wrote on them, you know, and Augustine. Thousands upon thousands of martyrs. Men, women, children. Insisting on death. Beheaded, burnt alive, roasted on gridirons, thrown from cliffs, mauled by animals, hacked to pieces. . . . What a tiresome bunch! Tertullian forbade them even to try to escape persecution, he loved blood himself, he taught that God would reward the martyrs and roast their persecutors in hell, and of course they could watch, from above. An extraordinary era! And yet, you know, I've often thought that the Donatists were simply obeying a profound human instinct, the most immediate and primitive instinct . . . I could sympathize with them if there had not been so *many* of them. I detest crowds.

You say there's an instinct for suicide, Owen says slowly, not raising his voice, but there's an instinct for murder too—isn't there? And wouldn't the instinct for murder satisfy the other instinct? Isn't it really the *primary* instinct? The Donatists as I understand them weren't really committing *suicide;* they were escaping sin, going to heaven, getting revenge on their persecutors; this revenge was their form of murder. And if they could have satisfied it directly . . .

May draws back, nodding and smiling. Around his neck are several thin gold chains; a small medallion, nearly lost in his frizzy chest hair, catches and loses the light. A priest out of costume, Owen thinks. But May is saying rather boldly: For a suicide's child you have a remarkably subtle mind.

Owen winces. But his schoolboy pride has been touched. I lived a long time before I became a suicide's child, he says. I wasn't born that way.

And have you any brothers or sisters? May asks.

A sister.

Older, younger—?

Younger. But possibly more subtle.

May drops a hand lightly on Owen's shoulder. And draws it away at once, in the same gesture. I find that difficult to believe, he says.

More—serious.

Serious—?

About being a suicide's child. About being *his* child.

You both intend to escape the doom, the boring doom of it, May says, don't you?—every psychologist with an M.A. knows that the children of suicides are drawn to suicide: I mean, it truly *is* boring. A general truth becomes so boring one halfway suspects it might be false.

Owen feels his heart clench and beat. Behind May, on the terrace near the caterer's portable bar, a number of people—old friends of Isabel's—are glancing in Owen's direction. The Degler woman and her lover Jack Fair; Eve Neilson in a red pajamalike costume; Charles Clayton—who has been testifying, under subpoena, before the House Ethics Committee. And is Isabel among them? Nearby? In the house? Peering at him through a window? Is she with Nick or accompanied by another friend—a diversionary tactic?

What's wrong, what are you looking for? May says, slightly annoyed, I thought we were having an interesting conversation. Are you waiting for someone *very* special to arrive—?

She won't come while I'm here, they've warned her, Owen says, laughing quietly. They've been watching me.

They—?

With exquisite tact Ulrich May does not turn to glance over his shoulder. He winds his watch with thumb and forefinger concealed beneath the cuff of his shirt; his sigh is languid. *Who* is it? he asks. A lover? A lover with whom you've quarreled?

The suicide's widow, Owen says. A notorious Washington whore.

He finishes what remains of his drink. The melting ice cubes fall against his teeth; liquid trickles down his chin. But he doesn't mind. Whiskers conceal. He dealt himself twenty milligrams of Dexedrine before crashing the Moultons' party, smoking mere dope up at school has made him too amiable and shuffling, he wants to frighten people a little now. *The wrath of the lion is the wisdom of God,* he murmurs softly.

But May has picked up on Isabel, the fact of Isabel, he says happily, One never really thinks of Isabel de Benavente as a widow because one never exactly thought of her as a wife—forgive me! And now I have to absorb the astonishing fact that she is a mother as well, of a young man your age. As for her being a whore—well—I won't comment.

Yes, says Owen, his shoulders shaking with quiet laughter, there's that embarrassment. That she has a son of my age and my size.

Your girth does surprise me, May says.

Well—I'm in mourning. I want another drink. It makes me nervous, people watching me, though I like it—I want it—it's why I came, in fact—I'm doing my own investigation of the case—all very informal of course—a sort of undergraduate approach—I thought I'd get more sympathy, being aboveboard and ingenuous, but the whiskers—they're new—d'you like the idea?—my sister doesn't—the whiskers are meant to intimidate too—I want it both ways. I think I'll get another drink. Gene Parr has just come in, the esteemed Senator, that fat-ass in the red Bermuda shorts, I'd like to intimidate *him*.

Your investigation, May says, I assume you mean—? Into the circumstances of your father's death?

Suicide, murder, whether anyone was actually hired, whether— you know—there are grounds for retribution. Owen sniffs and wipes at his eyes and notes that Eve Neilson is surely telling Parr about him, for the old boy is glancing fatly at Owen over his shoulder. (Has he bothered you, has he telephoned?—did you receive one of his letters? Do you think Isabel knows? Should we tell her? But of course she must know—she and Nick must both know—someone must have told them by now— maybe it isn't our business. But hasn't he changed, jowly and queer-eyed, and growing a beard! His own father wouldn't recognize him.)

Retribution, May says lightly, so lightly the word is questioning without being precisely a question, and again he winds his invisible watch, though his expression shows only a courteous patience. Ah yes —I see—retribution. You haven't faith in the police investigation or in the House committee—you don't take your father's confession at face value?

Owen doesn't trouble to answer. He is feeling both mellow and edgy, the edginess contained within the mellowness, a nice hard bitter stony pit inside the sugary fruit of his body. At first, at school, after the Great Change in his life—that is, the March visit to Eyre—he was simply in a walking daze, and though he was drawn to acquaintances and even to strangers who dealt with their own disasters by getting high as regularly and as thoroughly as possible (but mainly by smoking dope: Owen's university is conservative by nature), it wasn't until someone said disdainfully of Owen in Owen's presence, He's always plugging into somebody else's high, that he made the necessary move and began to buy his own dope. The ceremonial nature of the business bored him, the physiological effects—drowsiness, wooziness, a beery affability—struck him as inappropriate, a violation of his true zombie state, which he rather coolly diagnosed as a natural and temporary consequence of the blow his sister had given him, the wound he had absorbed. A dead body revenges not injuries, only the living revenge injuries, but the prospect was so overwhelming, so grotesque and unlikely and necessary and exciting . . . *Don't lie to me, don't pretend, you know what I want, you know what we're going to do,* his beautiful sister whispered, stroking his arm, though the words were inaudible, though she was some distance from him and he spied upon her only in a mirror: a mirror delicately steamed, as in reverie, from the heat of her bath. *You know what we're going to do,* she whispered. *Both of us—both of them. You know. You know.*

Suddenly he is trembling. The Dexedrine thrums along his nerves, more than he can handle. He sets his drink down on a table—does not notice that the glass tips and rolls and only May's alacrity prevents it from shattering on the floor—backs away trembling—for they *are* looking at him—they *are,* after all, Isabel's friends and conspirators—they too have profited from Maurie's convenient death—there are surely F.B.I. agents at the Moultons', unobtrusive guests—he and Kirsten haven't a friend in Washington—it was absurd for him to come here—of course Isabel is spying on him from the house—Isabel and Nick—she is grasping his wrist hard and saying, Oh God now it's Owen too—a psychopath—a psychotic—both my children—what can I do—how can I get them committed—how can I get them the *help* they need—

But Ulrich May, his new friend, takes him firmly in hand. Says in a kindly fatherly affectionately bullying voice: You have the revolutionary's logic, my friend, but not much else. Have you ever ridden upon a flying carpet?

In May's penthouse bedroom with its enormous plate-glass window framing resplendent Washington—the lights of Capitol Hill, the lights of the Washington Monument—Owen, giddy with the height, giddy with the queer undefinable texture of the carpet beneath his bare feet, and with the puzzle of the photographs of May's elegant white silk wallpapered walls which, though he stares and frowns and squints, he cannot *quite* decipher—Owen is not flying but quite simply suspended: risen with the fabulous hair-and-feather carpet a few feet off the floor. But then he and May are some fifty stories above the earth. It is a place for the miraculous, a place for secrets to be shared. This must be the first to go, May says, pinching the flab at Owen's waist another time, and Owen wonders why he doesn't shove the fairy bastard away—why the pinch is so familiar, and so welcome.

Research

Evidence assembled in bits, fragments, scraps. Notes scribbled to himself which turn out to be illegible—a stranger's handwriting. He tears out news articles from last summer's *Post* and *Star* and *New York Times*, crouching back in the library stacks, daring anyone to accuse him. Sometimes he smuggles a newspaper past the control desk and takes it into the men's room where he has more privacy.

Everything significant is tossed into his research bag—his sturdy plastic takeout bag from *That's Some Chicken!*

I shall bring my talent for undergraduate success, Owen declares to his sister, his only friend, my knack for precision and thoroughness, my indefatigable *patience* with library research—after all I lack genius, I require ballast—to bear upon the investigation of our father's murder. Since the police have been bought off. Since the committee down there is hopelessly corrupt.

Should you talk like that?—I mean where are you calling from? Kirsten asks nervously. Sometimes, late at night, her voice is so small and frail Owen hallucinates her as a very young child.

His sister, his coconspirator?

From my room, he says. The door is shut.

But his irony does not register. Kirsten says: Any telephone call, you know—I mean didn't they tap *his* phone—they just have to go before some judge down there and get a ruling—I think—or maybe not if it's the F.B.I.—or the Pentagon—but they do it anyway—they can break the law anytime they want to—we shouldn't talk like this—you're going to ruin everything—

Did you hear that Giallella was killed in Chicago, Owen says, it's only been a few weeks since he talked to the assassination committee—the Senate—Kennedy, King—this is the third or is it the fourth—of course it's been a long time—years—

Who? says Kirsten. What are you talking about?

Luigi Giallella, he gave testimony down there, of course he didn't really say anything, but—

Who? Luigi who?

Giallella! Owen shouts into the phone. Don't you for Christ's sake read newspapers up there? The Senate is investigating the assassinations of Kennedy and King—I mean a committee—I *know* it isn't the same thing but it's instructive—we need to be aware—if anyone was hired it was probably a syndicate man—

But Kirsten is silent. He imagines her thin hunched-up shoulders, her pale stubborn face. Her eyes are shut tight—probably. Too much information confuses her, he is becoming disappointed with her capacity for theory, he may end up doing everything alone. If she breaks down he will do it all alone.

Oh go to hell, he says suddenly, and hangs up.

The yellow and red plastic bag, carried everywhere on campus with Owen Halleck. My research bag, he says. He is growing a beard, evidently—or has forgotten to shave—then one day he shaves extravagantly—and dresses in a sports coat and tie and pressed trousers: My interviewer's costume.

Evidence assembled slowly. Slowly. Knowing the probable outcome of his investigation should speed its progress, yet doesn't.

An hour-long interview with a professor of political science whose reputation at the university is daringly leftist: but the man is guarded with Owen and answers his questions in a slow halting voice, professing to know very little about the Chilean business, the GBT investigation, the Commission's case, the Halleck bribery charges . . . the suicide. His specialty, he tells Owen, is the Far East. If you want to talk about the Lockheed bribery business I can help you with that, he says, smiling nervously, but—the South American connection—copper—the C.I.A.—all that—I probably don't know much more than you do if you've been keeping up with the papers. He pauses. For several seconds. Owen, fussing angrily with his Panasonic Auto-Stop recorder (a gift from Isabel freshman year; he could record lectures and save himself the tedium of note-taking), knows that the tight-assed bastard is deliberating about whether to say *I understand your concern and your grief, it was a terrible thing, I wish I could help you* . . . but in the end he says only *Sorry.*

An abortive attempt to record a telephone conversation with one of the old Commission men in Washington—an alleged friend of Maurie's. Each time Mr. Carlyle was about to come on the phone Owen pressed the *on* button; but another secretary spoke; or another assistant. It was Owen's strategy not always to identify himself . . . he knew word would spread in his mother's and Nick's circle quickly enough . . . yet his false names elicited no respect. And when he did get through to Carlyle at home the conversation came to nothing. Absolutely nothing. Zero.

Owen, I'm afraid I can't help you, I've told my version so many times, you must understand, it's all in the public record, I haven't falsified anything or held anything back, I'm still sick about Maurie and I understand your concern, I understand what you're doing, but I can't help you, there simply isn't anything further I know. . . . Owen?

Fucker, Owen whispers. And hangs up.

Tossed in the research bag: a *New York Times* article on a thirty-three-year-old chemical researcher at West Virginia University in Morgantown, West Virginia, who had dealt himself an anticoagulant named warfarin because he thought it would prolong his life—allow him to live for two hundred years. (He had also taken BTH, a chemical used in food packaging to retard spoilage.) Owen had difficulty reading the article all the way through because the ending was sad but he skimmed it several times and felt a powerful sympathy for the young researcher who had evidently miscalculated the potency of his drug and was found in bed in his apartment, blood on his clothes, soaking the mattress, and on the kitchen and bathroom floors. The young man had called warfarin the Fountain of Youth. It must have been an agonizing death, the assistant state medical examiner said.

And a lengthy article in the student paper, the consequence of undergraduate investigative reporting, about C.I.A.-funded research at the university between the years 1950 and 1973. This is the real thing, Owen thinks, they've got the bastards now, they've got them by the balls. A $25 million project of "secret mind control" research. Code-names MK-ULTRA, Project Bluebird, and Project Artichoke. Two private institutions underwrote the C.I.A. program: the Geschikter Foundation for Medical Research and the Society for the Investigation of Human Ecology. In New York City brothels "unsuspecting subjects" were given mind-control drugs and their behavior was observed in two-way mirrors. Prisoners at the Bordentown Reformatory in New Jersey were subjects of experiments, as were "sexual psychopaths" at the Winona State Hospital in Michigan. Five professors at the university were paid consultants—and paid quite well—and the president of the university stated that it was "not a university matter at all." Ah hah, says Owen, now we've got them, their names in print, right out front for everyone to see. . . .

But nothing happens.

Nothing happens.

He brings the subject up at his eating club. But his friends are not terribly interested. You know of the Nuremberg Code, we are supposed to follow it, he says, medical research and that sort of thing—you know —after the Nazis—the Nazi doctors— But no one is terribly interested, only a young man with cowlicky blond hair and a perpetual dissatisfied frown who is rumored to be failing two subjects. Those suckers are getting it where they deserve it, he says, I hope it makes the *New York Times*—I hope it goes out over UPI— Someone suggests that every university in the country would have leapt for that $25 million. And the Russians are doing worse things—if only we knew for sure. And in any case it all happened a long time ago, one of the professors isn't even on the faculty now.

We signed the Nuremberg Code, Owen says, keeping his voice low and level and courtroom steady, why did we sign it if we aren't going to follow it?

What's the Nuremberg Code? someone asks.

Oh Christ, don't get him started, someone murmurs, just loud enough for Owen to hear.

Owen leaves a note for his thesis advisor, whom he has been avoiding. The campus is small enough, it is possible to run into the wrong people two or three times a day. And Owen must use the library. *I will be postponing my thesis,* he types carefully on a clean sheet of paper, *I am shifting my research priorities to another field. This means I will not graduate. I will not enter Harvard Law. I hope you are not disappointed.* He laughs quietly to himself, seeing paunchy sweating unshaven Owen Halleck careening around campus with his plastic tote bag. *That's Some Chicken!* He finds it amusing that since his father's death—or, to be absolutely accurate, since his meeting with Kirsten in Eyre—the same old body trundles through the same spaces though *everything has changed.*

To the casual eye he is just Owen Halleck, Owen Jay Halleck, Maurie's and Isabel's good-natured son. But his secret is: *Everything has changed.*

A kid he had known only slightly at Exeter, now attired in amusing preppie gothic—tight jeans, L. L. Bean boots, a LaCoste shirt rakishly unbuttoned to show a pale, somewhat concave chest—deals him

Dexedrine capsules, though fewer than he requires. I can take every-thing you have, Owen says, I'm your only customer, come *on*, but the kid is already moving, he has other customers, other obligations. Don't be a pig, Halleck, he says with a sweet smile, already out the door.

All things conspire, all things rush into focus. For instance: his research problems have grown so difficult, he wanders restlessly through the library, his tote bag thumping against his thigh, his lips silently moving, and suddenly he has collided with one of the student workers at the library and suddenly a heavy volume falls to the floor and suddenly, squatting, Owen Halleck is staring at a photograph in the opened book—men who gradually emerge as soldiers in the American army of 1899, standing posed for the camera atop a curious little moun-tain that gradually emerges as Owen stares and stares ignoring the young man's impatient remarks as a—can it really be?—yes—no—yes certainly—*a hillock composed of enemy bones.*

Owen begins to laugh. He points at the picture, he grins up at whoever is beside him, Look, he says, hey look, you see, Filipino bones, we're standing on Filipino bones, we're all in uniform, look at the bastard fooling around with the skull—see him? Oh it's going to happen all right, he says, rubbing at his eyes, giggling quietly, it can't be stopped, it should have started long ago.

He rips open Isabel's letter, takes out the check. His fingers are trembling. She is buying him off, here's a check for $250, he can't remem-ber what he asked but it wasn't that much, she has been buying him off for years, he must maneuver himself into a *spiritual space* in which his acceptance of her money isn't a collaboration in her evil but a strategem for eradicating that evil. I take your check, Isabel, he says, but I won't read your contemptible, lying letter.

Later, he finds himself rummaging in his wastebasket for the letter—usually no more than a single stiff sheet of stationery, folded once—but he can find only the torn envelope.

Either Isabel did not choose to write him a letter this time, or one of his suitemates took it out of the wastebasket.

The former, he thinks. Yes, the former. (For the latter is not probable, is it. Not yet.)

So she has stopped writing, he thinks with a thrill of despair. O you bitch, you know, don't you?—you know what's coming.

All things conspire, all things rush into focus.

For instance: it is possible for Owen to continue his research while sitting through five consecutive evenings of Buñuel films. He learns a great deal from *L'Age d'Or,* even more from *Viridiana* and *The Exterminating Angel. Belle de Jour* excites him greatly: the shots of Deneuve's feet, legs, hands, shoes, stockings, and undergarments are absolutely riveting. Deneuve—that, is, Séverine—that is, Belle de Jour—is not Isabel de Benavente except in the cascades of blond hair, the unperturbed staring eyes, the vacancy, the absence. The little mannerisms, the accent. Glimpsed through curtains, windows, peepholes. If the film does not end with her violent death it is only because it has been seduced by her, contaminated by her. It is so shamelessly her own dream . . . !

But Owen will change all that.

The Mirror

Yes, Ulrich May will tell Owen some weeks later, all things conspire. You are quite right. There are moments that pierce like knife blades—moments in which the course of your life is suddenly clear.

And after that? Owen asks with a shaky grin.

After that? You resist less frequently.

More evidence: a memory of Isabel that startles him with its clarity, its obvious *significance*. (And how idiotic of him, Owen realizes, not to have grasped its significance at the time.)

Isabel reclining on a couch. The telephone cradled lazily on her shoulder. Owen had answered it downstairs, it was Nick Martens, could Maurie come to the phone?—but of course Maurie wasn't home, Maurie wouldn't be home at that time of day—late afternoon, not yet six—then may I speak with your mother, Nick asks reasonably and Owen shouts upstairs and Isabel takes the call and it is all perfectly ordinary.

Isabel in her white silky dressing gown, lying on the couch in the room that has come to be known as "her" bedroom, though it is supposed to be a guest room and in any case she "really" sleeps in the master bedroom with her husband. Isabel sullen and lazy, her face denuded of makeup, the forehead glaring, the jaw rather square. In a low voice she is saying, Of course it was all right . . . they came with a towtruck . . . they were surprisingly efficient . . . yes yes all right I know . . . yes I suppose it was . . . I *was* . . . didn't I show it? . . . oh hell . . . what are you trying to say . . . yes fine I *know* . . . I *agree* . . . if we'd had a real accident, if one of us had been hurt or the car really damaged. . . . Then again maybe we are both exaggerating. . . . What? I think it's almost six, I got back just after five, of course I'm fine, a man from the garage drove me home, the car will be ready on . . . Yes I *know*, I *agree*. . . .

It is not Isabel he sees, exactly, but her reflection. In a floor-length mirror. Just inside the partly opened door of her room. Owen is twelve years old and heavyfooted and he hasn't any idea how he has managed to get upstairs—so quickly and so quietly.

Of course I'm not angry, Isabel is saying, why would I be angry, her voice is low and resigned and there is a strange intimate laziness in her very posture: the hair disheveled as if windblown, the dressing gown carelessly tied at the waist, stockingless legs, bare feet. She sighs, she laughs, she says with a puzzling cheerful bitterness, *Why* would I be angry . . . !

And then she glances up and happens to see Owen watching her. In the mirror.

Just as Owen cannot recall how he got upstairs—he had answered the telephone in the kitchen—now he cannot recall *exactly* how Isabel looked at him. He seems to remember first of all her silence: her stiffening into silence. She lies on the pretty peach-colored couch static and perfect as a jewel in a setting. A woman in a mirror, slanted in a mirror. He sees her reflection and she sees his reflection and in the next instant Owen strides by the door—he's on his way to his own room, after all, he has just come home from somewhere, in a jacket, perhaps even in boots, he cannot recall the precise time of year but thinks it may have been winter, in any case he isn't interested in his mother's telephone conversations, in any case adults bore him terribly.

Isabel's stricken look. A queer and quite uncharacteristic stiffening to her face. . . . Or is the expression one of simple irritation (for both her children irritate her with their demands, their commotion, their voices, their presence); or one of . . . simple surprise?

But Owen, striding by the door, is not interested.

The Investigator

Can't I come with you, Kirsten begs, but Owen is adamant: Certainly not.

He wants to be unencumbered. He doesn't want *emotion.*

Will you telephone me? Kirsten says.

I can't promise, says Owen. I want to keep in motion.

You aren't . . . going to do it yet, are you? Kirsten asks. Her voice is so faint, so distant, he really cannot hear. But he knows exactly what she has said.

Why shouldn't I? he says.

She does not reply. The line is absolutely silent.

Coward, Owen thinks, grinning, now who's the coward, *now* who's in the driver's seat.

But he says aloud, with a scolding impatience he halfway means: *Of course not. It isn't time.*

The guilt is a foregone conclusion, Owen reasons. But the steps —the legal procedure—the orderliness of an investigation (however informal)—the habit of sanity itself: all demand caution.

Sunday, May 11. He takes the Metroliner to Washington. Equipped with his Panasonic Auto-Stop recorder, his journal (it has a blue cardboard cover, the word *Record* stamped in classy fake gold, lined pages), a wallet fatly stuffed with bills. The plastic tote bag has been left behind in his room in the residence hall. He has packed his evidence carefully in a leather hand grip along with a change of clothes and a few toiletries. Nothing excessive.

Claudia Lleyn, he checks off his list, Charles Clayton, Bobbie Tern, Reid Silber, Hal Seawright, Phillip Moulton, the journalist Preston Kroll, Morton Kempe, "Tom Gast" . . . if the contact man "Tom Gast" actually exists . . . and others. This won't be an interview, he will say with a frank clear-eyed smile, certainly not an interrogation, I'd just like to reminisce with you about my father. My father and his friends. You don't mind the tape recorder—?

It occurs to him as he passes through Baltimore that Morton Kempe is now an old man dying of throat cancer. An old broken-down dying rummy. Formerly a famous general. Scratch General Kempe, Owen thinks, he was in love with Isabel too but he's beyond doing anything about it.

Scratch Charles Clayton too. A secret supporter of Nick Martens who quickly went public when the Halleck scandal broke. Eager to wash his hands of Halleck, eager to put distance between them. . . . Of course I knew that Maurie Halleck was going through a very difficult time but I thought it was a personal crisis, I mean I know his work at the Commission was affected, but I thought it was the strain of separation . . . marital problems . . . I had never heard of Gast, I had never heard that the Commission wasn't pushing all it could for extradition of the alleged assassin of . . . I am profoundly shocked and saddened and . . . *Many are deserving of punishment,* Owen notes in his journal in a bold dark hand, *but few will receive it. There isn't time.*

He pretends to be reading a discarded *Wall Street Journal* but really he is spying on his fellow Metroliner passengers. Men with attaché cases, men in three-piece suits. A scattering of women. A young mother with a single fretting baby. Owen has chosen a strategic seat—a seat at the very end of the car, with no one behind it.

Isabel's friends, the sillier ones, used to joke about sitting with their backs to the walls in public places. But the courtly Portuguese Ambassador who came to dinner with his young wife *did* wish to sit in the "safest" position in the dining room at 18 Röcken.

Anthony Di Piero, flying Swissair from Rome to London in the mid-seventies, had been present at an attempted hijacking by members of the Italian *Brigata Rossa;* but Owen knew no details. (Tony doesn't talk about such things, Isabel cautioned her friends. Don't even mention you read it in the paper.) And there was Nick Martens—poor Nick, mortal for once!—almost taken hostage by Palestinian terrorists in Khartoum.

And Maurie's life had been threatened several times. Or perhaps more frequently—Owen wouldn't know. The first occasion was long ago, before Owen's birth, something to do with Ku Klux Klan thugs in Georgia. Later: This is Mr. Carpelan, Maurie said to Owen, he'll be driving us to the seashore today, and Owen stared blankly at the tall smiling man who had suddenly appeared in their life: a man sent by the government to "make things easier" for them. Owen might have been six years old at the time. And then again he was thirteen, and a Mr. Boyers came to spend two weeks at 18 Röcken, pink-faced, with a soft Mississippi drawl. (Daddy's investigating the Mafia, Owen told Kirsten, speculating freely, we could be blown up any time . . . a bomb in the car, a letter bomb . . . there's a special bomb hooked up to a telephone and they send a radio wave to detonate it . . . all kinds of things. You'd better be careful.)

The former Chilean Ambassador to the States Orlando Letelier and a woman assistant were assassinated in the car they were driving on Sheridan Circle, three years before Maurice Halleck's death, and the open rumor in Washington is that the administration—for the usual "diplomatic" reasons—refuses to put pressure on the Chilean government to extradite the men who ordered the murders; there is another rumor, less substantial, about a young American couple, former Peace Corps workers and alleged leftists, who were found clubbed to death in Mexico not long ago, under usually mysterious circumstances—and again the government, which in this case may mean the Ministry of Justice, seems to be going slowly in its investigation.

Connections?—of course there are connections. But Owen must control his thoughts. He must not allow his head to flood.

He pages through his notes, he rereads newspaper clippings, frequently puzzled over their significance—their relevance to *his* investigation. The C.I.A.-supported conspiracy that led to the assassination of commander-in-chief of the Chilean army, René Schneider, a decade ago . . . the infamous murder of Salvador Allende . . . multinational copper companies, GBT, Kennecott, Anaconda . . . truckers' strikes, trade union riots, Nixon's and Kissinger's covert policy of "destabilization" of Chile. . . . *Murderers,* Owen thinks helplessly, *but what can we do? There isn't time.*

If they ordered him killed, Owen reasons, it was political. If he killed himself it was love.

Claudia Lleyn is not visibly distressed at his questions or his appearance. (What *is* my appearance? Owen wonders, too late. Hasn't he shaved? His fingers encounter bristles, quills.) She is soft-spoken, gracious, perfumey, even motherly, a handsome woman Isabel's age, but looking considerably older: which comforts Owen. Because, of late, his sexual fantasies have become rather peculiar.

The Panasonic recorder gives him some trouble. But the trouble, at least, is something to chat about: I'm just not mechanical-minded myself, Claudia laughs. She is being helpful. He notes the high arch of her handsome butterscotch shoes, her slender ankles.

Did the two of you ever share—well, Tony Di Piero? Owen wants to ask. A wave of laughter threatens to break.

Can I give you a hand? Claudia asks, leaning near.

Claudia is one of Isabel's oldest friends in Washington. They were classmates at Mount Vernon college, though Isabel dropped out after her first or second year. Claudia of course knows *everything* about Isabel and Isabel knows *everything* about Claudia. —Was Nick Martens ever *your* lover? Owen wants to ask. His fingers tremble so, he cannot fit the goddam cassette in place.

They talk "freely." Owen encourages her to "say anything" about Maurie. He stares at the floor, nodding, grunting in agreement. (Maurie was one of the most . . . Maurie was so . . . The first time we met, I think it was in 1955, Isabel had called me and told me . . . so much in love, he was going to be the man, of course I was astonished . . . when we met I could see . . . I was so happy for her. . . . The sweetest kindest most gentle . . .)

Yes, says Owen abruptly, all right, now about Nick . . . ?

Nick?

Nick Martens. Nick.

What about Nick? Claudia says.

Owen suppresses a smile, still staring at the floor. The woman's legs are crossed, one slender foot swings just a little, just a little. Perhaps it is the pulsation of her blood.

Do you mean the friendship between Nick and your father? Claudia asks.

I mean the friendship between Nick and my mother.

Claudia is silent for a moment. Owen raises his eyes covertly and sees that she is affecting an absolute innocent blankness. One hand fusses with a tortoiseshell comb in her shagged "frosted" hair; the other rests on her knee. She is wearing a black silk blouse, yellow linen trousers, a square-cut diamond as big as Isabel's. Wealthy woman, Owen thinks, wealthy cunt, wanting to bury his face in her breasts, press his great yearning trembling body against hers.

The friendship between Nick and my mother! he half-shouts.

Claudia stares at him. Frowns, tries to smile, clasps both hands together, says falteringly that she doesn't know of any special friendship between Isabel and Nick . . . it was always the three of them, wasn't it, Maurie and Isabel and Nick . . . poor June never did fit in, exactly. . . .

Isabel and Nick, says Owen bluntly. I'm here today to talk about Isabel and Nick.

In another part of the house someone is thumping about: probably a cleaning woman. Outside, in the terraced garden, a mockingbird is singing. Claudia is silent but he can sense, oh yes he can sense, her scrambling thoughts.

There isn't anything to tell you . . . about Isabel and Nick.

Isn't there?

I don't know of anything.

My mother and my godfather were friends, weren't they. Close friends. Are friends. I mean—aren't they? For years.

Claudia says stiffly: We are all friends.

Oh, come off it, Owen laughs, you know what I mean. She was screwing around with Di Piero and she was screwing around with some doctor, I remember his cute little green Triumph parked on Röcken, a plastic surgeon wasn't it, and there was the time Charlotte Moulton was cracking up and you were all comforting her, even Isabel who was probably screwing her husband—or maybe you all were—and I remember overhearing you and Eve Neilson joking with Isabel about a marksman—an F.B.I. man, maybe—someone at the Pentagon—my sister and I weren't exactly deaf and dumb all those years.

He pauses, breathing hard.

That's—ridiculous, Claudia says.

Oh yes, is it ridiculous? Is it?

Absolutely ridiculous.

My mother was always faithful to my father?—always faithful?

The brevity of Claudia's hesitation is masterful. Yes, she says, so far as I know.

Always faithful? All those years?

So far as I know, yes.

But you know her very well. You've always been close.

Not that close.

Oh—not that close?

Isabel is rather aloof, she isn't that accessible.

Really?

We all lead our own lives, Claudia says.

Which means—?

Which means that I don't know everything about Isabel, we have always respected each other's privacy.

But you said she was faithful to my father.

Certainly. So far as I know.

So far as you know.

I really don't like to be interrogated, Owen, Claudia says. This is extremely unpleasant.

It is unpleasant, Owen says, nodding, panting. So you respect each other's privacy, you don't share secrets, you and her?

I think you'd better leave now, Owen.

If she has secrets—you don't know them?

Isabel is a very busy woman, her life overlaps many lives, of course we see each other constantly—socially—and we try to get together for lunch once or twice a month—she visits me in Nassau, when Henry was alive, at his post in Stockholm, she came with Kirsten and stayed for a lovely month—June—Kirsten was just a baby then and Isabel was feeling rather depressed—I don't mean *really* depressed, clinically depressed—but not quite herself—so she came to Stockholm to visit—the residence was lovely—Henry and I adored having Isabel, she was so immediately popular—she learned a little Swedish—the embassy people were greatly taken with her—the Mexican Ambassador, the French Deputy Chief of Mission and his wife—she even had a few East European friends—I mean, she is that kind of person, Owen—immensely friendly, immensely popular—she always has been—Nick Martens is one of many friends—it was really Maurie who—I mean the real friendship was between Maurie and Nick—Isabel has always had her own friends—I think you're very young and I think you're ignorant and I think you're being grotesquely unfair—

She went to Sweden and left me behind, Owen says, but with equanimity. She left Maurie behind too but that doesn't matter—that isn't important—we're here today to talk about Isabel and Nick.

I really think you'll have to leave now, Owen.

So you can get on the telephone and yak it up with Isabel?

Have you been home? Haven't you seen your mother?

How many Swedes did she fuck? Or did she prefer the Mexicans —the Spaniards? She seems to avoid them in her hometown, the Latin boys, the greasers, she goes for the Aryan types—it's better for the image. But of course you and she don't share any secrets.

I realize you're very unhappy about your father's death, Claudia says carefully, I understand that it will take a while . . . a long while . . . to absorb. But . . .

But you want me to leave so you can telephone her and warn her her son is back in town. Not that you're close or share any secrets. Right?

Haven't you been home yet? Did you just come down from college? What are you doing?

Assembling evidence, Owen says calmly. Look: I'll leave if you tell me a single simple truth.

You don't look well, Owen, you don't look as if you've been sleeping. . . .

Never mind the maternal shit, I think we can dispense with that am I eating right too etcetera etcetera, we'll just skip that and move on, tell me if Nick and Isabel are still a couple now or what.

What?

Are Nick and Isabel still a couple at the moment . . . or are they lying low because of Maurie . . . because of the death. Just tell me.

Owen, please—

And is the divorce final, from June. Just tell me. I need to know if they're planning some new strategy.

I don't know what you're talking about.

Are they going to get married! Owen says, suddenly shouting. He brings his big fist down on the glass-topped table. Are they going to get married, the two of them, he says more softly, staring at the hair-thin crack in the glass. Kirsten and I . . . we need to know . . . we need to know if . . . if my mother is going to get married again . . . and how soon . . . and . . . and . . .

Owen blinks and the crack disappears. He rubs at the glass with his damp fingers but it seems to be gone.

Why don't you ask your mother? Claudia says. She must be frightened but her voice is low and steady.

I can't ask my mother, Owen says. I can't step in that house.

But—since when?

Since—since a while back.

But why? I don't understand. You were so helpful at the funeral, and afterward—Isabel needed you so—she was so devastated—we all tried to help but she depended upon you—she told me you had matured so quickly, you were the man of the family, she didn't know what she would do without you—I don't understand what has happened—

Evidence, Owen says, grinning, snuffling, the passage of time, external circumstance. I may have been a little numb at that time. My mind may not have been working efficiently.

You were so attentive to her, so loving—

Never mind the maternal shit I think I said, Owen murmurs, I don't mean to be rude but I haven't much time, if you could tell me a single believable truth I will leave and never trouble you again, Mrs. Lleyn, maybe your sympathy for my mother arises from your common widowhood or something else you have in common but I really haven't time to pursue it—do you understand?

Don't shout at me, Claudia whispers. How dare you shout at me.

I wasn't shouting, Mrs. Lleyn, I was speaking clearly and distinctly for the record, in case this is being transcribed—is it being transcribed?—and so there wouldn't be any ambiguity in your mind. I am asking you: Are Nick and Isabel seeing each other *at this moment?* Are they—to use a term from the gossip columns—*still a couple?* All that I hear, all the shit that gets through to Kirsten and me, she's been running around with someone named—Payne?—I don't know who the hell it is—someone said he was a lawyer and someone said he was at State and someone said he was a "philanthropist"—I like that, a "philanthropist!"—they're the best!—but I need to know if this is a stratagem and she and Nick are planning to get together in a while when things quiet down—or—whatever.

I think you'll have to leave now, Owen. I can't tolerate your behavior.

Listen—when he died she kept saying *Your father* this and *Your father* that, *Your father has disgraced us, your father has made a fool of himself, your father was insane, your father did this deliberately.* . . . Screaming and throwing herself around—Spanish abandon—oh very very grief-stricken—aged five years in a week—the shame of it, the surprise, the headlines in the paper—photographs of poor Maurie—television coverage—reporters calling the house but *not* to interview her for her charity work or her beautiful face: poor Isabel the Washington girl, the Washington hostess, what a scandal! *Your father should never have accepted money—not in that idiotic way,* she said, I was struck by that observation, Kirsten and I were both struck by it, of course Isabel knows her way around and my late grandfather Luis was quite a professional, he could have given his son-in-law pointers on how and how not to accept bribes, I can grasp all that, the logistics are clear, except the one thing Kirsten and I wondered: Didn't she know our father at all? I mean—didn't she know him? At all?

Owen, please. This is enough.

Are they plotting to get together, that's all I want to know, Owen says more calmly, wiping at his damp face. Because if— Well— That's all we want to know.

You are asking if Isabel and Nick plan to marry?

Yes, right.

I wouldn't know.

You wouldn't know.

That's right, yes.

But Isabel is seeing someone else—?

I think she is seeing a number of people, Claudia says carefully, but no one important to her. She's begun to go out again, she's begun to recover.

Right, says Owen, laughing softly, it's important to recover, that's the main thing. Resume an active sexual life. Otherwise—the body organs atrophy, wither. The female breasts shrivel. Right?

Claudia gets to her feet. She must be frightened, Owen thinks shrewdly, but she gives no indication. Wise hard-faced bitch. Aloud he says: This isn't being taped, is it? You don't have this place wired?

Why would I have it wired? Claudia asks. Don't be silly.

You'd only be incriminating yourself, Owen says. All that you've said—all that you've eluded saying—it would be on the record.

I'll call Juan, Claudia says, he can drive you wherever you're going next.

So you refuse to tell me, Owen says.

Owen, I have told you. I have told you. I don't know your mother's secrets. I am not a—

You don't know that my mother has been having a love affair with Nick Martens for years, you've never heard of such a thing, right?—never heard a word!—that's the bullshit you're handing down, is it—you collapsed old bag, Owen says, rising clumsily to his feet, gathering up the Panasonic, oh you filthy lying collapsed old bag, he says, sniffing, wiping his nose on his sleeve, I wish I had time for you, *I wish I had time for all of you.*

Bobbie Tern's office will not put Owen through to Bobbie Tern, or even indicate—he has asked courteously—whether Bobbie Tern is in fact in Washington at the present time. Reid Silber, next on his list, is revealed to be living in New York City—but when did they move?— Owen can't remember—and the number is unlisted and no one Owen calls seems to have it handy or even to know for whom Silber is now working. Owen makes an appointment with Preston Kroll, however, and is so excited that he finds it necessary to leave the hotel and buy some sleeping pills at a late-night drugstore, he can't bring himself down otherwise, Dexedrine and adrenaline are pulsing too fiercely, he is circling in, tightening the noose, Claudia Lleyn all but blurted out the truth and Preston Kroll will know even more: he's that sort of journalist, mean-mouthed and wickedly funny and colored with cynicism as if with jaundice: his days of protecting Isabel Halleck are over since (Owen seems to know) his pursuit of her, back in the exhilarating Watergate era, came to nothing. Too morose, Owen thinks gleefully, too ugly, any woman would prefer Nick.

Over-the-counter barbiturates are notoriously weak but Owen hasn't time to prowl about disco bars and he hasn't the inclination to drink—beer makes his stomach gassy, liquor is too festive to swallow when he's alone—so he lies awake for quite a while studying the neon reflections on the ceiling of his hotel room (they are birds' wings, they are galloping giraffes) and listening to traffic down on Nineteenth Street which subsides only slightly as the hours pass. Then he is seeing a naked woman in a movie greedily peering into a black lacquered box but he is in the movie too, greedily taking up too much space, trying to snatch the black box out of her hands. Horns interrupt: there is traffic commotion down on the street: Owen wakes with a shudder and turns on the light and sweats with the need to talk to Kirsten though it is almost four o'clock in the morning and the switchboard at the Eyre Academy for Girls is certainly shut down for the night.

Has Kirsten boy friends now? he wonders. She went out from time to time in the past, her first "date" at age thirteen or perhaps younger, and naturally Isabel and Maurie were upset, but . . . you have to see these things in the proper context, Isabel finally said . . . with her magnificent philosophical resignation. (Her Spanish blood, Owen thinks with a sneer. Aristocrat and peasant meet in that blood: laziness and moral indifference masquerading as wisdom.) But does she sleep with them? Owen wonders uneasily, has she ever slept with them, does she . . . *know?* He believes not: there is something tight and stubborn about her, a virginity of the will. It would not have been difficult for Owen to poke about and discover whether his kid sister was taking birth control pills—no doubt Isabel would have told him if he'd asked—but for some reason he had had no curiosity. Up to the present time.

What about Di Piero, he asked her several times, and she said that nothing much had happened—nothing at all had happened—only that in his oblique way he had managed to implicate Isabel and Nick in Maurie's death, it was possible or even probable that they had had him killed to get him out of the way, look at all the money Isabel would inherit, Grandfather Halleck's estate. . . . Possible or probable? Owen asked eagerly. Possible, Kirsten said, her voice receding over the crackling line, oh, I don't know maybe *probable* . . . he did look guilty . . . I had to beg him to tell the truth . . . you know I think he has always hated Nick. . . .

And then? Owen said.

And then what? Kirsten said.

You and Di Piero.

What about me and Di Piero?

Did he—how did he act?—did he want you to go anywhere with him, did he make any—you know—suggestions—

For Christ's sake, Owen, Kirsten said irritably, we were walking in the goddam park all the time, what do you think?

She was fucking him too. Di Piero. Off and on. Do you think he's in love with her? What's the story about that?

I don't know, I have to hang up. This call is costing too much.

Do you think he hates her too? Which is why he might have told the truth about her?

I have to hang up, Owen, Kirsten said.

But Di Piero—

Enough of Di Piero, Kirsten said. The line clicked, the dial tone hummed.

Owen jerks convulsively out of his light slumber, sees that it is five minutes past four, why is the lamp switched on, why is he dressed in his underwear?—the elastic band of his shorts cuts into his flesh and has become unpleasantly damp.

I won't get through the night, he thinks.

He might telephone Lynn Fischer, she is comforting to talk with, but he remembers that they are no longer friends, something terrible has happened, why is he losing everyone? His suitemates avoid him, his adviser is "disappointed," the red-haired theater major in his history seminar no longer suggests they have coffee at the Annex. . . . My car broke down on the Deegan Expressway, he told Lynn, hours late for their meeting, I'm in the goddam fucking Bronx, please forgive me, I'm not in a good state of mind for communication right now, can I call you back tomorrow? And of course she was sympathetic. In fact gravely concerned for his safety.

But subsequent dates, broken, have dissuaded her of Owen Halleck's affection. And even his sincerity. Or his capacity for monitoring the truth.

I'm going through some problems right now, he said, I can't explain over the phone, I'll try to write, he said, suddenly bored with the need to explain or the need to believe he should explain the ambagious maneuvers of his psyche to anyone not his sister, his twin. But when will I see you, Owen, Lynn said impatiently, and he said, Sometime, and she said, Sometime—when is that? and he had to stifle an angry yawn, disturbed by the violence of blood rushing into his penis, which he guessed was not for Lynn Fischer. She seemed to sense his emotion for she said in a voice edged with tears: Then go to hell! Go to hell and don't come bothering me again!

And so he has not, he has not bothered her again, or any other young woman of his acquaintance.

Which is one of the reasons, he supposes, that his sexual fantasies have become so lively and so lurid and so engrossing of late. And so shameful.

Kroll

It doesn't surprise me that Preston Kroll was a disappointment, Ulrich May says. The propaganda of the word—as opposed to the purity of the deed—is always disappointing.

He was the only person who seemed sympathetic with my father, Owen says. He did a long piece for the *New Republic* last November. . . . And his reputation here . . .

His reputation! May says. You will learn how little "reputation" means . . . how little it means to *us*.

No one else will talk with me now, Owen says slowly, marveling. The network must be tighter than I had thought. It must be sensitive and quivering as a spiderweb. . . . I telephoned an old friend of my father's named Seawright but his secretary wouldn't put him on. I telephoned his home but a maid answered. Then a man, I don't know who. . . . I called this contemptible little Bobbie Tern, you know, the gossip columnist, but couldn't get through. If I give my name they don't want to talk with me and if I give a false name they don't want to talk with me.

A false name? What is your false name?

Oh—anything. Snatched out of the air. A billboard, a magazine cover.

I'm just curious. Sometimes a false name is revealing. You don't recall? May says with a soft encouraging smile.

It wouldn't be revealing, Owen says vaguely, scratching his jaw. It would only disclose . . . a certain poverty of imagination.

233

Such as—?

I really don't remember. Brown, I think. William Brown.

Ulrich May considers the name doubtfully. "William Brown," he says as if testing it. —Yes, I think you're right, Owen, a certain poverty of imagination. It calls no significant associations to my mind.

Preston Kroll poked the ice cubes in his drink with a knobby forefinger and spoke rapidly, in a somewhat slurred voice, of matters Owen knew or half-knew or had assumed from his own research. *That's Some Chicken!* had been carelessly stuffed with this information. The conspiracy charges to be brought against the copper companies, the scandal of American involvement in the overthrow of Allende, Nixon and Kissinger and probable assassination orders, the more recent deaths of Allende's former ambassador to Washington Letelier and a young couple named Naumann found bludgeoned "to pulp" in a Mexican village near Mazatlán, on the ocean. . . . Owen listened politely, tried not to fidget. It was difficult to interrupt Kroll or even to direct the angry flow of his words.

He asked about this alleged contact man "Tom Gast."

Gast, said Kroll contemptuously, Gast is a pal of Di Piero's and they've both disappeared.

Di Piero hasn't disappeared, Owen said. He lives in New York.

Gast has been bought off handsomely, I don't mean for the original work he did but for the cover-up. He's in Geneva. Or Rome.

But who exactly is Gast? Owen asked, confused. Someone said it was just a name—there wasn't anyone—

Gast has a law degree from Fordham and trained for the F.B.I. in Louisiana and was assigned to a West Coast bureau for a while . . . then he dropped out. I had some talks with him in the sixties, I was doing that series of articles on the F.B.I., you might recall, exposing not just their tactics but their asininity . . . their utter mind-blowing incredible asininity. You might recall. There were six articles and they appeared in a local newspaper with delusions of being national, Kroll said bitterly, I won't bother to say the name because we both know it, they appeared and caused a great deal of stir and there was a rumor about the Pulitzer . . . but the paper pulled the rug out from under me, betrayed me, I won't bore you with the details. I knew Gast then.

Is this Gast a friend of—my mother's? Owen asked shyly.

I knew Gast then but not really: he was an opportunist, a wise guy, he embroidered tales about the F.B.I. I would have swallowed if I hadn't checked them out. But the essential point is, the blundering and incompetence and naïveté of the Bureau. The banality of evil—that sort of thing.

Gast— Is he a friend of—

Maybe I made my point too often, maybe I was too shrill. They said that about the Cambodian series too. What do you think?

What do I think? About—?

My series on Cambodia. Or don't you read the *Times?*

I—I—I wasn't very political then. This was a few years ago?

Gast is sharp, you have to hand it to him, Kroll said, waving for a waiter. Di Piero too. I knew him for a while—he was poking around in Hong Kong when I was assigned there—drug trade—quite a network —Di Piero had delusions of being a great journalist and thought he'd plug in with me.

Journalist? Di Piero?

You're quite right: he stinks. No style.

I don't think Tony Di Piero has ever been a journalist, Owen said, actually he's an old friend of the family, I mean I know him a little, I think you're confusing him with someone else. . . . He works for a bank. International finance. I mean, he studied international finance after college. He and my father knew each other when they were . . .

He's a common criminal, Di Piero. A pig at the trough. Like all of them. What can you expect?—Agnew, Nixon. No point in getting caught in the cross fire. I've taken a vow of silence, it's my only form of protest, I refuse to expose corruption if no one gives a shit about it, I'm fed up to here, he said, drawing his finger across his Adam's apple. Go tell them. Your parents' friends. Nick Martens—he's a friend, right? Go tell him. *Preston Kroll has taken a vow of silence.*

What do you know about Nick Martens? Owen asks. His fingers pluck at his jaw, a stranger's whiskers. I mean, was he, was he one of—

Nick and I used to meet for a drink now and then, back in the early seventies. He admired my writing, he said, the vividness of the descriptions, Vietnam, Cambodia, he said he could sympathize with my disappointment—that readers stopped reacting—editors stopped being really interested. Wars like that drag on, material becomes repetitious. That's why everyone loved the Six-Day War. My prose style never slackened, my eye for the precise detail never failed, but it was—what the hell— it was like the performance of a medieval martyr—who am I thinking of?—some saint who helped his torturers pull out his guts—yards and yards of them, more and more, hand over hand, I mean it's a clown routine actually—there *is* a saturation point—people start to yawn. Nick sympathized when I was called back home even though—you probably know this—he was convinced we had to do it.

Had to do it—?

Vietnam, Cambodia. He was convinced. Is convinced. Not a hothead, not an idiot, but he just has this . . . big rock in his head. The United States versus the world. Our allies too—they're not dependable. Only the enemies are dependable. That sort of thing, you can't argue, Kroll said in disgust, waving again for the waiter. Hey! Over here! You blind?

Nick is my godfather, Owen said shyly.

Law-and-order man, perfect choice for the Commission, Kroll said, not having heard Owen. Dress up the image a little. After the— you'll excuse me—fiasco your father brought off.

My father was innocent, Owen said, shocked.

He was innocent, he was *dumb*, Kroll said, that's innocent around here. Believe me. I knew Maurice, knew him to talk to, knew the old man as well, your grandfather, eh?—fascinating old guy. Close-mouthed, though. That generation was, unless they kept diaries, in which case— Christ! Fantastic. Can't begin to compete.

You didn't know my father, Owen said. He didn't know you.

Of course we knew each other, everyone knows everyone else in Washington, Kroll said, as incredulously as if Owen had reached over to pinch him. Where've you been, kid? In the seminary? Playing ostrich? I knew Maurice and Maurice knew me and we respected each other, I mean once I allowed for the man's limitations. Sweet but dumb. Killing himself for chicken feed—negotiating for chicken feed.

What are you saying? Owen cried.

You don't think $250,000 is chicken feed? Well, it is. Around here, these times, it is. Your father must have known. Sweet man, very patient, very kind, but he couldn't see how GBT would just outmaneuver him, it's done every day. Make the bid and play around with it and threaten to withdraw and plead nolo contendere and meanwhile giving lots of parties, presents, PR crap, big glossy ads in the magazines, public TV, specials, weekends in Puerto Rico or Haiti. That sort of thing. You can't compete.

Did Nick Martens have anything to do with—

He was a C.I.A. man, did you know?—maybe still is. No secret. Sent on missions to the Mideast, to Italy. I mean, you're a friend of his, what the hell, nudge him in the ribs and he'll tell you some juicy stories. I fought them for years, I exposed them, Nixon and Kissinger and the others, long before Watergate, I wore myself out in the jungle, I tried to say what I saw, what I knew, let the reading public draw its own conclusions, be vivid, be dramatic, go for the jugular vein, but . . . the fuckers have no mercy, they lose interest fast. And once your prose style slackens the intelligentsia writes you off.

But Nick— Did Nick—

We flew to Frankfurt together once, early sixties, he was on his way to Stockholm to check out the anti-American flak there. Had a long conversation. You have to admire the man for his style, his energy, even when his ideas are shit. This whole upsurge of American patriotism—shit.

Owen stared sightlessly as a black waiter brought Preston Kroll a third martini. His blood pounded hotly in his ears. He said, after a moment, Your piece on the incident was sympathetic to my father. You came very close to making explicit charges against certain individuals. And now you seem to be saying—

I *was* sympathetic to your father, I *am* sympathetic to him, Kroll said with a weary impatience, sympathy is a way of showing unsympathy for the opposition—get it? The enemy.

What enemy? Who?

He was a sweet guy, just too trusting. Maybe a little stupid. Lamb among wolves—that sort of thing. I used to watch him up there, handling the big-time stuff, some of those prosecutions he worked were elegantly done—though maybe that was Martens's touch: they were a well-balanced team—and *did* surprise a lot of us who are supposed to know what is about to break. But I thought—that guy's time is running out. It's getting too hot. It can't last.

I don't understand, Owen said.

What's to understand? Kroll said carelessly, swallowing a mouthful of his drink. Who's asking?

Owen hid his face in his hands. He was not crying but his shoulders shook.

Look, kid, Kroll said in a gentler voice, tapping him on the arm, hey, kid, look: you'll get over it. Okay? You hear? You'll get over it like the rest of us.

The Swimming Pool

Though it will not be a gun Owen Halleck will use on his mother it is a gun he grips tightly in both hands, in a dream of such ecstatic clarity that he realizes, even while asleep, it cannot be real.

They are in the swimming pool behind the house. He is pursuing her. She tries to swim to safety and he plunges after her and for a terrible moment nearly loses his balance. Her scream is silent but he knows she is screaming. Her face is hidden from him but he knows it is Isabel.

Owen Halleck, bent at the knees, his arms extended straight, two hands gripping the handle of the gun, his shoulders hunched as if to protect the back of his neck—a classic stance. He must have seen the posture in innumerable newspaper photographs without grasping its significance.

He pulls the trigger. There is a rush of thin quick pleasureless sensation in his groin. He wakes, moaning aloud, in an unfamiliar room —a room whose strangeness, in the moment before he recalls the hotel and Washington, draws all his concern.

He is to remember a swimming pool. But why a swimming pool, and which swimming pool? He goes into the bathroom. Avoids his eyes in the mirror. Why a swimming pool, he wonders in disgust. His mind is blank and soiled as the porcelain sink.

The Convert

Perhaps because of the strong drink Ulrich May has given him, on a
near-empty stomach, perhaps because of the nervous exhilaration of the
day—which has involved not only the meeting with Preston Kroll but a
determined walk past the Halleck house on Röcken, and an equally
self-conscious and agitated walk past the brownstone on N Street where
Nick now lives; or perhaps it is a consequence of the queer exaltation of
the night itself, which promises so much—but Owen has begun to feel
very strange, very strange indeed. His eyes cannot remain in focus, his
stomach is lurching. He cannot be sick. He will not be sick. He wonders
if his face is as blanched as it feels. . . .

Midnight. Or later. And he is standing in his bare tender feet on
the extraordinary Uruguayan carpet (made not with synthetic hair after
all but genuine human hair, gorgeously black—hence its special appeal)
and staring at the photographs on the stark white walls of Ulrich May's
bedroom. He *cannot* be sick.

You're very quiet, May says, surely you have some response. . . .

A dozen photographs, black-and-white glossies, framed in unobtrusive metal. One shows what appears to be a littered concrete floor,
wet with puddles of oil. Uniformed men are grouped in conversation,
unaware of the camera. Another photograph shows a demolished helicopter, bodies, a single jump-suited figure with his arms stretched to the
sky. Another photograph . . .

Owen blinks and rubs at his eyes. He cannot be seeing what he
is seeing.

You're quite right about suicide as aborted murder, May is saying. Cowardly murder. The bourgeois reflex. *We* prefer to strike at our enemies instead of internalizing them.

We—? says Owen weakly.

We in a manner of speaking, says May at once. Not literally.

Owen makes an effort to study the photographs. He stumbles against a little lacquered table. May sets it aright and gives Owen a friendly push, saying, This photograph of the Lod attack is possibly my favorite. I mean, one is struck initially by the composition—the sheer formalism of the thing—which the photographer caught quite by accident. Photography is such an extraordinary art, isn't it!—capturing the moment, the half-instant, the dazzlingly ephemeral. And it always seems anonymous, which is the highest praise.

Yes, says Owen, staring at a large starkly black-and-white photograph over the bed. Distorted shapes, eerie slashes of light and shadow, the harsh texture of concrete. . . . He blinks and is seeing bodies. Blood, damp, debris. His stomach lurches.

The Japanese Red Army, says May, *Rengo Sekigun,* three of their bravest men, back in 1972. Certainly this was their finest moment. They simply arrived in Lod Airport—in Israel—and claimed their luggage—and calmly opened fire—automatic assault rifles without stocks, shrapnel grenades. They sprayed the crowd—it must have been chaos! —imagine the screams, people scrambling for cover, no one comprehending, no one even knowing where death was coming from. It lasted only a few minutes, of course. One of the soldiers was killed by gunfire and another by his own grenade and the third—unfortunately—was captured when his ammunition ran out. I say unfortunately for of course he should not have outlived this extraordinary piece of revolutionary theater. . . . Do you remember the incident, Owen? The bourgeois press made much of it.

Yes, says Owen, I don't know. I . . .

The sensation in his stomach deepens, grows heavy. He turns away in alarm. His distracted gaze roams the high white walls, the oversized bed with its black satin cover, the enormous window overlooking the city, a single broad mirror which should give him his own reflection but appears blurred, misted-over. . . . He wonders where he is. Why he has allowed this man to bring him here. What will happen. What has already happened. Shouldn't he simply go home?—find a cab and go home to his own boyhood bed? It isn't too late. Isabel will forgive him.

The Red Army revolutionaries were allies, of course, of the PFLP, May is saying conversationally, but the Israeli security people were totally surprised. Three young Japanese tourists—what could be more

innocent? They had volunteered as soldiers in the Arab struggle knowing that they couldn't escape from the airport—their act was sacrificial
—their courage extraordinary. *We three soldiers, after we die, want to
become three stars of Orion,* the survivor said. *The revolution will go
on and there will be many more stars.*

Yes, says Owen, swallowing carefully. Ulrich May seems to have
awakened from his amiable languor and is speaking now in an almost
urgent voice. Owen listens, nodding faintly, tasting something darkly
sour at the back of his mouth.

May would like to tell Owen of his "conversion."

Conversion *is* an authentic phenomenon, he says, it's absolutely
—authentic. If you have any doubts it's simply because you have never
had the experience.

No, says Owen. He finds himself nervously sipping from his drink,
which has a powerful medicinal taste. I mean—yes.

Of course my role in the struggle is only as an observer, May
explains. I give sympathy, I see myself as an amateur theoretician, I am
not committed to any single group. I don't give money or supplies—I
don't even help with passports—though I've given loans to individuals
occasionally—the poor Naumanns—but—I don't give money or supplies,
you must understand.

Owen murmurs assent. Out of the corner of his eye he watches
May, whose fair, smooth skin glows a little with the lamplight and with
the emotion underlying his speech. —I was rather slow to awake, in fact,
May says with a low incredulous laugh. Slept through most of Vietnam
—Cambodia—all that slaughter—too absorbed in my own insular life. I
may have mentioned earlier that I am an amateur historian—working
with family archives primarily. My family is so wonderfully "old"—they
arrived *before* the Mayflower! I'm now dissociated from them so I won't
bore you with a recitation of their public offices and their private crimes
except to mention that Samuel Sloan, you know, the architect who did
your house on Röcken—he's one of my ancestors, one of my favorite
ancestors. You do live in that stone Georgian on Röcken, at the end of
the street?—yes?—it's a jewel inside and out. A small house for the
neighborhood, wonderfully compact. I haven't been a guest of your
mother's for a decade now—we move in somewhat different circles,
generally—but I recall being agreeably surprised at the interior. A lot
of rococo-Chinese things that quite fit in with the spirit of Sloan's inten-
tions, and some exquisite painted panels in the dining room. . . . And, my
God, that mosaic-thing by Klimt, a sleeping woman with long tangled
hair. . . . May I freshen your drink, Owen?

No thank you, Owen murmurs.

It isn't disturbing—my mentioning your home? You seem rather upset.

I—I—I am not upset, thank you, Owen says with a shaky smile.

But you *despise* your home, is that it?

I despise its inhabitant, Owen says, clearing his throat. For a moment he feels less precarious; the weight in his bowels seems to have settled.

Quite right, May says with a shudder, she's an absolutely virulent creature. If May is aware of Owen's startled response he gives no indication but continues, conversationally: Your mother isn't so much depraved and vicious and selfish as she is utterly worthless—litter—a piece of trash. I mean actual *litter* on the face of the earth. She's the daughter of a fascist gangster who surely deserved to die a far more fitting death than he did . . . he simply died of a stroke, didn't he? There *is* no justice.

Yes, says Owen, he died a few years ago . . . of a series of strokes.

You're right to despise them, your instincts are unerring, May says, leading Owen to inspect another of the photographs, which showed only a single corpse: a strikingly handsome young man with shoulder-length hair, a dark mustache, parted lips. Owen looks away but May urges him to turn back. A hero of the revolution, an anonymous young Basque, May says, executed without trial by firing squad. . . . He was a member of the Revolutionary Anti-Fascist and Patriotic Front and I know nothing about him except the fact that he was brave, he was willing to sacrifice himself for the struggle, he died without sentiment. At this time Franco was still alive but he too died a couple of months later. After these executions, May says contemptuously, the so-called free world made their usual paltry protests—withdrew ambassadors, gave speeches at the UN—scolded Spain in the press—but the furor quickly died down. He's so very beautiful, isn't he, in death?—skin that resembles marble, black silky hair. . . .

Owen blinks tears out of his eyes. It is absurd. He is being absurd. But it strikes him as intolerable that the corpse is lying on the ground . . . in the dirt. A young man not much older than Owen himself, sprawled limply on the ground, his head turned to one side, hair loose, eyes partly open, mouth arrested in a grimace of alarm. . . .

And here, May says, slipping his arm around Owen's shoulders, here is something more encouraging, you see here . . . one of the Milan bombings. Several groups took credit but it's generally known that Bertoli did it, Gianfranco Bertoli, one of the most interesting members of the Italian resistance . . . I call it "resistance," of course because that is what our struggle essentially is. . . . The corpses are those of enemies only. It was quite a slaughter—quite a coup. That headless body you can tell by its uniform was a policeman. . . . Unfortunately

Bertoli was arrested and imprisoned for life and I don't know of his fate since then, the Italian situation is so extremely complicated. The *Brigata Rossa* has been going through such unhappy crises lately, this past year. . . . I really don't know what will happen. But the revolutionary spirit certainly will reemerge. Perhaps in even more extraordinary forms. Don't you think?

Yes, says Owen. He presses his glass against his forehead but the glass is no longer very cool.

You're *sure* I can't freshen your drink?—you look a little pale.

Thank you, no. I feel fine. I don't even feel tired. I—I feel fine, Owen says.

You've undergone a considerable experience, May says quietly, and you are nearly out of it—I can tell, I too possess certain unerring instincts—you have nearly come through. But of course the process *can* be accelerated. One *can* be converted in a single night.

Yes, says Owen, I believe that. I understand.

One goes slowly, and then one goes quickly. Baby steps and then a single giant step. Yes? *A revolution moves at the pace of a dove,* the admirable Nietzsche said, which is absolutely true, and so is the reverse true—at a somewhat later stage. We move slowly in order to one day move quickly.

Slowly in order to move quickly, Owen says. Yes. I see.

Do you see? Do you see any kinship between us? May asks.

Owen slips away from the warm weight of May's arm, though he does not find it unpleasant: only sinister. Kinship, he whispers, staring at the photographs, beginning to be mesmerized by them or by the secret exhilaration of the night or simply by Ulrich May's patrician voice, in which pride and humility are oddly mixed. This is Ulrike Meinhof, Owen says, startled that a face should be familiar, isn't it?—the German terrorist—

Revolutionary, May says, yes it's Meinhof before she went underground—years ago. Not *terrorist* but *revolutionary.* Are you composing copy for the bourgeois press?

She committed suicide, Owen says, studying the hard handsome unsmiling face. A woman in her thirties, with the eyes of a man, her intelligent gaze affixed to his. She committed suicide, Owen says almost reproachfully, hanged herself in her cell. . . .

A necessary act, May says reverently. Done precisely at the right time. Not only necessary—inevitable.

Is death a triumph, then? Owen asks.

Only when it's inevitable.

She looks so strong. So certain of herself. Those eyes. . . . She had no weaknesses, then? Owen asks hesitantly.

She married—she had children—twins, in fact. At one time she was a pacifist. And she underwent brain surgery, for the removal of a tumor. There was a metal clip implanted in her head, May says, peering at the photograph, but of course you can't see it. . . . Of course she had weaknesses, she was a human being like you and me.

I couldn't hang myself, Owen says.

Certainly you could—if it was necessary.

I'm a coward, I'm terrified of pain, Owen laughs, count me out. . . . Her friend's name was Baader? Is his picture here? What happened to him? The Baader-Meinhof gang, wasn't it?

Rote Armee Fraktion, May says with a slight edge to his voice. Baader isn't here but this is Holger Meins, still alive, near the end of his ordeal . . . his hunger strike. An unforgettable picture, isn't it?

Owen nervously studies the photograph, which is positioned over May's bed. A young man in his early thirties is lying on what appears to be, oddly, a bier . . . the fluffed-up pillow beneath his head is edged with prominent dainty lacework, as is the comforter that has been drawn up to his shoulders. His skeletal arms lie atop the cover and his long-fingered hands are crossed. Black limp hair, a very black beard, thick black eyebrows. He wears unusually small wire-rimmed glasses with perfectly round lenses and his eyes are shut—the black eyelashes emphatic as lines drawn in ink.

He isn't dead yet?—but he looks dead, Owen says quietly. And then, almost reproachfully: He looks like Jesus Christ.

That observation has been made by more than one person, May says.

Are they all dead? Owen asks scornfully, waving at the photographs. All? All of them?

Of course not, May says. Don't be absurd.

Owen strides about the room fueled with a strange sickish energy. The bloodied corpses of schoolchildren; the famous photograph of Huey Newton ("Minister of Defense, Black Panther Party") in his regal bamboo-backed chair, a rifle in his right hand and a spear—is it a fishing spear?—in his left; Japanese college students looking young as children fighting one another with iron bars and poles. Stark whites, starker blacks. Some of the photographs are dizzy with motion. Owen draws breath to speak but cannot for a long moment say a word.

He points almost at random, at the photograph of the smashed and flaming helicopter. This, what's this? he asks.

Munich, May says, 1972, one of our historic moments—the Olympics—remember?

Oh yes, Owen says, excited, I do remember, Kirsten and I

watched it on television—we were alone together—I don't know where
my parents were—I remember—Jesus, it was awful—I'll never forget
—oh yes—we were watching the Olympics and then *that* happened—I
was really scared—and Kirsten too—it went on and on and we couldn't
turn it off—we just sat there—we wouldn't eat, we wouldn't come away
from the television—the cook begged us but we wouldn't come—it was
terrible, the Israeli athletes—the hostages— And then, how did it end?
—I think they were all killed. Jews and Arabs, all killed.

Nevertheless it was a glorious moment, a real triumph, May says,
one of the best examples of the propaganda of the deed. Because it
involved so many millions of people. Because it moved so inexorably to
its flaming conclusion.

Black—Arabs? Palestinians? What did they call themselves?

Black September, May says. That's a Septembrist commando
leaping into the air, with his arms outflung. He has only a few seconds
to live. Perhaps in fact he is already dead.

How many died at Munich? Owen asks.

Not many, says May. That isn't the point. The point is the gesture,
the international attention, the triumph of the Arabs. It was quite right
that they were given heroes' funerals in Tripoli. The Black Septembrists
at their prime were an extraordinary group—geniuses of a sort—I mean
geniuses of the body—absolutely dedicated—fearless—the will made
flesh. Now that Haddad has been killed, however—the future is uncertain.

But how many did die, Owen asks. I seem to remember—a lot. A
lot.

No, only sixteen. Eleven Jews, five Arabs. Seventeen if you count
a German police officer killed by gunshot.

I seem to remember a lot more, I would have guessed thirty or
forty, Owen says slowly, pulling at his chin whiskers. Poor Kirsten was
so frightened . . . I was almost afraid to go to bed myself. My father,
you know, off and on, and probably more frequently than we were told
—his life was threatened. Bodyguards were assigned, F.B.I. men I suppose, the Munich massacre really scared us, Kirsten and me, we thought
they might bomb the house some night, or put a bomb in Daddy's car
. . . or we might be out walking somewhere, on the street, going to a
movie or something . . . he sometimes took us to movies on Sundays
. . . and a car would drive by and spray the three of us with machine-gun
bullets.

Owen is half-smiling. Because he feels the violent need to cry. He
stands swaying, turned slightly away from May, and for a long embarrassing moment he cannot speak.

May says softly, touching his arm: Of course your father was killed, but not by revolutionaries, you must know that. He was simply doomed. He couldn't have escaped. And I hope I won't upset you, Owen, by suggesting—hesitantly enough—that your father, as an official in the U.S. Government, as the Director of the Commission for the Ministry of Justice—absurd title!—was contaminated by his association—he *was* doomed—I mean morally and spiritually—though I'm willing to believe that he was the best of the lot. He *did* want to act against the fascist regime in Chile, he *did* build a case, however feeble. . . . But it was hopeless, it was and is doomed, there's no possibility for justice within the context of the existing society. The enemy is everywhere: the enemy *is* this nation, and particularly this ludicrous city. Imperialist, capitalist, racist . . . simply doomed. Are you all right? Are you terribly upset?

He didn't deserve to die, Owen says, biting at his lip. I mean—he was innocent. They killed him, they ran him off the road, he didn't deserve that fate, drowning in a swamp, in mud. . . . You didn't know him, you don't know the first thing about him. . . .

I can see that you loved him very much, May says with equanimity, but consider: he was a lawyer, an officer of the court, he swore to uphold the U.S. Constitution, he was a salaried employee of an utterly corrupt and criminal government. I am willing to believe that he was a good man and a good father, or at least that he impressed you as such, but, after all . . . It isn't my role in life to humor people, and certainly not a young man with your intelligence.

He was *innocent,* Owen says. He didn't accept any fucking bribe —he didn't write those notes—he was railroaded—he was coerced—they hired someone to follow him and harass him and eventually run him off the road—

"Innocent" in your terms is simply irrelevant, May says, squeezing Owen's shoulder. You're a very confused young man. In fact, anyone who worked for the Commission for the Ministry of Justice certainly *should* have accepted bribes—he might reasonably have demanded them—given that the entire Commission is a joke, and the present government of the United States an outlaw fascist government. When one is at war one can't afford the luxury of minuscule moral distinctions.

War? Owen says, blinking. Are we at war?

I knew your father socially, and I liked him very much—socially. In that context. But he was one of the enemy and in a sense—in a very broad sense—I hope I'm not offending you?—he did deserve to die: but only because he was the salaried employee of a murderous government. Within that government, inside that context of utter rot—there can't be any innocence, only evil. The connecting glue is evil.

Who's at war? Owen says. I don't understand.

For instance, Maurice Halleck headed an office that once barred a young lawyer friend of mine from meeting with one of his clients, a Black Panther guerrilla awaiting trial here in Washington—in fact my young friend was arrested. The charges were that the defense counsel was acting as a courier—carrying messages in and out of jail—and your father's office was totally unsympathetic with the situation.

He didn't deserve to die, Owen cries.

They *all* deserve to die—don't you see? May says with a throaty laugh. But—unfortunately—we don't have that much time.

Ulrich May's conversion, it turns out, had taken place in March 1973, in Khartoum, as a consequence of the Black September guerrilla raid on the Saudi Arabian Embassy.

But my godfather Nick Martens was there too, Owen says excitedly, the two of you must have met—

I was acquainted with Martens long before Khartoum, May says stiffly. You seem to forget: everyone knows everyone else in Washington. It's a version of hell.

You were there in Khartoum—both of you?—taken hostage at the same time?—in the Saudi Embassy—

We weren't taken hostage, May says, the commandos were very discriminating. They kept five or six people—Americans, Belgians, the Jordanian ambassador—and released the rest of us. It was an extraordinary experience. One minute we were all chattering in the luxurious garden of the Saudi Embassy, the next minute—eight guerrilla fighters had forced their way in. Everything came to a stop. A full stop. *Our* illusory social world gave way to their world . . . it simply collapsed, surrendered. You have no idea.

May falls silent. Owen wants to ask him again about Nick, but hesitates. What an extraordinary coincidence! It is simply another example of how *things rush together. Into focus.*

Aloud he says in a calm voice: You must have been terrified. You could have been killed.

But I could be "killed," my dear boy, at any time, May says lightly. Mugged and beaten on the street, stabbed on a whim, hit by a car—the traffic problem in this city is getting worse every day. Isn't that right? Even bringing you up to my apartment is a risk, isn't it?

Owen does not look at him. He says guiltily, A risk? Me—?

Of course. I approached you at the Moultons' because you *did* look—shall we say—distraught. And lonely. Murmuring and laughing to yourself.

I wasn't murmuring and laughing to myself, Owen says sharply.

Phillip was worried, he and Charlotte didn't know how to proceed, of course they're fond of you and of course they're sympathetic—they feel such *guilt*. And they wouldn't want to offend your mother. So, May says with an expansive sigh, I simply volunteered. Let me talk to the boy, let me take care of the situation, I told Phillip. Don't sic your bodyguards on him.

They hadn't better have touched me, Owen murmurs.

Befriending you—I could see that you badly needed a friend—and bringing you here tonight was a risk I thought worthwhile, May says. My own life—well—I detest personal "confessions"—but it's hardly a secret that my own life is of very little significance—not just because of my class, my background, but in general: my physical cowardice, my moral impotence. . . . I, Ulrich May, could never be capable of the acts of heroism required by the revolution, I only stand and wait, as it were, offering sympathy, sometimes a little more. . . . So while bringing you back with me might have proven dangerous—you could suddenly go berserk, I know that tenuous preppie restraint—I went to Choate and Princeton, myself—at the same time I reasoned that you are, after all, the son of Maurice Halleck; and that your father's death, ignoble as it was, might be having a salutary effect upon you.

No one had better touch me, Owen says, shivering. And then, looking up: My father—? You said—?

It occurred to me that his death might have awakened you to the fact of our war, if not to its ambiguous nature.

War, says Owen, chewing at his lip, yes, war, I think so, yes . . .

Not so much because of the death itself but because of the revelations that have attended it, and have received an unusual amount of publicity in the press—the very press, I should say, that refused to publish the real news about Chile at the time these things, these crimes, were being perpetrated. But now this old "news" is marketable. We have Chile, we have the Dominican Republic, we have the example of Nicaragua, in fact nearly the entire "free world" . . . the fascist-imperialist empire, supposedly invisible. So I looked at you and saw not the flabby slouching grimacing half-drunk kid who might be, from the rear, middle-aged: I looked at you and thought, *He is one of us.*

You did? Owen says sharply. *One of us* . . .

A soldier. A commando. A guerrilla. In embryo. Awaiting birth.

A guerrilla—! Owen says, laughing, choking. His teeth click on the rim of his glass. Oh, that's fantastic, that's—oh, you don't know—Jesus, I wish my kid sister was here—

What does your sister have to do with us? May asks irritably.

A commando, a guerrilla, oh, that's—fantastic—that's almost too much, Owen says, wiping his chin. Can I telephone her? What time is it? He rises from the edge of the bed on which he is sitting but sinks back again helplessly. Hey look—it's really too much—I think I'd better call her—

How old is your sister? May asks.

Seventeen.

Seventeen is too young.

She's in love with Nick Martens, Owen says, laughing. She wants to kill him. Assassinate him.

May says nothing for a brief while. And then, casually: He was a C.I.A. agent in the seventies, we're quite sure. The evidence suggests it was so.

He killed my father. He's responsible. Nick and—her.

He was probably in the Mideast spying on his own people, May says. I had the impression from the Foreign Service officers that they were a little wary of him . . . though I can't be sure. *He* killed your father?

It was a conspiracy. There were at least two people, Owen says.

I would have thought . . . there were more than that, May says.

Owen laughs airily and rolls his glass between his palms. Oh hey, it's too much—I *should* call her—unless the switchboard is turned off —what time is it?—no, damn, it's too late—

You and your sister are very close?

Oh, very very close, Owen says, actually we're twins, Siamese twins. Always have been. But lately—lately—the cord is pulling tight.

She has a fantasy about killing Nick Martens? May says, amused.

Tell me about him, what do you know about him?—the two of you were in Khartoum together—

I was a private traveler, winding my way through the Mideast— not for the first time: I've always been very idle—I'd spent two weeks in Teheran, some time in Turkey (which, incidentally, is a fascinating country), and of course Israel (which I didn't realize was an outlaw state at the time—I rather liked the Israeli people) and of course Egypt—the Nile trip, the pyramids, and all that. So I came to visit friends—acquaintances, really—I haven't any friends—in Khartoum—Foreign Service officers—and Nick Martens was there at the same time—not such a coincidence as you might think, Owen, since Americans in that part of the world always run into each other. Whether he was a government agent or not I really don't know and at that time I had no thoughts on the subject: my life was insular and utterly self-absorbed, like most lives. I was a somnambulist during the imperialist slaughter in Vietnam and

Cambodia . . . amazing. My conversion came rather late in life, I was almost fifty years old, but at least it did come . . . I'll be able to die with my eyes open.

Didn't they kill Americans there? Weren't you afraid? Owen asks, puzzled. How many did they kill?

Only three of the hostages, May says. But it was a triumph for Black September.

Did they kill—friends of yours?

Only one. The incoming ambassador.

But you didn't care? You weren't upset? —I don't understand, Owen says.

It was a great achievement for the Black September guerrillas— but then they've been one of the most spectacular commando teams all along, despite their small numbers. You might know that they were originally a splinter group of Al Fatah?—and their particular rage and grief derives from an unspeakable massacre of Palestinians by Jordanian troops in the pay of Israelis. It's a tragic part of the world, May says, shaking his head. You can't know.

I would have thought, Owen says slowly, that you might hate them . . . I mean, since they killed . . .

My emotions aren't that superficial, May says coldly. I can see, Owen, that you really are a stranger to the revolutionary code. I suppose you're sympathetic with the hostages in Iran!—no, don't bother telling me. I realize you're young and you are a Halleck, you descend from stock as contaminated as my own, not to mention—I won't mention—the unspeakable Spanish line, I realize all that, I must try to be patient, I mustn't get emotional, for after all my own conversion was long in coming. It's a failing, in fact, of most converts, the inability to sympathize with those who are yet blind. . . . Excuse my outburst.

They killed a friend of yours, and you didn't care? Owen asks weakly.

I *cared,* don't be absurd. As a private person of course I cared, how could I not? But in a larger sense . . . once my eyes were opened . . . of course I didn't *care,* in fact I applauded the execution. Do you know the writings of Laurent-Tailhade?—*What matter the victims, provided the gesture is beautiful?*

Nick Martens came away hating them, Owen says. The Palestinians, the Arabs, terrorists. . . .

Your friend is a fascist, Owen, your "godfather" as you fondly call him, and if you ever speak with him again—which I don't advise— you might tell him that all acts of terrorism stem from governments. Enormous tides of horror, suffering. . . . Incalculable atrocities. . . . I noted an article in the press not long ago that made the statement that the "terrorist toll" for 1979 was a "new record" . . . an absurdly paltry number of deaths . . . something less than six hundred! Six hundred! Which is nothing, nothing, set alongside the deaths caused by governments, or even the deaths caused by traffic accidents. . . . No, it's too laughable, I refuse to become excited.

Owen says in a slow dazed detached voice: But you didn't hate them. They came that close to you . . . and you didn't hate them afterward.

How could I "hate" such courageous men? May says simply. Black September guerrillas are simply extraordinary. They're organized in very small cells, they're highly professional and in contact with other revolutionary groups and *yet* . . . and yet they have no headquarters that I know of . . . no offices, no constraining ideology . . . in a sense, no soul. They're fiercely nationalistic, of course, but one thinks almost of the body's will . . . the physical organism . . . rather than anything so superficial as "spirit" or "soul."

They came that close to you, Owen says slowly. Without souls.

He blinks, he is having difficulty keeping his eyes in focus, something both alarming and wonderful is happening to him, the suspension of time, the rising floating miraculous carpet . . . which, too, drifts in and out of focus. Human hair, delicious human hair, jet-black and shining, gleaming, woven with feathers, his toes writhe convulsively, he has never experienced such a sensation in his life. . . . The hair of enemies, Ulrich May has told him, gloating. Oh, take off your shoes. *Take off your shoes.*

But May is still speaking. The voice goes on and on. A lullaby, immensely comforting. Hadn't his father read to him, many years ago, by his bedside . . . and when he was confined to his bed with colds . . . chickenpox . . . measles. Don't stop, Owen thinks. Oh, please.

Aloud he says in a voice that is surprisingly lucid, the kind of voice he summons forth for his seminars at the university: I find that remarkable, that you could detach yourself from your own emotions. From something so basic as fear and hatred . . . and a desire for revenge.

May grips his knees with both hands, the fingers interlocked, and lets his head fall slightly back. Ah, well—! Well. It was easier for me to feel simple visceral contempt for the embassy guests who panicked when the guerrillas ran in with their rifles—some of them even scrambled over the garden walls—and comic they were, too—like frightened chickens!—yes, it was much easier. Your friend Martens, and I, and a few others—Saudis, in fact—and the doomed Belgian—simply stood there, paralyzed with fear. I seemed to have turned to stone. Perhaps our panic was deeper than theirs but at least it had the appearance of dignity. . . .

How strange, Owen says dreamily, that he was there. And you. And now I'm here. The cord gets tighter.

The cord *is* tight. Very tight. Between each of us.

In the distance, a siren solitary and lovely as an owl's cry: one of those long-eared owls that haunt the woods surrounding Bitterfeld Lake. Owen, who has been easing slowly forward, his arms on his knees, pauses for a moment and listens. —I'm so unhappy, he says.

You'll transcend your emotions, May says bluntly, and rise to the point of being neither happy nor unhappy—only enlightened. But the way is difficult. The way demands discipline.

I did so much research, Owen says, laughing, I've always been a good student . . . the best of second-best. God *damn* it.

In the morning you can tell me about your sister. You can even telephone her, if you like.

She's very unhappy too. It came to me from her—the infection, Owen says. But she's right. She's right.

My conversion really began many years before Khartoum, of course, May says softly. His voice is low, level, consoling, melodic. A radio playing on and on. For now the siren has vanished and there is nothing else for Owen to fix upon. —My father, George M. May, was Ambassador to Argentina for six years . . . in the thirties . . . before Perón, it was that long ago . . . and though I was a very young boy at the time and completely sheltered from Argentine society, like most Foreign Service children, I was aware nevertheless of sporadic violence . . . uprisings . . . "guerrilla warfare" that was of course suicidal because it initiated such terrible reprisals. *Siempre la violencia!* When I was ten years old my father asked to be transferred to another part of the world —to a civilized part of the world!—and State sent him to Canada where he nearly expired of boredom; and we were so close to home, my mother and I were in Washington most of the time. So my foreign service days ended abruptly. But I think I remember the Argentine revolutionaries, I must remember their courage, their audacity, their physical strength . . . their tremendous will . . . which still lives in the Montoneros . . . though I have no contact with them, even indirectly. So my conversion was prepared for me. It lay dormant in me. You call us *terrorists* when you mean to say *martyrs*. You accuse us of trying to provide simple answers to complex questions when in fact we don't offer simple solutions, we don't offer solutions at all.

No solutions at all . . .

Owen's whisper is hoarse and tentative.

No solutions at all, my God yes, *yes*, no solutions at all. . . .

Fatigue overwhelms him but it is not a disagreeable sensation. He sees uniformed soldiers atop a great hill of human bones, he hears a woman's light jeering laughter, he sees again a boy hurrying past his mother's bedroom and not pausing to look inside, and then, suddenly, the boy is prowling in the basement of his house, he paws amidst soiled laundry, locates a pair of white cotton panties . . . a silky beige nightgown . . .

May is saying slowly: It has always seemed to me embarrassingly bourgeois, and tacky, to wish for *solutions*—not unlike the contemptible sort of mind that requires *causes*.

Yes, Owen says, laughing silently, yes, you're right.

The wave of fatigue deepens. He has never felt so exhausted: and yet it isn't a disagreeable sensation, for he is safe now, he will be taken care of, he will be understood. Ulrich May lowers his voice, to speak more gently, more soothingly, it is a lullaby he offers, a litany. O don't stop, Owen begs, don't leave me, I'm so lonely, I'm so afraid.

To his immense relief he feels May's fingers in his hair, gentle, stroking, fatherly, distant, O don't ever stop.

VI. The Game

Bitterfeld Lake,

July 1967

The Red Clay Court

Maurie Halleck and Nick Martens are playing a casual game of tennis late one Sunday afternoon on the Hallecks' new red clay court. The clay is the color of dried and faded blood, and dust from the men's rubber-soled shoes rises from it in startled spurts.

This has class, this has style, Nick has called out several times, meaning the new court. This is the real thing.

The old court was made of asphalt. For years it had been allowed to deteriorate: cracks, weeds, ground swellings, a rotted sagging net. This year the Hallecks—the "young Hallecks," that is, Maurie and Isabel—decided to tear it out and build a new court. The red clay was Isabel's idea though she rarely plays tennis and finds the game boring.

Hey, this is beautiful, Nick said when he first saw it, staring, smiling. He strode out onto the court and tapped it vigorously with his foot. What was here before, another court?—I don't remember.

A long lazy summer weekend. Houseguests at Bitterfeld, guests coming for dinner. Isabel is up at the lodge giving instructions to the cook—an amiable but slightly deaf woman in her sixties who appears to be, unless Isabel imagines it, part Indian; and who is in any case a staple of the camp, a long-time employee of the elder Hallecks not to be "let go" for another few years. Marrying into a family like the Hallecks, Isabel has noted to her woman friends, demands all the wiles of diplomacy: you can never exactly say which of their "gifts" is unwanted. And then after a while there's the danger that you won't remember.

Nick in white rumpled shorts and a T-shirt and blue tennis shoes;

sockless; his hair still wet from swimming, so dark it looks brown. Nick lazily returning Maurie's serves, which strike even the smallest children as both funny and desperate. He calls out: Not bad! from time to time and Maurie shrugs his shoulders, pleased and embarrassed. But Nick's own game this afternoon is loose and haphazard and only randomly inspired. For some years after college he had kept up his tennis, but gradually let it go. Though he and June joined an indoor club in Boston, and a luxurious one at that, it was always difficult for him to take the time. . . . He has been working so hard, so very hard, this past decade.

Shit, he says, slamming one of Maurie's high-sailing easy shots into the net; and then, recovering at once, calling out cheerfully: All right! Great! Your game!

Was that serve going to be good? Maurie asks doubtfully. I don't think it was.

On the line, Nick says. Great. Let's go.

How did it look to you? Maurie asks the children, his forehead crinkling. I think Nick was being generous, I don't *really* think . . .

Come on, Nick says, laughing, let's change sides.

So they change courts, and the green ball is thwacked back and forth, sometimes with startling precision, sometimes not, and Nick makes small stupid mistakes—not letting the ball drop enough before he strikes it, not troubling to bend his knees, misjudging distances, misjudging the strength of Maurie's backhand—and Maurie, like a boy, laughs in surprised delight whenever he makes a point.

It is soon clear that Maurie Halleck, by tradition an excellent loser, is a most discourteous winner: because, no doubt, he has had so little practice at winning.

So Nick instructs himself to calm down, to get serious, to make every stroke count; and he experiments with some techniques he hasn't tried for nearly a decade; and sometimes the ball smashes into just the right spot, and poor Maurie Halleck can't return it to save his life, and even if he gets his racquet up in time the ball is spinning so wickedly it will surely go out; and sometimes the ball smashes into the net, with a maniacal force that is rendered rather comic under the circumstances.

When Maurie returns a difficult shot Nick cannot help but be taken aback, and subtly insulted, as if some imposture is being perpetrated, some sly jest, and he must restrain himself from slamming the ball as hard as he can—for after all it's only a game—it's only a game —he's delighted, really, that Maurie is acquitting himself so well—he calls out, Great! Fine! Keep it up!—and settles in to play even harder, imagining how he looks on the court, his grace, his style, his ease, in contrast to Maurie's exertions, but then something goes wrong—a shitty idiotic mistake—and even if he wins a point it's a cheap point—and what is his little audience thinking, how are they assessing *Nick Martens,* do they give a damn that his serve is so ambitious, or that the sun is shining directly in his eyes, so that he is forced to squint almost continuously? —and where is Isabel?

That's enough for me, Maurie says, laughing.

Hell no, Nick says, it's your serve.

Twenty guests for dinner tonight, twenty-two, twenty-three, the Blondheims and the Averys are driving over from Saranac Lake, from the Blondheims' five-hundred-acre camp, and perhaps they are bringing a few other guests with them . . . and the Martenses and the Silbers are here for the weekend, Isabel is counting on her fingers, twenty-six, twenty-seven. Her hair is tied back with a red scarf in a fashion that appears to be casual. Her dress is a simple dark shift slit to mid-thigh at the sides. She is not thinking of the men playing tennis; she is not even thinking, at the moment, of Nick.

June Martens and her little girl Audrey and the Hallecks' little girl Kirsten walk by in their bathing suits, headed for the courts, and Isabel, on tiptoe, watches them pass but does not call out. I don't think she likes me, Isabel once told Nick, I think she senses something, and Nick said, June wouldn't like you anyway: you aren't her type.

The Silbers' shy daughter Ellen drifts into the kitchen and asks Isabel if she can help—set the table, maybe—arrange flowers—and Isabel resists the impulse to say no curtly (for *she* is hostess and supremely in charge in her own house, and nothing quite intoxicates her like party-giving and even its tedious preparations—how happy life is at such times, and how simple!)—though in fact she does say no, no thank you, Ellen, with her beautiful smile so placating that the girl blushes with pleasure and stammers a few inane remarks about the mountains, the mist last night that made everything so queer and scary and beautiful, and how she wishes she could learn to water-ski like her brother, and how exciting it is, the turn the investigation has taken, what can Senator Ewing say *now* . . .

June Martens and the little girls have joined the group at the tennis court, and are soon drawn into the game: for there's no denying it, the rhythm of the ball is hypnotic, the flying, the soaring, the crashing, the occasional volleys that go on and on and on despite Nick's powerful shots and Maurie's grunted returns: no denying it either that Maurie, scrambling about the court, even leaping into the air, panting and clumsy, is the favorite.

Poor Maurie! In his baggy seersucker shorts and yellow shirt, a pair of amber plastic lenses clipped to his glasses, out of breath, inconsistent in even the most elementary maneuvers, poor dear funny Maurie: it's impossible for the children, even Nick's child, to resist applauding him.

Of course the game is only a way of passing the time. It's harmless, it's good exercise, it isn't meant to be taken seriously. So Nick makes a show of being, suddenly, lazy; and even slovenly; for it *is* only a game and he has more important things on his mind than games. . . . After the long Fourth of July there will come Wednesday morning and everyone will return to court, real life will resume, play must be forgotten. I think we're going to eviscerate that old bastard, Nick has told Maurie and Reid, hardly daring to smile, he feels so certain, so exhilarated, I think we're going to suck his blood and the marrow of his rotten old bones. . . . Maurie thought it bad luck to say such things beforehand; but the old man *was* rather contemptible, wasn't he, blandly lying under oath, even when the evidence was out on the table. You might almost wonder, Maurie said, whether he really has forgotten: whether the pressure of the case has so affected him, he's lost his judgment. And Nick said irritably: No, he's just an inspired actor, they all are, mouthing that "Great Society" crap until I want to puke.

Still, said Maurie, it's hard not to feel sorry for him, or to feel something . . . his face is so blank, his eyes are so glassy. . . .

An inspired actor, Nick said.

Now the game is fifteen-love, now thirty-love, Maurie is staggering, perhaps Nick can win this set flat out and they can quit: but then, somehow, Maurie manages to return a vicious shot that Nick clearly didn't expect returned: and there is a brief volley: and Nick, his face reddened and contorted, slams the ball into the net.

Shit.

He wipes his forehead and covertly scans the figures at the edge of the court, but she isn't there, she isn't a witness, why the hell should he feel greatly humiliated, after all he *is* winning, and if he didn't hold back he could run Maurie into the ground. . . .

June waves impatiently and asks if this isn't the last game, after all it's nearly seven, they will be taking showers, won't they, hasn't this gone on long enough. . . .

My knee is killing me, Maurie says, laughing apologetically, but Nick is already in position to serve, rearing back, bringing the racquet down with that wicked twist he had worked so very hard on, in college, and the ball clears the net with a savage spin and strikes poor Maurie's feet and all the children giggle and Nick's heart swells near to bursting and he calls out: We have plenty of time, we're just getting hot, don't distract us.

Night Song

There: the glance, the spark, the tremulous incredible sensation: so deep inside it must be impersonal, remote and pitiless as the beating of her heart and the unfailing machinery of her organs: how to call it *hers* at all! A visitation, a lightning stroke, a feather's touch. But so fleeting.

She gains it, loses it. The angry need to draw it up again and give it strength, shape, focus: moving herself against him, her pelvis grinding wildly against him: I love you, oh please, don't, don't leave me—

Nick's warm weight upon her. The broad shoulders, the muscular sweat-slick back. The slap of their bellies. His mouth, his teeth, his tongue. He makes his claim again and again and again. She grinds herself against him, her eyes shut tight. The facial mask contorted. There is a sudden fury in her—to take him as deeply into herself as she can, to grip his shoulders hard, so hard her fingernails dig into his flesh and he winces. Oh yes. Like this.

I love you.

You and only you. You.

Don't leave me—!

Her eyes are shut tight, the skin at the corners crinkled with strain, panic. If he should draw away. If he should leave her, fail her. Her eyes are shut but she sees the shadow-streaked ceiling of the room, the bedroom in the northwest corner of the lodge; or is it the ceiling of the bedroom at 18 Röcken, the French wallpaper, silky silvery green and mauve flowers. . . . Suddenly her lover is standing at the far end of the room. Naked. His unsmiling face is taut and accusing with love. His stiffened shoulders, the brown chest hair, the bush of pubic hair, his erect penis. . . .

Come here, why are you waiting, no one will know, Isabel whispers. Her mouth is dry with terror that he will reject her.

Then she is kneading his flesh as if it belonged to her by right—she grips his buttocks—squeezes him—slaps him. Flesh is flesh, no mystery to it. Hasn't she given birth? Twice? Three times? Don't play games, she says. I know who you are.

I want, I *need* . . .

She writhes frantically against him. The sensation in her loins, so rich and full a moment ago, has begun to ebb. She must call it back. She must call him back. Her mouth is an anguished O, a fish's mouth, agape. No one should see her like this—not a lover—not even a husband—here is a shame more strident than childbirth—the witnesses crowding close to stare between her blood-smeared legs. There, *there* is the mystery—emerging from between her legs. But how to call it her own, how to make *her* claim. . . .

Don't leave me, she begs, help me, she sobs, I love you.

Turning the pages of an outdated glossy magazine in the beauty parlor some weeks ago—in early June, this is, the day of a much-awaited but finally disappointing White House reception: such crowds! such vulgar Texans!—Isabel happens upon an essay titled "Sex, Death & Fate: Why *You* Are In Love." Smart and sophisticated and breezy and edged with cynicism, but amusing too. Like most prose in these magazines. (The advertisements and fashion features, however, are totally serious.)

Isabel Halleck is not a conscientious reader these days—she scans society and gossip columns in the important papers, looking eagerly for her own name, then, with dread, for the names of her enemies; then for the names of her friends. She scans the prominent news articles and editorials, and the popular and "controversial" columnists—ah, but there are so many these days!—a consequence of the "mess" in Vietnam —and she makes it a point, a duty, to "read through" books presented to her and frequently inscribed to her with admiration or affection or even love by the countless writers of her acquaintance (journalists primarily, but high-ranking journalists whose specialties are the Far East or the U.S. human rights policy or the United Nations or the Third World or Latin America or global nutrition; and there are historians too, most of them associated with prominent universities; and biographers—Isabel finds the biographies easiest to scan, she greatly enjoyed a book on Eleanor Roosevelt not long ago, and another on John Foster Dulles, a Book-of-the-Month Club selection): all this material is imminent conversation at dinner tables and receptions, sometimes she crams for an evening while soaking in her bath, turning the pages of the *Washington Book World* which everyone reads, more or less. In odd sequestered pockets of time—under the hair dryer, for instance—she might read articles on new fashions, cosmetics, "ready-to-order" cosmetic surgery, vacation resorts in the Dominican Republic, South Africa, Rio, Marrakesh. This afternoon she reads "Sex, Death & Fate: Why *You* Are In Love."

Sex, it seems, is a "new" means of reproduction. By which is meant "new" in terms of billions of years of evolution. Amoebas bud and clone, mechanically, automatically, on and on they go and never die . . . unlike organisms that mix their genes. *Why* mix your genes, you might ask, and it's a good question. Well—life set sail upon highly problematic, risky, and exciting waters when it began to *evolve.* Which means "to grow from a primitive to a more highly organized form" *(The American Heritage Dictionary of the English Language).* Which means greater variation among individuals, of course—and a greatly improved ability to adapt to the environment. And since earth's climate and geological features have always been in a state of change you can see that survival of certain species was greatly enhanced by this strategy. And so—the invention of sex and death!

(Isabel reads impatiently, a little skeptically. "Sex" to Isabel has always meant men and women; its biological definition does not interest her at all. As a matter between men and women "sex" interests her, it must be said, greatly. Constantly. And the obsession, she supposes uneasily, is likely to increase.)

The invention of sex and death. Sex in order to mix genes, death because "individuals" are a new notion in the cosmos, and in any case the old generations must be cleared away. Only their genes are valuable, and only those genes of the experiments that worked. The rest—worthless. Clear it all away! Oblivion!

Life is heartless and greedy, Isabel reads, beyond the human sphere. When we were asexual creatures we were immortal but now that we are sexual creatures we are *very* mortal.

What are the advantages of this "new" state of things, you might ask. There are many. Just think: consciousness, language, mobility, freedom, memory, a concern for justice, goodness, and beauty, a love of *truth.* All social customs, all social pleasures. And romance. Romance! Death gives us romance and the exhilaration and despair of desire, the ecstasy of love and the anguish of love, the . . .

Isabel thinks, alarmed: I should have been stone, rock, what came before . . . A mineral, a jewel . . .

She turns the page and begins an article on fall designer fashions and the droning warmth of the hair dryer puts her gradually to sleep; and when she wakes the magazine slides to the floor and she's too lazy to retrieve it and in any case her hair is certainly dry by now.

Nick, she says, begging, whimpering like one of her own children, come here, come inside me, now, fuck me, do it, don't turn away—

He turns away in distaste. The pulsation in her loins subsides.

Nick—

He is lying heavily on her, teasing, laughing, tickling her with his fingers and tongue. His tongue. In that cave, that child-sized cave where they crawled to take refuge from the storm. Where they might have crawled. They laugh and pummel each other. Greedy as teenaged children. On the beach, in the wet sand, shameless. Her hair pulled loose, the gold dove slipping, now at the back of her head where it hurts, pressed against a rock; so she tears it off and lets it fall. I don't know you, I don't love you, this isn't right, this can't be happening, everyone is waiting for us, my fiancé is waiting for us—I don't even know your name, she says, which is of course a lie.

He kisses her full on the lips and makes his claim. Unsmiling.

The cave where they might have crawled.

An abandoned shanty at the edge of the marsh, where they might have gone. To take shelter from the storm.

Don't be afraid, she begs.

I don't love you that much, he says.

But you love me. You love me.

I love you . . . but not that much.

To hurt him, you mean?

What else have we been talking about, he says irritably.

She seizes his hand, kisses it, presses herself against him. A blaze, a delirium. Beautiful girl. Her breath comes in short gasps as the sensation in the very pit of her belly takes strength again, suddenly, surprisingly. Hurt me, she says, pressing his hand hard against her breast, I know you want to hurt me, slap me, I know what you want to do, I know who you want to hurt and it isn't *him*. . . .

But Nick turns away. Her lovely body: her breasts, belly, legs. She knows she is lovely. She studies herself as if she were a work of art, but one in need of both constant maintenance and adoration. She knows, she knows. Idiotic to pretend otherwise. But Nick turns away. I can't, we can't, he says. Luis once took hold of her chin with his nicotine-stained fingers and said *You'll do after all* and then, without affection, *You'll do better than your bag of a mother,* breathing his stale liquory breath on her, staring, assessing. He had custody of her but she rarely saw him. Her mother had "relinquished" custody of her and gone back to St. Paul to live with her family. The Kuhns of Minneapolis-St. Paul? people inquired, as if the name were significant, but Isabel did not think it was significant: she hated the whole tribe.

Only two Kuhns had actually made their way to Washington as anything other than Congressmen and one of them was Secretary to the Treasury under Chester Alan Arthur, during the last year of Arthur's term, and the other was appointed by McKinley as Deputy Secretary of State a few weeks before McKinley's assassination. Now they were tire manufacturers, fussy civic-minded citizens, a Kuhn had run for Governor of Minnesota in 1957, and lost, on a "strict censorship enforcement" platform hastily drummed up by the Republican Party.

You'll do, Luis said grudgingly, *I can help you invest it,* but perhaps he was joking, his heavy pale face, his thick eyebrows, his doggish jowls often quivered with secret amusement. His suits were made by a London tailoring firm that sent tailors to New York and Washington twice a year, his shoes were custom-made in Spain, he was handsome, lethargic and frenzied by turns, fired by schemes, plots, maneuvers to borrow money and to invest it and to "recoup" losses, stratagems in which he achieved revenge for financial or personal injuries or perhaps anticipated the injuries by deft betrayals of his own: and then again he was bitterly disappointed, disillusioned, "finished" with the human race, plunged into long inert wintry periods of what Isabel diagnosed as not quite clinical depression, which might have been treatable. He was gallantly verbose and "good-humored" when Isabel introduced him to Maurie Halleck, but said afterward, as soon as they were alone, with an amused sneer: *You might get him but you won't keep him unless you're very, very careful.*

Nick cups her chin in his hand and gazes at her speculatively. Her lovely face, her robust good spirits, her famous energy. Quick and bright and shallow and irresistible. Though he decides he will resist.

Then again he does not: he follows her to Stockholm.

They become lovers in Stockholm, in the grandiose Royal Hotel where Nick has a suite.

They become lovers here at Bitterfeld Lake, in the pine woods above the lodge.

They become lovers—suddenly and casually—in Washington, shortly after Nick accepted the offer from the Commission for the Ministry of Justice which Maurie negotiated for him, at a salary very close to Maurie's own. Nick is in the city for two weeks, staying at the Shoreham. June and Audrey are in Boston, there is some difficulty in persuading

June to make the move but Nick tells Isabel that he's "confident" she will see things his way, eventually.

Now we can see each other anytime we like, Nick and Isabel tell each other, as often as we like.

The Martenses visit the Hallecks in the Röcken cul-de-sac in their elegant residential neighborhood; the Hallecks visit the Martenses, at first in their attractive apartment in Park Fairfax, and then in their Chevy Chase home. They are frequently seen together around town though the couples never exactly become "friends" as couples—June's failing. No one notices that Isabel Halleck and Nick Martens shy away from kissing each other in public, or even brushing their lips lightly against the other's cheek by way of a greeting, nor does anyone notice that, at large parties, they inevitably drift into the same corner of the room, two remarkably attractive young people who would have, as a couple, shone powerfully in the Kennedy circle. They are both performers certain of an audience, perhaps they are even exhibitionists, but marvelously winning, charming, entertaining: Isabel tells the funniest tales, wild and droll and convincing; Nick can talk on virtually every subject—he knows the lives of "great men" from Julius Caesar and Hadrian to Napoleon, Bismarck, Stalin, Hitler, F.D.R., Mao, he knows bizarre but evidently true anecdotes about their personal lives, and is scandalously amusing on the secrets of American Presidents not ordinarily revealed in history books. Sometimes Isabel has to grip his arm, begging him to stop, she and his other listeners are overcome with convulsive laughter. . . .

In her wide-brimmed straw hat with the green felt ribbon Isabel gives her name to the security police and makes her way across the lawn, her gloved hands lifting her long skirt, her silver-blond hair, just cut, swinging heavily an inch or two above her bare shoulders. A lavish reception for the Shah of Iran and his queen. Greetings and handshakes and embraces and kisses. Nick is spying upon her and will telephone her the next morning: he couldn't bring himself to approach her, it would have been all over, they would have to tell Maurie, they would have to terminate the masquerade, the subterfuge. And what of June, Isabel asks gaily, a little feverishly, and Nick says—Oh, of course June, of course, of course. And after a moment he says: Are you sorry I was a coward? Isabel? What are you thinking?

I don't know, Isabel whispers.

They become lovers, however, in the most idyllic setting possible: Claudia's Nassau place, the white stucco guest house overlooking the sea, it is the holiday season, white and red poinsettias everywhere, Nick tells June he is called away on Commission business, confidential business, in Latin America. They are frenzied as puppies, gay and breathless and daring; they cannot get enough of each other. Do you love me—only me? Do you love *me?*

Isabel is greedy, Isabel is insatiable.

Isabel bursts into hoarse heartrending sobs.

A black macramé shawl to her ankles; silver jewelry, Peruvian, that droops elegantly to her shoulders; eyes outlined in what appears to be violet ink. She hates him and will not even glance his way, cannot bring herself to say hello to his wife, allows drunken Morton Kempe to hug her and kiss her wetly on the cheek, allows the tedious doomed bores X and Y of the Pentagon to fawn upon her, has a bright dazzling absolutely natural smile for the peppy hangdog Vice President whom—as everyone knows—the President is treating like, well, shit. I want you, Nick begs over the phone, half-sobbing, look, Isabel, please, Isabel, shall I come over, what shall we do, and her voice is airy in reply as if she felt no rage, as if one conversation might be very much like another. Go to hell, she says, go back to your wife, go fuck your secretary as you've been doing, go fuck yourself.

But they become lovers, on Mount Dunvegan Island. That day.

They become lovers here at Bitterfeld Lake—despite the presence of so many other people, and their own children, nuisance Audrey hanging on her father's arm.

They become lovers in the unused maid's room on the third floor of the Hallecks' house, while below some thirty-five guests chatter and laugh noisily, and Maurie drifts off into his study for a troubled talk with Charles Clayton. (June, pleading an infected ear, has stayed home.)

They become lovers with a passion, a brutality, that frightens them both. Hurt me, Isabel demands, I know what you want to do, I know the kind of pig you are. . . . In the woods on the far side of the lake, back on one of the old logging trails, the two of them having driven out for . . . for more beer, more liquor . . . though one of the servants would surely have been sent? . . . clutching at each other, pulling at each other's clothing.

He enters her. She cries out. It is so simple!—done.

She sobs, striking him weakly on the arm. Startled, he laughs and draws away.

You're crazy, he says. You don't mean it. It's a game.

He discovers her allowing the Belgian Ambassador, a Francophobe of immense charm, to stare at her with absurd raw longing in the presence of her own husband.

What a bitch you are, he says.

He enters her crudely, and as masterfully as any lover making his claim, seizing what is only his by right. If he hurts her—if she squirms with pain—that too is his right, and increases the savagery of his pleasure. But of course she does not resist. It is not her privilege to resist.

Look—you know how I feel, he tells her, could it be more obvious? Don't make a complete idiot of me.

She stares at him, her pretty lips parted. She is six months' pregnant, with Owen. Her maternity outfits are filmy, airy, fussy with ribbons, she wears exotic wide-brimmed hats to summon the eye upward. Despite her frequent headaches and constipation and nightmare bouts of terror about giving birth she has never looked more beautiful, as everyone comments. To her, and to her husband.

Suddenly she is frightened. It is no game, her fluttering eyelids, her faint voice, her hand lightly falling on her belly as if to protect it. I . . . I don't know what you're talking about, she tells her husband's friend, his friend from boyhood, the friend who—ah, how often she has heard!—saved her husband's life; I don't understand, she says, her voice faltering.

Certainly you know, Isabel, Nick says. Certainly you know, Mrs. Halleck.

She takes him to her, into her, her knees spread. A simple act. No diplomacy needed. No anguish, tears, guilt, grotesque accusations. If you love me, if you want me—the hell with love!—come here, put it in, God damn you.

She has never wanted any man the way she wants Nick Martens. It is a fever, a curse. A physical obsession that shades now and then into the nearly philosophical—*Can* the flesh betray? What are bodies? Does anyone care? Would Maurie care? Would Maurie know? The best man at the wedding, subdued, distracted, rather melancholy. She sees him with June Penrick and murmurs to herself, Give me time, give me time, virginal and gloating in her white satin bridal gown with the heavy Halleck pearls around her neck and snug in her ears, insured for—she hasn't asked, she discovers the fact "by accident"—$25,000. Give me time.

Now she buries her face in his chest hair, in his stomach. Unembarrassed, coarse. Her lips, tongue, teeth. Taking his erect penis in her mouth. Its size, its warmth, its strength. His desperate fingers close in her hair and he begins to whimper and her own heart is close to bursting.

But the sensation abruptly ebbs.

No.

She can't love Nick Martens that way. "Blowing," "sucking off," the unspeakable disgust of the semen in her mouth . . . and would he kiss her afterward. . . . She can't love any man that way.

Suddenly she is exhausted. With a sob she gives up.

I can't, oh, leave me alone, get it over with and leave me alone, I can't, I can't . . .

She is so exhausted, her heart seems barely equal to the strain. She says aloud, I'm sorry, I can't . . . I can't.

And in another two or three minutes the sweaty ordeal—growing infrequent since the birth of their little girl four years ago, and shortly to become more infrequent still—is over.

I love you, Maurie whispers. Sleepy, content, his labored breathing gradually slowing, his hand loosely cupping her breast. Her husband. As if he doesn't know. And perhaps he doesn't.

The Angry Gnome

But who *have* I married? Isabel wonders.

She is reasonably certain that she knows *why*, but not always certain that she knows *who*.

It was in the third or fourth year of their marriage, after a noisy, protracted, and altogether marvelous dinner party in Georgetown, to which Maurie had not wanted to go, that Isabel, who had assumed she knew her companionable, industrious, and doting husband as well as any woman could know a man, was forced to conclude to her chagrin that she hardly knew him at all.

The party was made up of bright lively well-informed hard-drinking people of what might be called junior rank, and in that setting Isabel, resplendent in a white silk pants suit with a low-cut neckline and her hair in a tight French twist, matched quips and witticisms and anecdotes with the most amusing and audacious of the guests. She told the long, convoluted, sadly hilarious story of X, a certain high-ranking State Department official now openly on the skids, and fair game for Washington gossip: it was a story whose source was Esther Jackson the columnist, who had had an affair with X for several years, a negligently kept secret around town, and who knew the most *extraordinary* things about the poor man.

The story was a great success. Isabel had already acquired, in high school, the art of being wicked and funny and richly informative all at once, and since her marriage—since "coming into her own" as a

popular Washingtonian—she had even perfected a sort of droll innocence as well. In her lightly inflected voice, with her beauty as a shield,
she seemed to be saying things too bizarre for her to quite comprehend
—which was part of her malicious charm. If women did not find her as
amusing as men they nevertheless laughed along with the men, and
went about town saying how winning Mrs. Halleck was. She *could* be
warm, on an individual basis; she *could* be subdued and even shy in
certain company. Which might have been part of her strategy, though
the women did not yet understand that.

Maurie had wanted to leave the dinner party at eleven-thirty,
which was disappointingly early, and for a few minutes the Hallecks
debated—should he take a cab home, should Isabel stay on for another
hour by herself and then drive home; or should Maurie take the car and
Isabel a cab; or—and this was more probable—might Isabel get a ride
home with one of the guests? There were a number of single men—
bachelors, divorced men, men ambiguously separated from their wives
—who would have volunteered with alacrity. But in the end it was
decided that Isabel and Maurie would leave together.

She noticed on the drive home that her husband was quiet and
withdrawn and not inclined to reply to her remarks. His driving was less
methodical than usual. His profile was that of a much older man—
fatigued, settled in upon itself, even a little censorious. He was exhausted from his work at the Commission, Isabel thought, where he was
expected to put in a routine day of ten hours or more: for though he was
still at junior rank he was already entrusted with highly sensitive work,
primarily as a consequence of serious problems the Commission was
having with one of its assistant deputy directors, Maurie's division head.
And then he disliked, or anyway did not like, what he persisted in calling
the "social pace" of the city. This is our life, Isabel said defensively, this
is the element in which we live. But tonight she conceded that it hadn't
been a really *remarkable* evening . . . one or two of the men had drunk
too much, the women were even more boring than usual.

It was not until they were preparing for bed that Isabel realized
something serious might be wrong. She spied on her husband through
the mirrored door of her dressing room—which was in an alcove of the
bedroom—and saw him standing motionless on the carpet, half-
undressed, his knobby and somewhat foreshortened legs bare. He was
in his socks and his boxer shorts and his white shirt, the cuffs loose. His
mouth worked; he was shaking his head just perceptibly, as if quarreling
with someone in silence.

Maurie—? Isabel whispered. But he did not hear.

In this particular setting, furnished with beautiful things—some were Halleck heirlooms, some were impulsive gifts from old Luis, and the French chaise longue Isabel had picked up herself at an auction—poor Maurie Halleck looked like an intruder: a gnome with a boyish but prematurely crinkled face who had blundered into unfamiliar territory. He was sad, he was slightly comic, even a little alarming. . . . Isabel saw that his fingers were wriggling, and he was certainly talking to himself under his breath. And he had had only two drinks since seven o'clock, which included a single glass of white wine.

He's mad, Isabel thought, panicked.

And in that instant she recalled two things: a long-forgotten remark of her mother's—*Your father is insane—it happens to them—men—it comes and goes—you can't live with them—don't make my mistake*— made when Isabel might have been as young as six or seven; and a curious remark Nick Martens made when she was still in the hospital after Owen's birth, and he had flown down to congratulate the euphoric parents and to be the baby's godfather: If anything ever happens, Isabel, I mean if . . . if Maurie ever . . . If anything goes wrong between you . . . If he ever . . . It's difficult to say this, but . . . at Bauer, and at college . . . he could sometimes get rather peculiar. . . . He's a natural eccentric, he's essentially a loner, of course it's marvelous for him that he broke free of that shell and has married, and now he's a father, even, and it's made him so happy . . . changed his life . . . but I'm not sure that he *can* change his life . . . do you know what I'm saying, do I make any sense at all? Or am I merely offending you?

Offending me, Isabel had said coldly.

When Isabel approached her husband in her long silk nightgown, her hair loose on her shoulders, her eyes clean of mascara and eyeshadow and her face clean of makeup, and very lightly creamed for the night, he glanced up at her and then stared for a long unsettling moment. She was an apparition, *she* was an intruder, it did not matter that she was a great beauty or had pretensions of being one.

You—! he said in a hoarse whisper.

And then, before Isabel could reply, before she could ask this absurd little man what on earth he was doing, Maurie Halleck began, incredibly, to stammer—to weep—to berate—to accuse—so taking Isabel by surprise that she stood paralyzed and silent, merely looking at him in amazement. She had *never* before—! *Never* since their marriage—! Such anger! Such sputtering fury!

His words were disjointed, she was too alarmed to grasp them all, the outburst went on and on, his voice trembled and his hands shook, even his knees trembled, she recalled suddenly that Nick had gone on to say *if he ever cracks* and the substance of his message was *call me immediately,* and she stood motionless staring at her husband who adored her, who was silly and puppyish and besotted with love for her, and the words tumbled about her head, and she made no attempt to defend herself—for how could she?—and no attempt even to understand what the words meant.

How could you—simply to entertain—to make fools laugh— how could you fabricate—distort—lie—the irresponsibility—the cruelty—cynicism—inventing reality for the sake of amusement—such contempt for the truth—it's criminal—it's unspeakable—the injustice—served up to fools for their diversion—how can you—Nick as well—I can't tolerate it—I won't—such imperialism—grandiosity— contempt—malice—half-truths and lies—appropriating a human being for a story—a joke—all the complexity, the personal history— the humanity—it's intolerable—you and the others—and Nick—I've tried to explain—I've tried to speak to you—to you both—the appalling disregard for—the contempt for—despising of—not just your victims but your listeners too—and the truth—what the truth is—*justice—balance—community—law— How* could *you, my wife—!*

Not immediately, in fact not until a week or ten days later, did Isabel telephone Nick in Boston, at his office, to tell him about Maurie's outburst. By then the fury had naturally subsided, Maurie had apologized, Isabel had given every indication of having forgotten. . . . Of course I know you didn't mean it, she told her anxious husband. Of course I know you love me.

She told Nick about the accusations but did not mention that he too was involved, however obliquely. She told Nick that in that instant she had seen a Maurie Halleck she hadn't known before—a lawyer, an officer of the court, a man with an allegiance to something she could not grasp and perhaps did not care to grasp; it was too abstract to be of interest to her. She told Nick that she had not defended herself at the time, or afterward, because she knew that, by her husband's code, she was indefensible.

And forever afterward Isabel Halleck was to tell her wildest, funniest, most irresistibly wicked stories when her husband was not present.

Strife

Do you know the Greek legend of the "Judgment of Paris," June Martens asks oddly, during a pause in the game. (Maurie and Nick have stopped for some iced tea, which Isabel brought down from the house.) I was just reading it last night . . . an old copy of Bulfinch in the library of your house, Isabel.

Oh yes, says Isabel.

I used to love those Greek legends, Florence Silber says, but I get them all mixed up. The gods were always changing into something else . . . or making mortals change . . . it didn't seem quite fair, no one had a chance against them. What's the "Judgment of Paris"?—I don't remember.

I just happened to be reading it, quite by accident, Audrey was fretting so I thought I'd humor her, June says in her low, rather throaty voice, smiling across the red clay court and into nowhere—into the woods. Isabel, watching her husband and Nick, noting the ripple of muscle beneath Nick's damp T-shirt, and the frizzy bronze hair on his legs, answers absently. (Yes, she too reads to Kirsten, Kirsten loves to fall asleep to a story, thumb in mouth, but Owen—of course Owen is too old now: he does his own reading and is quite the critic!)—The Greek legends are very interesting, June says slowly. I hated them when we studied them in college—in ancient Greek—because they're so crude and merciless, and I think because they tell us such implacable truths about ourselves. Truths that don't seem to change across the centuries.

As I recall, Florence says, inhaling her cigarette and letting the

smoke mushroom merrily about her face, the legends were mainly
rather risqué. Is that a word still in use?—risqué? It was used in the
fifties when we all grew up.

June laughs at Florence's remark; and Isabel joins in, though she
is distracted by the men. It worries and annoys her that Maurie looks
so drained, and yet insists upon continuing the game: he seems to have
developed a perceptible limp. And Nick, why is Nick so sweatily ebullient, why do his inane jocular remarks to Maurie carry so clearly across
the court. . . . (It has occurred to Isabel frequently that her husband and
Nick, in each other's company, are not *really* themselves. Neither has
the dignity, the charm, the intelligence—even the simple physical attrac-
tiveness—he has when alone. She wonders how they behave together at
the Commission. She wonders if Maurie watches Nick so keenly, and if
Nick is so expansive, so self-consciously brash. Their friendship might
very well irritate their associates because it is fueled by so many oblique
allusions, so many uncompleted sentences that nevertheless communicate their meaning . . . which is partly to exclude others.)

Zeus transforming himself into a shower of gold in order to rape
some poor fat virgin, Florence says, or into an ox—or was it a bull?—
neither is very tempting. But a shower of gold—! You wouldn't know
what hit you.

Yes, says June, laughing, a catch in her throat, there is a great
deal of rape in Greek mythology. It seems to have been on everyone's
minds.

On men's minds, Florence says. Did you read, by the way, the
other day in the paper—some experiment a psychologist was doing—
college students, I think it was—of course they were anonymous—they
were shown a pornographic film, a rape sequence, the woman suffered
a great deal and the film was *very* graphic, and afterward the boys said
in a poll that if they were guaranteed they wouldn't be caught they'd
"probably" like to do the same thing.

I don't think that can be right, June says quietly. Where did you
read that?

In the *Times*. The other day. Yes, I *did* read it.

But that's impossible, really, June says, looking up, squinting, I
mean—college boys—after all— It isn't as if the experiment had been
conducted in a prison—

Oh yes, I read it, I read it, Florence says. Now look: the game is
starting again. Poor Maurie looks so hot. . . .

I really don't think that report can be accurate, June says, not
looking at the players, though Nick is preparing to serve, and stretching
his shoulders and arms rather elegantly.—Things get garbled in news-

papers. It just doesn't seem believable. The kids are so upset right now about the war, napalm, Vietnamese civilians—

They're upset about the draft, I think, Florence says.

But *college* boys, rape—

Only if they don't get caught: that's the hitch. But why should you be surprised, Florence asks, amused, you were just saying about the Greek myths—nothing changing across the centuries?—weren't you?

Fifteen-love, Nick calls out. Maurie has returned his serve into the net.

But—says June.

Why don't we watch the game, Isabel says, smiling, stooping to touch June's shoulder, to calm her. If Isabel is concerned about the growing lateness of the hour—her guests on their way from Saranac—her husband's flushed face, Nick's aggression, a certain rowdiness among the children—of course she gives no indication. This is Bitterfeld Lake and she is the young Mrs. Halleck and here, in this territory, she is queen.—Maybe they will get it over with, then, a little faster—we can have drinks up at the house and relax—

The "Judgment of Paris," I don't remember that one, Florence says. Didn't Paris kill someone? A girl? And she turned into a tree?—or she turned into a tree before he could kill her—

No, Paris was a mortal, June says slowly, you're thinking of someone else and he didn't try to kill her, he tried to rape her—

I meant rape, Florence says, what did I say?—kill?—I meant rape of course. *Did* I say "kill"?

June clears her throat and begins to speak and Isabel, annoyed, moves just perceptibly away. Schoolmarmish, bossy, *always* lecturing when she is with other women . . . not revealing herself to men . . . particularly not to her own husband. (Your wife is so very forceful in her quiet indirect way, Isabel tells Nick, and Nick says, surprised: Really? I haven't noticed.) Isabel has tried to be friendly with June but June has resisted: there's a stubborn little pit of hatred in her which Isabel senses quite clearly, though her own manner to June couldn't be more warm. So you're afraid of losing him, my girl, Isabel thinks, so you're frightened: good, you've caught on. Isabel is the only person apart from Nick and June who knows that June knows of Nick's two or three "harmless" infidelities in the eleven years of their marriage . . . and knows, in rather close detail, of June's response to Nick's confessions: hysteria, disbelief, anger, tears, resignation, "pity" (which has sounded fabricated, to Isabel's sensitive ear), forgiveness; and dread.

She watches June covertly. An unattractive hair style, limp and straggly in the heat; no makeup so that every pore on her nose—in this sunshine—is revealed; slumped shoulders; cut-off jeans and a sports shirt that are really *too* casual. As if she and her family had gone on a camping weekend in the mountains, and were not guests at the Hallecks'. As if she were invisible, immune. June has never quite adjusted to the move to Washington, she claims not to "understand" the city, the people, which Isabel interprets as an incapacity to understand why she isn't happy there. Though she must have realized that Nick—brilliant, ambitious, energetic Nick—couldn't possibly have stayed in that firm another year, tolerating the sort of abuse they handed out to him: as if they didn't realize who Nick Martens was! A promotion with an insultingly small increase in pay, a frankly ugly office, no secretary of his own. . . .

Doesn't she want you to be happy, for Christ's sake, Isabel asked.

Well—she's afraid.

Afraid of what?

Afraid.

Isabel gripped the telephone receiver hard and raised one bare leg so that she could examine her toenail polish. It pleased her, that it was still in good condition after two days. She said: I can't agree. June is an absolutely stable, self-determined, *responsible* young woman. She went back for a master's degree in—what was it?—social work—while she was pregnant, and she isn't afraid to disagree with you about Vietnam, and she's—well—wonderfully unaffected: the kind of person who cuts her own hair, around behind where she can't see it—or cleans her glasses by licking the lenses with her tongue and wiping them on her blouse.

Nick was silent. He did not laugh. After a moment he said quietly, That isn't worthy of you, Isabel.

I suppose not, Isabel laughed.

Now June is telling Isabel and Florence about the Greek goddess Eris. Which means "strife." For one day Eris threw an apple "for the fairest" in front of three goddesses—Hera, Aphrodite, and Athena. Of course the goddesses argued—each thought she was the "fairest"—and Paris was brought in for his opinion. (Paris. A mortal man. But the most handsome mortal on earth.)

The legend tells us how each of the goddesses tried to bribe him, offering her own special gifts: Athena offered wisdom, Hera offered divine power, Aphrodite offered the most beautiful mortal woman for his bride—which was Helen of Troy, June says. Her manner is chatty and conversational but Isabel is uneasy. Of course it isn't any surprise that Paris chose Aphrodite . . . he chose Helen . . . and he had to kidnap her . . . and this was the start of the Trojan War.

Oh yes, says Florence, of course, the Trojan War. The first of the great boring wars.

The point is, June says quickly, the point that struck me last night when I was reading to Audrey—nothing seems to matter except physical beauty, not even wisdom, not even *power*. Just physical beauty. Helen of Troy, the most beautiful mortal woman, and so on and so forth . . . it *is* completely boring. And the man is the judge. Paris is the judge. He's only a mortal but he has the power to judge goddesses because he's a man. Because they give him the power. It doesn't say why they give him the power. . . .

A long volley: Nick and then Maurie and then Nick and then Maurie and who will miss?—the children are exaggerating their suspense, Owen is clowning idiotically, his hands over his eyes.

I mean why, June asks, looking up at Isabel and Florence, smiling, squinting, unaware of her somewhat coarse skin and the faint white lines beside her eyes, the whole thing just struck me last night: *why* give a man this power?

The volley ends when Nick slams the ball down just inside the net, at an extraordinary angle, and poor Maurie lunges forward—not only missing the ball but staggering into the net.

Ah now, Isabel cries, clapping her hands, Is it over?—you've both been playing marvelously but I think it's getting—

Thirty-love, Nick says, positioning himself for his next serve. We have plenty of time.

A Bad Smell

Isabel de Benavente, prettiest of the girls in her graduating class at the Hays School for Girls, Georgetown. But Monika van Steen is pretty too. And Jeanette Bolling. Eating banana splits in the Golden Goose Ice Cream Parlor, giggling arm-in-arm in the shops on Wisconsin Avenue, strolling on Saturday afternoons through the National Gallery, the Phillips Gallery, the Smithsonian. Birthday luncheons, theater parties, slumber parties, teas. The Crocker house on Thirty-third Street—the "most sumptuously decorated private home in Washington"—with its queer dormer rooms on the third floor that echoed laughter so spookily; the Bolling house with the mural by "Giovanni Battista Tiepolo"—as he was called—in the drawing room; the May house near Dumbarton Oaks where, dunking for apples at a rowdy Halloween party, Isabel overhears someone murmur *Hola her head under for a long, long time.* Raiding for fun the upstairs of the van Steen house one afternoon when no one seemed to be around—Monika rifling her mother's drawers and closets for what she called "loose change." Raiding the Stimsons' for fun too one dismal rainy Saturday morning not long before Mr. Stimson is to be publicly exposed for his role in the "debacle" of the Washington Permanent Community Trust. Chauffeured limousines, tea dances on the rooftop of the Clareton Inn, Isabel is a Cherry Blossom Princess, Monika is in her court and never forgives her. Field hockey. Art classes with "Monsieur Roland" for one year only. Preparing for the debutante season. Isabel with an admirer from the Costa Rican Embassy; Jeanette Bolling with an admirer from Thailand. Whispers, peals of laughter.

Plotting revenge against certain teachers. Mr. Bolling's "illness" for which he has to be treated in a private sanitarium in Virginia, about which Jeanette never speaks and her friends never ask. A tearful good-bye party for Alice—"Allie"—Ventor whose father is leaving for Iraq as Deputy Chief of Mission. A savage whipping with an actual riding crop across her bottom—not her bare bottom, poor screaming sobbing Isabel is allowed the minimal dignity of her white cotton panties—after Mr. de Benavente learns from Mrs. Arthur that there were boys present "for at least part of the night" at Deedee May's slumber party.

Isabel's mother has gone to visit her family in St. Paul, Minnesota. She is gone two weeks, a month, three months. My mother misses her own part of the world, Isabel will explain if anyone asks. My mother hates Washington, Isabel will explain. She might even confide to her closest friend Monika—but perhaps Jeanette is her closest friend? —that her parents' marriage doesn't seem to be working out. Luis is gone all the time, there are strange telephone calls, quarrels when he returns, tears and shouts, slammed doors, Mrs. de Benavente locked away in her bedroom for days at a time, drinking. My mother wants me to come with her but it's too damned cold in that part of the world, Isabel will explain brightly, if anyone asks. Though why anyone should be interested in Mrs. de Benavente who is forty-five at least and looks older, Isabel can't really imagine: after all, the poor woman's life is over. In any case, no one inquires.

Art classes with Monsieur Roland, Monday and Wednesday afternoons. Isabel is impatient with pencil drawing—she works too fast, nervously and carelessly—does five or six sketches to her classmates' one. The object of the exercises is to draw without lifting the pencil point from the paper and without glancing down at the paper but Isabel finds this "asinine." The class moves on to watercolors. Which are difficult. Which are *very* difficult. Monsieur Roland is cautious in his criticism, however, for Hays girls are excitable young ladies, and their parents pay a fairly high tuition which barely covers "extras" like classes in art, dance, and theater. Talent among them is unevenly divided.

I want to paint something cheerful, Isabel says, but her watercolors turn out not only blotched and runny—all the girls' watercolors are blotched and runny—but morose as well. "Depressing," in her words. Her trees possess the lugubrious slump of mourners, her skies harden to mineral, the tiny faces of her flowers sneer. Her most successful effort is a still life—apple, pear, grapes—presented to Luis, who praises it and assures Isabel she has talent but does not, to Isabel's secret mortification and rage, send the watercolor out to have it framed.

And then the class moves on to sculpting.

A final three weeks of sculpting.

And Isabel de Benavente discovers a queer excitable sensation in her fingertips. She works even more quickly than usual, and with more of her high-spirited carelessness than usual, but the results are not always disappointing: she tries figures, animals, trees, human hands, and finally heads: and the heads turn out surprisingly well.

Look at what Benavente is doing, her friends say, and even Monsieur Roland is impressed—it would seem genuinely impressed. Aren't they funny! Aren't they something!—Heads the size of a man's fist: children, mature women, elderly men. The class crowds round. Isabel, though blushing, is immensely gratified.

Oh—this is just something I'm doing, she says. I like the way it feels, the clay.

She is eager for class on Mondays and Wednesdays, and stays in the studio afterward to continue working. Sometimes she drops in for an hour on other days—just to "fool around." Monsieur Roland encourages her at first but then suggests she move on to other subjects. After all—why heads? And why so many?

Monsieur Roland is a fattish man in his late thirties with a prim little mustache the girls giggle over in secret, and appealing semi-Bohemian costumes: loose flowing smocks, paint-splattered denim jeans, a wine-colored beret. Though his manner alternates between a diplomatic geniality and stony silence he has, on occasion, irked or teased or amused his students, alluded daringly to the "Hays mystique" and the "hothouse atmosphere" of Washington in general. Benavente is kind of good, isn't she? Isabel's friends ask him, eager for his approval, his *real* approval, but he says only, with a fluttery wave of his fingers, The dear child is certainly *our* resident genius—!

Isabel stays after school three days in a row, working feverishly. Now her fingers move even more rapidly—it's amazing—it's almost alarming—her eyes grow glassy and unfocused—she works in a kind of trance. A queer little blind smile, damp prickling skin. I'll meet you later, she tells her friends vaguely, hardly hearing where they are going or when she should meet them. *Don't* come barging into the studio—okay?

Three days in a row. Four. Five. The heads are gradually growing larger. Isabel, Monika says, you aren't *serious* about this . . . are you? Now she comes into the studio every afternoon and on Saturdays as well, since Monsieur Roland has been coerced into giving her the key. This isn't really any fun, is it, Monika asks, I mean—is it? Standing here all the time, just *standing* here?

The heads are striking, and rather skillful, but very odd. Very odd. And as the days pass they become odder still.

Old men, oldish women, and young children. But never girls Isabel's own age. Isabel ruthlessly smashes the earliest heads, the small ones. You broke my favorite one, Deedee May says, you were going to give that to me, Isabel! Isabel says vaguely, Which one?—I don't remember.

The heads grow larger, and queerer. By the time Isabel abandons the project in early June they will have become life-sized, and *very* queer.

How funny, everyone says, perhaps uneasily. How ugly, they begin to say. Isabel's English teacher drops by the studio, intrigued by the girls' reports, and stares at the rows of clay heads; she says, finally, Is that how you see the world, Isabel?

Isabel blushes with annoyance. I'm just fooling around, Miss Thayer, she says. She flexes her clay-stained fingers restlessly.—You know, seeing what happens. What turns out.

The headmistress drops by one morning when the studio is being used by another class, and according to gossip she does nothing but stare at the heads on Isabel de Benavente's shelf for some three or four minutes, in silence; she does not even trouble to talk to Monsieur Roland, who hovers at her elbow. If Mrs. Cox forms any judgment on Isabel's talent she tells no one about it, including Isabel.

Oh, Isabel, Monika says, what fun is it?—those ugly things.

The faces are uplifted but the eyes are usually half-shut. The expressions are those of derision and mockery, sometimes fear. Even the children have been visited by monstrous thoughts. Lips are drawn back from teeth, facial muscles are cruelly bunched. There are furrows, creases, demonic grins, dimples like small pits. Cords in necks stand out rigidly—one can almost feel the tension. Eyes grow smaller, noses longer and thinner. Several of the men's faces are shaped with such precision that one might almost think them life-masks—except for the peculiar malevolent expressions.

"Bad Smell" might be the caption for this one, Dottie Arthur says with a delighted giggle.

"Bad Smell" might be the caption for all of them, another girl says.

Isabel laughs and raises one of the heads—that of a pompous old man with tightly pursed lips, puckered up as if for a kiss, and wicked slanting eyes that are practically shut, and pinched nostrils that comically suggest extreme, perhaps even psychotic, disgust—and kisses it on the lips. He's my favorite, she says, I mean I hate him the most!—*isn't* he ugly—Her eyes are bright and her clayey fingers twitch.

The heads accumulate, though Isabel is industrious about smashing the earlier ones that no longer strike her as quite *right*. What are you doing, Isabel, the girls say, puzzled, why do you break them if you spend so much time on them—? Isabel shrugs and says she doesn't know: Just fooling around.

And then, one Monday afternoon, Monsieur Roland "exposes" her —and the head-sculpting period comes abruptly to a close.

It happens like this: Monsieur Roland announces to the class that he has managed at last to discover the model for Isabel's work. It has taken him a long, long time . . . he has been poring through art histories and encyclopedias . . . and, finally, after many hours of searching he has found one Messerschmidt: Franz Xavier Messerschmidt who lived from 1736 to 1783—a German sculptor—Munich—famous in his time and now forgotten—or *nearly* forgotten—for of course clever little Isabel de Benavente knows his work well!

And, smiling angrily, blushing, Monsieur Roland holds up a book —an oversized book of photographs—and points to the busts of this Messerschmidt, from whom Isabel has plagiarized.

Of course Messerschmidt is much better, the man was an authentic artist, a genius, Monsieur Roland says, a *real* artist, but you can see the connection clearly enough, can't you!—please observe.

Isabel stares, too astonished to protest.

Messerschmidt? A German sculptor? Heads like *her* heads?

He is famous for having done sixty-nine heads, Monsieur Roland says quickly, as if reciting facts only newly acquired, quick before he forgets, executed in lead and stone. . . . Some of them are found in museums in Vienna, and in Hamburg, and . . .

The girls crowd close. And there they are, heads heavier and squatter and uglier than Isabel's, yet rather like Isabel's at the same time—masculine versions of Isabel's, it might be said. Far more skillful than Isabel's, of course.—Franz Xavier Messerschmidt was considered the leading sculptor of his time, in his part of Europe, Monsieur Roland says gravely.

Isabel too stares, incredulous, crushed. Surely there is some mistake . . . is Monsieur Roland teasing . . . he has always been curtly flirtatious with her, or so she thought, and perhaps . . . perhaps this is a good-natured joke. . . .

Messerschmidt's heads are queer mocking sardonic things, faces screwed up in disgust, grimacing like lunatics, with elongated chins and noses and ears. . . . They are caricatures of such hideous tension that one can barely look upon them. Ugly, supercilious, sneering, repulsed, fearful of drawing breath, as if the very air were feculent!—every muscle in the faces is a protest.

I did not copy him!—I did not copy those heads! Isabel finally cries. Monsieur Roland—*I did not copy those heads.*

He ignores her. The other girls ignore her, peering at the book, giggling, pretending to be surprised and shocked and "embarrassed" for her. She strides forward and strikes the table, wildly, and waves her fist at Monsieur Roland—she really doesn't know what she is doing, the entire world has burst into flames—and stammers, You nasty old liar, you fat ugly old frog-shit, *I did not copy those heads and you know it!*

And she runs out of the studio. And no one follows her.

She stays away from school for the rest of the week. And on Saturday morning Mr. de Benavente's driver comes to the school with a letter from Mr. de Benavente for Mrs. Cox, who reads it with some anxiety, and then, evidently quite relieved, leads the young Puerto Rican upstairs to the art studio and allows him to pack the clay heads—more than two dozen of the ugly things—in cardboard boxes, and take them away. And Isabel stores them for a while in the damp basement of the house. And, months later, seeks them out again, and studies them, and makes her calm decision: she smashes them with a hammer, one by one, and never thinks of them or Monsieur Roland or sculpting or "art" again.

Except once, and briefly, she brings up the subject of her "strange period," her "crazy hobby," to Maurie. In the eighth or ninth year of their marriage. When matters with Nick are in a kind of equilibrium—not placid, not frantic. Maurie immediately asks if she would like to take art lessons again. Isabel says no, of course not. Not only hasn't she time (this year she will be cochairman of the United Cerebral Palsy Association Benefit Ball, this year darling little Kirsten will be a flower girl at the second most important Washington wedding of the season, lavishly and a trifle vulgarly laid on in the Shrine of the Immaculate Conception at Catholic University) but she doesn't really want to endure anything like that again: a strange period in her life when she had worked so hard, so feverishly, day after day, forgetting her friends and everything else, her mind circling one thing and one thing only, tirelessly, obsessively: she hadn't even any appetite for food, she tells Maurie with a contemptuous laugh, at a time in her life when she loved banana splits and French fries and hot buttered popcorn, she hadn't even the ability to sleep through the night . . . at a time in her life when she loved nothing better than to dawdle in bed as late as possible. And what the hell did I have to show for it? she says. Her pert upper lip curls back slightly from her strong white beautiful teeth, and her nostrils pinch in faint revulsion.

She does not tell Maurie about the specific nature of the clay heads, or even that she was sculpting heads; and she is never to bring up the subject—or art itself except in the most general impersonal terms —with Nick Martens.

General Kempe's Secret

Many and varied are the guests who are to pass through Isabel Halleck's salon in the handsome stone house at 18 Röcken, in her foreshortened but brilliant career as a Washington hostess: embassy people from every part of the world; White House officials and ladies-in-waiting; United Nations people, Pentagon people, public relations people under various titles; lawyers, businessmen, lobbyists, Congressmen, Senators (even—once—the formidable Senator Ewing in the days before the Commission for the Ministry of Justice turned the attention of its most scrupulous young investigators to the possibility of "conflict of interest" in the Senator's career as a public servant and a property owner of evident wealth in his home state); journalists and editors and columnists and "experts" and university professors; famous athletes; theater people, film people, ballerinas, musicians, television people, photographers; bankers, financiers, out-of-town philanthropists, visiting millionaires; military men both active and retired; hairdressers, fashion designers, models, "secretaries," "assistants," widows; influence peddlers, unclassifiable people, members of entourages, exiles from despotic regimes, memoirists, former revolutionaries, former kings, blackmailers, ecology experts, executives, owners of tobacco plantations in unknown countries (Malawi), and steelworks in improbable cities (Calcutta); World Bank officials, Rio Tinto men, nuclear engineers, architects, sportswriters, rock singers, "active" clergy, feminists, high-ranking bureaucrats, a former Secretary of State, intelligence men under various titles; liaison men; prime ministers, shahs, premiers, presidents, kings, bodyguards under various titles.

Many and varied are the political "opinions"—by no means simply pro- or anti-Vietnam, during the days of that war—by no means simply "liberal" or "conservative," White House supporters or White House detractors—representatives of the "public sector" and representatives of the "private sector": many and varied are the unusual personalities. (As in, You gather such unusual personalities about you, Isabel, I'm frankly jealous—a frequent remark made by women friends and acquaintances and rival hostesses. But then of course—your life with Maurie Halleck is so stable.)

Among all these guests no one comes to Isabel's more often, and no one is more devoted to her, than General Morton Kempe, a former chairman of the Joint Chiefs of Staff.

What are you doing with your time these days, General Kempe, people ask, and General Kempe replies: What I've done with it all my life —observing fools and knaves and keeping my distance.

General Kempe, an acquaintance of Mr. Benavente's, and possibly even a business partner of his upon occasion, has known Isabel since she was a very young child; but to Isabel's eye the old man does not seem to have changed in three decades. Everything about him is outsized, striking, unsettling: he is about six feet seven inches tall, his head is massive and "leonine," his face is that of a bloated bulldog's, his enormous pouched eyes are sleepy and yet stare—at women in particular— with a powerful cold passion. In recent years his clothes have become threadbare, out of negligence and indifference; he was once seen, at an inaugural ball, at the White House, in a black evening jacket with satin lapels and an ordinary red and black plaid flannel shirt from Sears. General Kempe dresses like that to insult us, people say, hurt, but Isabel defends him: Not at all, not at all, the dear old man simply doesn't see himself—quite literally he doesn't look in mirrors. He told me that at the age of sixty-five he stopped looking in mirrors forever.

How extraordinary! Can it be true?—But when was he sixty-five?

I have no idea, Isabel says.

He must be in his eighties now, don't you think. Eighty-five, eighty-eight. . . .

I have no idea, Isabel says, curtly, as if the discussion of age— even General Kempe's age—is slightly obscene.

One thing about General Kempe that *has* changed, over the decades, is his breath. Since Isabel's childhood it has grown progressively more dank, more cold, more fetid. . . . In recent years it has become so awful that people who stand too close to him simply cannot, at first, grasp the fact; they cannot register it. Those who know the general better station themselves at a comfortable distance from him, and in fact he prefers listeners fanned out before him, four or five feet away, for though he is hard of hearing it isn't usually necessary for him to hear. He is one of the great Washington raconteurs.

Tales of war: World War II and the "Korean conflict" in particular. Blunders. Idiocy. Barbarism. Corruption. Statistics. (291,557 battle deaths in the war, 33,629 in the "conflict.") Tales of Dwight Eisenhower, Omar Bradley, Matthew Ridgway, Douglas MacArthur. Tales of Truman, F.D.R., Chiang Kai-shek, Churchill. Franco and Hirohito and Mussolini and of course the Nazis—he knew them all. He was, he says, quite a Nazi man at one time: a Nazi expert, that is. (What of the Vietnam war, General?—he is often asked, but he rudely declines to give an opinion except to say that it's an "unprofessional" war. Isabel suspects he knows little about it.)

Sometimes, however, when General Kempe has been drinking straight Scotch for hours, and the party is depleted, and only two or three avid listeners remain before him—always men, at this hour—and rather "odd" men at that—his stories are about his early experiences in combat, many years ago. No colorful military leaders, no famous names, no ribald wild implausible anecdotes. Only battle skirmishes, exhaustion, rain and mud and fatigue, hunger, panic, hallucinations, terror. And profound surprise. *What is the body's reaction to the news that it is mortal?* General Kempe asks with a grin,—*profound surprise.*

His descriptions of explosions, gunfire, toppling buildings, deaths and woundings in "interesting" modes are so physical, so graphic, yet delivered with such cold oratorial zest, that even male listeners have turned aside, sickened.

(As the years pass General Kempe drinks more heavily, and begins to concentrate on this second kind of story, which to Isabel's fastidious ear is always the same story in different settings, involving different means of death, the same ugly implacable pitiless story . . . and quite naturally his popularity falls off. Who wants to hear, time and again, of a single figure, at dawn, a single young soldier, wandering across a smoldering landscape heaped with the faceless dead, his "buddies" . . .? At about the time Owen Halleck is old enough to drop in casually on his mother's parties the poor general will be relegated to a corner, or a strategic position beneath an archway, where he will stand for hours, drinking steadily, his gray hair thick as ever and wild and erect in a profane aureole about his head, his cold sleepy ironic gaze prowling the room. Chattering people, laughing people, handshakes and hugs and kisses . . . ! General Kempe watches, General Kempe knows.)

Yet there is obviously a sentimental streak in the old gentleman: consider his devotion to Isabel.

His numerous gifts to her and, less frequently, to her little boy and girl—whom he loves, he has told Isabel confidentially, more than he loves his own grandchildren. (His own *grand*children! Nick Martens snorts. His own *great*-grandchildren, he means, the old goat.)

Over the years General Kempe has given Isabel costly gifts for her birthday and Christmas—a strand of cream rose pearls, a Japanese cape threaded with actual gold, a short fitted jacket of dark brown sealskin that had belonged to his second wife, now dead—and Isabel has accepted most of them, reluctantly, under pressure from the old man, who can be quite tyrannical when the mood seizes him. She is caught between not daring to offend Morton Kempe (infamous in Washington for "severing connections" with his first wife, an unhappy local beauty whom he shut out of his life after a quarrel and to whom he refused to speak though, dying in the hospital of cancer, she begged for him) . . . and not wanting to offend his heirs (Byron Kempe, for instance, a son from the general's third marriage, is making a considerable name for himself over at State; and Isabel encounters his pretty, aggressive young wife virtually everywhere in town).

Just before the Hallecks left for Bitterfeld Lake Morton Kempe dropped by, ironic and wistful, not *quite* hinting that he was free for the Fourth of July weekend . . . sitting in Isabel's charming little drawing room and drinking one Scotch after another and devouring, with a chilling impersonal zest, a box of chocolate-covered cherries. Isabel felt sorry for the old man. She knew, if pressed, Maurie would consent to inviting him up with the family . . . Maurie always gave in, in the direction of being "generous," "charitable," "kindly toward outcasts" . . . and though the children were afraid of him, and shrank away from his cold touch and fetid breath, they could be cajoled into accepting him . . . and in any case the children's wishes were not important. (Isabel, like her father, does not believe in spoiling children—it ill equips them for the world.) But Nick Martens would be furious.

She smiled cruelly, imagining Nick's handsome face if he arrived at Bitterfeld and found General Kempe there—!

So she said apologetically to the general, while freshening his drink, that the weekend in the Adirondacks is really a working vacation for the men—Nick Martens and Reid Silber and Maurie. The hearings on Senator Ewing, the immense amount of thinking and planning and rehearsing that go into a single day's session . . . the men want to get away from the city, of course, it's a wretched summer, but mainly they want to work.

General Kempe stared and for a long moment did not speak. His eyes were the most peculiar slate color—inhuman and yet—queerly—rather beautiful: and their intensity flattered Isabel.

Finally he said, as if only reluctantly granting her point, and forgiving her, yet subtly blaming her as well: Since it's in the public interest—running the old fox to death—tearing him to pieces with their teeth—"Great Society" blather, my ass!—a pity you can't touch Johnson too—*there's* a master criminal, an expert hog at the trough—since it will go in the history books—as a footnote at least: all right. But I'll miss you, dear. Away up in the mountains with your men.

How can you allow that old murderer to touch you, Nick frequently asks. How can you even allow him in your house?

He's a lonely old man, Isabel says slowly. He's deep, he's complex —he *isn't* just a murderer, there's much more to him.

Her wit is so sly, her manner so gay and charming, that for a moment Nick doesn't seem to have heard. Then he explodes into laughter. He squeezes her hand, hard, laughing, and then releases it—even pushes it away as if she is a naughty child.—So you do admit he's a murderer!

Only in the service of his country, says Isabel.

Yes?

In the service of his heritage.

And what about his wives, and his stepson?—that one who jumped off the George Washington Bridge?

It wasn't the George Washington Bridge, it was something less impressive, Isabel says slowly, trying to think, a long time ago . . . the Queensboro Bridge, I think . . . and the young man had been suffering mental problems for years, it was hardly Morton's fault. As for the wives . . . what can you do about alcoholics? . . . it's an illness, it's no one's choice.

The second wife died, didn't she, in some sort of mysterious way. . . .

She fell down a spiral staircase in their house, Isabel says, but she was drunk, she'd been drinking for days, all the servants said so . . . the rumors were really slanderous, poor Morton might have sued if he had known how cruel and unfair they were! . . . you misjudge him, Nick, he's really a sad lonely broken old man. He seems to need me.

I asked—how can you let him touch you?—breathe into your face? Nick says irritably.

He doesn't *touch* me, Isabel says with a smile, not very frequently . . . about as frequently as you do.

Nick stiffens; his reaction is so pure, so spontaneous, that Isabel believes he really hadn't expected her to say what she did . . . though the motion of many of their private conversations, its general game plan, is toward this charge.

He doesn't actually breathe into my face very often, Isabel continues, I think he wants to spare me . . . he's no fool, he *knows* . . . he knows that he isn't quite as attractive as he once was to the ladies.

He doesn't know anything, Nick says, flushing in anger. He has absolutely no self-awareness and he doesn't give a damn about anyone, including you, it's just your face or your innocence or your youth he adores, don't flatter yourself it's *love.*

Love isn't flattering to me, much, Isabel says. My children love me —more or less. And Maurie loves me. It's really quite automatic.

Nick is now supposed to say, *Look, you know I love you, let's change the subject,* but he sits stubborn and red-faced and silent. Several strained seconds pass.

Isabel says, faltering, baiting: My husband doesn't mind the general. He isn't jealous in the slightest. He feels sorry for him too . . . his spirit is generous enough to enfold all sorts of cripples.

Maurie isn't home for your parties, Maurie's conveniently absent, Nick says. And then, as if unaware that he is contradicting himself: Yes, he does mind. He minds a great deal. Don't kid yourself.

Has he told you he minds? Isabel asks.

Nick says nothing.

Has he told you? Do you talk about me, the two of you? Isabel asks, casually. I'm just curious, I can't imagine you and Maurie talking about anything except your precious work.

Nick shrugs his shoulders and says evasively: We talk of innumerable things. We're really quite human.

"Human"—?

I mean as men, as husbands. Men are really quite human.

Do you talk about me, do you talk about June? Isabel asks.

June, rarely.

Isabel smiles a small sad gratified smile. And adroitly changes the subject since it is one of the unarticulated rules of their game that whoever pursues a certain too-familiar topic beyond a certain point is gauche, and the loser by default. She says: If you insist I will sacrifice the old man. Never invite him to any party you're likely to attend.

But what about the others? Nick asks.

The "others"—? Are there other friends of mine you hate?

The other parties. The ones I don't attend.

Do you want that too! Isabel laughs, startled. Then you want everything. You're jealous after all.—But do you insist?

Of course not, Nick says coldly.

Of course not, she mocks.

It isn't my privilege to insist about anything, in terms of your life.

It isn't your inclination, Isabel says. And a moment later, sullenly: It isn't your strategy.

One New Year's Eve shortly after the Hallecks moved into the house on Röcken, Maurie's and his family's gift for his beautiful young bride, General Kempe confided in Isabel: murmured his drunken "secret" in her ear.

He had been going to kiss her, perhaps, but drew back, seeing her frightened smile, and said instead that he'd tell her his great discovery —his secret, secret revelation—if she promised to tell no one, not even her husband; or that man Nick Martens who always hung around.

Isabel promised, inclining her head obediently.

The secret that nobody knows, General Kempe said with a chuckle, though in fact everybody knows—everybody right in this room —is that we're all dead and nothing matters and it was painless after all and no one can touch us!

Isabel blinked. She must have misunderstood.

Yes? she said faintly. What—?

Really dead, the old man whispered in triumph, teetering over her, his breath in an almost perceptible cloud about her lovely blond head, the whole bunch of us—the old ones especially—just hear them celebrating!—it's more evident tonight of all nights of the year but it's clear enough at any time—just crowd us all in one room—hand out the drinks—everybody knows.

Isabel smiled and swallowed and stared at the floor. It was a protocol violation to move away from the general until dismissed. I don't think I understand, she said.

You will, you will, General Kempe said heartily, giving her a little squeeze before he stepped away, a pack of ghosts—cheerful horde of ghouls—but never mind—it was painless and nobody can touch us now —you know it the second after the bullet strikes—nobody can touch you again—there isn't even any mystery about it.

And Isabel *did* keep General Kempe's secret, and keeps it still.

Love

The game continues.

Another can of smart fresh lime-green balls is opened.

The angry thwack of the strings. The pounding of rubber-soled shoes on the court. Audible panting. Nick's shouted query and Maurie's mumbled reply and the game continues.

It is nearly seven-thirty and the game began at four-thirty and it is clear that Nick will release Maurie from the red clay court only when he wins a game completely—without Maurie making a single point. It is also clear that Maurie is too honest, too guileless, and too defiantly stubborn to lose this single point. So the game continues. One game and then another and then another.

Both men are winded and drenched with sweat. Maurie's glasses slide down his nose almost continuously, Nick's shirt sticks to his back in odd wet creases. Their playing is erratic—sometimes slaphappy, sometimes grim. It seems to be the case that Nick must play a "brilliant" game of tennis while not playing "seriously" in the eyes of his opponent and their small group of spectators. Nick has said, in regard to the Commission's current prosecution, that it isn't simply winning that matters—it's the style with which, publicly, one wins.

Men can't play games, June says quietly, rising to leave. They don't know what play is.

Reid Silber, dressed for evening in an open-necked silk shirt and beige linen trousers, sipping a drink, consoles Isabel: It sometimes happens like this on the court, a player gets hot who isn't ordinarily very competitive, his opponent is knocked off balance and when he regains control he wants—well, revenge is too strong a word—he wants, let's say, to reassert himself: surely you can understand?

The children have begun to bicker, the tension on the court has made them anxious, someone nudges someone, someone pinches an arm, there is a slap, an accusation, tears. June takes her weeping daughter away. Florence scolds her son.

Isabel stands watching the players as if mesmerized. Her anger is so deep, so massive, it has passed over into a kind of calm.

After a long pause she replies to Reid: I hate "understanding."

What's that? says Reid, cupping his ear.

Nick's strong legs which will never give out. His soiled white shorts, wet T-shirt. His hoarse cry: Fifteen-love! And then the nervous laugh, the sporty chuckle, the surreptitious glance to the side of the court—who is it, the woman walking away?—is she someone who matters?

Maurie's perceptible limp. The ache in his knee. (Sometimes, at night, the pain wakes him. And Isabel wakes as well. What is it? she asks, and Maurie says, Nothing—nothing, really, and Isabel says, Can't you sleep, what are you thinking of . . . ? though her voice is soft, soft, almost inaudible, not because she is sinking back into sleep but because she doesn't want an answer to her question. What are you thinking of, are you as lonely as I am, has "love" injured you, do you know how we cherish you, Nick and I, how we talk of you, how we betray you . . . ? Do you know anything? Do you suspect? Or is your pain only physical?)

Isabel and her lover are not lovers, technically. Though they have lain together. Though they have wept in each other's arms.

Can I always rely upon you, Isabel has begged. And Nick has said, Always. Of course. Don't you trust me?

Don't I trust you, don't I trust you. . . . So Isabel muses, alone, staring at her reflection in the mirror. Isabel is one of those persons to whom the mirror is a continuing consolation.

Nick's tireless ambition, Nick's lust. The ticking of his brain. (Which keeps him awake at night, he tells Isabel. Not that he is necessarily thinking—though of course he is, most of the time—he has a great deal to think about in this phase of his career—but the brain ticks on and on whether there are in fact thoughts to accommodate it, very late at night.)—June is unhappy. June is worried. She doesn't think she will be equal to all I intend to do, Nick says slowly.

Isabel considers telling Nick that "predictions" concerning the Martenses' marriage are generally negative. (People in their circle do talk a fair amount about one another, and about the Martenses—Nick, that is. And, yes, there is a sort of mock-grave consensus that June Martens will not be "equal" to all that her husband intends to do.)

Will you go into politics eventually, does that sort of thing interest you? someone asked Nick not long ago, in Isabel's presence, and she watched his face closely as he replied; but he did not dissemble.

That depends upon my luck, Nick said simply.

Good luck or bad luck—?

Nick laughed. Isabel laughed. It *was* an amusing quip—mildly. There is only one kind of luck in Washington, Nick said.

Isabel Halleck is Maurie Halleck's wife and it might be indiscreet to talk of Nick Martens and the possibility of a political future and luck of any kind in her presence, since Nick is an associate of Maurie's at the Commission and their work is what the newspapers call "sensitive" these days. But the conversation continues just the same. It is a very interesting conversation.

Isabel de Benavente Halleck has the reputation of being admirably discreet.

What a person is in secret, he becomes—in politics.

Isabel cannot remember who said this. Her father?—one of his friends? General Kempe?

The tennis game continues and Maurie wins a point and Nick wins a point and then there is a ferocious volley and Maurie nearly cries out in despair—or resignation—or exhausted humor—and after a pause there is another serve, a wild wicked crashing serve, and the game continues and now it is quarter to eight, now eight o'clock, the guests for dinner are arriving up at the lodge, three cars, their headlights burning because, in the mountains, in the pine forest, dusk comes early even at midsummer.

Everyone has left the red clay court except the players.

Maurie has turned the floodlights on.—Yes this is real style, this is the real thing, Nick says, smiling, trying to smile, something tight and hard about his jaw, tennis courts with floodlights, great, your serve—?

Ellen Silber walks with Isabel and her children, who are bickering. Isabel handles the squabble deftly—gives little Kirsten a shake, gives little Owen a brisk slap, and separates them. Ellen is flattered to be asked to take Kirsten's hand.

Such a pretty little girl, Ellen says.

Isabel ignores her. She is thinking not of the men playing tennis —those fools—but of the guests arriving in their cars. Cocktails and dinner and the heady exhilarating momentum of a party: which is, after all, nothing more than people crowded into a set of walls, and yet miraculous: her salvation.

Such a darling little girl, Ellen murmurs.

Ellen Silber has been shyly courting Isabel for a long time, and Isabel half-sees with amusement that the girl has tried to fashion her hair into a chignon—one of the styles in which Isabel wears hers. But the chignon is ineptly done. And not attractive. The girl's profile is not attractive.

I should hope she's a pretty little girl, Isabel wants to murmur, vexed, I should *hope* she's darling. . . . She's my child, after all.

But she says nothing. Her silence may be interpreted by Ellen as haughty, or troubled, or contemplative—or the natural silence of a beautiful woman who need not reply to every inane compliment thrown her way.

I'm looking forward to the dinner, Ellen says, it was really nice of you to invite us up—you and Mr. Halleck—I love it here—I could stay here forever—

Could you, says Isabel.

She hears, rising from the red clay court, Nick's sudden hoarse voice: *Fifteen-love!*

VII. Night-Blooming Cereus

Washington, D.C.,

August 1980

The Surprise

What is it?—a species of cactus, actually—an American cactus—it blooms only once a year around this time, late summer—and only at night—

Once a year?—do you mean this is it, tonight?

This is it, tonight, Claudia says with a high delighted laugh. Tonight.

But how wasteful. . . . How beautiful.

Someone counts aloud: there are fourteen large buds on the plant. Several have begun to open. Kirsten stares, transfixed. The petals are moving, the petals are actually moving as she watches. . . . Would you like a flashlight, Kirsten, Claudia asks, offering her a pencil-sized flashlight, or can you see well enough by the moon? We're so lucky the moon is out this year, last summer the sky was overcast and it began to rain and I was heartbroken. . . .

Kirsten's first instinct is to refuse the flashlight but in this newer phase of her life she accepts it with a courteous smile. Thank you, Mrs. Lleyn.

Thank you thank you thank you Mrs. Lleyn and all of you, you are most helpful.

Collapsed old bag, Owen had called the poor woman. Perhaps she remembers. Kirsten and Owen were convulsed with laughter when Owen recounted in detail the fruits of his numerous investigations back in May. I had no method then, Owen admitted. My mission was doomed. And yours as well—we were idiots.

Chagrined, Kirsten is inclined to agree.

Ah, aren't they beautiful!—the blossoms are so *large*—

Wherever did you get such an extraordinary thing, Claudia?

Is it rare?—is it expensive?—is it temperamental?—I have no luck with temperamental plants!

You can actually *see* the blossoms opening, can't you. I didn't think they would be so large, they're the size of a fist, a man's fist. . . . But so delicate. . . .

Are those spikes around the petals? I mean—prickly spines?— like cactus needles? Are they sharp?

Oh, I wouldn't touch—

I'm *not* touching it, I'm just looking—

It's pink, isn't it, actually, a *pink* flower—

Pink shading into white—

More white, I think—

This little one up here is all pink—

Aren't they beautiful!—Claudia has such luck with plants—of course you really have to love them, you have to coax them along—take them very seriously.

Do you suppose it's aware of us?—all the attention it's getting tonight?

It must certainly be aware of something unusual. An agitation in the air, voices, vibrations—of course I'm not one of these people who thinks that plants are—well, people—that they have souls—

This blossom is the color of your dress, Isabel—isn't it?—almost?

Such a lovely color. . . .

Ah, look, another bud is opening!—over here.

It's the most *amazing* phenomenon. . . .

Claudia has such lovely things in her home, from all over the world, where did she say this plant is from?—South America?—what's it called again, ceresus—?

Cereus. She said it's a cactus.

It doesn't look like a cactus.

Is there a bar set up?

I don't think there's a bar, actually, I think Claudia is just asking people—no, wait, there's a waiter—over there—can you get his attention?—or maybe we should go over.

It's getting crowded, what time is it?

Quarter to nine.

Isabel, shall I get you a drink?

Your daughter is looking beautiful, Isabel. . . .

We haven't seen each other for a long time . . . I think it must have been . . .

. . . a long time.

Damn, he's going in the other direction. What would you like?

Kirsten, what would you like? A summer drink, something light?
—a glass of white wine?

No thank you, Kirsten says absently, staring at the blossoms.

Perrier water, fruit juice. . . .

No, says Kirsten.

They move away and she is left alone, studying the cereus. She has heard of the night-blooming flower before—she has in fact heard of Mrs. Lleyn's enormous plant—but she has never seen a cereus, to her knowledge, and she has certainly never seen it in bloom.

Let me pick you up tonight, around sunset, Isabel said over the telephone. Her voice was quite steady, even resolute. "Cheerful." "Maternal" but not "bullying." She did not sound frightened, she did not sound determined, she did not even sound as if she were "trying for a reconciliation." A little surprise, an unusual little outing, Isabel said. Only an hour or two.

Are you coming alone? Kirsten asked.

I don't go anywhere alone, Isabel said.

You don't go anywhere alone? Kirsten repeated, struck by something queer in her mother's voice. But—what do you mean? Why did you say that?

Because it happens to be true, Isabel said.

But—I don't understand.

You understand.

For a long sweating moment Kirsten gripped the telephone receiver and could not speak. She knows, Kirsten thought, she knows what Owen and I are going to do. Kirsten gripped the receiver, her pulses racing so hotly she was in terror of fainting, then she thought calmly, No, it must be a misunderstanding, she's just afraid, just afraid—of everything.

Isabel took up the conversation again, cheerful and maternal and positive, for after all wasn't she just suggesting an outing, a pleasant evening, mother and daughter, wasn't it all entirely normal?—no loathing, no apprehension, no danger. I'll pick you up around sunset, we won't be gone more than a few hours, she said, coaxing, as if Kirsten were once again a very small child, stubborn enough to resist fun.

A surprise, said Isabel. At sunset.

Sunset, Kirsten said, laughing nervously. Why do you put it that way? That's an odd way of putting it.

Because I don't remember what time the sun goes down any longer, Isabel said, and our surprise has something to do with sunset. With dusk.

What is the surprise? Kirsten asked.

It wouldn't be a surprise if I told you, would it? Isabel said. And now the "cheerfulness" thickened into a low unconvincing laugh.—Let us pick you up, Kirsten, it's only for an hour or two, right here in the neighborhood, I promise not to ask about Owen or try to get you to come home. . . . I think you'll find it a very beautiful surprise.

Do you, Kirsten murmured.

Now the blossoms are opening as she watches and they *are* beautiful, there is something quite remarkable about them, Kirsten is a child again gaping at tropical plants in the botanical garden, Maurie is holding her hand, there is no Isabel there is no Owen the air is warm and thick and moist the rubber plants are enormous there are giant ferns wonderful spiky leaves she brings her face close against one of them and feels the light tickle against her forehead . . . a *tickle* that reverberates through her body and makes her want to laugh and sneeze.

She counts the blossoms for herself. Fourteen. Of which ten are open, or nearly. The plant *is* a kind of cactus, you can see that, standing about seven feet high in its clay pot (which has been placed in the ground). Rather ungainly. In fact—she steps back to judge—almost monstrous. The individual flowers are beautiful but the plant as a whole is monstrous, propped up with sticks.

Beautiful ugly thing, Kirsten whispers.

She looks around the terrace, her head slightly bowed, her eyes working quickly. Tall slender Kirsten Halleck. The daughter of. Yes, a pity, isn't it. But recovered now. Evidently. She is wearing white trousers that hug her small high buttocks and a red shirt—one of those flimsy muslin things on sale in "Oriental" bazaars—and the shirt is open to show, as if deliberately, her narrow chest and the tops of her small pale breasts. It cannot be said even by well-intentioned relatives and friends of the family and other affable liars that Kirsten is looking beautiful "again" but her face has a carved ascetic starkness—the hard cheekbones, the staring accusing eyes—that is arresting to even the casual observer. She gives the impression of being rigidly under control: restrained, ferociously calm. When her hair falls in her eyes she brushes it back in a gesture that is slow enough to appear studied. . . . Beautiful ugly thing, Kirsten smiles.

A surprise, her mother promised. For you.

For me, Mommy? For me?

For you.

For *me*, Mommy?—and no one else!

For you, little sweetheart, and *no one else*.

And you aren't angry with me, you don't want to punish me—?

But Babylove, why would I want to punish you?—why would anyone want to punish you?

Cruel Isabel, sly sneering Isabel, perhaps she had been a secret witness that afternoon in Di Piero's apartment, perhaps she had overheard Kirsten's frightened sobbing, or did Tony afterward recount the episode in full, for the amusement of his Washington friends?—brave little skinny little virginal Kirsten Halleck steeling herself not to wince and not to gag and not to burst into baby-tears, as of course she eventually did.

Di Piero was incensed, Di Piero was not amused, after all she had broken her promise not to cry; after all, despite her bravado, she hadn't acquitted herself with much style. And as she left she said spitefully that she knew now why Isabel referred to him as a "beautiful pig"—though she didn't exactly see the "beautiful" part of it.

Don't confuse yourself with your mother, dear, Tony said lazily, not troubling to accompany her to the door, —you and Isabel aren't in the same league.

Late that afternoon, at the usual time, Owen telephoned to ask if there were any "developments" and Kirsten had to restrain her excitement because, today, for once, she had something to report.—We're going out tonight, she said. Isabel and me. And her boy friend.

Going where? Owen asked. Eager and slightly—or does she imagine it?—envious.

A surprise, Mother said. I assume it's a party somewhere nearby. Though it could be an old "friend" of mine she's unearthed . . . or an unexpected Kuhn from Minnesota she doesn't know what to do with . . . or maybe we'll go swimming nude in the pool, the three of us. A variation on the nuclear family.

She fell silent. Owen said: You don't think it might be to see *him?*

Kirsten had thought of that probability. That possibility. But she rejected the thought—it was worthless.

I doubt it, she said, annoyed; for she and Owen had talked about this subject so very many times. That wouldn't be part of their discretion right now. Their strategy.

They must talk on the phone, Owen said. I'm sure she's told him all about me—all she knows. He might even have someone following me. . . . Uli thinks this is probably the case.

Doesn't Uli know?

He doesn't know *everything.*

I thought he did, Kirsten said. I thought—

Let's change the subject, Owen said, we were talking about Isabel and Nick and their telephone conversations and the fact that, if you moved back home, you could monitor them. You could make this all much easier.

That's Uli's idea, Kirsten said, isn't it.

I don't want to talk about him right now, Owen said.

You wouldn't make me move back home and live in that . . . in that place, Kirsten said. She was silent for a few seconds, and noted Owen's shrewd silence, which she had grown to respect. (She had not met Owen's friend Uli and did not know his last name. But she had no doubt of his existence for he had effected an extraordinary change in her brother. Uli, Uli, what kind of a name is that, is it a foreign name, Kirsten said, it sounds—Swedish?—is he a foreigner?—someone connected with one of the embassies?) Why don't *you* move back in, she said hotly.

You know I can't, Owen said.

Why not.

I *can't.*

Why the hell not.

I'm only going to cross the threshold when she's there to . . . to pay my final respects to her, Owen said quietly. You know that.

Kirsten did know it. But she needed to hear it repeated.

Oh again and again and again . . . !

Her brother's sobriety intoxicated her. The secrecy of his life now. His discipline. Purity.

Kirsten did know his plan, his vow, but she said in a childish tone: Well—I can't either, I can't stay under the same roof, imagine eating meals with her—! And her lover or bodyguard or whoever. And General Kempe—he still visits—a male nurse drives him over, wheels him in—it's too ridiculous. Don't ask me to do something you can't do yourself. Just for the sake of spying on her and Nick. . . . And she's too clever anyway, she wouldn't talk over the phone if I was around, she wouldn't talk to *him.* They must meet somewhere. Or telephone from different places. She knows that we know and . . . well, she knows.

Yes, said Owen, his voice quavering—though whether with joy or apprehension, Kirsten could not gauge—she *knows.* But she can't foresee the future.

What is now proved . . .

. . . was once only imagined!

Kirsten has no need to pretend an interest in the night-blooming cereus. She is genuinely interested. She studies the lovely slow-spreading petals—white, creamy pink, pink—and overhears a garrulous fool offer the widow condolences. (Where has he been? Out of the country for more than a year?) And for the ten thousandth time the widow murmurs her gracious thanks. Stoic and soft-voiced and brave and so very beautiful even in bereavement.

Black becomes you, Isabel Halleck!

Slender clinging voluptuous black, black silk, St. Laurent, Pauline Trigère, Oscar de la Renta. A charming little fitted sweater top with a cape-collar, subdued navy blue stripes, by Adri.

But tonight, for a casual evening at Claudia Lleyn's—accompanied by her daughter and her most recent gentleman escort—the widow is wearing cream-colored linen culottes and a "simple" sleeveless rayon sweater to match. For of course—after fourteen months—she is no longer in mourning.

For the ten thousandth time she murmurs words and phrases her daughter has no need to overhear. Yes, unseen, tragic, shock, trauma, children, financial snarls, legal complications, difficulties, adjustment, necessary, passage of time, medication, cruelty of media, scars, ghouls, support of friends, sympathy, generosity, travel. . . .

It is a curiosity of this society, Owen has told Kirsten, his speech-rhythm as well as his words not entirely his own, but very seductive, very very seductive, one of the most murderous societies in history, that death is assumed to be *causeless*. That it just "happens." That no one is responsible. I mean really responsible. Bad luck, the wrong place at the wrong time, should have known what would happen, he was asking for it, she was asking for it . . . the usual. Not one of Father's friends has said to Isabel: Look, you had kicked him out of the house, right?—you were negotiating for as much money from the poor bastard as you could get, you wanted a divorce, you've been having a love affair with another man for twenty years, what is all this *widow-shit*—! Not one of Father's friends has come up to her and said: So how did you kill him —directly or indirectly?

Your daughter is looking lovely, the voice continues, that *is* your daughter, isn't it, Christine?—oh yes, Kristin—I mean *Kirsten*—of course—is she starting college next month?—no?—oh, I see—well, that's a very *good* idea—that's a very—yes of course—languages—less pressure—right here at Georgetown—Spanish is a lovely language, I studied it myself in college—but you wouldn't know it now!—though I adored Spain when we went there, it must be eighteen years ago now —beautiful country—mountains, coast—And how is your boy Owen? I believe he graduated from—?

Kirsten would very much enjoy hearing her mother's response. But babbling interrupts: more guests, more embraces and kisses. And of course Isabel's voice is lowered whenever she negotiates this particular topic.

The contemptible thing about the theft, the unforgivable thing, Isabel said, several days after the hysteria had passed, is that I can't notify the police and I can't file a claim with the insurance company and the little bastard was counting on that.

Kirsten, somewhat intimidated, biting her lip, guilty though she had—in truth—no reason to feel guilty, could not think of a reply.

I can't notify the police and I can't file a claim with the insurance company and the little bastard was counting on that, Isabel said slowly.

Nick Martens might be dropping by tonight, Claudia says casually.

To Isabel.

To Isabel, whose face Kirsten cannot see, from this angle. But whose slender back in the creamy beige sweater does not stiffen or otherwise show alarm or surprise or interest.

It's been so long, I thought I'd telephone, he's never in but, but I thought I'd give him a ring, such a *long* time, since the funeral in fact, of course his life is very complicated these days, that pipe fitters' union, or the syndicate, whatever, I don't know any details but I was reading in the *Post,* threats against his life, that poor young woman . . . wouldn't you know it, a brilliant young girl just out of law school and such a promising career and I don't blame her a bit, I think these feminists in the papers are absurd, they're nothing but bullies, any one of them in her place would have resigned too, I'm not a sexist but I think there are such risks we don't have to take, I mean women, it's tragic enough that men must take them, of course it was a shame it said in the paper there were four hundred applicants for her job at the Commission. . . .

Kirsten watches her mother's back, covertly. And Claudia's pleasant attractive face. But really there is nothing to see. There is nothing to interpret.

Nick Martens. It's been so long. And June, what of June?—oh yes, I suppose it was over long ago—but not an actual divorce, was there? —oh, was there really?—and now the poor thing has dropped out of sight—well—I suppose she's moved back to Boston or wherever—I never thought she fitted in here—she was too *serious*—I mean at dinner parties—it's tiresome—the men get that all day long and in the evening —yes, exactly—they want to relax and enjoy life a little—and to find yourself seated beside someone who wants to discuss the "issues" without knowing all the facts—and of course we can't know—of course most of it is confidential—but I didn't actually know whether or not there was an actual divorce or whether it was just one of those depressing marriages that go on and on and on with people living in two places. . . .

Kirsten's heart beats calmly and steadily. Which she notes with pride. Which she will certainly report to her brother.

Look: my hand isn't shaking, it's as steady as yours.

The Telegram

On the afternoon of May 14, 1980, Owen Halleck sent the following message by Western Union to his sister Kirsten, at the Eyre Academy for Girls, Eyre, New York: LIVE BE BEAUTIFUL AGAIN NO QUARTER FOR OUR ENEMIES ALL IS CHANGED AM ON MY WAY UP LOVE O.

Kirsten studied the message for a very long time and did not in fact manage to sleep during the thirty-six hours between the delivery of the telegram and her brother's arrival in Eyre. She spent much of the time reading the message aloud, testing the pronunciation she might give to the word LIVE. It did not take her long to deduce that it was an imperative but the imperative so excited her, she thought she might be in danger of going mad. She thought she might be in danger of running wild and crazy and injuring herself.

The Raid

Since her husband's death and the unpleasant publicity surrounding it Isabel Halleck has traveled extensively, alone or with companions: she has visited Nassau, Mexico, Guatemala, Rio, Geneva, Rome, Florence, Venice, the Costa del Sol, and Gibraltar . . . and has plans to spend three weeks in Paris, in October, and then fly down to Morocco to stay with friends.

A moving target, it seems.

It was during the Italian tour, in June, that the house at 18 Röcken was raided.

Owen Halleck chose this strategic time to return to his former home—alone, without a comrade—and appropriate a number of reasonably valuable items. He let himself in by way of the front door with the key he has always had; he said a few friendly words to Mrs. Salman, the housekeeper (who reported to Isabel afterward that Owen was so much changed she hardly recognized him!); he went upstairs, ostensibly to his room, "to pick up a few books," and within an hour had cleared the master bedroom and the guest suite of the most valuable small objects he could find. Silver and gold trinkets, an ivory figurine, a Chinese urn . . . carried back downstairs and out the door in a handsome tartan plaid canvas suitcase that was in fact his own suitcase.

He had not, of course, been able to open the safe in the master bedroom, so Isabel's jewelry was left behind.

He had not had access to the downstairs, because of Mrs. Salman's presence, so the silver tea service that had come down through the

Halleck family, and the flatware, and crystal, were left behind: a regrettable loss.

But the raid was a "triumph," as Owen reported to his sister. And only the first.

The Revolutionary

Kirsten has graduated from the Eyre Academy for Girls—they didn't dare fail me, she tells her brother, laughing, they didn't want me back next term—and is now living in her aunt Harriet Fletcher's house on Thirty-second Street, a ten-minute walk from Röcken.

A strategic location, Owen has observed.

It worked out quite by accident: Aunt Harriet is spending six weeks in Switzerland with her married son and his family (her son is a U.N. official with a permanent post in Geneva) and, though of course there are servants to take care of the house, she was particularly anxious that someone in the family look in now and then. Naturally she was *delighted* that her niece (her grandniece, in fact) was willing to move in.

She doesn't think it's . . . strange? Owen asks. I mean that you're so willing. To move out of your own room. To move away from Mother at this delicate time.

"At this delicate time" is given a light ironic nuance.

Kirsten says: Aunt Harriet doesn't examine motives, she isn't naturally suspicious, you know what she's like. Just a nice silly fussy old woman who worries about her plants. She doesn't think the maid will water her plants *gently* enough . . . that's where I come in.

A nice silly fussy absolutely worthless old woman, Owen says absently.

Kirsten looks at him. She wants to say, But Aunt Harriet *is* nice —don't we love her?—but the words fail to come.

"Worthless"—? she says faintly, hesitantly.

Worthless, her brother says. The word has a hard flat irrevocable weight.

At a sidewalk café just off Nineteenth Street, beneath a lollipop-striped umbrella, Owen instructs Kirsten in "short- and long-range strategy."

Your mission is simply to stay as close to home as possible, and of course—*if* possible!—try to reestablish contact with Martens, Owen says. He speaks quickly and calmly and reasonably. I mean—you mustn't force it. You mustn't call attention to what you're doing. Be inconspicuous. Just be—well—someone's daughter—hanging around for the summer—taking a course in Spanish at Georgetown.

I hate Spanish, Kirsten points out.

You can't hate a language, Owen says, not troubling to glance at her, you can't hate an entire *culture,* don't be idiotic. I forbid you to talk that way in the future.

What way, Kirsten says.

That way. Like an empty-headed spoiled-brat American kid.

I hate Spanish because of Grandfather Luis and you hate it too, Kirsten says. Anyway I've taken a year of it, I got a C without even studying, why can't I take a course in French or German?

Spanish, says Owen curtly. And then, maybe, if things work out, in a year or two—Italian.

Really! Kirsten cries, staring at him.

Spanish, yes. And then Italian. But not immediately.

Really, Kirsten says, more softly. She has been sucking at a lime drink through a lollipop-striped straw but now, half-consciously, she pushes the tall frosted glass away.—You seem to have plans for me. You seem to have given some thought to me.

Yes, Uli and I. And the others.

. . . some thought to *me.*

Yes. They agree with me that you can be of use.

. . . that I can be of use. Of *use.*

You sound like a parrot, Owen says, annoyed.

And then he is embarrassed that, in public, a few feet from a busy sidewalk, his sister has begun to cry.

Live, Owen commanded, *be beautiful again,* was the charge, and so Kirsten has returned to life: she eats breakfasts and lunches and dinners, she tries to sleep eight hours a night, she has cut down the dope-smoking and other pastimes though it hasn't been easy. . . . I feel so alone, she says. I mean when I'm awake. When my mind is absolutely clear and it's high noon and no shadows or blurs or corners to hide in.

Don't be insipid, Owen says. Your self-pity is tiresome.

Is that self-pity? Kirsten cries, as if struck by a revelation. Oh, I see. I see.

Of course it's self-pity, what else would you call it, Owen says sharply, all this drivel about emotion. . . . I was strangling on it myself, I should know.

But I feel so lonely, Kirsten says. I *am* lonely . . . I'm alone. . . . Shouldn't I feel that way? After Daddy died . . .

Don't get on that subject again, please.

But . . .

You're doing remarkably well, Kirsten, you look so much better than you did, Jesus, the way you looked back in March!—Mother might have been able to have you committed to a hospital, the state you were in—but—anyway—my point is that you're doing remarkably well and in fact better than I might have given you credit for—so think of the present, think of the future, think of your mission. And forget about your insipid emotions, which are of no interest to anyone except yourself.

But you never want to talk about Daddy anymore, Kirsten says.

What about the Spanish course? Owen asks.

I enrolled, Kirsten says evasively. Then, after a pause: It's a six-week course. Taught by a Jesuit. He seems fairly nice. Maybe a little too demanding.

What about Mother? Owen asks.

Well—naturally she wants to see you, Kirsten says. She drops by at Aunt Harriet's, she telephones, she's being very—what is the word —solicitous—bright and cheery—her boy friend waits outside in the car —they have a midnight-blue Corvette, I guess you haven't seen it. She says she knows we are in contact but she isn't accusing us of anything —she wants to see you or at least talk with you on the phone—she says there has been a "misunderstanding" between you and her but she can't explain it to me.

A "misunderstanding," Owen says slowly, with a smile. Oh yes. Yes. Truly. And is she still angry?—and is she afraid?

Mother isn't that easy to read, actually, Kirsten says.

The boy friend—who is he?

He was introduced to me as Robert something, he's about her age, maybe younger, he doesn't smile much, he seems to dislike me, we went out for dinner one evening and I asked Mother if Tony Di Piero was ever in town anymore and this seemed to annoy her, evidently Tony is not a good subject to bring up . . . but I did get the impression, which surprised me, that Tony never informed her of my visit. He never told her anything.

Are you certain of that?—that's important.

I can't be *absolutely* certain, Kirsten says, exasperated.

Owen makes his first nervous gesture: he inserts his thumbnail in the crack between his front teeth and for a long moment says nothing, simply stares into space. Finally he says: Di Piero. I wish I could trust you about him.

What do you mean, Kirsten says, faltering.

About what happened between you and him. That day. You know.

I told you everything that happened.

I know what you've told me. But I'm not sure that I can believe it.

I *told* you . . .

And Martens. How are you going to do it, with him. I mean, how are you going to get that close to him. You know what I mean.

I know, Kirsten says, swallowing.

You know . . . ?

Yes.

It would be . . . the first time? . . . with a man. Or wouldn't it?

Kirsten sits staring at her hands for several seconds. It is a very long time.

Di Piero, then, was he the first? . . . or wasn't he.

Owen is worrying the crack between his teeth, and then he is plucking at his beard in quick short surreptitious movements. Kirsten imagines a light film of perspiration on his face—she does not look directly at him—she hears herself say evenly: I'm almost eighteen years old. I'm Isabel Halleck's daughter. Shall we change the subject?

Owen draws a slow hoarse breath. He says, as if reading a written document: Our acts are to confirm justice. To restore balance. Equilibrium. They will not be acts of personal vengeance—we've gone beyond that. Do you understand? Do you agree?

Yes, says Kirsten, closing her eyes.

Sacrifices are necessary, says Owen, stroking and pulling at his beard as if it distracted him. But they will not be "personal" sacrifices.

Yes, says Kirsten.

Samira . . . that is, Fusako Shigenobu . . . was once a bar girl in Tokyo. And there is the great example of Charlotte Corday. And . . . and . . . there are many other examples, Owen says in a slow distracted voice, many other illustrations of the principle.

Yes, says Kirsten. I understand.

Live, Owen commanded, *be beautiful again,* and he arrives in her life fierce with his own strange unsettling beauty.

We are taking upon ourselves the sorrow of the judges, he says in a whisper. The sorrow of the executioners.

Does Isabel know? Can Isabel guess?

Impossible.

In raiding her house, for instance, he was quite considerate. He did not despoil. He did not deface. Not a thing destroyed.

Ah yes, he says, laughing gaily, fingerprints everywhere, he says, wriggling his fingers in Kirsten's smiling face,—my calling card.

Do you think Daddy is aware of us, Kirsten asks timidly, and then more boldly, do you think—I mean—if—well—if—

We are not superstitious, Owen says.

—if there *is* another world—spirits—life after death—I mean of course there isn't, but—

We are contemptuous of superstition, Owen says. Our religion is sanity.

In the post office yesterday I was looking at the wanted pictures, Kirsten says, excited, and I . . . I . . . I stared into the eyes of the . . . you know . . . the men and women . . . wanted by the F.B.I. . . . and I had such a strange feeling of . . .

Aren't you attending that course at Georgetown? Owen asks.

. . . their eyes. Their eyes are so beautiful. Because they're haunted—those people. Blacks and whites and some Spanish. Puerto Ricans. Do you know what I mean?

Your mind is drifting, Owen says. You'll have to learn to consolidate your strength. Even your posture . . . The backbone is the center of strength, of health. But first you must follow instructions: What about the Spanish course?

It's a hateful language, Kirsten says.—Do you remember, Owen, a long time ago . . . up at Bitterfeld . . . Daddy and Nick were playing tennis and it went on and on . . . and Tony Di Piero was there . . . I can't remember if there was a woman with him or not. And the Silbers. Yes. The Silbers. Ellen wasn't married yet, she was still in college, maybe. Do you remember? June was crying in the car. They left a day early. Something went wrong, there was a quarrel, they left a day early and Audrey was crying too and I missed her. . . . Do you remember that? Daddy and Nick playing tennis? And Mother was so angry.

I suppose so, Owen says. But what's the point?—I no longer dwell on the past.

I feel so lonely sometimes. Back then—I mean, thinking of it—

back then—there are more people there—you can summon them back—
you can try to—do you know what I mean?—even if they weren't happy,
even if they were quarreling. Do you know what I mean?

No, says Owen.

Daddy and Nick playing tennis. But I can't remember who
won.

You know who won, Owen says with a snort.

Who?—oh—*him.*

You know.

I might have been five or six then. I might have been just starting
kindergarten.

If you want to reminisce, Owen says irritably, you'll have to move
back to 18 Röcken. *She'll* be glad to oblige you with her own interesting
memories.

Then you don't think Daddy might be aware of us, Kirsten says
in a near-inaudible voice.

Which Owen prudently declines to hear.

Owen, handsome impatient Owen, with his new beard: short and
curly and brownish-red.

Owen with his secrets, his cloudy smiling gaze.

He swooped down upon her in May, in Eyre—wild wonderful
high-flying Owen—a great hawk with his wings outspread—after the
thirty-six-hour wait—during which she came rather close—or does she
imagine it?—no?—yes?—to cracking up. I've come to change both our
lives, he said. I mean—to save them.

And since then another Owen has intervened.

Whom she adores.

The beard, the posture, the new voice. The new forcefulness of
manner. He weighs 185 pounds; he exercises for hours each day; is he
in training . . . ?

Kirsten asks but of course Owen does not always answer.

I live differently now, he says simply.

What do you mean by that? Kirsten asks.

I mean that I live differently. I do different things, I have a different schedule, I'm not at liberty to discuss it.

But when will you tell me? Kirsten asks, hurt.

Sometime.

I don't even know where you're living, I don't even have a telephone number. . . .

I have *yours,* I'm in contact with you. That's the important thing.

But you're living in the city, aren't you?

Sometimes yes, sometimes no. Shall we change the subject?

Are you in training?—some sort of physical training?—I mean—

You look very good these days, Owen says, squeezing her arm. Are you in training?

But you never want to talk anymore, Kirsten says, I mean . . . about . . . certain things. . . . I feel so lonely, I almost want to go home. . . . I could talk to *her.* . . . We hate each other and we'd quarrel and she'd kick me out in a week but at least . . .

Do you mean that? Owen says, squeezing her arm. His manner is still playful; but Kirsten winces.—You don't mean that, my friend.

I want to get it over with, Kirsten says, her and Nick, the two of them, they poison the world for me. . . . But I never see him. I never hear anything about him. We wanted to get them alone together, in bed together, but . . . But if they get married . . .

You had that in mind, Owen says. I knew all along that it was impractical.

But they *might* get married! . . . in another year or two.

No they won't, says Owen.

Kirsten's heartbeat accelerates. But she does not look at Owen. She says, calmly: You never said it was impractical. You wanted it too —the justice of it.

It's melodrama, Owen says. I'm a pragmatist.

You're a pragmatist *now.*

In any case they won't be married, they aren't going to live that long, Owen says bluntly.

How long . . . how long will they live? Kirsten asks faintly. How long do they have?

That depends upon circumstances, obviously, Owen says. But not long.

But *we* are the ones, aren't we, Kirsten says, I mean, we, you and I, we are the ones who will . . . who will do it . . . aren't we?

Of course, Owen says with a small tic of a smile, who else?

He talks to her in his grave studious voice about "revolutionary politics."

Yes, she murmurs, closing her eyes.

A litany of crimes, outrages. Yes of course. She has always known.

The outrage of Vietnam, the exploitation of the world's resources, C.I.A. murders, Cambodia and Iran and Guatemala and Chile, ceaseless war, ceaseless revolution.

She has always known.

She loves her brother's voice when it is calm and strong and sonorous. She loves his voice when it begins to tremble—with apprehension, with rage?

Will I be given a gun? she asks.

The theories of Fanon and Guevara. The theories of Lenin, Bakunin, Kravchinsky. Prince Kropotkin. "Permanent revolt by the dagger, the rifle, dynamite." And Robespierre. And Arafat.

For capitalism, after all, is violence.

Yes, Kirsten murmurs.

Tupamaros. Black September. Holy War. *Brigata Rossa.* Sacrifice. Heroism. "A revolution moves at the pace of a dove." Guevara. Meinhof. Kirsten listens. Kirsten's eyes flood with tears. Owen grips her hand and says passionately: We are soldiers whether we wish to be or not, we are at war whether we acknowledge it or not. We are surrounded by enemies.

When should I do it? Kirsten asks. Will they help me—your friends? Will I be given a gun?

United Red Army. The Popular Front for the Liberation of Palestine. The Turkish People's Liberation Party. Yes, she knows, she has always known, she takes her brother's hand and presses it against her overheated face. She does not want to embarrass him with her tears but she cannot help herself.

The massacres of revolutionary blacks, American intelligence agents abroad, fascist death squads for hire, U.S. currency. Has she ever heard of the revolutionary Doves, an American organization, mainly students in the East, New York City, Boston, gone underground, five of their members executed in the past three years. . . . No, says Kirsten, yes, I think I've read something, I don't know, are these your friends? . . . when can I meet them?

Edith and Richard Naumann, killed in Mexico, in Mazatlán, by C.I.A.-hired assassins. Revolutionaries in their late twenties. Students of Sartre, Marcuse, Fanon. Latin American specialists: Richard Naumann had a Ph.D. from Columbia. Edith Naumann had made innumerable requests to the State Department, under the Freedom of Information Act, to be allowed to examine certain documents relating to the National Security Agency's role in Chilean politics at the time of the Allende overthrow.—The Naumanns were founding members of the Doves, Owen says. But of course I know very little about them.

When will I meet your friends, when will I meet Uli? Kirsten says, her face streaming with tears, I'm so lonely without you. . . . Are you ashamed of me?

Of course I'm not ashamed, Owen says.

I want to meet them. I'm ready. I've been ready for a long time. You know that. *You* know that.

It isn't quite time—

I believe everything you've said, I understand, I don't want to live unless it happens soon, I don't want to forget Daddy, they are poisoning the world for me, I don't want to lose him, tell them I'm ready, tell them I want to be of use, I know he's a murderer—Nick—I know he deserves to die—Nick and *her*—we're at war—there's always been a war—I understand, I'm ready—

For your own protection, Owen says awkwardly, at the present time, it's felt that, Uli thinks—and I agree—

Don't leave me alone, Owen, Kirsten begs, can't I come live with you, can't you move into Aunt Harriet's house?—but why don't they want to see me, don't they trust me?—Uli—what kind of a name is that —*is* it Swedish?—is it—I don't know—Spanish?—Russian?—doesn't he want to see me, doesn't he want to know who I am? I can't stay invisible—!

Actually, Owen says, Uli *has* seen you: he knows who you are.

He does? But how? When? When did he meet me? Kirsten asks, astonished.

He didn't meet you, he saw you, he was sitting at a table beside us, that day—do you remember?—the little café—Nineteenth Street—

He was sitting beside us—? He was listening—?

He was listening, he knows who you are, Owen says, smiling, taking her hands, he was very impressed. . . . Yes, he approves of you.

He approves of me, Kirsten says numbly. He was *there* . . . ?

He listened, he watched you, and of course he's judging partly by what I've told him, and partly by telephone conversations of ours . . . which he has heard . . . of course he's very scrupulous, he takes every precaution. It's a matter of life and death, after all. It's a matter of war.

He *approves* of me? Kirsten asks shyly.

Yes. Of course. You're my sister, after all, Owen says, suddenly grinning, and now his voice does quaver with an emotion she can understand, you're my Kirsten, after all—right?

The Lovers

From the expression on Isabel's face—a quicksilver rippling as in water —Kirsten knows that her mother's lover has arrived.

Isabel is standing motionless, staring past Kirsten's head. Her lips are parted, her wide-set eyes level. Beside her someone is speaking with the warm ebullience of the near-drunk but Isabel has given up all pretense of listening.

A wave of faintness rises in Kirsten but she does not give in to it.

It is important to remain calm. To remain still. Not to turn at the sound of his voice.

Isabel is staring at her lover, without love. She is not aware of Kirsten watching her; she is not aware of anyone except Nick. And then, abruptly, rudely, she turns away from her companion and walks into Claudia's house. Through the opened French doors and into the house. . . . Behind Kirsten Nick Martens's voice lifts in a greeting of exaggerated warmth.

Nick, for Christ's sake!—it's been so long—

It *has* been a long time—

His voice, his presence. So quickly. Kirsten bends closer to examine the blossoms of the cereus, her breath thin and shallow. She is not well. She has not been well. Since the drowning, the mud, the black tarry mud, mosquitoes and gnats and slugs. . . . It is important to remain calm. Not to turn at the sound of his voice, gay and childish. Throwing herself into his arms.

Nick. Nick.

Isabel has walked away. Isabel has retreated. There's no longer anything between them, Kirsten thinks, frightened, but the thought is too eel-quick to retain and in any case she must concentrate on the night-blooming cereus.

Giant creamy-pink blossoms, elongated, tubular, larger than a man's fist. Queer spiky thornlike petals surrounding the blossoms. A very subtle fragrance. Almost imperceptible. And now all are opened—nearly opened. Kirsten, conscious of being watched, brings her face close to one of the flowers and sees that it might open further still: there are recesses within recesses, vertiginous depths, delicate filose stamens and pistils, a pale yellow-striped tongue that quivers with life and sensation.

The plant is alive, conscious, tremulous.

Kirsten leans close. Her calm pale face, her beauty. Here is an eye staring into an eye.

You must play this scene very very carefully.

Someone is counting the blossoms on the plant—eleven, twelve, thirteen—is that right?—no, fourteen—there's another—and Nick Martens is behind her, approaching her, in conversation with someone Kirsten doesn't know. The false warmth, the slightly drunken camaraderie, the interruption of laughter that means nothing. Liar, Kirsten thinks, murderer, holding herself very still, not wanting to breathe, an eye staring into an eye.

Everyone on the terrace is watching covertly.

Everyone sees: Kirsten Halleck, tall and ferocious and utterly calm, her back to the man who destroyed her father. Kirsten Halleck, a young woman of queer staring unsettling beauty. Everyone has seen Isabel in retreat—Isabel Halleck walking away—and soon will be whispering: Poor Isabel, she *is* looking a little drained these days, isn't she? Hasn't she recovered after so many months? Is she going to crack at last?

Kirsten can hear the whispers, the murmurs. The secret laughter.

Why didn't you give me a gun, she will shout at Owen, I could have killed him as soon as he stepped onto the terrace—no one could have stopped me!

Suddenly he is a few feet away, not noticing her or not recognizing her. He is shaking someone's hand vigorously. False hearty enthusiasm that is part of his disguise. Nick Martens, a public man, a success, with his strained smile, his quick darting eyes, a tightness about the mouth and forehead Kirsten doesn't recall. And his hair is graying. And there are bruiselike rings of exhaustion beneath his eyes.

Kirsten finds herself moving toward him like a somnambulist. It is all very easy: her face is uplifted, her eyes calmly fixed upon his face. She does not think *Liar*, she does not think *Murderer*, she simply approaches him as a young woman might approach an attractive man, so bold with desire that the very boldness shades into innocence. She is struck by him, she is in a kind of trance, it is extraordinarily easy, why had she ever been frightened . . . ? Some garrulous fool is talking about the cereus—what a waste, such beauty—it only blooms one night of the year and in the morning the flowers will be hanging straight down— amazing sight—hideous—and did you know—this will amuse you, Nick —there's even a moth, a special moth, devised by nature for this particular plant—but Kirsten does not hear and Nick, having seen her, now staring at her, is clearly paying no attention either.

Nick is no longer smiling. His eyes are oddly pale in his tanned face. Kirsten extends her hand—it is all very easy—her face must be radiant with something like desire, how can he resist?—he quite naturally takes her hand and closes his fingers hard around it.

Hello, he says. Kirsten—?

VIII. The Handshake

Washington, D.C.,

June 1979

Deathday

On this day, June 11, 1979, Maurie Halleck will scribble the notes that constitute his "confession." In a shaky hand. So shaky he must steady it against the edge of the table.

So shaky, in fact, that after his death there will be some doubt—though not considerable doubt—about the authenticity of the confession.

On this day Maurie Halleck will grope his way through a tide of dreams that casts up to him—but not in chronological sequence, as popular mythology would have it—the jumbled visions that constitute his life. Old memories, voices, snatches of conversation; faces and ceilings and corridors and the deafening roar of the wild Loughrea; kisses hard and bright with the confidence of insincerity; children's embraces, children's tears; a friend's final handshake. So, a life. His life. Completed.

Birthdays, Maurie Halleck thinks. Deathdays. Why not a celebration?

Alone, he pours another inch of Scotch into the scum-ringed tumbler he seems to have been using for weeks, for months. In the cozy squalor of his bachelor solitude.—Only a temporary separation, you see. And I am taking a leave of absence from the Commission as well. A way of achieving emotional equilibrium, a strategy for "working things out," with the children to consider, and my wife.

Many die too late, and a few die too early, Nick once read aloud to Maurie in a tremulous histrionic voice, *the doctrine still sounds strange: Die at the right time!* Tall handsome Nick Martens, bold with the promiscuous energies of late adolescence. Bold with plans, plots, ambitions. His restless amused eyes. The heat of his skin. Were they at Harvard then, or still at Bauer. Probably Bauer: the days of their real intimacy. Since then a gradual estrangement. Thirty years. Twenty-seven years. . . . And was the quotation from Nietzsche, or was it from Camus, or Sartre, or Dostoevsky?—the icons of adolescent derring-do in the fifties. When we went through the motions of growing up.

Still, the doctrine is a rather beautiful one. And demands a celebration.

Maurie Halleck is scribbling notes, crumpling pieces of paper and letting them fall to the floor, waiting for the telephone to ring, to retrieve him. Maurie Halleck groggy, unshaven, alcohol-befuddled. A "separated" man. A doomed man. Father but not husband. Professional man now without a profession. In uncertain health. (There are queer choking spasms in his chest and stomach and bowels that might be pain, if he could feel pain. But he has other things to think about.) *My purpose is to clarify,* he writes, steadying his hand against the edge of the table, *My purpose is to put an end to rumor and speculation and . . .*

He glances up. A voice? From the front hall? Kirsten? Has she relented and come back to see him?

He stumbles to his feet but no one is there. The door is locked, the latchkey in place.

(Take care of yourself, Charles Clayton said, gripping his forearm, not quite meeting his eye. If there's a parking garage in your building, I mean one of those dark desolate places—can you park on the street?—or anyway don't use the garage late at night when no one's around. And don't answer your doorbell unless you know exactly who it is.)

Maurie Halleck, on a leave of absence from the Commission. His innumerable responsibilities—his "highly sensitive" work—will be divided up, of course, among his colleagues.

Only a temporary separation.

Maurie Halleck in his prosecutor's suit (three-piece, dark gray, wool gabardine: made at Isabel's insistence by the London tailors who did most of her father's "serious" clothes); Maurie Halleck in his old green plaid bathrobe with the frayed cuffs. (The bathrobe was a gift from one of the children. Aren't you going to open my present next, Daddy, here it is, Daddy, aren't you *excited?*—years ago. But now the children are grown up, now the children are embarrassed and distant and in any case very busy.)

Kirsten's tennis lessons, Owen's exams.

The error of having children, Maurie writes in his slow dazed scrawl, *the error of bringing life into the world. When one is not equal to the responsibility.*

Kirsten's harshly drawn breath, her extreme surprise. Why don't we kneel together, why don't we pray together, Maurie must have been drunker than usual, or more desperate, only a few minutes . . . together. Afterward he recalled the episode with grave embarrassment and telephoned his daughter to apologize but she was not home, nor was Isabel home to take a message.

And Owen . . . He does not want to think of Owen.

(Owen bragging of being invited to the wealthy X's home for a weekend. Owen bragging of having "really impressed" one of his professors. His grades, his eating club, his plans for law school, his plans for a future as a Washington attorney who will know everyone and move in every circle. . . . Even his tennis shoes are chosen with fanatic care for they *must* be the correct brand.)

The error of fatherhood in the "personal" sense, Maurie writes. *Believing that love should call forth love.*

His car keys, he thinks suddenly. Will he be able to locate his car keys.

I, Maurice Halleck, being of sound mind and . . .

His living quarters are temporary but it was necessary to sign a year's lease. Signing, he felt an absurd oversized tear slide down his cheek. How could you ever imagine I loved you in that way, Isabel asked calmly. Now he has an attractive one-bedroom apartment on the fifth floor of the Potomac Tower Apartments and his view is facing south, toward the Capitol. Closer in, his view is of the Holiday Inn, a companion tower.

He hesitated before signing the lease. But he signed it.

The telephone, Charles said.
Yes?
The telephone in your apartment—I'd be careful if I were you.
I don't understand, Maurie said.
Charles did not exactly look at him but Maurie felt the impact of his impatient pitying gaze. Asshole, Charles might have murmured. Aloud he said: Yes, I think you understand.

But the telephone rarely rings. Kirsten has called three or four times, but not recently; Owen is too busy; Nick Martens naturally does not call. And Isabel—naturally she too does not call.

Life is short, Maurie recalls, *but the hours are long.* He cannot remember who said this. Perhaps it is a folk saying. Perhaps it is one of Nick's cryptic observations, the implacable "truths" of Swedish folk-lore. *He who sees God's face must die*—which Nick claimed his Swedish grandmother had said. Maurie wanted to know more, what did the saying mean, was it part of a story or legend; but Nick did not know.

"A Day in
the Soviet Sky"

It was in the spring of 1971, when Isabel Halleck was thirty four years old, that a postcard from Nick Martens—sent to her from the Soviet Union, where Nick was on a three-week tour for the United States Information Agency—precipitated her into what might be called her "career" as a promiscuous woman.

The postcard was a color photograph of one of the oval mosaics in Moscow's Mayakovskaya Station. It was called "A Day in the Soviet Sky" and it showed a husky parachutist leaping into a turquoise void, his parachute just opening. The young man confronted his Soviet duty with a brave smile and he resembled, just perceptibly, Nick Martens.

Nick's scribbled message: *Cold up here! But I'll be down in a minute! Paella—? Love, N.*

Reading the postcard, studying the photograph, rereading the message—Isabel burst into unaccountable tears.

She cried for several hours.

She cried in her bathroom, where she washed her face with glycerin-and-coconut-oil soap, and rinsed it repeatedly with cold water. She cried in the bedroom, with the blinds drawn against a prematurely summery sun. She came to the dining table but was forced to leave—to the extreme embarrassment of her guests for that evening, and to her husband's alarm.

What is it, Isabel, he asked, stroking her shoulder as she lay across the bed, please tell me, he said gently, though she could hear, even in her agitation, the fear in his voice. So she told him that it had something to do with the spring air, the sudden warmth: she had found herself thinking of their baby girl, the infant, unnamed, who had died so many years ago.

Nick was due to return to Washington in eight days, and by that time Isabel had begun an affair—with Tony Di Piero, in fact, to whom Nick had reluctantly introduced her one day at lunch at La Cuisine. Tony told her that everyone assumed she and Martens were having an affair: he thought it "droll" that Isabel had remained faithful to Maurie all these years.

Droll and rather vulgar, Tony said.

Transgression

Long ago Maurie and Nick discussed the ambiguous politics of "doing good."

They were boys—they were *very* young men—and they took such matters seriously: *how* to live one's life, *how* to fulfill oneself; *doing* good and *being* good simultaneously!

Hours and hours, into the night. As if knowing that such truths must be discovered now, before they entered adulthood. But even then Nick observed: I don't give a damn about *being* good if it prevents my ever accomplishing anything—including "good."

Maurie observed with an uncharacteristic whimsy—or was it a premature cynicism—that perhaps one might neither "be" good nor "do" good, in fact. He smiled sadly, he said: Maybe it would be better not to do anything. Just to stay here.

At Bauer?—hell, Nick said.

Here.

It was only to Maurie that Nick spoke of his father, and of music. And of what he called "transgression."

Bernard Martens, now director of the Philadelphia Academy of Music Arts, had once been a highly promising young pianist. He had studied with Schnabel, he had even had some twenty-odd "secret" sessions with Horowitz. Schnabel told him, No one gets up at six in the morning to do nothing, but one might gladly get up at five in the morning to do *something*—that is, to do something of great significance, greatly exciting. This remark Bernard Martens habitually repeated until, at a certain point in his life, it was no longer applicable.

Nick spoke of his father in a low, rapid, and sometimes inaudible voice, his eyes fixed on the wood plank floor, his flushed face curiously alive with tics and squints and half-grimaces—a Nick Martens the other boys never saw and who would have astonished them. . . . Maybe a divorce, I can't keep it straight . . . she calls and doesn't make sense over the phone . . . crying . . . begging me to come home . . . claiming he's walked out and he's going to live with some girl . . . a mezzo-soprano . . . New York Opera . . . and then we hang up and I'm standing there nauseous . . . I mean *nauseated* . . . oh Christ! . . . oh shit . . . if they were both dead, if *he* was dead . . . if I didn't have anyone . . . anyone with my name . . . if I was just, you know, a person . . . a person without a family, without a history. . . . And then the telephone rings again and it's Mother again and now she's asking me if he has called and if I know where he is, if he has been confiding in me, and I tell her no, no of course not, I'm standing there scared shitless by her, by how crazy she sounds, I don't mean wildly crazy or even angry or anything like that but the *logic* she is suddenly using . . . that of course Father and I are conspiring against her and probably I have met the mezzo-soprano, probably we've all gone out to dinner together, haven't we, in New York . . . and she goes on and on . . . this was yesterday morning . . . I was late for history, you knocked on my door . . . then a few minutes later you came back, remember? . . . I don't know what I said to you but I'm sorry if I was rude, I didn't know what the hell was going on . . . my poor idiotic mother . . . my poor *boring* mother . . . because of course her every thought is about *him*: Bernard this and Bernard that, how cruel he is, what a liar he is, a hypocrite, a criminal, an adulterer, I can't know, I can't guess what an evil man he is: how deserving of my hatred.

Nick was silent. Maurie wanted to reach out to him—to comfort him, to console him. But of course he did not dare move. He did not even dare speak.

Bernard Martens began instructing his son in piano, and in a "general musical education," when Nick was six years old. The child was subjected to the usual technical exercises—much of Czerny whom he came to despise—and he was encouraged also to "compose" and to "use his imagination." Because of Bernard Martens's erratic schedule lessons were apt to be at peculiar hours of the day: seven in the morning, ten-thirty at night, special "makeup" sessions to compensate for missed days that might run for as long as three exhausting hours on a rain-locked Sunday. He was possessive and tyrannical and easily outraged by Nick's ineptitude, and then again he was easily—too easily—inflamed by hopes of Nick's "pianistic genius."

When Nick was ten years old Mr. Martens arranged for him to take lessons with a former colleague of his at Juilliard, which meant a great deal of commuting between Philadelphia and New York: commuting that became Mrs. Martens's responsibility. But then, after four months, it seemed to Mr. Martens's sensitive ear that his son's playing had *deteriorated* . . . and so he broke off the lessons with a single telephone call of perhaps five minutes' duration, and Nick never saw Mr. Roussos again. (He had grown nervously fond of Mr. Roussos who was gentle and kind and patient with him, and did much of his instruction seated at the piano, showing the child how a passage might be played, and how again it *might* be played—the option being the pianist's.)

So Nick returned to the turbulent lessons with his father. And then something was happening with the Academy: financial problems, quarrels with faculty, the need for what Mr. Martens called an "aggressive" public relations campaign: and perhaps there were marital problems as well. (Poor Nick once blundered into his father's office at the Academy, when Mr. Martens's secretary was not at her desk, and came upon a scene that did not impress him at the moment but was to haunt him for years: Mr. Martens was seated at his enormous cluttered desk, leaning back in a swivel chair with his hands clasped behind his head and his hefty legs comfortably crossed at the knee, and a young woman— a girl of perhaps nineteen—was seated on the edge of the desk toying with a letter-opener, jabbing the point lightly into the wood. The girl had long tangled red hair, she wore an embroidered "peasant" smock and a black rayon skirt and transparent black stockings, and though she was not pretty she had an arrogant puggish face and very bright brown eyes that startled Nick. That his father was so lazy, so relaxed and even amused; that his father, so easily annoyed at home, should be in this stranger's company so indulgent; and that both Mr. Martens and the redheaded girl should glance at each other in Nick's presence as if—as if, what?—as if they were united in an unfathomable rapport that excluded him, and was somehow amused by him, by his blushing timidity and his stammer—all this, though it failed to fully register in Nick at the moment, greatly impressed him as time passed. And what could he make of his father's mock-courteous patience in hearing what Nick had to say —a message from his mother, in fact—and then waving Nick out of the office with a lordly, genial, All right, thanks, now out, *out*—back you go, that had no anger in it, merely a bored disdain—?)

Nick never mentioned the girl to his mother, of course; nor did he ask his father afterward who she was. Though he wanted to know. He wanted badly to know: not her name, but which instrument she played. And if she was talented.

So there were unexplained lapses in Mr. Martens's interest in his son's musical education, and then again there were periods of intense concentration. Three-hour lessons, the punitive assigning of technical exercises to correct Nick's "natural" slovenliness, passages in Mozart that must be played over and over and over . . . until they were mastered. Nick was eleven years old, Nick was twelve years old. He received consistently high grades at a private Episcopalian school in Chestnut Hill but his "pianistic genius" was increasingly in doubt and Mr. Martens's temper was increasingly volatile. There were long fatiguing sessions during which father and son listened to records by "other" pianists —Rubinstein, Horowitz, Kann, Laugs, de Larrocha, Demus, Schnabel himself—playing the same piece; and then Mr. Martens would sit at the piano and ruminate over how the piece really *should* be interpreted; and then Nick would be called upon to play. Yes, Mr. Martens would say, nodding as his son echoed his playing, No, Mr. Martens would say irritably when he did not, Again, he would say, tapping with his big blunt forefinger on the sheet music. And still again. *Again.*

The absolutely "perfect" emphasis, the rubato just so, the fingering like *this*. . . . The sonata in C Sharp Minor, the so-called Moonlight, very familiar and very difficult indeed. . . . Nick had never played the sonata in its entirety but he certainly played and replayed certain challenging passages, from which he was released—forever—when his father said, usually quite abruptly: Yes. Very good. Fine. Stop. You have it. You'll remember it all your life.

Nick was thirteen years old when, practicing, believing himself alone in the house—alone, that is, with his mother who did not exactly "count"—he played a certain piece not as his father had instructed him but as he wanted to. Defiantly, with a great surge of angry elated gusto, he launched into an old worn exercise assignment of a Bach organ transcription, playing it somewhat wildly, but in his own way, and he heard footsteps—a rapid thumping on the stairs—Mr. Martens was home after all—and as Nick sat paralyzed at the piano his father rushed not into the living room but—oddly—out into the back yard: where he was to remain for some thirty minutes, pacing about, smoking a cigar.

I spied on him, Nick told Maurie, I hid by the window and watched him, and there he was trying to decide what he should do with me— whether he should beat the hell out of me, or what—and I was terrified —I could see the tension in his shoulders, his arms, the back of his neck —I felt like throwing up—my knees were actually shaking—it was so close, so close—no one could stop him from doing whatever he wanted to do—my mother couldn't stop him—she had never been able to stop him—and I stood there like a stupid fool watching him because I couldn't run away, I couldn't move—and finally he slowed down—finally he gave in—he sat on a bench and smoked his fucking stinking cigar and that was that.

So I stopped taking lessons, Nick told Maurie, grinning, squinting, picking at a loose strip of rubber on his sneakers. That was it: he was done with me. And I was done with him.

Not at the time—Nick was only thirteen, after all—but three or four years later, in recounting the incident, he was able to give a somewhat esoteric name to what had taken place: "transgression."

(The word must have been plucked, of course, from something the boys were studying that term, probably in their English class. It did have a marvelous theological weight, an almost musical ring.)

What I thought by the window was *I beat you, you old bastard,* I wanted to shout down at him, *You old bastard you old fart I beat you didn't I,* Nick told Maurie in an elated voice, but later on I felt sorry for him and felt very guilty, I think he started getting bad then, I mean really bad, drinking, staying away for days, he never touched the piano and he never bothered about me, he was the one who thought of sending me to Bauer, or anywhere, anywhere that was a big deal but wasn't close to home—and I felt guilty about it because I *had* beaten him but then I had to give up the piano too—and I loved the piano—I even loved doing musical calligraphy—fooling around—you know—and after that summer I just gave it all up and started getting interested in sports—I lifted weights, I did a lot of swimming—you know—I was just a different person, I'm a different person now, this isn't really *me,* now. . . .

Maurie was charmed and amazed and even a little frightened by his friend's story. And by his last remark: *This isn't really me.*

Nick continued, more slowly: I was right, but it was—you know —a transgression too. Does that make sense?

Maurie told him that it did make sense.

But *was* I right?—Nick asked, looking at him. I mean—was I— was it—was it *really* right?—or just a transgression?

Maurie told Nick, after a confused pause, that he couldn't answer that question: he didn't know Nick well enough.

Adultery

Isabel no longer breaks down in Nick's presence when she confronts him with suspicions—or explicit news—of another of his infidelities: she has begun to chide him lightly, one friend to another. Her languid smile, her lazy sensuous "Latin" tone, allows him to know that she too has certain experiences, certain secrets: about which she will not speak.

In any case it's too late for us, she says, lighting a cigarette and letting the silver case fall on the table.

What do you mean, Nick says, hurt, too late—? In what way?

We've run through all the things we can possibly say to each other, such as: We can't hurt my husband, we can't hurt our children, it isn't the right time in Maurie's career or in yours, and anyway he loves us—each of us—more than we really love each other.

This last remark is uttered with a negligence Nick finds chilling. What do you mean, he repeats.

You know, says Isabel.

I mean—*he loves us more than we love each other*—that isn't true—do you think that's true?—that's a lot of bullshit!

Or, says Isabel, exhaling smoke through her pursed lips, you love him more than you love me. You honor him. And you don't honor me.

Bullshit, says Nick, reddening.

Bullshit, exactly, says Isabel at once. But quite true.

It is after this conversation, in fact when Isabel lies naked in Tony Di Piero's bed, smoking another cigarette and waiting for him to un-

336

dress, that it occurs to her—the thought slides into her mind like a thin cold nail—that she has, for the past eighteen months, been unfaithful not simply to Nick Martens but to her husband as well. *Adultery,* she thinks, struck by the notion, *adultery*—after all. And so simple.

Schweppenheiser

It became a joke of sorts between Nick and Maurie, an uneasy joke, that Hans Schweppenheiser had resurfaced, in Washington.

I saw him again today, Nick might inform Maurie, passing him in the corridor at the Commission; guess who I saw today!—Maurie might say to Nick in a low amused murmur, passing near him at a party.

Schweppenheiser—aged, of course; but not *greatly* aged. Twenty pounds heavier, perhaps. And much better dressed. (Nick has seen him in a wine-dark overcoat with a sealskin collar, and a pin-striped suit he insists is Oleg Cassini—since he owns one himself; Maurie has spotted him in a suede sports coat and jaunty plaid trousers, just turning into the entrance to the White House, exchanging a curt greeting with the guard.)

But surely it *is* Schweppenheiser, Hans Schweppenheiser?—with his near-hairless bullet-shaped head, his stocky body, his small glaring eyes?

Nick first encountered him on a blustery November day in 1968 when Nick himself was still new in Washington. Schweppenheiser—or the man who resembled him—the man who very much resembled him— was just heaving himself out of a cab in front of the State Department, as Nick prepared to climb in: and it took Nick several seconds to grasp the situation: exactly whom he'd seen! By then Schweppenheiser was striding away. Mr. Schweppenheiser, Nick called, feeling quite foolish— for, after all, the man was dead—this *cannot* be him—and he felt some relief when the man simply continued on his way, up the front steps and into the building. That day, he wore a gray tweed overcoat that flared slightly at his broad hips, and a black astrakhan hat.

Nick telephoned Maurie that afternoon, and learned that Maurie had seen the same man—surely it must be the same man?—at a large reception at the embassy of the German Federal Republic some months before. But Maurie had supposed he must be mistaken. For, after all . . .

The years pass, and Maurie Halleck and Nick Martens catch glimpses of their old history teacher, usually at a distance. Sometimes he is alone, sometimes in the company of State Department officials. He has been seen upon several occasions in a chauffeur-driven limousine with State Department plates; once, Maurie saw him strolling on Capitol Hill with a prominent Senator and his attractive young woman assistant. Both Maurie and Nick have approached Schweppenheiser and asked—shyly but directly: Excuse me, but aren't you Hans Schweppenheiser? Didn't you once teach history at—?

Schweppenheiser, or the man who so uncannily resembles him, blinks in surprise and what appears to be courteous, and not mocking, bewilderment. His voice is gravelly—somewhat lower than Maurie and Nick recall, from Bauer—but the eyes are certainly the same. Piercing and wet and about to squinch up in a playful grimace. The pale lardy hairless face, the smooth bald head. . . . Excuse *me*, Schweppenheiser says politely, but my name is Fritz Messenheimer and I am really in rather a hurry at the moment.

It is Nick's opinion, later confirmed by Isabel, that "Fritz Messenheimer" must be a consultant of some sort over at State; he is not a government employee and he is not on any payroll. Isabel thinks the business is absurd, the man either died or did not die, in any case does it *really* matter? She simply asked a friend in German affairs at State if he had any knowledge of the mysterious "Fritz Messenheimer" or the still more mysterious "Hans Schweppenheiser" and he told her, after hesitating only a moment, that, yes, he knew Messenheimer—though not well—the man is a very highly paid consultant—considered very valuable—in a "sensitive" area of foreign policy.

Do you suppose he ever finished his book, what was it called—"The Madness of Greatness," Maurie says.

Why not ask him, Nick says. Next time you meet.

The Initiate

In Tony Di Piero's stylish bedroom with its chrome edges and its black lacquered furniture and its white-upon-white clinical chic (an ironic atmosphere, as it turns out, since Isabel will contract from Di Piero, or by way of Di Piero, an embarrassing genitourinary infection the only virtue of which is its swift banishing by penicillin) Isabel's passion for Nick appears to be negated but is in fact channeled into a passion for her new lover: not the lover so much as his body, and not his body so much as his sexual prowess, which is no less extraordinary than rumors among the women have suggested.

But since an affair with Tony Di Piero precludes emotion, Isabel finds herself speaking frankly with him, as she never would with another man: she complains bitterly of Nick Martens who is too ambitious, or not ambitious enough; who is angry over her alliance with Tony, or not angry enough. He never really loved me, she says, and Tony replies with equanimity, Of course he did, of course he does, he's simply like most normal men—he's terrified of women.

In the aftermath of passion that is, at times, savage in her, wracking her slender body with "pleasure" of a kind she imagines she has always craved or anyway required, Isabel weeps violently in her lover's accommodating arms and tells him that Nick Martens has ruined both her life and his own by not having the courage to marry her at the right time. (Now, to her angry despair, he begs to see her, he has offered or threatened to go at last to Maurie: to confess everything and to make his claim.) Tony listens without interrupting and

340

then says politely: I don't exactly see, my love, that either of your lives is ruined—you and Nick Martens are both extraordinarily successful individuals.

Since an affair with Tony Di Piero also precludes remorse, or shame, or elementary embarrassment, Isabel gradually—or is it rapidly?—learns to accommodate herself to the demands of the moment, and not to think a great deal of what her lover will "think" of her. He was correct in supposing her to be somewhat naïve and even, despite her social poise, charmingly prudish; he was correct even in supposing that beautiful Isabel de Benavente did not *really* believe she was beautiful —only that the illusion, in others' minds, must be maintained. But yes, says Tony, yes, insists Tony, you really *are*—and not just your precious face.

White walls, white ceiling, white louvered shutters; the glaring chrome fixtures; the pitiless digital clock on the bedside table. There are afternoons when Isabel collapses into tears and cries for an hour, or two hours, or three; there are afternoons when she arrives gaily drunk. She is in love with Tony for an autumnal month or two. She cries—so it seems—over him. And then again she shows virtually no emotion when his fiancée telephones and Tony talks idly and vaguely for more than half an hour, and Isabel has nothing to do but pace about and yawn and examine herself in the mirror, or brush her hair, or leaf through one of Tony's architecture magazines or a copy of *GEO* on his bedside table.

He bullies her into performing on his body certain acts that have always struck her as not only objectionable but positively disgusting; and she does find them disgusting, the first several times. The violence of her own sexual pleasure is such that the sensation—blood-heavy, rich, slumberous—stays with her for hours, and is so profound that she cannot really associate it with Tony Di Piero: it is crude, it is primitive, it is physiological, and can have little to do with personalities.

My secret is that I don't count, Tony says, laughing luxuriously, and it's no secret—but the statement is not entirely true: there are women who fall in love with him, women to whom he has even become engaged, though something always intervenes to prevent an actual marriage.

Your secret, Isabel says, running her hands lightly along her lover's sides, stroking his thighs, is that you are precisely what you appear to be. I don't mean superficial. But having to do with the surface. Because surfaces are mysterious too, mysterious and beautiful, the surface of water, for instance, a lake or a river. . . . Surfaces are just as mysterious as depths and far more reliable.

Isabel's passion for Nick Martens, diverted for some time into a "passion" for Tony Di Piero, never precisely subsides, but acquires an intellectual and therefore melancholy quality as the years pass. Infidelities continue to be defined in terms of Nick, however: which deepens Isabel's resentment of him.

After a bout of serious crying, Isabel tells Tony, a woman's face can age ten years, and it may take a week to repair itself. Is anything worth that?

Nothing, says Tony thoughtfully. And then adds: Only age.

Tony's affection for Isabel matches hers for him, in quality and depth. They are passengers on an ocean crossing, each concerned to amuse the other as a way of amusing himself. Isabel is not jealous of Tony's other women, though she comes to be, near the end of their affair, jealous of the fact of Tony's occasional sexual fatigue—she correctly gauges it as a loss of her own, a theft. Tony is not jealous of Isabel's interest in other men though he admits to being jealous of guests invited to 18 Röcken on evenings when he is not. (Most evenings, at larger enough gatherings, Tony naturally is included. It is at a dinner party for thirty people one evening in February 1978 that Nick Martens is introduced to Tom Gast by way of Tony—in Isabel's home, of course. But in all likelihood Isabel does not *precisely* know who Gast is or which corporate interests he represents at this time in his career.)

The affair ends gradually and painlessly. In a sense it never really ends. Isabel leaves a message with Tony's answering service, breaking a luncheon date with him, and Tony forgets to call back; and weeks pass; and then months. When they next meet at a brunch at Jack Fair's trilevel glass-and-aluminum house in Bethesda Tony is with a new "fiancée"—the daughter of a Brazilian steelmaker—and Isabel is with a new lover, a registered lobbyist who is also an excellent amateur golfer and who resembles, in his bronze-blond forthrightness and his energetic handshake, no one so much as Nick Martens. Tony comes to Isabel at once and kisses her hand in an elegant courtly gesture that is not entirely mocking. How beautiful you are, he says, how lovely to see you again, I've missed you, and he kisses her on the lips as he would never have done in public, during their affair. It is a valediction, a blessing. She has been initiated.

ŌM

There was a young man named James S. who was graduated high in his class at Yale Law School, and came to Washington in 1972 to clerk for one of the Supreme Court Justices, but soon grew impatient with the pettiness of his duties: for he was an active idealist, at heart a "revolutionary." So he resigned his coveted clerkship and came to the Commission for the Ministry of Justice in spring 1974, where he worked as an intern for one of Maurie Halleck's numerous assistants.

He helped research the Commission's investigation into the misuse of federal funds in a Cleveland urban renewal project in the late sixties, and he helped research the Commission's case against several pipe manufacturers who had worked out illegal arrangements for the allocation of contractor bids in 1970 and 1971. He was a tireless worker, and something of a perfectionist. The light in his cubicle of an office often burned late.

Maurie Halleck had several absorbing conversations with James S., by accident in the Commission cafeteria, and so he invited him out to lunch once or twice; and would have invited him home for dinner except that Isabel objected to such evenings—she claimed that Maurie's junior staff bored her to exasperation, they were so earnest and so young.

The Commission prosecuted both cases satisfactorily, though of course the convictions were immediately appealed. But James S. handed in his resignation. He refused to discuss his decision with Maurie, or with anyone: he resigned, and cleared his cell-like office, and disappeared.

Another young law school graduate, just out of Harvard, was immediately hired to take James S.'s place.

A year later, at a large reception in a new wing of the National Gallery, an acquaintance of Maurie's told him a remarkable story. He had heard it from another acquaintance, an economist on a tour through India for the State Department. Evidently the economist was told of a young American—formerly a "Washington official"—who was a disciple of Sri Makyomoy at an ashram near Benares. So he went to visit the ashram and there discovered James S., who had of course changed his name but made no secret of his past. (For if he was not ashamed of his present situation, why should he be ashamed of his past situation?—all phases of development are equally authentic.)

It was James S.'s discipline to meditate for as many as eight hours at a time, in a cell-like room with bamboo walls and a small unscreened window, in heat that rose to 120 degrees by midday. He seated himself in the full lotus position, naked except for a pair of navy blue bathing trunks, pressed his fingers in his ears, and chanted ŌM at the top of his voice. ŌM ŌM ŌM ŌM ŌM ŌM—in order to "cleanse his mind."

The economist was shocked at the young American's skeletal condition—his bones nearly protruded from his ashy skin, his eyes were enormous in his wizened face. Evidently he was in the process of "stilling appetite" and now needed to eat only two or three times a week. His graying hair fell coarsely to his shoulders, his manner was courteous, his smile benign.

The next stage of his discipline, he explained to the economist, was to learn from his teacher how to draw his tongue up into his nasal cavity and go into a meditative trance.

Some years later, in his handwritten and near-incoherent confession of numerous misdeeds at the Commission—his acceptance of several installments of bribe money from an intermediary for GBT Copper, his deliberate stalling of prosecution against that company, and actual sabotage of certain tapes, letters, memos, and documents—Maurie Halleck will include, in abbreviated form, an accounting of this "deplorable history." He will speak of "James S." as if the name were generally known and had an immediate bearing on his own case. He will speak of "cleansing," "stilling of appetite," and "ŌM"—all of which are to greatly perplex police investigators, his former associates at the Commission, and his friends and acquaintances. Isabel will say, holding the scribbled notes in a shaking hand, that she has never heard of any of this —"James S." or Benares or ŌM.

My husband and I had been separated for a long time, she will say, in a voice so bereft of tone, it might have been an official public statement.

The Confession

But how could you imagine that I loved you in that way, Isabel asks Maurie one otherwise ordinary winter morning, and finds herself coldly astonished by her own courage. How could you be so deceived, you aren't a fool, you should have known. . . .

Sipping at a glass of wine. Dry white wine, Isabel's staple, it looks so very beautiful in the glass and it has so few calories, one might sip it for hours, and suffer no visible effects.—That I loved you sexually, that you have meant anything in my real life, my physical life, my life as a woman.

So the words emerge. As if rehearsed. But in fact they have not been rehearsed—not exactly.

I don't want to hurt you, God knows I respect you and admire you, you're a wonderful man, you've been a wonderful father not like so many men, but—

She talks, slowly and not without poise, she sips wine, takes note of an annoying chip in her fingernail polish, and she'd had her nails manicured only the afternoon before at considerable expense: and when is her next appointment at Cecil's—? I don't want people to think I'm discarding him because of all the rumors, Isabel told Tony, because in fact I've waited a long time, I've probably waited too long, I'm the last person I know to get divorced and I seem to have been the first married.

She talks, and he listens in silence, his face drained of all color and of all emotion, I think I can count on him not to fight, Isabel told Tony, dear God I hope he won't cry, I do love him, I don't want to hurt him,

I don't know why he married me, am I to blame—? Now Washington is thrumming with rumors. There have been the usual "mysterious" leaks to the media, and cruel asides in gossip columns, and an abrupt decline in both invitations to the really important parties and acceptances to Isabel's own. Suddenly 18 Röcken is not so glamorous. Suddenly everyone is busy for that evening, or due to travel, or the call never gets through the secretary, the maid, the answering service. Another high-level official in trouble. It might be a professional matter exclusively, it might have a great deal to do with his marriage, or his family life, it might be an "idiopathic" breakdown of the kind fairly frequent these days, or some undiagnosed physical ailment, or a sudden paralyzing notion that he doesn't believe in what he is compelled to believe in, save as a highly paid servant: all these possibilities are reasonable, and are quietly discussed.

I don't want people to think I'm abandoning him when he needs me, Isabel said slowly, and for a long embarrassed moment Tony did not speak, and Isabel's throat constricted with the need to cry, but why make a fool of herself crying in front of Di Piero, why risk looking ugly?— she heard herself continue: But what better opportunity, after all, than right now?—it would be superfluous to abandon someone when he *doesn't* need you.

Tony grinned. Tony laughed. All the women adored him for his "warm and gregarious" sense of humor, which only emerged after intimate acquaintance.

She watches her husband covertly as she talks. How very queer the situation is, he listens, he stares at the floor, he even nods just perceptibly, as if he has suspected all this, as if he cannot protest, as if he finds himself in agreement, poor dear Maurie, Maurie whom everyone loves, Isabel hears herself explaining their marriage, their initial attraction for each other, wasn't it a case of mutual self-deception, wasn't it so very premature, did he know how eager all the girls were to get married, at Hays and elsewhere, even the bright girls, even the athletes, it was something in the air, no one could resist, no one even understood its malevolence. But I did love you, Isabel says, as much as I could have loved anyone at that age.

In Washington it is often a matter of delicate coordination and timing—the professional collapse, and the collapse of the marriage. And there are peripheral factors like increased drinking, moodiness, irrationality, surprising lapses in grooming: all of which, sad to say, poor Maurie Halleck has exhibited. And his hours of silence, pinched self-gnawing inwardness . . . He's changed and I can't accommodate him and I don't think I want to try, Isabel told Tony, I think it's simply too late: it's been too late for fifteen years.

You're Luis's daughter, after all, Tony observes.

What does that mean?—Isabel is genuinely puzzled.

I've had lovers, Isabel hears herself telling Maurie, I've been in love, she tells him, but not in a sobbing "confessional" voice, for Isabel is too cultivated for such drivel, please don't be upset Maurie but I've been in love and I know what I'm capable of as a woman and—forgive me—it was always a pretense, with you: and I think you knew.

No.

Yes.

The stiffening expression, the flicker of guilt. Yes. But no: impossible.

God knows I wanted to be your wife, Isabel says, hearing, half-bemused, a sudden "Latin" inflection to her voice, as if some small outward sign of emotion might be of aid, I wanted to love you *in that way*, but it was always a lie, it was a pitiful deceit, I felt sorry for you and I detested myself and perhaps it was no one's fault, the marriage was a mistake from the start, if we had it to do again we'd never . . .

Her words trail off into amazed silence. Does she mean it, and she would annihilate both her children?—so incidentally, so cursorily?

I think it's best to consider that we both made a mistake, and we're both to blame, Isabel says carefully, no longer able to look at Maurie. I can't honor my commitment to you any longer and I should have told you all these things years ago. . . . You really never knew me, Maurie: you never brushed near my real life, my inward life, my secret physical life: you were never really my husband.

Though she tells him these many astonishing "truths," intermittently frightening herself with her own daring, she never tells him a small baffling fact which she suspects is at the heart of their failure: that she could not forgive him for the death of their second child—for the loss of that unnamed unbaptized infant girl.

Drowning

When Maurie asks Nick his simple, terrible question there is a beat of perhaps three seconds before Nick replies.

No, says Nick slowly. Not to my knowledge.

Not to your knowledge, Maurie repeats.

It is a brilliant blinding winter day. Sunshine pours through the high plate-glass windows of Nick's corner office so fiercely that he is forced half-apologetically to close the blinds. Sometimes, he says, he even draws the heavy dark drapes.

Maurie Halleck is sitting in a leather chair with brass buttons, staring at his friend Nick Martens who sits in a similar leather chair, though with a swivel seat, behind Nick's large paper-strewn desk. He has asked the question he has rehearsed for weeks and it quite dazes him —Nick's lie—and the queer conversational nature of the lie—and the way Nick is looking at him. "Not to my knowledge" is a classic and even a comic reply but Nick's boldness is such that he doesn't seem to have caught the humor.

Maurie has rehearsed his quiet speech, his several questions. But suddenly he knows it is pointless. Evidence of collusion, papers misfiled or missing, the bewilderment of the younger assistants, Nick's estrangement from him . . . the rumors that have made their way back to him . . . leaks about the Commission's strategy in preparing their case for the grand jury. . . . (I think you should know, Maurie, a friend told him, that Nick has been dropping hints about you, always with an air of concern, he isn't critical and he isn't making one of his jokes, he pretends to be

—or maybe he actually is—genuinely concerned: he says you're obsessed with the GBT prosecution, that it's become almost a personal vendetta of yours, a monomania, it must have something to do with guilt —your own family's business. I'm sorry if I've upset you but I think you should know. And he goes on to talk about the way you became obsessed with things in school, you had an "unsettling Boy Scout earnestness" that could shade into fanaticism, the other boys were amused by you but disturbed, that sort of thing, it's always been Nick's style to some extent but until now he's never turned upon *you*. . . .)

Nick murmurs something about a lie. Lies.

Maurie leans forward.

My eyes, Nick is saying, rubbing them cautiously, they've become so sensitive. . . . I'm starting to get headaches. . . .

Maurie stares at him. Maurie is sinking, he cannot breathe, his own vision pulses white. Yet nothing happens. He does not reply, Nick continues speaking slowly, idly, as if nothing had passed between them, as if their friendship were not over.

. . . misery with June dragging on and on . . . and now Audrey seems to be affected, she wants to leave Exeter at the end of the semester and go to a school in Boston . . . I told her it would be suicide . . . academic suicide . . . I told her she shouldn't let her mother poison her life . . . poison her against me. To drop out of Exeter of all places . . . !

Maurie stares, blinks, sits in silence. There is a slow constriction in his chest but it is bearable; he can breathe.

And nothing happens.

Nick rubs his hand over his eyes less cautiously, more with an air of impatience now, sighing, murmuring something about middle age: Is it just middle age?—needing glasses? But his vision is unchanged, really, he can see perfectly well, there doesn't seem to be any deterioration of his eyesight . . . only this distracting sensitivity to light.

Always something, Nick says, glancing at Maurie. Always a problem.

Yes, says Maurie faintly. But his numbed lips do not move.

The final handshake, the handshake of dismissal?—that will come in another ten minutes.

June *does* poison the air. She is not "consoled" by an old friend's telephone call—she speaks rapidly and bitterly and in a voice Maurie does not recognize—Nick has done this and Nick has done that and Maurie was a fool to work so hard to bring him to Washington to engineer a position for him that would be *good enough* for him and wouldn't insult him and would allow him to save face with the law firm did Maurie think Nick was grateful did Maurie think Nick could be grateful for anything to anyone powerful enough to do him a favor that would mean anything to him—was Maurie that stupid, was Maurie that easily duped—and why was he telephoning, hadn't he telephoned only a few months ago, what was this peculiar *interest* in Nick's family since Nick has now so conspicuously moved on? You really don't have to bother, Maurie, June said, less angrily now but still without affection, I'm picking up the pieces, I'm doing very well, I don't need any of you, not even you, yes I know you're concerned and I know you're generous and I know you'd even fly up to see me but it isn't necessary, I know you're willing to do "anything you can to help" but I don't want your help, I don't want to see you again or talk to you again, you only force me to think of Nick, there's no connection between us except through Nick, please leave me alone, Maurie, please don't bother me again, I don't want your sympathy, I don't want your prying, you live a kind of life I used to admire and I tried to live the same way but it never worked —I'm not like you—none of you ever knew me—Nick never knew me, he never gave a damn for me—you know who he's been in love with all these years—you know—I couldn't manage that kind of life—I tried for twelve years—I'm not like you—I don't forgive, like you—do you understand? You don't mind your wife's infidelities but I mind my husband's infidelities do you understand will you please leave me alone will you please let me pick up the pieces by myself?—none of you ever knew me—

Maurie Halleck, sinking, drowning.

The constriction in his throat and chest: he must sit very still, very very still, breathing as gently as possible: otherwise he will suffocate.

The deafening roar of the river. The rapids. In the distance. And then so loud, so amazingly loud, you can't really hear it: you are in it, propelled through it, wild and dazed and laughing and gasping for air as the cold spray strikes your face.

He glances up and his face *is* wet. With embarrassment he recalls the tears in his eyes when he signed the lease—and there have been other tears, other awkward sessions—best to forget—for Maurie Halleck too requires pride—what is called "self-esteem"—Maurie is not a saint Maurie is really not a generous man in fact not generous at all for how can he be generous when he has nothing?—the wisest strategy is to forget: and anyway his face is wet with perspiration, not tears.

Do you want to marry Isabel? Maurie asks Nick.

It is not a question he had planned to ask, this morning.

It is not a question appropriate to Nick's office on the third floor of the twenty-year-old but still "modern" building of poured concrete and stark contours and flying-buttress–like columns of no discernible use that houses the Commission for the Ministry of Justice—a building now rather dwarfed in size and splendor by the new J. Edgar Hoover Building nearby.

I know—I think I know—how you feel about each other, Maurie says quietly. Perhaps it is a consequence of his profession, his calling: he is able to talk calmly and coherently and even rationally when in fact his mind has shattered and his chest is so queerly tight he can barely draw breath.—I think I understand, Maurie says.

And now Nick stares at him in genuine alarm. In fear. Where, a minute ago, he has been able to lie about a criminal act—*his* criminal act—and has been able to lie with terrifying equanimity, now he flushes and begins to speak and stops and begins again. He makes an angry helpless gesture, a wave of his hand.

I can't talk about that, Nick says.

You are in love with her, and she is in love with you, Maurie says, picking the words out of the air, yet giving no sign of his distress, though it is necessary for him to sit very still and to grip the arms of his chair. —You know Isabel isn't happy with our marriage, you know she has asked me for a divorce, I—I'm not angry—I'm trying to understand— I need to know—

Nick rises from his chair and stands at the window, rattling the blind. Maurie recalls the sweater he once loaned Nick: a cable-knitted skiing sweater: had Nick ever returned it?—Please don't lie, Nick, Maurie says. His numbed lips barely move and perhaps Nick does not hear.

One accepts a "contract of finitude" in agreeing to live, Maurie once read. He liked the expression: a "contract of finitude." You accept the fact that you are not immortal and not without limitations and not guilty as a consequence. . . . Maurie accepted, Maurie signed. But perhaps did not *entirely* believe.

Isabel wanted to name the infant girl who lived only a few days. Maurie refused. Defective heart valves, malformation of organs, probable brain damage. A life clearly not meant to be lived, and hence *named*.

Isabel wept, Isabel was hysterical. Then said greedily: We'll try again, yes?—right?—won't we?—yes? No one can stop me!

Nick is speaking but the roar in Maurie's ears is such that he cannot exactly hear. Yes, no, we couldn't help, we were terrified of hurting you. . . . Nick who can lie so skillfully, with such style, now flushing even darker and stammering; his pale eyes snatching at Maurie. I never meant . . . we never . . . we *weren't* . . . we did talk of . . . yes . . . but we never . . . and the children too . . . and June . . . and . . .

You are in love with her, Maurie says, but the question is a statement, his vision is going blank again, he is frightened of fainting in Nick's presence. Coward, he thinks, liar, meaning Maurie Halleck: terrified of drawing a full breath.

I love her, of course, Nick says with a helpless laugh, of course I love her, I've been in love with . . . but . . . but I never . . . we never . . . do you understand? . . . she was never unfaithful to you. For twenty years . . .

Maurie sits without moving. His sweaty palms are pressed against the leather arms of the chair.

Never unfaithful, he says. His lips stretch into a small bitter smile. He glances at Nick but his eyes cannot quite focus. He is sinking, he is drowning, he can't catch his breath, in another moment Nick will have to rush over to him and grasp him beneath the arms and raise him, save him. . . . But he grips the arms of the chair and steadies himself. Thank you, he says softly. Thank you. For telling me. For troubling to lie.

Months later he is scribbling his incoherent and perhaps implausible "confession."

I did this and I did this, I accepted this, with deliberation and premeditation I violated the sanctity of my office and the duties entrusted to me the oath I swore to uphold the Constitution of the United States the trust of my associates the faith of my . . .

His hand shakes so absurdly, he must steady it against the edge of the table. Which makes the procedure awkward. Which prolongs the effort considerably.

A simulated walnut dining table. With four matching chairs. Pale green simulated leather cushions. And a sofa in practical brown-green fabric, knobby to the touch. (A sofa-bed, in fact. In case Kirsten or Owen chooses to spend the night sometime.) One dazed afternoon in a department store at a mall off Wisconsin Avenue, mattress and box springs and headboard, lamps, a carpet, two carpets, how many chairs?—$50 down, C.O.D., very prompt delivery, a coffee table, end tables, bedside table, Maurie is checking off his list, then he cannot find his list, the salesman is sympathetic and not impatient, Maurie wants to break into laughter and clap him on the shoulder and inquire whether husbands "separated" from their families, asked forcefully to move out of their homes by their wives and their wives' attorneys, stop by here often at Park Lane Furniture in this slow-speaking smiling daze . . .

I am guilty, he writes.

So simple, and so irrevocable. *I am guilty. I am guilty.* The white water, the cold stinging spray, his foot pressing against the gas pedal, a gathering sense of déjà vu, the tightness in his chest, the thrill of panic in the bowels and groin, shapes whipping by on either side, a deafening roar, he must drive faster and faster not to escape the choking sensation in his chest but to plunge into it.

Déjà vu, Nick once said, reading something out of a book, that's when you think you've experienced something before, isn't it. When it feels like—you know—you've been in a certain place before—

Nick who lied so adroitly, Nick who had never heard—well, yes perhaps he had *heard*—the name Gast. Nick stammering, sweating. Will you have a drink with me, Maurie, he says, opening a cabinet below one of his bookshelves, we must talk this through, is the door locked, maybe we should leave, but a drink first, please don't be angry, no don't leave, are you all right?—you look so pale—

My purpose is to clarify, Maurie writes, beginning again. It is easier to begin again than to attempt to read what he has already written. *My purpose is to put an end to . . . In the first place is the error of marriage, in the second place the error of . . . Details confuse, there isn't time, I have already drifted past my birthday which was May 19 & I had planned to clear everything off my desk by then.*

Isabel says frankly: But how could you imagine that I loved you in that way, Maurie? Years and years . . . so many years. . . . I felt sorry for you, I did love you, I love you now, it's tearing me apart to say these things, but I have to say them, I am forty-two years old, Maurie, I have been married to you for half my life, Maurie, do you understand, the years and years of . . .

The error of marriage to that woman. The error of marriage to any woman.

You never came near me, you never brushed near, Isabel says, her eyes glittering with tears, it was my fault, I mean the masquerade was my fault, I lied to you I pretended certain feelings I simulated certain responses maybe no more than all women do—at times—in marriage—but—but—do you hate me—will you forgive me—I love someone else—I've had lovers, I've been in love—I respected you and I cared for you I care for you now I love the children I don't regret having children I've been married to you half my life everything is slipping past—rushing past—do you understand, Maurie?—please look at me, Maurie!—do you hate me—do you understand—but how could you have believed me—how could you—all those years—how could you imagine—I really loved you—in that way—I really loved you *in that way*—how could you with your intelligence and your sensitivity and good judgment *believe*—!

Will you shake hands? Nick asks, his voice trembling.

And Maurie is equal to the moment. Though sinking, though drowning, breathing thinly through his mouth, he manages to hoist himself to his feet and shake his friend's proffered hand as if nothing were wrong, as if nothing had been decided or completed or erased, and the queer thing is: the attack of vertigo lifts and he can see again: he can see again well enough to find his way back to his own office and sink into his own chair and fight the collapse for approximately forty-five minutes.

By then Nick has left the building. By then Maurie's secretary, concerned over his appearance (but how did he strike her, he wonders, was he ashen-faced, did he look as if he'd taken a blow to the head, or as if a vise were tightening around his chest?—did he look, to be blunt, like a dying drowning man in heart failure?)—by then Maurie's secretary is knocking at his door, knocking calling out, trying the doorknob, Mr. Halleck?—Mr. Halleck?—is something wrong?—why don't you answer your telephone?—why is the door locked?

"Stilling Appetite"

Isabel Halleck's women friends and acquaintances in Washington suffer from dizzy spells, migraine headaches, anemia, fatigue, and "nerves." They suffer from premenstrual tension, severe menstrual cramps, and menopausal embarrassments. There are frequent complaints of insomnia. There are anxiety attacks that necessitate tranquilizers, attacks of depression that necessitate amphetamines. Indigestion, constipation, chronic diarrhea. Flaming skin eruptions diagnosed by dermatologists as "idiopathic." Unexplained aches in odd parts of the body—elbows, feet. Heart palpitations. Generalized dread. One season there are a half-dozen hysterectomies, another season several mastectomies.

Of course there are numerous alcoholics—"secret" and otherwise. And barbiturate and diet pill addicts. And occasional breakdowns of the sort called "nervous."

Isabel, however, has always enjoyed exceptionally good health. (And will continue to enjoy it until the period following her husband's suicide when she is arguably "not herself," as a consequence of both her husband's suicide and her children's increasingly erratic behavior.) She attributes her good health to genetic disposition, perhaps; or her naturally sunny nature; or physical exercise. (Though in fact she is too lazy for exercise. She plays a little golf, she swims for perhaps twenty minutes a week, in the summer. She never walks and has been known to drive a half-block to the nearby home of an acquaintance.)

In secret, Isabel attributes her health and her equilibrium of temper to the number of parties she gives and attends, and the number of men she knows. She has a voracious and evidently insatiable appetite for both, the parties especially.

Parties and men: and the rest of life is, she has observed, *backstage*.

Appetite exists to be satisfied, and constantly "stilled"—for a while. Health resides in constant satisfaction and constant stilling. So Isabel reasons, considering the fact of her own body.

She takes voluptuous pleasure in bathing herself, soaking for long inert minutes in a fragrant tub. She takes pleasure in rubbing rich creams and oils into her skin. There is a distinct tactile pleasure in the way astringent dries on her face.

The bliss of sinking into bed, her mind extravagantly empty.

The bliss of the first cigarette of the day. The first drink.

The euphoria of parties: the first ring of the doorbell downstairs, or the moment of her entrance into another's house.

The euphoria, only slightly less reliable, of sexual pleasure: though it is becoming increasingly difficult for Isabel to attach individual men to her experiences.

Maurie astonishes Isabel one evening near the end of their marriage by saying suddenly, through a mild alcoholic haze: I have the dispirited feeling that nothing counts for anything, Isabel.

Isabel is offended, Isabel is frightened. She never does manage to accommodate this "new" Maurie Halleck—the brooding, ill-tempered, secretive Maurie—but knows enough not to blame herself for him, as of course everyone else does. (For it is primarily Maurie's abrupt shift in personality that inspires her to make her move—to demand her "freedom.")

I don't understand, Isabel says. "Nothing counts for anything—"?

A conviction I seem to have been infected with, Maurie says, unsmiling. By you. And others.

One of Isabel's lovers is a cosmetic surgeon who drives a green Triumph and whose specialization is traffic victims. She meets him while shopping for a surgeon to tuck up the soft, sad, and increasingly maddening skin beneath her eyes. He is the first doctor she interviews, and he refuses her as a patient: You're too beautiful, Mrs. Halleck, I wouldn't touch you for another ten years—well, maybe five.

Their affair lasts only a few months. He becomes too possessive, too jealous in an outdated way; most annoying of all, he asks too many questions about the Hallecks' "wide range of social acquaintances" and their private lives. He queries Isabel about prominent Senators, judges, State Department and Pentagon people, White House officials, the President and his family, and is reluctant to believe Isabel's assertion that most of these people lead quite normal, even boring, domestic lives. He finds it difficult to believe, though intriguing, that Washingtonians in Isabel's circle look down upon the President. (The current President, certainly, Isabel says. It's always awkward to deal with a fool who also happens to be a failure.)

A year or two later Isabel encounters the surgeon on a downtown street—he is leaving a restaurant, she is entering—and though she recognizes him at once and says hello he responds only politely. Since Isabel is wearing oversized sunglasses she takes them off—and still he does not seem to recognize her, exactly. Yes, he says, smiling, embarrassed, yes, it's very nice to meet you again, I—I'm afraid I—

But I'm Isabel, she says, Isabel Halleck, don't you remember?

Isabel, he says slowly. *Isabel.*

And then, finally, he does recognize her: his smile is even more embarrassed.

I should explain, he says apologetically, drawing Isabel aside so that her companion cannot overhear, I see so many faces and I didn't *do* your face—it isn't one of mine.

One of her more idiosyncratic lovers is a Pentagon SAGA man— from, that is, the agency for Studies, Analysis, and Gaming. SAGA devotes its time to war games of a classified nature and has a reputation for being "intellectual," but Isabel's lover Jebb describes himself as a "renegade" there. He has a law degree from Virginia, he has been divorced for six years, his children are ten and thirteen, both girls. He is an excellent marksman. Sometimes he takes Isabel practice shooting with him.

Jebb's duties at SAGA are unclear, as are the nature of his duties before joining the agency, but his conversation is liberally sprinkled with offhand references to prominent and little-known countries in the Mideast and Africa. He is evidently something of an expert—a contemptuous expert—on what he calls "homegrown Communist punk terrorists": Weathermen, Black Panthers, Symbionese Liberation Army, Doves. Isabel asks a few questions about the Symbionese Liberation Army, because of Patty Hearst, but is otherwise not much interested. That the Weathermen had killed someone in Wisconsin, that the Black Panthers had killed policemen, and the Doves are responsible for a few isolated bombings—a policeman assassinated here, a civilian there—strikes her as unfortunate, nothing more. Jebb seems to know a surprising amount about Basque guerrillas too, and is curious at Isabel's lack of interest in Spain and Spanish politics: Spain, that "dark" place.

I like the Costa del Sol, Isabel says.

I don't mean the Costa del Sol, Jebb says, I mean the real Spain where there's no sun at all.

Isabel says indifferently: I prefer Washington. I prefer our police.

On one of their frequent drives into the Virginia countryside they tramp through a field and Jebb asks if Isabel would like to do a little practice shooting and Isabel agrees, with polite enthusiasm, and soon she is watching this tall heavy-browed man in a windbreaker—a man she barely knows—firing methodically at red-winged blackbirds in a marsh. He calls the blackbirds "garbage birds."

Jebb carries a pistol in a shoulder holster at all times, even when he and Isabel meet in secret, and he may or may not have another weapon in the glove compartment of his car. He has told Isabel the kind of pistol he carries but Isabel has forgotten. Despite the noise of the shots she finds herself yawning, and daydreaming. She doesn't care to watch the birds being killed and so she gazes into the mottled sky and sees again, faintly, the Soviet parachutist leaping boldly out of his plane. She does not flinch or reject the image—it is not Isabel's strategy to suppress any emotion—and she notes to her satisfaction that the parachutist means very little to her now.

She has never been Nick Martens's mistress, technically. She has never seen the man naked.

His flesh, then, remains sacred to her.

There is an Isabel Halleck who is permanently in love with Nick Martens, as there is an Isabel Halleck who is permanently the mother of two children. It is a fact, a simple statement. In a sense she is always that Isabel Halleck—she is trapped inside her own flesh, certainly—but in another sense she strays, she drifts, she yawns and daydreams and diverts herself, she forgets a good deal.

To have gathered Nick Martens in her arms—*really* in her arms —to have been engulfed by him—to have surrendered her solitude to his: what a risk it would have been, what an act of rapacity!

Which may happen yet, she thinks idly. If Nick ever strikes her as seriously involved with another woman.

Jebb notices her daydreaming and in play shoots over her head— a comfortable distance of two or three yards. Isabel manages to laugh —she is at all times a very poised woman—but she breaks off her friendship with Jebb soon afterward, and one evening when General Kempe has come over just for a nightcap, by himself, she informs him of the very odd very unprofessional behavior of a Pentagon man who is "dating" a friend of hers. General Kempe listens to the story and says: His name, please.

Brean Down, Virginia

Maurie Halleck rummages through his pockets for the car keys. Then through the clothes in his bedroom. Among the papers and coins on his bureau.

Maurie Halleck leafs anxiously through the Bible. He has a queer faithless faith—that a voice, a mere word, might speak to him. Too late?

A sign. He is waiting. A voice. He awaits. The very voice the holy man Father de Monnier heard many years ago in a country parish in Quebec. *You will become a priest.*

But only silence.

Decades.

She wore a red polka-dot dress, she cried in his arms, selfish and winning in her abandon as a small child. It is a lie, her later claim, for she *did* love him. On their wedding night she wound her shining blond hair around her head, she peeked at him through a strand, teasing, shy, perhaps a little frightened, she whispered I love you I love you I'm not good enough for you you *shouldn't* have married me.... But I will try.

Silence.

He has taken only four or five books from the house on Röcken Place—the Bible; an anthology of twentieth-century poetry; a study of U.S.-Arab relations by a former member of the C.I.A., a friend of Joseph Halleck's; a copy of Aeschylus's plays which he has been unable to read —Aeschylus requires extreme concentration and a great deal of courage.

A half-rotation of the sun from his death, he reasons that it is too late for these books, for a spurious "wisdom." He tries to arrange them neatly on the simulated walnut coffee table.

The many pages of his confession too. For order is imperative.

A Kodacolor postcard selected from a revolving rack in a drug-store—Washington, D.C., in Japanese tulip tree season—Nick's name and address scribbled on it—a brief message *Thank you for the 27 years. M.*

(A postcard Nick Martens is to receive on the morning after Maurie's death. Three hours after he has been notified of the death by police.)

Silence. And then a boy's brash voice: That room facing the court-yard—you took it because it has the best light, didn't you? It's the largest room, isn't it?

Maurie cringes in astonishment, in shame.

No. Yes. Anything you say. All right.

But you *did* get here first, the voice acknowledges. There is a slow conspiratorial smile. An almost-granted affection.—You *do* have first choice.

No.

Yes. First choice.

No. Please. Whatever you say.

Kenosis. Christ's humbling of Himself, emptying of Himself of His divinity. For this too shall be taken from you.

Maurie's fingers close about the keys. His heart swells with sudden gratitude. It will not be happiness he is granted, and certainly not a sign—the gesture of God's acknowledgment of him. It will be instead a sudden gratitude—wave upon wave of calm—peace—lucidity—certainty. I die to clear the way for others. I die to erase shame. To shock them into the purity of soul of which they have always been capable.

The thunder out of the river. Vibration of the air, the earth. Harsh cold stinging blinding spray. Yet he is carried forward emptied even of terror.

A rock—another rock—to the right, to the left—a hunchbacked tree—water in his eyes and mouth—choking, gasping—elated—plunging—nothing can stop us, we will live forever—

He has tried to arrange the notes in sequence. But his fingers shake badly. Sentences leap and veer, words protrude, a stranger's handwriting. . . . As my faith in larger processes waned there arose in me a fanatic application to minor matters which I hid (I think successfully) from my associates. Overscrupulosity, monomania. A ravening pride. As if I grew to fear *looking up* from the matter directly before me. As if I grew to fear the very notion of Justice itself & the oath I had sworn to uphold the Constitution of the United States. Self-effacement = the most primitive fear. I made the attempt through the zeal of my labor & the excess of my devotion *to disappear* into my work. The Commission for the Ministry of Justice to which I had sacrificed my adult strength with its innumerable offices & corridors its jurisdiction over each of the fifty-one state divisions its labyrinths of paperwork files microfilm tapes evidence moldering in safes. The Commission for the Ministry of Justice which has drained my life's blood did not fail me as a worthy abyss into which one might fall forever. Forever. Without ever striking the bottom.

He searches for a pencil, he locates another piece of paper. Writes quickly, bent over the table. Must explain. Must make clear. The irony of his sacrifice if they don't believe—!

I am guilty, I alone am guilty. Cannot live another 24 hrs. with the sickness in my heart.

Another drink? But the bottle is nearly empty. A quarter-inch. A few drops. One, two, three . . .

A stamp for Nick's postcard! But he can find only a 15 cent stamp. And postcards require only 10 cent stamps.

He returns to the bedroom and rummages through the tossed-down clothes, the papers and coins and unspeakably filthy dried Kleenex.

His daughter would not kneel to pray with him. Pretty Kirsten in her white tennis costume. Slender tanned legs, close-cropped red-blond hair. Wide-set eyes like her mother's. A light dusting of freckles. She will not kneel on the carpet with him, she is repulsed by his sickly-sweet breath, his cobwebbed eyes, his pallor. A dying man. One heart attack —though it was so minor, must it be called, so clinically, an "attack"? —a fainting spell in his office at the Commission, no more. Of course an ambulance was called. Of course he was taken into the emergency room. How fortunate that his secretary was alert, that she didn't respect his "privacy." And by then of course Nick Martens had left the building. Had gone perhaps to telephone— To spread the alarm.

Kirsten knows about the "trouble" at his office, the fainting spell, the need for rest. Abstinence from both work and drink. Kirsten knows about the impending divorce. But she will not kneel, she is embarrassed, she has a tennis lesson at the club in twenty minutes. *Why don't we pray together, Kirsten. Prayer is stillness. The mind and the heart are one. No yearning! What is left to desire, Kirsten—that is God. That alone is God.*

Kirsten blushes scarlet. Kirsten stammers excuses. Her mother's glacial eyes in her child's oval face. Daddy no please no I can't Daddy I'm already late I have a tennis lesson look—I'll call you tomorrow.

Of Owen, why think? He will not think. I surrender my son to Washington, Maurie thinks. To his "career."

Ham-thighed, fast-talking jocular jovial "popular boy" Owen Jay Halleck. Not even his mother's son, really. His grandfather Joseph Halleck's boy. Most likely to succeed.—An exam in economics, a term paper, difficulty sleeping at night, anxiety over grades, admission to law school, you must understand, Daddy, you've gone this route yourself.

He will not think.

He cannot find a 10 cent stamp. Well then—he will be forced to use the 15 cent stamp.

Yet he must have shaken Owen's hand. Goodbye. Owen's car filled with luggage, boxes of books, clothing on hangers. Yes? He cannot remember. Goodbye.

Little Kirsten licking the long-handled silver spoon clean of ice cream. She belonged, or did not belong, to the infamous Hays suicide club. (Yet there are such clubs elsewhere, Maurie has recently read. Young girls. Between the ages of thirteen and seventeen. An eerie attraction as a group: why? For suicide, the taking of one's own life, now seems to Maurie a sacred act, to be performed only by oneself, in absolute privacy.)

Kirsten with her wide-set eyes, her mother's penetrating ironic gaze, an involuntary coquettishness about her every gesture—even the graceless ones. Even the dismissive ones.

Don't touch, don't come near, don't breathe in my face, don't make me *ashamed.*

No final handshake. But a quick perfunctory hug. Which might almost have become a genuine hug: he felt the child tremble, felt a shudder in her thin shoulders. Oh Daddy please be well Daddy take care of yourself don't think of *her*—she isn't worth any of us thinking of *her*—

Nick's handshake. The palm damp with sweat but the fingers strong, strong. In control. A gesture of dismissal, finality, completion. The heavy sullen blood beating in Nick's face, the pale alerted eyes. An enemy. A rival. Maurie responds instinctively, or perhaps it is his body responding: a flood of adrenaline: a sense of brute physical danger registered in his bowels and groin. The handshake terrifies by its mockery of a handclasp.

Go, Nick whispers, go and leave me, he is urging, go and leave us —how could you imagine we ever loved *you!*

While his lips move forming other words. An arrangement—so Maurie gathers, through the rising din in his ears—to meet the next morning, to talk. About these "developments." About the "future." But not of course in the Commission building.

By then Maurie is in the hospital. Where he will remain for a week.

Goodbye, he manages to say. His fingers lack strength: he cannot match Nick's.

He licks the stamp and puts it on the postcard. He switches off the light and immediately the windows come to life—the traffic on the avenue, the slow blinking lights in the sky.

A sense of certainty. Lucidity. He is not drunk, his mind is clear, he has never been more sober and determined. And already the elation has begun.

It isn't true that we live and die alone. Every hour of my life I am with others. Every hour of my life I am . . .

He is on his way to Brean Down, Virginia. Of which he has never heard. Nor does he notice the sign: Brean Down, Incorporated. Pop. 640. His elation rises, he is carried onward, it is all very easy, even making his way through the evening Washington traffic was easy, one needs only to imagine the car floating . . . being borne along by a swift-running current . . . everything in motion . . . weightless . . . rushing to its destination.

Headlights, expressway lights, the whipping red flashes of patrol cars, ambulances. But all floating weightless. Plunging forward.

To humble oneself, to empty oneself—even of goodness.

Christ's final sacrifice: the sacrifice of divinity itself.

He exits and leaves the streams of light behind. Gravity draws him west, into the dark. Countryside, hills, secondary roads and then smaller roads and then very small roads, hardly room for more than a single car. The swiftness of the current, here—! Maurie gasps for breath, he has never felt the euphoria of gravity before, the implacable incontestable *fact*.

His foot on the gas pedal. Absolute darkness behind him. The rich cool darkness of fields, hills, trees. A winding road, banking and climbing and sinking again. The damp night air. So rich. Intoxicating. He is carried forward into the thunder of the rapids, the rising deafening unbelievable roar. But he cannot drown, he cannot be injured. The current carries him along. An enormous hunched rock to the left, another rock to the right—the car's headlights illuminate a creature, suddenly, a deer

—standing paralyzed by the side of the road, her eyes ablaze—and then he is past, he is speeding, accelerating, at every turn his euphoria grows, his certainty, I die to clear the way for others, I die to erase shame, but the sheer power of the gravity that draws him forward overcomes his feeble words, his thoughts: how good and clear and simple his life has been, after all!—how swiftly and fearlessly he rushes to his destiny!

All his life he has awaited a sign but of course no sign came. For he had imagined it outside him. Outside the strength of his passion and his love.

All his life he has awaited—

But the wind rushing against his face blows his words away, his voice is too feeble, too faint, he has no need of it any longer, he has only to surrender to gravity, to plunge forward, not to escape the gathering constriction in his chest and the white pulsing in his eyes but to plunge into them, into it, into it.

IX. Twins

Washington, D.C.,

September 1980

The Dove

September 8, 1980. Kirsten's first telephone call comes at 8:50 P.M. and Owen, who has been waiting by the phone for two hours, snatches up the receiver at once.

Hello, says Owen impatiently, hello—you aren't *there* yet, are you?

Kirsten is still at home: that is, in the Fletcher house on Thirty-second Street. But now she is leaving. She is about to leave. And there is a slight alteration of plans: she will be meeting Nick not at his town-house on N. Street but at another house—she doesn't know whose it is, or where exactly it is—out Sixteenth Street. East of Rock Creek Park.

Oh Jesus, Owen says. Give me the address.

Kirsten gives him the address.

When did he change the plans? Owen asks. Why?

Kirsten laughs lightly. She says: He wants to slip away—in case anyone is following him. To protect me.

So you'll be taking a cab, alone.

Oh yes, Kirsten laughs, I'll be taking a cab. Alone.

Is someone following him? I assumed he would know. They've given him protection whenever he's requested it, haven't they? Owen asks. He is sitting in a straight-backed chair in an odd position—beside the room's only window, exactly perpendicular to the window, so that he can look down into Bidart Street without being observed. The room is on the third floor of a wood-frame house rented for $275 a month by "Shirley Kane," a young woman affiliate of the Doves who is not underground but who, in fact, works as a stenographer for one of the Mutual of Omaha Insurance agencies. The house is wedged in tightly beside two similar houses in a street of "mixed" composition—blacks, Hispanics, a scattering of whites. Apart from the occupants of 667 Bidart the whites in the neighborhood are transients, or elderly, or patients released to the "community" from one or another of the local mental hospitals.—But in any case that's better for you, Owen says. That might expedite matters.

Kirsten murmurs a cheerful assent.

And now she must leave. The cab—she thinks—is coming up the street—yes, it's turning in the driveway.

Give me the address again, Owen says. She reads it off: and he sees, astonished, that he had transposed a numeral!—he would have given his friends the wrong address. Is this a house or an apartment building, Owen asks nervously. Kirsten says she has already told him— a house. A house borrowed for the night.

Whose house? Owen asks.

But Kirsten must leave. She will telephone Owen again if she can —from a pay phone, maybe—or, failing that, at the house—as soon as she arrives. As they have planned.

Shall we go over your instructions? Owen asks.

I'm leaving, Kirsten says.

What are you wearing—?

But she has already hung up.

Owen, awaiting his sister's second call, begins his own preparations.

Dark clothing: inexpensive shirt and trousers and a sailcloth jacket with innumerable pockets, pouches, zippers, and snaps. Into which he slides his equipment. A flashlight, a loop of wire, gloves, the finely honed German knife Ulrich May gave him, a dark oversized handkerchief that can be used for a mask, if necessary. The four-ounce bottle filled with chloroform. Some Johnson & Johnson cotton swabs. A tiny red plastic pill box in which a single cyanide tablet rattles—perhaps the most extraordinary item in his possession.

A cyanide tablet!—Owen marveled. But how do I know it will work?—that it's the genuine thing?

Why would we give you anything else? Rita Stone asked pragmatically.

Owen Halleck, preparing calmly for the assassination of one "Isabel Halleck." And her lover. If her lover happens to be at 18 Röcken tonight. In fact—Owen is empowered to assassinate anyone at 18

Röcken if it is necessary for the successful completion of his mission, and for his escape.

"Innocent people?"—but there are no "innocent people" in wartime.

On the night of September 8, 1980, many extraordinary things will happen.

Buddy and Rita Stone and Adrienne and Smitty and "Shirley Kane" and, now and then, other Doves or Doves affiliates—young men and women—youngish men and women—with "real" jobs in the "straight" world—living companionably in the house at 667 Bidart. Within four miles of the White House. Where no one—so they believe, and Ulrich May believes as well—suspects them of even mildly revolutionary activity: no one knows they are there.

Owen, the newest convert, the newest Dove, naturally shows curiosity about his companions' pasts, and he is, as an intellectual, fascinated with revolutionary theory (which is both simple and complex, direct and circumlocutory—a wild Aristotelian logic), but in this phase of his career he tends to be rather absorbed in his mission. In fact he thinks of very little else. His sobriety, his taciturnity, the willingness with which he consents to his friends' suggestions—all are very impressive.—Owen will be the bravest of us all, Adrienne declared. Her dark damp eyes fixed hotly upon him. He reminds me of ——.

The others agreed. Smitty hesitated for a moment, staring—and then emphatically agreed.

Owen had not exactly caught the name. He is often missing names now, parts of sentences, connective tissue in debates that wind on and on through the night, like tinsel-ribbon, glittering and blinding. . . . We are continually at war, it is continual wartime in this country, though at heart we are at peace . . . we are repulsed by violence . . . even necessary violence. The Doves. The Silver Doves. Named for a legendary secret sect . . . Russia . . . pre-Revolutionary Russia. Buddy and Rita Stone and Adrienne and Shirley and Smitty and Brock. Amos, a week's stay. Sam, coming up from Miami, who never arrives after a succession of late-night telephone calls. . . . Taxi drivers, parking garage attendants, a part-time instructor (remedial English) at American University. Owen dizzily counts eleven advanced degrees among them. Though perhaps he is mistaken. A cook at Burger King, a stenographer at Mutual of Omaha, a near-Ph.D. in philosophy from Columbia who has been in hiding for the past three years: Buddy, the expert on Wittgenstein and explosives. Master's degrees, Ph.D.'s, a year or two of law school. Psychology, social work, linguistics, English literature, American studies. Years ago. Brock has actually taught at the University of Minnesota, Shirley claims to have nearly been offered an instructorship at the University of Pennsylvania. Now maps of the Eastern Seaboard, nuclear power plants, army and navy and air force installations, the larger airports, other "strategic" sites. We call ourselves the Doves because in our hearts we are peaceful and peace is the only hope of the world. In our essence there is no contention but a oneness, a unity, a symbiosis of all warring elements. . . . Plans for a fall offensive. To coincide with. To underscore. To dramatize. To awaken. Current social crises are accelerating the evolution of revolutionary consciousness on all class levels . . . not just among the workers and disenfranchised students. Scandals, corruption, hired government assassins. The candidacy of Reagan. Fascist-reactionary powers consolidating. Imminent police state. Takeover. Military. Educational institutions shut down. Censorship. Summary executions. War. . . . Rita Stone, former psychiatric social worker, Chicago. Talking with blacks and Hispanics in Washington. Mingling freely. Asking questions. Answering questions. *Might as well bring it all down*—America. The world. The city. The neighborhood. Flames to the sky, a funeral pyre. . . . The error of liberal thinking. Counterproductive. Retarding the revolution. Like Mother Teresa feeding the starving poor while her church forbids birth control and fights world reform. Fools, enemies. Rita Stone dismissed from her job for spreading the truth about the system. *Might as well bring it all down.* . . . Surveillance work on the streets, tracking pedestrians. A class in weapons handling, led by Buddy. Shooting practice at a commercial range in a suburban shopping mall. Marksmen, markswomen. Owen is praised in particular for his steady aim. . . . Praised too for his support, his quiet strength, the donation of the items taken from 18 Röcken back in June, placed with a "retailer" of Buddy's acquaintance. Couldn't we keep this ivory figurine, Adrienne said, but the others were furious with her, *just because it's beautiful!* . . . beauty is a luxury the world cannot yet afford. Perhaps will never be able to afford. . . . Beauty, luxury, bourgeois decadence. Corruption. Rot. Stink. The "perfect victim": not yet chosen. Purity, sanctity. Not Martens, not the Halleck woman, who are contaminated. And then—ransom or not? Ransom or not? Kidnapping and ransom, or kidnapping and (eventual) execution. Newspapers and television coverage. Selected interviewers. Journalists. Prestige. Adrienne to screen applicants, if necessary. Cover of *Time* magazine, *Newsweek*, first-person accounts in the *Washington Post.* Shirley MacGregor alias "Shirley Kane": the unedited uncensored story of my life. High school in Utica, New York . . . vice-president of the student council, cheering squad, female leads in three plays, president of the Methodist Youth Organization, delegate to Girls' State of the YM-YWCA, a member of the Honor Society, literary and special features editor of the school newspaper, elected to the court of the Senior Queen, called by teachers a "natural leader." Voted "most civic-minded girl." Scholarship to Cornell University where she met —— and became, under his tutelage, a devoted Maoist and eventually a member of the American Silver Doves Revolutionary Army. The high school yearbook photograph of Shirley (in her prom dress) is available for media reproduction. . . . Owen cashes his checks, Grandfather Halleck's trust, month by month, clockwork, absolutely reliable, hands the cash over to Shirley who keeps the books, pays the bills, does the shopping, tireless and cheerful and pretty, twenty-nine years old. . . . War, wartime, sleepless nights. Spies. Maneuvers. We of the American Silver Doves Revolutionary Army do hereby declare NEVER to submit to the murder, exploitation, and oppression of the world's population in the name of American Fascistic Capitalist Imperialism. We of the American Silver Doves Revolutionary Army do hereby declare NEVER to submit to mind-slavery and brainwashing tactics of the Police State. We do hereby declare PERPETUAL WAR upon the Fascist Capitalist Class and all their employees, agents, sycophants, and dupes. We do hereby declare ourselves SELF-EMPOWERED under the RIGHTS OF MAN. We do hereby declare FREEDOM and JUSTICE for our children and our children's children throughout history. . . . Buddy sitting on the floor, hugging his knees, studying Owen thoughtfully while Uli May speaks. Uli's mellifluous words. A velvet ribbon winding on and on. Buddy in his bib overalls, workman's shirt, leather boots. Studying Owen. X-raying Owen. "Tuning in"—as he calls it—to Owen's "subconscious" mind. Wittgenstein, explosives, a Midwestern drawling innocence. B.A. from Kalamazoo College, M.A. from Columbia, thirty-one years old, a high school kid, bashful smile, queer nicks and tucks in face, slight acne scarring, freckles, moles, small colorless warts, crooked teeth, an incisor that veers sharply to the side, the (unofficial) leader of this cell of the Doves, *The Tractatus*, railroad worker's denim cap, bombs filled with roofing nails and gunpowder, patient drilling of bullets to be filled with cyanide, *Objects are what is unalterable and subsistent; their configuration is what is changing and unstable*, winking (can it be? winking?) at Owen as Uli speaks, tear-gas bombs, sticks of dynamite and alarm clocks and batteries and wires and blasting caps in his workshop, the only door routinely locked, the key kept in *Buddy's* pocket, his amused calm glass-green gaze, impressed by Owen's "logic" and by Owen's "centeredness" and by Owen's "physical discipline" these past six arduous weeks, a security officer's badge pinned to his shirt, *The expression of doubt has no place in the language-game*, the clarity at which the Doves aim is a *complete* clarity which means that all doubt is eradicated as the optimum state is approached, we are not actively seeking martyrdom or sacrifice but will not draw back from historical necessity, refused Rhodes scholarship, was on the track team in high school, Marquette, Michigan, *If in the midst of life we are in death, so in sanity we are surrounded by madness,* so with the American Silver Doves Revolutionary Army surrounded by bourgeois capitalist imperialist society, men, women, and children, and children yet to be born, midnight detonations to coincide with the culmination of the missions of Owen Halleck and his sister Kirsten (spied upon by several of the Doves but not yet brought to 667 Bidart for security reasons, or allowed to meet any of the members *for her own safety*), spontaneous sites, chosen by intuition, Smitty and Rita Stone in the van, cruising, two bombs to place, soldiers in an undeclared war, coordinated "strikes," awakening of revolutionary consciousness, workers, disenfranchised students, blacks, Puerto Ricans, Cubans, Iranian students under F.B.I. surveillance, middle-class citizens, the elderly, teenagers, welfare victims, veterans of wars declared and undeclared, fallout casualties, drug casualties, *What can be said at all can be said clearly, and what we cannot talk about we must consign to silence.* . . . The anarchist Johannes Most, "mass slaughter in public places" a fundamental strategy, national liberation, people's struggle, Jean-Paul Sartre, Sartre's student Jules Régis Debray, the catharsis of violence, the health of dynamite, the cleansing power of death, a total class war with no compromises no negotiations no bargaining no mercy, the spirit of improvisation, the spirit of intuition, guerrilla and commando warfare, twenty-four-hour alert, *The people's army will be the nucleus of the party, not vice versa,* Debray on trial in Bolivia, *Naturally the tragedy is that we do not kill objects, numbers, abstract or interchangeable instruments, but, precisely, on both sides, irreplaceable individuals, essentially innocent, unique for those who have loved, bred, esteemed them, this is the tragedy of history of revolution it is not individuals that battle but class interests but those who fall those who die are persons—we cannot avoid this contradiction, escape this pain.* . . . Letters prepared for newspapers, television stations, national networks. The fall offensive. Death sentences on the heads of (unnamed) men and women, some thirty-five persons, marked as enemies of the Revolution. . . . Smitty, Rita Stone, Brock, Shirley, Buddy, Uli, not perhaps so real as Owen would like them but the pace is accelerated now, the heartbeat cannot slow, he is set upon his mission, he is weightless bodiless soulless without volition without pity without emotion or intellectual weakness without "personal history," a missile, a cyanide-filled bullet, a gleaming knife blade, even Kirsten is becoming less precise, We don't know them, she has said, half-sobbing, Owen please listen we don't know them, not even Daddy, we don't know any of them, whatever we do to them we will have missed them. . . . But no time, no rest, no solitude, a "strike" planned for September 8 and beyond that: "improvisation" defined by existing security conditions, underground strategy continued until such time as the Hallecks (brother and sister both) can be safely transported to Arizona to New Mexico to the border to the secret compound in Mexico where Uli will join them. . . . Loyalty, treason, pledges of allegiance, betrayal. Immediate and summary punishment for traitors. An army, a unified field of consciousness. Absolute harmony. Comrades and enemies, revolutionaries and reactionaries, undeclared war, perpetual. The beginning of the Industrial Era. The Crystal Palace. Striking workers fired upon in the snow. Women, children. Blood. Blood that must be shed. Endless flow, the world's wound. Stanchless. History. *This is the tragedy of revolution, it is not individuals that battle but class interests,* we take upon ourselves the burden of the judges and the executioners, a lonely vigil, the eradication of all future misery, exploitation, injustice. . . . Puerto Rican *Fuerzas Armadas de Liberación Nacional.* Propaganda by the deed. Elections in West Germany, in the States. The most reactionary candidates must win. Provocation of spontaneous uprisings, rebellions. Workers, students, welfare victims. Bologna martyrs: the start of fascist offensive countenanced by the Police State. . . . The victim must be selected with great patience and care. Or: Rita Stone's and Uli's preference, following Johannes Most: mass slaughter *regardless of civilian status* for the most successful historical gesture and media coverage. . . . Laurent-Tailhade, Trotsky, Mao, the Tupamaros. Edith Naumann's important publications on Mao before the onset of her own subversion which then infected her husband Richard. . . . The panel truck, driven by Smitty, Rita Stone, and (possibly) Buddy. Safe escort for Kirsten Halleck after the completion of her mission. . . . Radio beams, X-rays, Buddy's "subconscious" powers. Owen listens, agrees, Owen is taciturn, stoic, muscular, bearded, purse-lipped, in a trance of concentration upon interior musings. It is his assumption that after the mission is completed—his mission, and Kirsten's—he will enter a new phase of his life, a "radically altered vision," in Ulrich May's words. Both he and Kirsten. Baptized in blood. "Crossing over." And— but why should it be otherwise?—with nothing but the future to move into. And so, then, on the other side of that turbulent river, which his companions have already crossed (or claim to have crossed: in fact none of the Washington-based Doves is wanted by the F.B.I. for suspected murder—it isn't clear whether they are precisely *wanted* by the F.B.I. yet at all)—on the other side of that river he and Kirsten will have a good deal of time to think and to listen and to absorb and to experience. But at the present time he hasn't the patience or perhaps the intellectual capacity for background, for history, even for gossip about former Doves and their fates, or broken-away Doves, or fugitives in Denver, Vancouver, Mexico. He isn't a theoretician, he isn't greatly concerned— at the moment—with the outrage of the presidential nominees or the outrage of the bankrupt American fascist-capitalist two-party system or, in particular, the outrage of "reactionaries" in faraway Peking who are desecrating Mao in order to promote their own political careers. He is concerned of course with the impending assassination of Nick Martens who will represent the corruption of "justice" in the United States in world-consciousness—but primarily, obsessively, he is concerned with the impending assassination of one "Isabel Halleck." A woman by happenstance his mother.

Shirley MacGregor aka "Shirley Kane" aka "Auguste" (self-named for one of her revolutionary models, the anarchist-martyr Auguste Vaillant who was executed in Paris in 1893) is responsible for preparing documents for publication and distribution: *The American Silver Doves Revolutionary Army Newsletter*, a bimonthly printed on inexpensive pulp paper and usually averaging about fifteen pages; reprints of early Doves material—*A 17-Point Strategy for the Dissolution of the American Feudal State; "I Accuse!": Travels in Fascist America; A Call to Arms.* She has also arranged for reprints of classic revolutionary tracts, paying for the printing costs out of her own salary: the great Johannes Most's *Science of Revolutionary Warfare: A Manual of Instructions in the Use and Preparations of Nitroglycerine, Dynamite, Gun-Cotton, Fulminating Mercury, Bombs, Fuses, Poisons, Etc.;* excerpts from Frantz Fanon's *The Wretched of the Earth;* poems and meditations and teachings of Mao. With a calligraphic pen she has prepared the two death warrants, on stiff parchmentlike paper—

AMERICAN SILVER DOVES
REVOLUTIONARY
ARMY

EASTERN SEABOARD UNIT

.————————.

Know all Men That it is Hereby
Declared After Due Process of Law
Under the Natural Rights of Man the
Sentence of Death Without Appeal
Has Been Passed Upon a Criminal
Subject of the International Fascist
Capitalist Class. Vengeance for the
People!

SUBJECT: _____

WARRANT ORDER: Execution

WARRANT ISSUED BY: The People's Court

DATE: 8 September 1980

The names are to be neatly typed in.

Owen brings the knife down sharply. Without hesitation. One stroke, and another, and another. The air is rent with his exertions—he hears panting—his heart swells and would burst—but in another moment all is calm, all is routine. Traffic passes on Bidart Street; a city bus creaks and sighs and releases poisonous exhaust.

Owen is awaiting his sister's second call. For she *will* call—she has promised.

It is nine-five. It is nine-ten.

A voice—a radio announcer's voice—rising through the floorboards of the house. Adrienne turns the dial aimlessly, nervously, seeking out "news" she knows is distorted, if not completely false. There is station WKWG-FM. There is the twenty-four-hour news station. The hostages in Iran, the uprising in Poland, rumors of discontent and rebellion in rural China, the presidential campaign at home, Owen holds himself stiff with contempt and will not shout down the stairs for her to turn the fucking thing off or he'll slash her throat.

Kirsten and Nick. Kirsten and Tony Di Piero.

Can it be possible?

Does it matter?

I am an instrument, Owen murmurs aloud, running his thumb along the finely honed knife blade. We are all instruments. But impatient —dear God, impatient!

He waits. Buddy is downstairs in his workshop, completing—he calls it "playing with"—the compact little bomb Owen will carry to 18 Röcken. For no one felt that the execution would be sufficient: discussing it, discussing its symbolic dimensions, all felt—though Owen himself was the first to articulate the thought—that something more striking, more "public," was necessary.

Bring it all down, Owen said. And said no more.

An involuntary and singularly graceless moan escaped from Uli: That house! One of the Sloan houses!

A moment's silence. The young people exchanged glances—they hadn't any idea what Uli May meant *this* time—Buddy rolled his eyes —*Sloan?—what?*—and then Uli conceded: Well, yes. I suppose so. Neighboring Dumbarton Oaks, after all.

Kirsten's pale-gleaming face, tendrils of hair stuck to her forehead. A heat wave in Washington. Day after day, motionless heat. Isabel is out of the city—Isabel is spending a week with friends on an island off the coast of North Carolina—Isabel is due back soon—Nick has gone away somewhere, probably to Mount Dunvegan Island—but will be back after Labor Day—after Labor Day a great deal will be possible.

Kirsten clutching at Owen's hand. A begging grasping tiresome child.

We don't know them, Owen, she says. Even Mother. Even Daddy. We don't know who they are . . . who they were.

Owen is faintly repulsed by his sister. Yet the odor of desperation in her excites him.

He says in Ulrich May's haughty tone: *Doing* is a way of *knowing*. What we *do* to them will compensate any failure of *knowledge*.

Kirsten brushes hair out of her eyes, regards him with her bright-hot glassy stare, considers. It is often the case that this young woman surprises him with her subtlety, her intransigence, the very quality of her doubt; and she does so now by murmuring, half-apologetically: No. I think you're mistaken. *Doing* is only *doing*.

Ulrich May weighs the handsome gleaming knife in his hand, his open palm, speaking gently, coaxingly, as if after so many weeks it might be coaxing Owen Halleck requires and not restraint. Out of cold curiosity I sought her out, Owen—I move easily in those circles, as you know—and even I with my experience was repulsed by her: her appearance, her behavior, her circle of "friends." Her new lover is this creature Tim Fox, you must have heard of, yes?—a so-called journalist, a television "personality," a self-appointed investigator of private lives—And old General Kempe among them, in his wheelchair, shrunken and ghastly and mute, but managing at times to grin—*hideous* man. Perhaps the cancer has been arrested, or perhaps he's simply numbed by morphine: I hadn't the heart to ask.

Where was this? Owen asks quietly, his eyes fixed on the knife. What was she wearing?

Your mother—! Ah, Isabel de Benavente! I don't recall what she was wearing—I do recall that she'd had something frantic done to her hair—a kind of fried frazzled spiky kinky look—rather too young for her, but attractive—she has the facial bones to carry it off. She seems to have acquired an unfortunate shrill laughter of late. The quintessential howl of the female drunk. Not that anyone in that circle would notice, of course. . . . I drew her aside as if we were old friends and for a gay moment or two we *were,* she smeared her lipstick on my cheek, hugged me, I asked her the usual social questions—the usual palaver—and rather naughtily eased onto a certain subject: How are your children, Isabel?—leaving for school soon, I suppose?—you'll miss them.

She started to reply—she was going to brazen it out, I suppose —then she simply froze—drew away—looked away—said not a word.

Your two very attractive children—? I said coaxingly.

But no, no: not a word.

Owen has been listening closely, his head cocked. Now he snorts with laughter.

Uli continues expansively: This Tim Fox, what a creature—one of the most pernicious parasites of our time—castigating "folly" as he calls it in others—his vicious columns, his vicious television shows—he really must be marked for execution, I think—I'm going to insist upon it—if —if things work out—but no more of that at the moment: Do you know, Fox championed a Soviet dissident poet a few years ago, I forget the poor man's name, Grigory something, Fox made a lot of noise about bringing him to the States—he'd defected in Paris, I think—and was quite poor—couldn't speak much English—in a very bad state—so Fox drummed up support and donations and Grigory came to the States and there was a flurry of parties and interviews and some New York publishers made well-publicized bids for his work—the usual thing—and then Fox arranged for a reading here in Washington, at the Kennedy Center, the box office to go to Grigory—or most of it, anyway—and a big crowd did show up, it was quite *the* occasion of the week—I must admit I went myself, I'm always curious about "dissidents"—and poets—and the evening was a disaster: Grigory stood on the apron of the stage reciting his poetry in Russian, a completely unintelligible stream of gibberish, he swayed back and forth with his eyes shut, he was passionate, he was perspiring, it was *quite* the real thing, and naturally quite moving— diverting—for a while. Of course there were translators on stage and they were supposed to translate into English, but Grigory went into a sort of trance or pretended to do so, and refused to allow them to read —and gradually the audience drifted out, in small guilty groups—until only a few of us were left. But everyone said, afterward—and it was reported in the press!—that the man was "courageous" and a "marvelous poet."

Owen joins him, laughing. Owen's broad shoulders quiver. He says: *Your two very attractive children,* you asked her—? I wish I could have seen the bitch's face!

In the old days, in the old years, anticipating summer camp— Owen was shipped up to New Hampshire for several years, and then, once, to a "fat camp" in the Catskills—he would place on the floor of his room, sometimes two weeks beforehand, the single large suitcase he would be taking. The prospect of camp always excited him tremen dously; he had, as a child, an excellent facility for forgetting disappointment. So the suitcase would be taken from the closet, the child would be humored, Mrs. Salman would help him arrange his underclothes, socks, towels, toiletries, as if he were leaving in the morning, and he would spend a good deal of time simply gazing at the opened suitcase, and looking through the glossy color brochures for the camp, and rereading the instructions that accompanied his Polaroid camera. By the time the morning of departure arrived he would be in a near fever of anticipation.

So, now, in the cubbyhole of a room assigned to him at 667 Bidart, Owen Halleck lays out across the cot his assassin's clothes, the German knife, the loop of fine strong pitiless wire, the dark suede gloves, the taped flashlight, the vial of chloroform, the little red pill box. He does not pace about the room: he stands motionless, staring, contemplating. The other Doves do not interrupt him, even to summon him to meals. He is in a state of suspension, he is in a state of sanctity, and perhaps they reason too—for they are fairly shrewd young men and women—that he is restraining himself as an attack dog might be restraining itself and might be—*might* be—for other Doves and Dove-affiliates, over the years, have sometimes behaved in surprising ways as the time of a "strike" approached—might be considered dangerous.

In any case, a convert of rare zeal and dedication. A Dove-to-be of possibly heroic proportions.

He lays the precious items out one by one, tenderly. On his neat little bed. He contemplates them, arms folded. One and then another and then another. . . . The pill box fascinates him though in fact he will never be required to open it, he will never have to jam the tablet into the very back of his mouth and swallow hard, *swallow* hard. (As he has imagined. As he has rehearsed.)

At the end of the day he lifts the items from his cot and sets them aside, reverently. Day after day, weeks, has it been months and even years, he is waiting, he has longed for this, he is in a state of holy suspension.

Isabel's piercing scream wakes him. Her fingers clutch at him as she falls. He might imagine her pretty fingernails breaking, he might imagine blood bubbling from her mouth.

He rises from her, knife in hand. They are in the large bedroom perhaps, or in the adjoining bathroom, the "new" one—there is the appeal of the smooth clean antiseptic ceramic tile. Owen steps carefully over the body. There will be blood, naturally. He plans not to be alarmed or even especially surprised by blood; he will not make the mistake of getting his shoes stained.

In a small spiral notebook he scribbles what he calls "flight plans" —*Do not step in blood*—and places a row of ###### beside it.

Buddy hardly glances around at Owen as he speaks. His fingers continue to move deftly and expertly.—I didn't even realize I was tuning into her, he tells Owen, I mean after all we had *trusted* her, she knew everything about us and so did her husband, they joined only a few months after I did . . . but there was this business of them going off together, on walks, in their room with the door closed, and then they wanted to leave the compound, and Richard tried to take a certain typewriter with him—he claimed it was *his* but it was communal property. Anyway, says Buddy, his tone sharpening for a moment, the principle we must maintain is that of unity. And for unity we must maintain discipline.

Yes, Owen murmurs. It is Buddy's fingers that interest him.

An army without discipline isn't an army, Buddy says. You can't tolerate people going off in all directions thinking any thought that flies into their heads. . . . You know the principles of radio beams? I think it must be like that. On a certain level of frequency. I can pick up thoughts if there isn't too much static and if I don't *will* myself to do it. The static comes from the—shall we say—upper brain, the newer brain—and as long as the actual thoughts are on a lower level of frequency I have no trouble interpreting them. So it was with Edith. Unfortunately for her —the traitorous bitch.

Yes, says Owen, watching his friend's fingers.

Buddy too is tender, leaning over his workbench of marvels. Sticks of dynamite; gunpowder in small but quite heavy packing cases; alarm clocks in various appealing stages of dismantling. It is all so precise, it is all so magnificently *real, Objects are what is unalterable and subsistent; their configuration is what is changing and unstable,* Owen enters into a blissful state approaching Buddy's in intensity, simply watching: that he should have found his way here, to this house, to this secret room with its black shades and clinically glaring 150-watt bulbs!—that he should have discovered, without any plotting, any preppie calculating, so extraordinary a friend—how unhesitating this boy's touch, how irrefutable the fact of dynamite and the simple fact of a clock with its minute hand moving, moving—the comforting tick of a machine—

Owen who rarely thinks now of the past, and never of his "personal" past, suddenly recalls an anecdote told to his political science class by their professor: The scene was Athens, the professor was a guest at a banquet in honor of the prince of Saudi Arabia, the prince turned out to be a B.A. from the University of California at Santa

Barbara and an M.A. from Harvard where he had studied under Henry Kissinger—that most "charming," "articulate," "clear-headed" of men. Years later Kissinger as Secretary of State went to Saudi Arabia, met the prince in a reception line, recognized him at once, and said: Don't believe what I told you in those Harvard lectures—*this is the real thing.*

So too, Owen muses, watching Buddy's fingers, is this the real thing, the irrefutable logic of . . .

I place my faith in machines, Buddy says softly. In machines that run along a continuum of time. In which case, you see, both the *machine* and *time* are extensions of our brains. In the global revolutionary war to come this fact will be of immeasurable significance.

(Owen has been told, though not by Buddy, who is modest, that he has masterminded innumerable "strikes" over the years; he is one of two or three bomb-making geniuses in the movement. When he lived in New York he helped the Puerto Rican group *Furia* with their incendiary and bombing maneuvers at Rockefeller Center, Park Avenue, and Wall Street; the most famous strike of the era, FALN's bombing of a Wall Street restaurant where three people died and dozens were injured, had been part of Buddy's general strategy—though he would have preferred an office building or better yet the World Trade Center instead of a restaurant. Such strikes only stir up old tedious distracting arguments about "innocent" victims.)

Yes, Owen murmurs, the *machine* . . . and *time.* Yes. I see.

There is *his* bomb, being assembled. Dynamite, batteries, wires, an alarm clock. An inexpensive alarm clock bought at a drugstore up the street.

Owen, busy-minded Owen, has never spoken with Buddy, or with any of his new friends, of his father and his father's death: he has never had time to bring the subject up. Nor the fact of the swamp, and the unspeakable insult of the Brean Down coroner's office. And so abstract and so sentimental a notion as "betrayal"—what has it to do with the Doves, and with him?

Buddy glances around at Owen and smiles a faint startled smile, as if he had forgotten Owen's presence. He hasn't shaved for several days but he looks boyish and ingenuous and rather sweet.—I'll set it for midnight, he says, according to the plan, right?—though of course you could always delay the detonation simply by moving the alarm ahead. What time is it now? When are you leaving?

The telephone has just begun to ring in the other room. It is 9:35. It is surely Kirsten. Owen rouses himself as if from a deep sleep and says, licking his dry lips: Yes. Midnight. Thank you.

Failures

The first time, nearly twenty years ago, after the death of Isabel's second baby. A female, unnamed. Premature by eleven weeks. Defective heart and lungs, malfunctioning liver. Nick flies down alone from Boston to visit Isabel at Mount St. Mary's Hospital where she is weak from shock and loss of blood, white-skinned "as an angel"—in the possibly inappropriate words of one of the nuns.

Nick, another woman's husband, sick with grief for Isabel. Love-sick with grief.

He brings flowers—daisies and white roses—and dares to clasp her hand while Maurie grips the other.

Finally there is a telephone call and Maurie must excuse himself and the lovers are left alone. Except of course they are not lovers: the dead infant is not Nick's.

Isabel draws her hand out of his, perversely. There are hair-thin blue veins in her forehead, there are fine white cracks in her lips. She looks at Nick with hatred: I knew the baby was going to die—I knew—don't feel sorry for me—you and *her*—don't pity me—we'll try again, Maurie and I—don't worry about us—don't trouble yourself—it wasn't your fault, was it—it wasn't your baby, was it—which is what you are thinking—I know—I know—

Nick tries to console her. He tries to quiet her. (Her voice has been steadily rising, she is about to become hysterical, he cannot silence her by force and he cannot flee the room.)

He grips her hand hard. And finally she stops, in the middle of an accusation. She hates him, she cannot bear to look at him, she begins to cry—a relief!—and says only: It was our punishment anyway. It was *mine.*

And then upon impulse—desperate impulse—Nick flies to Stockholm for a weekend in the spring of 1965, simply to see Isabel Halleck who is "unhappy" and separated from her husband, her son, and Washington life for a "brief exploratory period," having brought her baby girl Kirsten with her.

A bright blowy Swedish June. The American Foreign Service people congratulate them on their good fortune: the weather has finally turned!

Nick is jealous of his friend's wife's popularity in Stockholm. Among the embassy people. Among the Swedes. She does not strike him as "unhappy" after all: she does not strike him as his friend's *wife,* precisely, in this place. There are receptions, there are cocktail parties, there are luncheons, there is even an interminable elegant dinner in the ambassador's residence. Nick is rarely alone with Isabel, and then she insists upon bringing her baby girl with them.

I want to know only one thing, Nick says quietly. Are you and Maurie really separating?

Why do you need to know? Isabel asks.

I came all this distance to see you, to find out, Nick says. And now you treat me like shit.

Isabel turns her lovely face to him. She is blankly astonished, she is slyly delighted, she says with a smile: *Is* that how I've been treating you?

It might be their time of sudden passion, their time of intoxicating romance, a Stockholm honeymoon braced by the chilly sun of the Baltic Sea: but something is wrong.

Without Maurie near?—without Maurie to define them?

Isabel refuses to hear Nick's complaints about his marriage, Isabel speaks of having gone to the ballet—a Parisian troupe—with a Swedish cultural officer, a few nights previously. They walk through the Djurgården without seeing it, they visit the open zoo at Skansen, for Kirsten's sake. (And the child loves it—at first. But then she tires and begins to fret and her small face burns with temper.) They become almost gaily drunk at a canal-side restaurant. They are sobered and chilled by the Munch paintings in the Thielska Gallery—those tall lovely cadaverous females whom Isabel cannot help envying.

Nick drinks a great deal of Swedish beer in extraordinarily tall glasses. He hears himself say in anguish: You can't leave him! You would destroy him.

Isabel visits Nick at the Grand Hotel—once: and brings whimpering Kirsten along.

Their last evening together is ruined by a small crowd of demonstrators—protesting the Vietnam war, protesting America in general—in front of the United States Embassy. Nothing happens, no one is injured, but Nick becomes almost physically ill with rage, like several of the other Americans attached to the embassy.

The bastards, he mutters, the fuckers, what do they mean—criticizing *us!*

And then again, six years later, after much has happened between them, and has failed to happen, Isabel is driving rather fast along an expressway and Nick is berating her for her recklessness—her involvement with Di Piero: Doesn't she care how she is hurting other people! Doesn't she care about the danger to her marriage, and to her children!

Isabel says nothing.

And all for what, Nick says contemptuously, surely you don't think Di Piero would stand by you—

Isabel interrupts: "Stand by me"?—a curious thing to say.

You know what I mean, Nick says.

Would *you* stand by me? Isabel laughs.

They have met for lunch, for the first time in many weeks; they have had a fair amount to drink; there were the usual involuntary—perhaps obligatory?—moments of despair and tenderness and exhilaration. But now the afternoon has shifted, it is a truly malevolent glowering late-winter sky. Isabel presses down on the gas pedal and Nick tells her to stop behaving like an idiot and Isabel shouts for him to leave her alone, simply leave her alone, how dare he lecture her on her life—on *her* marriage.

He tries to comfort her, sliding his arm around her shoulders. She beats him away, frantic and sobbing as a young girl. It is one of their manic episodes, it is not exactly unfamiliar, but suddenly the car skids out of control and sideswipes the concrete median and Isabel screams and Nick is thrown forward to strike the windshield with his forehead —fortunately not hard: the glass isn't shattered, his skull isn't broken.

The car has stopped. Isabel is still sobbing. Nick is silent and very white, rubbing his forehead, blinking, dazed.

The car has stopped but traffic on the expressway continues. My God, Isabel whispers.

Ten seconds, twenty, thirty.

Isabel does not look at Nick and, after a while, Nick takes her hand and squeezes the cold limp fingers.

My dear God, Isabel says. I almost killed you.

They look shyly at each other. Nick's forehead is bleeding.

After another pause Nick says: I must leave. I can't be caught here with you.

Yes, Isabel says faintly.

Traffic streams by: enormous rattling semidetached trucks, city buses, cars. Isabel's eye is fixed upon the rearview mirror. A patrol car? Already?

I must leave, Nick says, are you all right—?

Yes, says Isabel.

Still he doesn't move. They sit close together, dazed, staring at the median and the traffic, in an utter nullity, a blank. Again Isabel thinks she sees a patrol car, again she is mistaken.

If the newspapers printed— If Maurie—

Yes—

I must leave—

Yes—you should hurry—

Nick embraces Isabel and burrows against her, suddenly, desperately, kissing her throat and her mouth, rubbing his hot damp face against her breasts, and then he pushes away, he opens the door, he says: I'll have to run for it, will you be all right?—the police should be here in a minute.

Yes, says Isabel. Be careful.

You *are* all right?

Of course, yes, go on—hurry—

He climbs out of the car and hurries back along the median and she watches him for a while in the rearview mirror, then she notices the smears of blood on her face, and wipes them off with a wetted tissue, totally absorbed in her task when the police arrive.

And then again, a final time—twelve days after Maurie's funeral.

When Nick's fumbling touch is abrasive against Isabel's skin, and Isabel's hair burns his cheek.

They draw back from each other, baffled. But Nick's fingers *do* hurt, there are dull red marks on Isabel's forearm; and his skin stings lightly where her hair has brushed against it.

We did it, Isabel is whispering, we killed him, we'll be punished, but Nick makes another attempt to hold her as if he hasn't heard. He reasons that she must cry, in his arms, it is crucial that she cry in his arms; they must cry together.

But Isabel stands stiff and ungiving. It is only with an effort that Nick is able to embrace her—and still she resists, holding herself from him. Her hair smells acrid as if newly bleached, the scent of her skin is faintly repulsive, the minute bracketing lines about her mouth will only deepen, cruelly, with age. We killed him, Isabel says tonelessly, I hate the two of us and I hate him. . . . It's all over.

Nothing is over, Nick says, frightened. No one knows.

And then, as if it were possible to contest the point, he continues: Maurie didn't hate *us*.

Isabel says angrily: You killed him that day you lied to him—it's as simple as that. He never recovered from it. He didn't even try. If only you could have told him something—anything—you might have said you were in debt, or being blackmailed—that your family was threatened—or you might have broken down and he would have forgiven you—he would have forgiven you *anything*.

I didn't want his forgiveness, Nick says.

God damn Tony, says Isabel, and that crude bastard Gast—I hope he *is* dead—have you heard anything more about him?—all of you meeting in *my* house—in poor Maurie's house—I didn't know what was going on—I truly didn't—you lied even to me—you never explained—

I didn't have to explain, you understood perfectly well, Nick says irritably, don't play games with me now, Isabel. You were there from the start.

No. You're wrong.

You and Di Piero.

No.

Yes, certainly, you and Di Piero—don't trouble to lie.

So he's dead, Isabel says, and for what?—everything is over. We'll be punished.

No one knows, Nick says angrily, we *can't* be punished.

He should have let you go to jail, Isabel says. He should have prepared the case himself.—No, it's all over. I hate us. We will be punished.

Her upper lip curls just perceptibly, in contempt. It crosses Nick's mind that he has never loathed any person the way he loathes Isabel Halleck.

He has been meaning to show her Maurie's postcard—Washington at blossom-time—*Thank you for the 27 years*—which of course he has shown no one, prudently: but now his great need, his almost visceral hunger, is to get as far away from this woman as possible. He says, walking to the door: We *can't* be punished.

The Fly

A mistake?

A dangerous mistake?

But in any case an interesting mistake, Nick Martens thinks. A profound diversion.

So he awaits Kirsten with mounting excitement. He finds himself prowling the house, drink in hand. Nine o'clock. Nine-five. His friend's daughter. His mistress's daughter. Squeezing the very tips of his fingers, leaning up to him, her pale hard face uplifted and unsmiling: You don't want to give me a chance, she says hoarsely. And when he pretends not to understand she says: You know what I mean.

The high narrow new-brick townhouse, borrowed for the night. An elegant but sparsely-furnished pied-à-terre belonging to a New York acquaintance, divorced like Nick, and like Nick rather unsettled at the present time. Two small bedrooms upstairs, a small bathroom; unnervingly steep stairs; a living room, a kitchen that is hardly more than a pantry, a tiny foyer, grillwork with a "New Orleans" flair across the ground-floor windows. The house smells of newness—parquet and polish. Very few rugs. The fluorescent tubing in the bathroom hums with remarkable vigor.

Nick is restless, agitated. Grateful for the sweating glass in his hand. Grateful for the anonymity of the place. (He has borrowed it for the night several times in the past—it has always been satisfactory.) Too many people know him now, or at any rate recognize him. Restaurants, hotels. Crossing busy streets. He is restless and agitated and yet quite at home: the odor of parquet, the odor of disinfectant in the toilet, the odor of Scotch. He will make Kirsten a drink when she arrives. Will she have a drink? He will make her one.

She leaned up to him with startling boldness. He hadn't been prepared. Her cold fleshy mouth pressing against his. Pressing. Hungry. Alarming.

A light had been burning by the front portico of the Fletcher house on Thirty-second Street, where Kirsten was evidently staying with her aunt. But Kirsten led him by the wrist along a flagstone path to a side door, past enormous hulking rhododendron shrubs. Shadows, warm summer darkness, a young girl's audacity. He did not resist. He smiled. He joined her caprice, her light tinkling laughter. It was an adventure, after all—being coerced into taking Isabel's daughter home from a party —being a conspirator—though it hadn't been clear to him whether Isabel and her escort had already left the party, or whether Kirsten and Isabel had simply had a disagreement. In any case he hadn't seen Isabel in the gathering. He had been spared.

She pushed herself against him, leaned up against him, making a joke of it, grinning, then unsmiling, petulant, demanding as his own daughter—that rapid change of mood that did in fact excite him. You don't want to give me a chance, she said, accusing him with a little poke in the ribs, you don't even want to know who I *am*, the awkward seductive boldness of adolescence, the sheer surprise of it. His friend's daughter, after all. His mistress's daughter. Whom he had not always—not *always*—found irresistibly charming. (In general he had preferred Owen. A solid forthright intelligent industrious boy. Nick's only godson. Whose admiration for him—and the admiration *was* embarrassingly clear at times—did not spill over into tiresome requests for Nick's time.)

You don't know a goddam thing about me anymore, she said, laughing, tightening her arms around his neck, you don't know the *first thing* about me, Nick, and he gripped her shoulders to push her gently away but did not push her away: and for a long, a very long, a very long delirious time Nick Martens was actually kissing Kirsten Halleck— standing with her in a shadowy doorway, fugitive, panting, faint with lust as any high school boy.

Are you afraid of me? the girl whispered.

Out on the street Nick's companion—the young F.B.I. man assigned to him for several weeks—waited in the car, turning the radio dial, half-smoking and discarding cigarettes. Nick feared not the young man's disapproval but his professional silence, his social—which is to say, Washingtonian—tact.

Had he absorbed the fact of the girl's youth, and that queer bright unnerving insouciance that came with alcohol or drugs or fatigue—the way she chattered, laughed, went abruptly silent, teasing Nick with a vague and highly provocative story about her meeting with a man in New York not long ago, a friend of Nick's (this would be Di Piero, of course)? Had he absorbed the fact of the girl's identity—?

Of course, Nick thought. The young man knew everything he was required to know, of an evening.

Why don't you come inside, no one will know, Kirsten whispered, but Nick extricated himself from her, made his excuses, his apologies, his promises—which he hadn't meant at the time—for why on earth would he choose to become involved with *this* one?—and hurried back to the street, to the car.

Where the silence, the professional indifference, the chilling tact awaited him.

A friend's daughter, Nick mumbled, not very happy at the present time. . . . He was going to say "going through a phase," which was one of Maurie's philosophical assessments of his children, but instead his words trailed off.

Where now, Mr. Martens? the young man asked, stubbing out his cigarette.

He stands at the narrow window of the front bedroom, the bedroom they will use, watching the street. A mistake, an error, another of his half-deliberate miscalculations?—he is too excited to greatly care.

Do you know *me*, Kirsten, he thinks, sipping his drink, do you imagine you know *me*, little girl?—and he smiles to consider the fact, the rather marvelous and horrific fact, implacable as a pebble-hard lump in his flesh, that he uses the phrase "little girl"—that he has become, or seems to have become, a man in a pied-à-terre borrowed for a night's assignation with a teenaged girl—a girl he is gloating over—whom he addresses as "little girl" as if imagining that might disarm her.

It is all there, still—coiled up and slumbering—anxious, malevolent with sheer energy—hunger. It is all there, Nick's spirit. It has not drowned with Maurie after all.

His ambition, his old lust. His tireless plotting.

Nick Martens as he knows and values himself. Nick Martens as the world observes him, pious with envy.—Let me exist, to begin with, Nick has often wanted to say, to shout, in angry justification of himself: let me for Christ's sake *exist* and the rest of the world can fall in place around me.

Five minutes after nine. Ten minutes. She is on her way—greedy and eager as he—breathless over the telephone: she cannot be stopped. Even if Isabel knew. Even if Maurie.—Not my house, the neighborhood is too risky, I swear there's some celebrity-hunter or local madman who watches me with a telescope from his redwood deck to my redwood deck, they've checked him out and say he is harmless, a CPA in fact, but we won't bring you there, and hotels are out, and your aunt's place is out —enormous as it is—and I can't get away for more than a few hours, I must be in the office by eight-thirty tomorrow morning—so come to this address, at this time— And he gives her the information as if dictating to a secretary.

If she thinks he is being abrupt and peremptory—if she thinks he is being rude, not offering to pick her up, instructing her to take a cab —of course she gives no indication. But she has no such thoughts, surely. She is too young. She is too inexperienced.

In the morning, too, she will take a cab out of Rock Creek Lane. Early. No later than seven. He will call the cab—he will make the arrangements himself—well in advance. He has learned in this phase of his life to be pitilessly efficient.

No one gets up at six in the morning to do nothing, but one might gladly get up at . . .

Shall I repeat the address, dear? Nick asks. Do you have it?—and the telephone number if something goes wrong.

Yes, says Kirsten, her voice hoarse, gleeful, yes thank you, Nick, but nothing will go wrong.

But to know at last what one is, Nick murmurs aloud to Maurie, the corners of his eyes crinkling, to know the most magnanimous perimeter of one's soul: not just one's value on the market, but one's worth in secret!—and he finds himself smiling at the sudden image of an enormous buzzing fly hovering . . . lowering itself with its many legs extended . . . squatting . . . quivering greedily . . . on a great unspeakable pile of shit.

Interviews, articles, profiles "in depth." Nick Martens the Director of the Commission for the Ministry of Justice. Replacing the late disgraced Maurice J. Halleck.—Watching himself on a taped television interview show, filmed in New York, Nick is coldly impressed with his own ability to speak—to summon forth, on the spot, felicitous quotes— alluding to Aristotle's *Politics* ("It is evident that the State is a creation of nature, and that man is by nature a political animal. And he who by nature and not by mere accident is without a State is either above humanity or below it . . ."), Oswald Spengler ("It is the hallmark of

Faustian peoples that they are conscious of the direction of their history"), Franz Kafka whom he has not troubled to read in twenty years ("I am a lawyer. So I can never get away from evil"); he is coldly impressed with the affability, the graceful logic, of his lies.

A lengthy and nearly entirely favorable interview in the *Washington Post*, with an ambitious young woman journalist not known for her charity toward men of power. An even more flattering—though less factually precise—profile in *Time* magazine: there is a cover story on several men, including Nick, an allegedly new, dynamic, professionally rigorous breed of government officials, idealistic, apolitical, "contemptuous" of old-fashioned party politics. . . . Nick scans the story, which is called, boldly, "The New Washington," to see if he is exposed, or even suspected, but it is a deeply gratifying piece, a confirmation of the wisdom of his appointment to the rank of director. His friends and acquaintances and associates and assistants congratulate him. He even receives telegrams. Who are these people? He rereads the article with a growing sense of astonishment that the journalist should have understood him so well . . . and then it occurs to him that of course it isn't Nick Martens the journalist has written about, but Maurie Halleck. Idealistic, apolitical, contemptuous of party politics. Committed to his work. To his profession. Incorruptible. And feared—as a consequence of his very incorruptibility.

Maurie Halleck, yes. But the name in the slot is *Nick Martens.*

(But then he emerged from the House Ethics Committee's investigation looking very good. Very good indeed. Shattered by the tragedy of his close friend's death but not contaminated by it. Deeply shocked. Grieving. But not debilitated in the slightest. *Nick Martens.*)

To Maurie he tries to explain, ceaselessly pleading his case: I gave in because I had come to feel that we didn't really have enough evidence anyway—it was all so circumstantial, the witnesses were so unreliable —and the regime has been gone so long, so very long—everyone dead —Allende forgotten—and now there's Guatemala—and tomorrow there will be another scandal: United Fruit, Gulf and Western, Lockheed, GBT Copper: which is which, and why, and when, and how can it possibly matter? To accept so-called monies in order to retard an investigation that was doomed in any case, to sabotage a prosecution that didn't require sabotage to look insubstantial in front of a shrewd judge . . . it appealed to my sense of humor.

Maurie has no reply, Maurie shows no response.

They were all lying, Nick insists, our witnesses as well as theirs. Who killed whom . . . who actually pulled the trigger . . . who beat in whose heads . . . which government agency financed the strikes, the truckers' demonstrations . . . who bombed the newspapers . . . who flooded Santiago with leaflets . . . who shot Schneider and who paid off Valenzuela and what exactly Kissinger ordered the C.I.A. to do and which documents are missing and all the rest of it: the great stinking pile of shit: how can it possibly matter if a half-dozen American businessmen got their hands dirty too? *How can it possibly matter so many years afterward?*

It appealed to my sense of humor, Nick says angrily, my sense of style. *You* wouldn't understand.

A car, a yellow cab, is moving slowly along Rock Creek Lane.

Nick hurriedly finishes his drink. Yes, he thinks. Kirsten. At last. It's time.

He presses against the window, spying on the street, his heartbeat accelerating foolishly. Little girl, he thinks, staring, swallowing, so you really *have* come.

How remarkable, how . . . improbable. For of course her mother had never crossed over. Like this. With such recklessness, such insistence. Such hard queer frightening desire.

Nick watches as the cab stops at the curb across the street. (He had instructed Kirsten to give the driver that address—the address of a high-rise apartment building.) Now the back door swings open and Kirsten climbs out, long-legged, eager, energetic. She stands in a halo of light from a very bright street lamp, paying the cabdriver, talking with him. Of course she is wonderfully unconscious of Nick—unconscious of being watched. In an ankle-length mauve skirt, an embroidered saffron-beige blouse with long sleeves, the usual open sandals. Bracelets, necklaces. Her generation. Her youth. Windblown red-blond hair, slightly straggly behind. Very narrow waist. And hips. Her shoulders are probably wider than her hips. Nick stares, motionless. How can it be happening, how can such things happen, the whole thing is preposterous, an unfunny joke, he will send her away again at once, he will not even answer the door, absurd, grotesque, unthinkable . . .

She leans to one side and her oversized bag swings heavily from her shoulder. It is a gaudy purple, probably made of macramé—Audrey has something like it, a smaller version. Audrey who now detests him.

Affluent middle-class American children, Nick thinks as he watches Kirsten, with their peasant handicrafts, their harmless trinkets made by slaves. They wear costumes the colors of macaws, made of coarse lacework, they favor the "primitive" but of course they are charming. . . . And this one isn't my daughter.

It all appeals to my sense of humor, Nick will tell the next interviewer. My deepening sense of the comic.

Since Maurie's death very little matters. For the universe has shifted—subtly but irreparably.

Very little matters: what Nick does, or what is done to him.

An "orderly" demonstration took place last Monday morning, overseen by television cameras, on the sidewalk in front of the Federal Commission for the Ministry of Justice. Of course Nick knew about it beforehand. Nick knows everything beforehand.

The leader of the "Americans for Peace and Justice" was granted a ten-minute interview with Nick; he was even allowed to tape the interview. He did most of the talking, as it turned out, though Nick made encouraging sounds now and then, and nodded from time to time with an air of only slightly distracted sympathy. Our organization stresses peaceful and legal tactics, the young man explained, but not at the expense of being denied a hearing for our cause.

Yes, Nick said.

The "cause" at the present time was a Vietnam veteran, a black, sentenced to death for first-degree murder in Fresno, California. One of Nick's innumerable young assistants had supplied him with a folder of information about the case, some of which he had had time to read, with a dismaying sense of déjà vu. The veteran, now thirty-two years old, had made what might be called a poor adjustment to civilian life since his discharge from the army. Several arrests for drunk and disorderly behavior, an arrest for burglary, another for armed robbery . . . and finally for the "unprovoked" murder of a Fresno policeman, also black. Newspaper articles had focused upon the fact, sworn to by witnesses, that the veteran had gone berserk on a crowded Fresno street, firing into the air and shouting "Vietnam, Vietnam . . ." His defense attorneys had spent a great deal of time questioning acquaintances of the accused, and psychologists, and doctors, in order to stress the fact that the man was not only obsessed with his military experience but physically affected by it: there was medical proof that he had been "poisoned" by defoliant, and consequently subject to erratic behavior. Yes, said the prosecution, but did he know right from wrong?—and they established to the jury's satisfaction that he did know right from wrong, had in fact intended to do "wrong" by very deliberately firing a pistol in the face of another man.

The California Supreme Court had heard the appeal, and upheld the verdict. The United States Supreme Court had declined to review the case.

Nick listened to the impassioned and surprisingly articulate plea of the leader of the Americans for Peace and Justice, and gave every impression of being seriously concerned. Though the stale air of déjà vu made it difficult for him to breathe. Though he had to resist a witticism: Just because we've all been poisoned, have we carte blanche to kill?

Since Maurie's death very little matters. Even Maurie's office. Even Maurie's chair. —I want to thank you for your time, Mr. Martens, the young man said, his voice quivering. I realize you're very busy and I—well, I want to thank you for your time. I hope I'll be hearing from you—

Yes, says Nick, not at all, I mean—you're welcome.

She rings the doorbell and he opens the door and she steps inside, bold, laughing, into his embrace. They are both very warm. —I was afraid I might have the wrong address, Kirsten says, kissing him, and Nick says, Don't be silly, how could you have the wrong address?—we made sure of that.

She draws back from him, looking around. She brushes her hair out of her face. Breathless, as if she had run to him. As if she had had to fight her way to him.

Nick asks if she would like a drink. She murmurs a reply, it sounds like yes, all right, if you want one. She is looking around, her eyes moving quickly but vacantly from place to place. He dreads her asking —Whose house is this? Why are we here? What sort of things happen here?—but of course she says nothing. She *is* out of breath, her small breasts rise and fall, loose inside the peasant blouse. A queer wide bright smile, wet teeth, glistening eyes. But she isn't crying. He hopes she isn't crying.

Yes, says Kirsten, a drink would be fine. Ice cubes. I'm so warm.

And then, a moment later, with a half-embarrassed laugh: I'm so shaky.

He asks her why she's shaky, why should she be apprehensive, and she says no reason, no reason, brushing her hair out of her eyes again, staring at him, smiling so that her pale gums show, and her hard wet white teeth. Nick feels an uncanny faintness in the backs of his knees, his groin, his bowels. Kirsten Halleck is not altogether real to him and yet here she stands—and what is he to do with her, to her?—the darling little scamp who ran into Isabel's drawing room at the age of six, scarlet lipstick smeared on her mouth, rouge on her cheeks, her pretty little white nightgown falling off one shoulder—the hard-breasted panting girl who pushed herself against him one night a few weeks ago, forcing him to kiss her, sucking at his lips, his tongue.

She is laughing at something, suddenly—her laughter is surprisingly raucous, like any teenage girl's—she holds out to him a brochure or a pamphlet and asks if it belongs to him, she found it on the sidewalk: Nick takes it from her, glances at it, a religious or political tract. *The American Silver Doves Revolutionary Army Newsletter,* crude pulp paper, black and red headlines, HAITIANS EXPLOITED ALONG EAST COAST, SUPPORT FOR OUR IRANIAN COMRADES, BROTHERS AND SISTERS OF LIBYA. He tosses it aside, of course it isn't his, just a flyer, junk mail. And now —should he make them each a drink?

Anything, says Kirsten. With ice. Maybe some lime.

I don't have lime here, Nick says, amused.

Lemon?—a twist of lemon?

I'll look in the refrigerator, he says.

He kisses her and the faintness deepens in his knees, in his bowels. His mouth feels parched. Blood rushes into his penis—his penis is becoming a club—a small hot throbbing club—absurd—grotesque—altogether delightful.

You *are* alone here? Kirsten says with a wan smile.

Nick laughs. I'm always alone, he says.

She has to make a telephone call, she tells him, her aunt Harriet Fletcher is so solicitous of her—the kind of sweet old well-meaning biddy who forces you to lie—does he mind?—is there a phone?—and Nick tells her of course he doesn't mind, help yourself, the telephone is in the vestibule.

He leaves the kitchen door open. Overhears her dialing, speaking: Hello, Aunt Harriet? Yes. Sure. I'm fine. Yes, it *is* a house party—yes, that address—Sissy Lathrop—yes—no it was Miss Pickett's—she wasn't my roommate *exactly*—of course it is—of course they expect me —everything is fine—I have my overnight things—I'll see you sometime tomorrow, maybe the afternoon?—I don't know. Good night. And *please* don't worry. . . .

He emerges from the kitchen, drinks in hand. His agitation is delightful: his teeth are lightly, very lightly, chattering: but of course the girl cannot see. She herself is fairly trembling, fixing him with her queer wide terrified smile.

They look at each other. They find themselves laughing—it is all so peculiar, so marvelous.

Shall we go upstairs? Nick says. Here's your drink.

Oh God, thank you, she says, taking it from him, sipping at it, her eyes closed. A pale blue vein flutters in her temple. Lovely girl. Smelling just perceptibly of perspiration. Perhaps she does not shave her legs, perhaps she does not shave beneath her arms, he can imagine the damp curly kinky hair, red-blond, secret, utterly charming. —Shall we go upstairs now, Kirsten, he says lightly.

Yes, she says, leaning against him, and he slides his arm around her shoulders, he kisses her mouth, her throat, her ear, she shivers and giggles and shrugs, pushes him away as if involuntarily; and then she pauses, she turns, she says: I'd better take this along—leaning to pick up the macramé shoulder bag from the floor.

The Sunken Tub

A party. There is always a party at 18 Röcken.

Owen Halleck in his sailcloth jacket and dark trousers lets himself in the front door—which isn't locked—and walks boldly into the living room, in which a single light is burning. Everyone is on the terrace. It is a warm September evening and the pool is illuminated and there are cicadas in the trees.

No one greets him. No one has noticed. Owen the son of Maurie returned home, and no one has noticed.

He spies on his mother and her guests through the French windows. Voices, laughter, shadowy figures. Always a party. White wine and vodka and pink caviar and pâté with cognac and green peppercorns. The party is Isabel Halleck's life and when it comes to an end her life must come to an end.

He stands very still, observing. He is invisible. In his dark clothes, in his close-cropped beard. The cicadas in the trees emit a sawtoothed thrumming that would hurt his nerves under ordinary circumstances.

Someone is talking nearby, perhaps in the dining room. In the kitchen. Owen is not alarmed. The explosive he carries is set for midnight and this is a fact that inspires confidence. For now it is nine-thirty and the party must come to an end. When did the guests arrive?—five-thirty, six?—they must be leaving soon—unless it is a different sort of party— in which case they must all die and it will be no one's fault.

Buddy has commented on Owen's "perfect sanity." Which he feels, now, to the very tips of his fingers. To the very tips of his toes.

He has not slept for some time so his keen burning insomniac's eye is pitiless. He contemplates the length of the living room and pronounces his judgment: Beautiful. And worthless.

The arched windows, the brocaded drapes, the blond travertine mantel from Florence, the eight-foot Chinese scroll with its sparrows and trees and dream-fluid landscape, the white balustrades at the staircase. . . . A jewel of a house, a Washington prize, Isabel Halleck's triumph: *Bring it all down.*

He has the warrant, he has the tranquil ticking explosive. The future into which he is being carried. The future into which *she* is being carried—though at the moment she laughs with her guests on the terrace, she squeezes hands in farewell, accepts noisy drunken kisses.

He is not Owen Halleck. He is a soldier, a guerrilla. He will ascend the stairs and await her in the bedroom. To bring it all down.

Quick—running with a tall pyramid of eggs in his arms!—before he drops them and they shatter!

But the voices in the other room retreat—someone is leaving, by a side door—and Owen finds himself prowling the downstairs, light on his feet, invisible in his dark clothing, somber, curious, hungry.

He has not eaten in twelve hours or more. It isn't significant: in this phase of his life he requires less food, just as he requires less sleep. But the odor of something agreeable draws him forward and he finds himself in the darkened dining room, and then at the door to the kitchen pantry, and then he has poked his head into the brightly lit kitchen where Mrs. Salman is rinsing glasses and setting them in the dishwasher.

She does not notice him at first. A portly woman in her late fifties, thinning gray hair baked in tight curls, blue plastic harlequin glasses—she has worked for Isabel since the mid-sixties and though Owen knows her very well he has never contemplated her before. A victim, he thinks finally. But not innocent.

For no one is "innocent."

There is a gaily oversized red-orange plastic hors d'oeuvres tray on the counter, and on this tray there are leftovers that absorb Owen's interest: cheese and bacon puff pastries, stuffed mushrooms, a single shrimp spiked with a green toothpick. Who looks upon my face must die, Owen thinks, but in the same instant he leans against the swinging door and pokes his head farther into the kitchen, a teenaged boy home for the night, hi, hello, what's to eat, where is everyone . . . ?

Mrs. Salman glances around at him. A startled moon face, brackets around her mouth that relax—at first—into a smile of recognition and affection. But then she sees that it is not Owen the teenaged boy but Owen who has caused his mother distress and the smile stiffens.

Hi, murmurs Owen, hello, Mrs. Salman, are things kind of winding down here, where's Mother, d'you mind if I . . . Snatching up two of the puff pastries and putting them in his mouth. Chewing. Smiling. His eyes bright and keen.

Mrs. Salman stares at him. She wipes her hands on her apron in a gesture he supposes is classic.

Are you on your way home, Owen asks conversationally, chewing, stepping forward without urgency, his bulky knapsack swinging at his side, is the party almost over? . . . nice warm night isn't it. A little humid. Have they been swimming? Where is Mother? D'you mind if I . . . these are *good.* . . .

Mrs. Salman begins to speak but Owen silences her with a raised hand. —You can go home now if you want to, he says, you shouldn't be working this late, the hell with it, right?—just this once. I'll explain to Mother.

He snatches up the shrimp and chews it, a forlorn rubbery taste, no taste at all, and again Mrs. Salman starts to speak, to protest, or is the woman actually frightened of him, and again he silences her, this time by taking hold of her arm—the upper arm, which surprises him with its plump flaccidity, surprises and saddens him, Mrs. Salman has become an old woman without his having noticed.

In here, he says quietly, walking the astonished woman into the room adjoining the kitchen—a servant's room that has always been Mrs. Salman's room for the day, and on those occasions when she stays overnight. In here, let's close the door, no need for conversation, Owen murmurs, forcing the woman across the bed, you couldn't help me anyway could you—you're on *her* side. Of course she has begun to scream but he hardly hears her, he is calm and ruthless and very much in control: the little bottle of chloroform, the clean cotton swab, gripping her shoulders and head in a wrestling hold, one simply waits, holds one's breath and waits, all resistance ceases with time and the properly applied strategy.

How long?—two or three minutes?—or less? Impossible to calculate. He simply does what he must. "Owen Halleck" is not involved: a skilled mechanism is involved: one simply holds one's breath and waits and the danger passes.

An unconscious woman, heavy-set, pale fat blue-mottled knees and thighs, mouth open, dentures offensively bright and wet. . . . She is breathing hoarsely. Gasping for air. The chloroform stinks. Owen gags, turning away. Perhaps it is an error: the stink of the chloroform. It has no place at 18 Röcken.

But what is done is done. History, Owen thinks, tugging at the woman, trying to arrange her on the bed, her bulk, her fat, her offensive weight, history and necessity, a future that rushes back to meet us . . .

He rises from her, panting. A droplet of perspiration runs down his forehead.

Is this part of the plan? A wheezing woman lying on a pink chenille bedspread, one eye partly open? —But no matter, Owen hasn't the time or the authority to undo any act, he must continue as if this were merely the first step in a series of steps (their precise number unknown) leading to the successful completion of his mission. And to his "crossing over."

And so he shakes more chloroform onto another cotton swab and holds it against Mrs. Salman's mouth and nose. The wheezing grows louder, her head jerks to one side, but she does not otherwise struggle —her big soft body has sunken into its natural place in the center of the mattress.

He moves quickly about the room, improvising. No longer needing, exactly, to think. He turns on the little air conditioning unit, he opens a closet door and finds a light wool blanket, he shakes it open, drapes it across Mrs. Salman, removes her glasses, switches off the light. He pauses, contemplating. Is this part of the plan? This, and this?—this? When the Doves review the night's actions one by one how will they assess this phase?

A tall shaky pyramid of eggs. Carried in his arms. Owen can half-see them: bright lacquered colors, ceramic eggs perhaps, lovely, yet fragile, breakable: in his trust. He must run swiftly with them or—

He switches on the light again, and again shakes more chloroform onto the swab. Presses it against Mrs. Salman's face. How long, how long is advisable, they told him to count to—to count to twenty?—or one hundred—he can't recall—but in any case he isn't panicked or even very much alarmed or disturbed or annoyed—perhaps he should count to five hundred or perhaps he should not trouble to count at all—improvisation is the poetry of revolution, someone has told him, the absolutely unanticipated but necessary act, the act that changes the course of history, one must only be in the right place at the right time, audacity is all.

When it is time to stop he stops, and again switches off the light, and leaves the room: and the first phase of his mission is completed.

Weightless, near-bodiless, he ascends the back stairs, chewing on a Norwegian rye cracker smeared with liver pâté—it had been lying, with a stubbed-out cigarette, on a paper plate in the kitchen.

When he reports to headquarters he will tell them of the *perfunc-*

tory and *reactionary* nature of his physiological responses: though he is not hungry his mouth floods with saliva.

The bravest of us all, one of the young women murmurs. Owen has forgotten her name. Hot dark liquorish eyes, a nervous unpretty mouth. Perhaps he was meant to stumble to her bed in the dark—but he has grown to despise certain physiological responses.

In Isabel's bedroom a single light is burning. A small slender lamp made of mosaiclike pieces of glass, perched atop a mirrored cabinet. Owen steps silently into the room—the pale pink carpet is thick beneath his feet—and at once he feels an overwhelming sense of relief: he is here, this is the source, that bed, that cocoon, the larval nest, the place of his own conception.

Anyone here? He asks boldly. Anyone in hiding—?

There is a buoyancy in his legs, in his strong muscular calves, which springs from his sense of safety. Here, in this room, amid the perfumy heaped clothing, the tumble of shoes in the opened closet, the coffee cups and glasses and crumpled linen napkins on the bedside table. Here, in Isabel's bedroom which is still known as the master bedroom.

Safety, relief, a mission drawing close to completion. For what can stop him now? Who can stop him?

He unloads the knapsack, lifts the clock-bomb tenderly from it, sees that it is still very early, very early indeed. Not yet ten o'clock. And so much time ahead—

Like this, Buddy says, giggling at his timidity, the thing won't go off, for Christ's sake!—it's a *clock*. It's a *machine* and I am a *master machinist*.

Yes, says Owen, I see, I'm not afraid, he says, reddening, though his hands tremble slightly. And then again, upon another occasion, when Owen picks up a wire, experimentally, or perhaps playfully, it is Buddy who grabs at his wrist—Be careful, Buddy says.

The bomb is a clock, the clock is a machine. You are in the hands of a master, Uli promised.

You know what I want, a voice urges, teasing, you know what we're going to do, and Owen, squatting, placing the mechanism beneath the bed, murmurs an assent.

Of course. Yes. No choice.

You know, the voice teases, yes you know, fat boy, big phony shit, you *know*, don't play games.

He draws the death warrant out of the knapsack and examines it without reading it. (He has already read it. And refrained from wincing at the language. *Vengeance for the People!*—why should he, Owen Halleck, give a damn for the "People"?) He does not read it, he examines it through half-closed eyes, it is quite appropriate for the circumstances, it is perfect.

He places the document on the bed, on the satin cover, and partly hides it with something of Isabel's—a nightgown or a negligee.

Yes. Fine. Good. And now.

He stands contemplating the bed for several minutes. His eyes sting with an indefinable emotion. Here, in this bed with its carved mahogany headboard and its quaint old-fashioned posts, here in this secret place—something extraordinary happened.

Owen the son of Maurie. Owen the son of a dead father.

Or perhaps it was quite ordinary after all?—a marriage bed like any other, a place of necessity.

I am an instrument, Owen says, of necessity.

Slowly, ceremoniously, he takes the knife out of his pocket. It is a handsome enough weapon, a work of art, as Uli insists, and reassuringly heavy. The gleaming steel blade is imprinted with magic words: EL. HERDER KG SOLINGEN GERMANY MOLYBDENUM-VANADIUM STAINLESS INOX.

Yes, Owen said, primly, chastely, I want to do it correctly, I want style.

But it is the tub, the luxurious sunken tub, that truly engages his interest.

As soon as he enters the bathroom—switches on the light—absorbs the glaring beauty of the tile—the white and blue Spanish tile of the floor, the walls, the deep conch-shaped tub—he sees that *this* is the place, the obvious place, ceremony demands it, style and economy and good manners as well. The beautiful sunken tub Isabel requested when the bathroom with its antiquated fixtures was remodeled. . . .

Yes, he thinks, nodding. Good. Here.

He squats at the edge of the tub, examining it. Quite clean. Though perhaps—if one looks closely—there are stains, blemishes. The brass faucets are slightly tarnished at their base. A blond hair is trapped in the drain.

His heart beats calmly, he is fully in control, he has only to wait. The time?—his watch reads nine-fifty but perhaps it has slowed.

Voices downstairs, voices on the terrace. Farewell. He tests the edge of the knife with his thumb and penetrates the skin, not for the first time, so that a hair-fine line of blood appears.

He turns on the hot-water faucet. Watches the water trickle and then gush. Drain away. An impulse to fill the tub with water—warm soapy water—and bathe himself—for, after all, he *is* sweaty and dirty

—and when has he bathed last?—or showered—the fear of the cock-roach-haunted shower at 667 Bidart—the fear too of the water, the noise, drowning out other sounds: but of course he hasn't time now, Isabel will come upstairs at any moment, he can hardly strip himself of his clothes and crouch in the tub naked when she flings open the door.

But the moments pass. Minutes pass. In handfuls, in yawns. There are voices on the street, car doors slamming, car motors, still his watch reads ten minutes to ten though he gives his wrist a petulant shake.

Mother, he murmurs, his smile curling, it's you I want. Hurry.

But she does not hurry. He lowers the toilet seat and sits and allows his gaze to wander freely over the hard gleaming surfaces, his brain a blank, a comfortable nullity, smooth as tile. In a room like this —spacious, in fact, like most of the bathrooms in the house—the mind that falls shadowlike *out there* is safely contained, in restraint. The situation is under control. Space, a high ceiling, yet intimacy too. . . . He experiences a sudden almost irresistible urge to take off his clothes and lower himself into the tub and bathe in hot soapy water. Long ago, they played and splashed in here.

The sunken tub, deep and fluted as a shell. The blue counter with its double basins, deep, round, and also grooved: one for Mother, one for Father. Brass fixtures, a brass soap dish, a large mirror in which a bearded young man with sad pouched malicious eyes assiduously avoids Owen's gaze.

Her lover will enter the room first, Owen thinks. Perhaps it will be a man Owen knows?—perhaps not. But no matter. Owen will be fully prepared for him: he will be standing behind the door as it opens, he will seize the intruder by the jaw, bend his head sharply back, and with a quick hard well-practiced sawing of the knife he will cut the throat as a hog's throat is cut. So easily will the act be accomplished, so vivid is the splash and spray of blood, that Owen blinks, startled, to see that the tile is still so very clean—and that no body has defiled it.

Or, shall he allow his mother's lover to enter the room?—to stoop over the sink, running water, bathing his face, his eyes—to wipe his eyes brusquely and raise his head and happen to see, in the mirror, Owen lunging forward with the knife?—the frisson of that instant, the stare exchanged through the mirror, would be extraordinary.

No time for a struggle. No time even for shouting, screaming. No resistance. This and this and this and this, Owen grunts, and *this* . . . and in a few seconds it is over.

Strong as an ox, Owen Halleck. Muscles primed for action.

He will allow the body to fall to the floor, he will retreat to a corner, observing. The man's identity is of no significance—one or another or another, how can it matter?—for of course the man will not be Nick Martens, and no other man *does* matter.

He will retreat to a corner. Watching the spreading blood. Inky, a dark blossom. Remorseless. Common sense demands caution: he must not get his feet wet. He will perch atop the toilet seat if necessary and wait a long patient wait for Isabel if necessary.

Mother, he murmurs, I want you, where are you. . . . Hurry.

He has killed one, he has killed two. Downstairs. Elsewhere. He has successfully crossed over and he is baptized in blood though his fingers are not stained, and even the bathroom tile remains clean.

Mother, he whimpers angrily.

She has abandoned him to lie with other men. It is not his fault.

"Adulteress"—the word is biblical and quaint and precious on his tongue. He says it again, wonderingly: "Adulteress." An *amusing* word.

An evening that began in summer, now shading into autumn. So long. A film of oily perspiration covers his body, he *should* strip and bathe himself before she comes upstairs, he *should* prepare himself with more ceremony, more dignity, like a warrior; but the humid air is growing chilly, he has begun to sweat and shiver simultaneously, he resents the long tedious wait—which is typical of his mother's thoughtlessness, oh sweet Christ how typical only Owen knows!—though at the same time his gaze drifts and darts unimpeded along the tile, into the corners of the room, slowing, accelerating, bemused by the sunken tub and the brass fixtures and Isabel's innumerable bottles, jars, vials, and soaps. . . . The frosted window, the fluorescent tubing that hums warmly along the length of the mirror, the twin basins, one for Mother one for Father: he is not impatient, he is not *waiting* at all: he is merely in place, an instrument, a machine, superbly primed.

The Death of
Isabel de Benavente Halleck

She will be wearing a long fuchsia skirt with an oyster-colored sash and a matching bodice of narrow pleats and tucks, by Pauline Trigère.

She will have kicked off her high-heeled glazed-straw sandals and left them somewhere outside—probably by the pool.

Her pierced pearl earrings, the very small ones, will be in place, but her rope of pearls—the cream-rose strand, General Kempe's gift—will be broken, and the lovely pearls scattered, all over the sticky bathroom floor.

She will be forty-three years five months old.

She will have outlived her husband by fifteen months.

She will leave her estate—the "estate" that has come to her by way of her late husband, her late father, and her late father-in-law—in a state of considerable confusion.

She will of course be panicked when her assailant rises to stalk her—she will be terrified—paralyzed—unable to scream for help until the stabbing, the pain, actually begins—and yet it will strike her assailant that she is not really *surprised:* her flushed face, when she opens the door, will gleam with a queer hard gratification.—Owen. Yes. *You.*

Thirty-seven stab wounds, most of them superficial, several very deep, piercing throat, lungs, stomach. The face untouched except for a blow—perhaps inadvertent—to the right cheek with the heavy handle of the knife.

She will be wearing her hair in a new autumn style—thick and wavy about the face, buoyant, rather "romantic," in a touching nostalgic effect. And not quite so blatantly platinum: a honey-gold tint for the honey-gold autumn months.

It is quite true, she will not be *surprised:* only terrified.

Owen. What are you doing here. What do you want.

She will not stride lazily into her bedroom and into the bathroom and into her fate in a petulant mood, despite a good deal of provocation: the quarrel with her lover at lunch; the general poolside quarrel about the presidential campaign, which was more serious and consequently less amusing than the hostess would have liked; the peculiar behavior of Mrs. Salman—falling into bed like that, and leaving the kitchen counters a mess; and one or two additional vexations. On the contrary, and rather surprisingly, Isabel Halleck will say goodbye to her guests and lock up the house and turn off the lights and ascend the stairs to her death in a hazy elated state: feeling, in fact, quite good.

She will not be drunk, only pleasantly and charmingly intoxicated.

She will put up a considerable struggle, after her initial shock.

She will scream, she will shout, she will accuse: she will even threaten her son with a curse.

She will weigh one hundred eleven pounds.

She will of course recognize her assailant immediately, despite his weight loss and his beard and his mad eyes and his ludicrous costume, a navy blue jacket of some coarse synthetic material, all zippers and snaps and buckles and tiny belts.—Owen. Yes. You. What are you doing here, what do you want. *What do you want.*

She will try to stop the knife—seize the plunging blade—with her hands.

She will slash at her assailant's hair and face and clothing, so that her shapely fingernails—painted a delicate cream-rose to match General Kempe's pearls—break and tear back into her flesh.

She will have completed arrangements, just that morning, for an extended tour out from Morocco in October—to Egypt, for the Nile cruise.

The Master Machine

Within a five-hour period on the night of September 8 the capital is "rocked"—the word is used repeatedly by the media, in newspaper headlines and on television—by several premeditated and linked acts of violence claimed as "Acts of Revolutionary Justice" by an underground organization calling itself the American Silver Doves Revolutionary Army. Three deaths, one vicious and near-fatal assault, four bombings, damages totalling more than $2.5 million. . . . Photostated letters sent to the *Washington Post*, the *Washington Star*, the *New York Times*, and several Washington television stations proclaim a "Fall Offensive" to be launched by hundreds of thousands of "Revolutionary Americans" in protestation of a "Corrupt and Contaminating" government; the letters are issued by "The People's Court" with "The American Silver Doves Revolutionary Army" as its official agent.

The acts of violence are:

The explosion at the Maurice J. Halleck residence, 18 Röcken, at 12 midnight, in which three bodies are found in the rubble

Three less serious explosions at the headquarters of the Commission for the Ministry of Justice, Constitution Avenue; the headquarters of the Selective Service System, F Street, N.W.; the Export-Import Bank of Washington, Vermont Avenue, N.W.

The attempted assassination of Nicholas Martens, Director of the Commission for the Ministry of Justice, at a residence in the Rock Creek Park area

(The bodies found in the collapsed house at 18 Röcken are in too mutilated a condition to make immediate identifications feasible, though the unofficial word is that one of the dead is surely Mrs. Maurice J. Halleck, the widow of the late Director of the Commission for the Ministry of Justice. Another body, missing part of the head, is believed to belong to Mrs. Harold Salman, an employee at the Halleck residence. Nicholas Martens is in critical condition at Mount St. Mary's Hospital, suffering from stab wounds inflicted by an unknown assailant or assailants. —*Vengeance for the People!*)

The Cradle

You know what I want, Mother.

Owen does not speak. He has no need to speak. But his words explode into the white gleaming air. His words fly against the tile, the splattered mirror, the porcelain, the brass.

Come here. In here. Here. Hurry.

She is not surprised, seeing him. Though of course she is terrified. Though of course she knows why he is here, why the enormous blade rises and dips, lifting, darting, so quick no eye can follow it, only the flesh can gauge it, struck, shuddering, recoiling in incredulous pain.

In here. Where it's clean. Where it will all wash away. Here.

She pushes against him. She is screaming now. Shrieking. Begging. No no no no. This cannot be happening, such things do not happen. The steel in the white tile, in the great blank pitiless mirror, reflected in the ceiling, in the floor. Two struggling figures. Two contorted faces.

You know what I want, Owen whispers. Bitch. Cunt. Murderer. *Mother.*

She scratches at his face but her pink fingernails break and tear. She screams but her voice cannot escape the tiled walls. At the rim of the beautiful sunken tub she fights all the more convulsively but of course she is no match for him: her terrified rage is no match for his: the struggle is over within a space of, say, three very long very protracted very dreamlike minutes.

A master machinist, Owen thinks, washing the handsome knife—blade and handle both—in one of the ceramic sinks. A master machine.

He had intended to avoid being splattered by blood, and he had certainly intended to avoid stepping in blood. But it seems that blood is general in the room. A skein of blood has even flown—how?—against the frosted window.

If there were time he would strip naked and bathe himself, and rid himself of every smear of blood, every drying glistening ribbon of blood, and he would shampoo his hair too, and scrub his scalp; he would wash his beard; his chest and pubic hair; his feet. Between his toes. One by one by one, between his toes, in the sunken tub, where they played and splashed as children. Toes and fingers and elbows, tricky corners where dirt hides.

But he cannot bathe himself in the sunken tub. He cannot even look into the tub.

The splattered mirror is, fortunately, opaque at that point—at the point at which he might inadvertently see the tub and what is in it. He washes the knife tenderly, and his hands, his wrists, his arms to the elbow, and the faint scarlet water whirls and rushes and drains away in the handsome scalloped basin. His forearms, his wrists, his hands, between the fingers, but he hasn't time for the fingernails which are ridged with dark blood, it appears to be black blood, he hasn't time at the moment, he will make a note to clean his fingernails assiduously in the morning.

Will they airlift him, he wonders vaguely, idly, as he wipes his hands on a thick powder-blue towel monogramed *H*, there was talk of a compound in . . . The towel is crooked, he pauses to straighten it, now one side is longer than the other and Isabel would be offended, and Owen's eye too is offended: minor things of course but significant: like the boys at school who did not mind paper napkins. Like one of his suitemates freshman year who wore white cotton socks at all times.

Headquarters in Colorado, north of Denver; or is it outside Tucson; or somewhere in Mexico. Ulrich May's elderly father's estate. You will go into hiding, Uli says, lightly stroking his shoulder, the back of his neck, we expect great things from you, the propaganda of the deed, the beautiful irrevocable gesture, the crossing over, the baptism by blood into your deepest truest self. . . . You will go into hiding into retreat into sanctuary, you will be redeemed, how I envy you and your courageous sister!

If there were time he *would* strip naked and bathe himself but he suspects there isn't time. (Though his watch has stopped. The crystal has been broken, the minute hand is bent.) Blood in sticky curls in his hair, clots in his beard, everywhere on the sailcloth jacket, great dark wet hideous stains on his trousers as if he had lost control and urinated on himself like a baby. Pig, he thinks, fastidiously, filthy pig, he murmurs aloud, wiping roughly beneath his nose, peering at his bloodshot eyes in the mirror, but then, suddenly, he forgives himself: there isn't time.

His hand is so wet and sticky, the doorknob will not turn.

He tries the other hand—the fingers slip.

He waits, breathing calmly. The complex machine that is his heart continues to work with magisterial authority. He is not in danger; no one can stop him; in fact it is too late—he has accomplished his mission, and it lies in the sunken tub behind him, utterly still.

He tries the doorknob again and again it slips, but only because his fingers are slippery, he wipes them on his thighs, flexes them, and tries again. . . . An army without discipline isn't an army, Buddy has told him, frowning seriously. Glass-green eyes. Slightly pocked skin. Not the sort of boy Owen Halleck would be rooming with, hardly the sort of boy Owen Halleck would find seated beside him at his eating club, but Buddy is a natural-born leader, Buddy cannot be charmed or deceived, Buddy is modest about his ability to assemble clock-bombs and read thoughts on the "subconscious" level, so if Owen Halleck is trapped inside the bathroom at 18 Röcken Buddy will sense his predicament and come rescue him.

As for Kirsten: the panel truck, the painted-over dry cleaner's truck, has been parked discreetly down the street from 9:30 P.M. onward, the plans were 9:30 P.M. to (at the outermost limits) 11:30 P.M., no further time being deemed necessary or advisable under the circumstances. (The circumstances are those of the Fall Offensive and the need to meticulously coordinate activities.) Consequently Owen reasons the truck *has* picked her up, Smitty and Adrienne have hauled her aboard, greeted her with warm handclasps and embraces, made her welcome, slid the door shut after her, driven her away to 667 Bidart and to safety. . . .

Of course, the shabby olive-green truck isn't very real to Owen, though he has ridden in the front seat, on the torn leather cushions, and he has even squatted in the back, on the metal floor, being driven about Washington on "maneuvers" that were, in truth, not very real to him either. Smitty and Adrienne and Rita Stone and Shirley and even Buddy and even Uli: none is very real though Owen has tried to make them real: and now time is running out.

The odor of blood is a *warm* odor, Owen thinks suddenly. Because blood is *warm* and *warming* as it circulates through the body.

The doorknob turns easily, the door opens easily, Owen finds himself in the bedroom, a far fresher air. He breathes great gulping mouthfuls, immensely relieved.

So easy. So easily done. Why had he ever sought mere *solutions* to life . . . ?

He will leave the bedroom, taking the lovely German knife with him. But leaving behind the death warrant and one or two printed pamphlets—material his new friends pressed upon him. (Asinine stuff, he thinks, kindergarten crap, and in bad taste too—but this is a thought that, for safety's sake, he has managed to jam with static before Buddy can read it.) He will walk out of the bedroom . . . he will descend the stairs . . . he *is* descending the stairs . . . near-silent, near-bodiless . . . making his casual escape . . . having no difficulty with the front door . . . opening it, stepping out, closing it carefully behind him.

And so, to safety. His own car parked a half-block away.

And no trouble starting it, either.

And no trouble with traffic, or inquisitive police, or nervous driving.

He walks out of the master bedroom forever. He descends the stairs, his fingers lightly brushing against the railing. (Fingerprints? But of course. The identity of the soldier-guerrilla can never be in doubt. That is part of the beauty of the strategy, as Uli would say.) He makes his way along the darkened hall to the front door. He steps outside into the clear night air, alive with crickets and cicadas and june bugs, a dense jarring network of sound, a crosshatching of sound, more raucous and perhaps more sinister than the cries of birds, but he steps fearlessly into it and strides out the walk and turns to the left, unhesitatingly to the left, and goes to his car which is discreetly parked. . . .

Fatigue settles upon him, a heavy black-feathered bird, smelling of dust and dried blood and vomit, he must rest before making his escape, he will wait just a few minutes. The house is absolutely still; he is in no danger; perhaps Buddy is monitoring his thoughts, or Maurie himself, from the other side, looking on with disapproval of course but finally with love. Justice, Father, and not revenge, Owen reminds him, easing his weight onto the edge of the bed, sighing luxuriously. He checks his watch: not quite ten o'clock.

The bed is not a cradle, it is far too big, but in this room, beside this bed, there *was* a cradle—he is certain of that. Isabel would know; Isabel rocked him in it. Owen remembers it suddenly, his eyes filling with tears. Yes. A cradle. Not very large. Wicker, painted white. With green velvet ribbons. Yes? And stuffed animals. A fuzzy woolly green blanket.

The cradle is beside the bed, in the near-darkness. He stands on tiptoe to look inside it and sees himself—a baby!—a small red-faced big-eyed drooling baby!

But it isn't Owen, it is his new sister.—Look here, look, aren't her

toes beautiful, Mother says, hugging him, the tremor in her body communicating itself to him, making him want to shout and laugh and
scream and kick, yes she's beautiful yes she's going to live with us her
name is Kirsten she's your sister you will love each other—oh *aren't* her
toes beautiful!—her lovely little eyes, her eyelashes—

He would slap the side of the cradle, he would clamber up and spit
into the red-faced creature's eyes, but yes he does love her, he supposes
she *is* beautiful, the size of a puppy, the right size to hug. Mother draws
him into her lap beside the new baby. The two of them in her lap. Now
look, look here, patty-cake, like this, she says, giggling, her long hair
falling loose, Owen snuggles up beside her and touches his tongue
against the new baby's cheek because he knows it will please Mother and
it does please Mother who squeals with delight.

My Babylove, she calls them, my Babyloves, just the three of
us—!

Owen sits on the edge of the bed, his shoulders slumped. Not long
ago he ascended the stairs with a wonderful vigor, a delectable buoyancy, concentrated in his legs and thighs; now he feels—frankly—exhausted.

Fatigue in his shoulders, in his feet and ankles. A dull tinge of
nausea in the pit of his stomach. He recalls the pâté smeared messily on
the cracker—the lardy-tasting cold puff pastries—and for a horrific moment the nausea deepens.

So tired, he thinks.

Suddenly his eyelids are heavy, the creature on his shoulders
rocks from side to side, perhaps a quick nap?—a five-minute nap?—and
then he will be on his way—and then he will have enough strength to
continue. The drive back through Washington to the sanctuary at—he
has forgotten the precise address but of course he knows the direction
—and then, what were the plans?—smuggled from state to state from
commune to commune an "impeccably organized" underground network, his new friends assure him, innumerable Doves and Dove-affiliates
and comrades in brother organizations, loyalty, faith, absolute commitment, generosity, selflessness, soldiers, guerrillas, undeclared war,
Owen a hero, Owen the bravest of all, to have struck down the fascist
capitalist-murderer *at the source:* he rocks from side to side, lightly,
jamming his thumb against his teeth, the nail hard against his teeth, if
only he weren't so exhausted, his eyelids so heavy, he yawns and his eyes
fill with moisture and he lies surreptitiously back on the bed, cuddles
against the pillow, his thumb in his mouth, his eyes closing, only a
minute or two of sleep, he is so very exhausted, he has come so very far
in a single evening, crossing over, baptized, he gropes for a blanket or

something to cover himself with, pulls the bedspread loose, pulls it over his shoulders, the room grows swiftly dim, someone is shading the light with her cupped hands, Owen?—Owen?—are you asleep?—stooping to kiss his overheated forehead—brushing a damp strand of hair out of his eyes—but, mischievously, he does not reveal that he is awake—he pretends he is asleep—just for another minute or two—he is very still, not wanting to giggle, not wanting to give himself away—for she is stooping over him, watching—she is smiling at him—Owen?—are you asleep?—and he keeps his eyes closed because he *is* very very sleepy—he has never felt so sleepy in his life—the sensation washes over him—the sensation is so dark, and so delicious—he doesn't open his eyes—he can't open his eyes—his mother is a dark plumed bird—a beautiful plumed bird—bending near—the silken feathers brushing against his cheeks—he is so very sleepy—the light fades, the room recedes and darkens, he can't open his eyes and he is pretending to be asleep and he is asleep and nothing, nothing, nothing is more delicious.

4:00 A.M.

There's a man injured here, there's a man maybe bleeding to death, Kirsten says, her mouth close against the receiver, her breath moist as a baby's, you'd better call an ambulance and come get him, she says, giggling, sniffing, he's one of *yours*. . . .

She steadies herself against the telephone booth, trying not to breathe deeply—the interior of the booth smells of urine.

Traffic on the wide trembling street. Late-night buses heaving themselves from the curb. Neon, headlights, a porous sky lightening to orange. Her thighs ache from straddling him. The skin is raw, abrasive as sand. This and this and this, she screamed, and *this* . . . finally dropping the knife when her fingers lost their sensation.

Someone is asking her a question. Repeating a question.

He's bleeding because he has been injured, I think he might be bleeding to death, she says, more slowly, cupping her mouth with one stiff clawlike hand. There's a lot of blood. Soaked into the mattress and on the floor. The carpet on the floor . . . It's been a while. Three or four hours. I don't remember. He can't take care of himself, he isn't conscious, I think he must be bleeding inside too. . . . I couldn't finish the job.

Someone is asking where she is, where she is calling from. Where is the injured party. Someone says in a level unexcited voice, *Don't hang up.*

Kirsten wipes her eyes clear. She tries to focus upon the traffic, the separate hurtling cars, a yellow taxi cab, perhaps she can hail a cab and be taken away, safely away, back to Aunt Harriet's house—since of course the van Owen promised is nowhere near: she had in fact forgotten about it entirely until she walked out of the house and found herself, dazed, blinking, flexing her stiff fingers, on an unfamiliar street.

You will be picked up by my friends, by our friends, Owen told her, and taken away into hiding into our secret headquarters into a part of the city you've never seen before!—and after that, after that, he said gravely, his voice quickening, the two of us will be treated like royalty and protected and smuggled west until such time as—

Kirsten began giggling, pressing her fingers against her mouth.

Owen frowned. And continued:—Until such time as it's believed safe to transport us across the border. And out of the United States forever.

"Like royalty"?—really? she said, now grinning broadly. But why?

Owen frowned, and plucked at his beard, and began at last to grin too; and, at last, to burst into high nervous delighted laughter.

"Out of the United States forever"! Kirsten crowed, throwing open her arms, letting her head fall back. *"Out of the United States forever"!*

Where are you calling from, the patient voice is inquiring, where is the injured party, please don't hang up, Kirsten knows very well they are tracing the call: the crudeness of the trickery fills her with contempt. She says: Rock Creek Park. D'you know where that is? Off Sixteenth Street. A private home.

She steadies herself against the side of the booth, watching the traffic. An all-night diner across the way. A darkened Sunoco station. Die, why don't you *die,* she wept, enraged, bringing the knife down as hard as she could, gripping it in both hands, yet without strength: weak as a child. Straddling him, his bare thighs, his pale slack stomach, his mouth bubbling blood, stinking of alcohol. A drunk old man. A drunk graying balding old man. Flab at the waist, flaccid thighs, the buttocks bluish-white, a funny ghastly lardy color, tiny broken veins, she wanted to jeer and laugh wildly at him, into his ashen face, *how did he dare impersonate Nick Martens!—how could he show himself naked to any woman!*

She had not anticipated the hard work. She had not anticipated the simple resistance of flesh. And bone, when struck. Bone! The knife flew from her damp fingers and crashed against the floor.

He was too drunk, too exhausted, to rouse himself. His arms flailed about. She had circled the snoring man in the bed for a very long time—for ten minutes—fifteen minutes—an hour?—only the light in the bathroom burning, behind her—and the faint light from the curtainless window. Panting, stinking of perspiration, her own and his, and his semen; his semen that ran down her leg. —Like this, like this, *this*, she whispered, as if praying, and stabbed wildly with the knife, gripping it in both hands, going for the throat.

But the throat too was dense with bone. Tendons and muscles, cords, resistance.

He cried out, dying. It would be over in a minute!—she found herself crouched in a corner of the bedroom, trembling convulsively, her vision blacking out, her strength draining from her. She must continue her work, she must not be afraid of him, of the blood, of his writhing, his desparate struggling—now the body crashing to the floor, kicking, the arms flailing, in the throes of death—

She could not move. And then forced herself back.

And then, and then—

She strikes at him and screams and he is an animal in pain, in desperate pain, dangerous, resisting, struggling not with her or even with the knife which his blind fingers cannot grasp but with pain itself: which must be lightning-quick and terrible, flashing about him.

I can't do it, she whispers.

I couldn't do it, she whispers into the telephone.

He was dying, surely. But then—he did not die. Minutes and hours, the astonished groaning, the seeping of blood, a man's naked body on the floor writhing, and curling and shuddering. . . .

How long does it take for them to die, Kirsten wonders.

She backs away. Crouched. Her teeth chattering. No sound but the hideous wheezing of his breath, the moaning, fainter and fainter— for of course he is dying, she has stabbed him a dozen times in the throat and shoulders and chest. The carpet is dark with blood, the smart polished parquet floor gleams with it.

Impossible, Kirsten thinks, shaking her head to clear it. This cannot be happening to *me*.

She backs away and descends the stair. Unpleasantly steep stairs, and slippery. She will telephone Hannah. What time is it?—which day of the week? The thought of Hannah fills her with an inchoate longing, an almost bodily distress: her closest friend, her only friend: turning away from Kirsten with tears in her eyes. How quickly it can happen, Kirsten never ceases to marvel, though she has been a girl for her entire life, a mere child, easily hurt and easily hurting others, causing pain, tears, that sullen flushed pouting . . . How quickly it can happen, your closest friend turning away angry, tears stinging your eyes, I hate you I don't like you any more please go to hell, will you—leave me alone.

She will telephone Hannah in the morning.

She descends the stairs and prowls in the dark, not knowing what she does. Upstairs he is dying, of that she is certain. A matter of time. The blood seeping in the mattress, in the carpet, across the parquet floor. . . . Common sense instructs that it is only a matter of time. And of waiting quietly, cautiously. Not panicking. Not becoming hysterical.

She switches on a light. The shadows are warm and humid and comforting. Where did he drop it?—that newsletter—that pamphlet Owen gave her—and she has the death warrant as well—a stiff sheet of paper—fancy black handwriting—rather exaggerated, silly—though of course she must see it in another way—serious and grim and necessary —a consequence of the class struggle, the undeclared war—*the sentence of death without appeal has been passed upon a criminal subject of the international fascist capitalist class*—

Tomorrow's newspapers, she thinks, with a sudden thrill of satisfaction. News must after all come from *somewhere*—and now it is her and her brother's turn.

Waiting for him to die she busies herself eradicating "evidence." She washes both their glasses in the kitchen sink, she wipes every smooth surface, spitting in a tissue, humming to herself, peering closely at the smooth white refrigerator door which appears to be clean but perhaps she had brushed against it earlier. . . . She uses the tissue until it shreds in her fingers. Then uses a damp dish towel. Humming, biting her lip, utterly occupied. If there is a vacuum cleaner at hand . . .

She is tranquil for ten or fifteen minutes at a time; then the wave of panic rushes back over her and she begins to shiver convulsively. Her bowels feel loose. No, she thinks, her eyes shut, gripping the counter— no. And she stands motionless until the attack subsides.

His wet arrhythmic snoring, earlier—! How she had hated it!

A groveling burrowing teary-eyed old drunk, Nick Martens. A pig. Panting, Sweating. The thick flesh of his back—muscles going soft —the surprising looseness of flesh at his waist—the graying chest hair —the ugly quivering penis of which he seemed, even in his grunting desperation, to be ashamed. Kirsten, he murmured, Kirsten oh please, begging, half-sobbing, a pathetic aging man who stank of alcohol: *Was this Nick Martens!*

There is an old story, a sort of teasing joke, that Kirsten's diaper once overflowed into Nick's lap, or into his arms. Where this happened, or when, Kirsten doesn't know: but the allusion always filled her with a violent hot mute rage.

She hates the two of them, their secrets, their laughter—sometimes it is loud and braying and shameless. Even when Maurie is near.

Waiting for him to die she hums under her breath and wipes away all her fingerprints. The doorknobs the top of the coffee table the door-frame the railing leading upstairs. . . . A matter of time, a matter of being very scrupulous, she is not impatient, she will make no crude silly mistakes. Undeclared war. Revolutionary combat. Invisible. It's true enough, their enemies *are* criminals, they surely do deserve to die, a matter not of revenge but of simple justice. As her great-great-great-great-grandfather said . . .

Waiting for him to die she runs water in the kitchen sink and washes herself with a bar of soap someone has left in a blue plastic "shell" on the counter. It is important to get very clean, to get the stench of him off her: his sweat, his semen, his blood. The enormous penis poking at her. Impossible. Incredible. He began to sob, he began to babble, Kirsten forgive me Kirsten oh Christ oh Jesus Christ stop I don't mean this I don't want this—a heaving sweating man, a stranger, in her thin arms. Impossible, she thinks, rolling her eyes in embarrassment, not very practical, she would explode in a fit of giggling except for his weight, which is a matter of some seriousness. (I can't breathe, she whimpers, panicked. Wait, wait—I can't breathe—I'm choking.) So too did Maurie want her to kneel beside him. Let us pray for a few minutes. Let us still our minds in prayer. Prayer is stillness, the mind and the heart at one . . . at rest. Kirsten? Please? Will you? *You have been told, man, what is good, and what does the Lord demand of you but to do justice and love kindness and to walk humbly with your God. . . .*

The water gushes from the faucet warm and comforting. She soaps herself lavishly. Her hands . . . her arms . . . her shoulders . . . her breasts . . . her belly . . . between her legs, the sticky pubic hair . . . her thighs . . . her legs. The warm soapy water trickles down her leg. Now I can't go back to him, she thinks suddenly, I *can't* get dirty again.

By now he has died. The hideous wheezing has stopped.

Was there a rattle in his throat?—but, downstairs, with the water running, humming busily to herself, she has heard nothing.

She peers at the small clock in the kitchen range, trying to read the time. Her eyesight is uncertain. Her head rings with fatigue. Upstairs Nick is dead which means she is free which means she will never have to think of him again. Or Isabel. (But can Isabel be dead? The thought suddenly strikes Kirsten as unlikely.)

She slips the blouse over her head, shakes out the sleeves, checks the cuffs to see if they are stained: they are not. And the skirt is untouched. Only a little wrinkled. And her necklaces, her bracelets?—one by one she hunts them down.

No trace of her will remain. No evidence.

She wanders about the house, avoiding the room in which he lies in a puddle of blood on the floor. Though she hears his breathing she tells herself that unless she checks his pulse, unless she lays her ear against his chest, she cannot *really* know that he is still alive.

Why do they take so long to die, she wonders, biting at her fingernail. Suppose I telephone Owen . . .

She locates the amber necklace, the thin gold chain, the coral bracelets. Steps into her sandals. Fresh and clean even beneath the arms, even between the legs, smelling of Ivory soap. Why don't you die, she says softly, you bastard, you liar, you ridiculous hairy drunk old man, sticking your thing at me like that . . . She holds her breath to listen: but he's there, still: he's *there.*

She locates the knife where she has dropped it. And rouses herself to try again—one last desperate plunge—but her bowels constrict and there is the terrible danger of losing control, of succumbing to utter physical helplessness. And she has just washed herself.

You'd better come get him, you'd better send an ambulance at once, she tells the policeman at the other end of the line, clearing her throat, her voice steadying against two speeding automobiles hurtling south on Sixteenth Street.—He's bleeding to death. It must be internal too—hemorrhaging. Rock Creek Lane. Yes. The second house from the end.

And she slips the receiver into its cradle and walks quickly away.

Where to, miss? the taxi driver asks, eying her curiously in the rearview mirror. He has a dark Hispanic glow, a heavy mustache, round rimless eyeglasses that give him a rakish schoolmasterish look.—Running away from your boyfriend?

Kirsten is not intimidated by him. She brushes her hair out of her eyes in a slow contemplative gesture; she sits back in the seat, her macramé bag on her lap. She says, in a voice as poised as her mother's: Away from here. North. Just start driving.

Epilogue

Exiles

After I died, Nick Martens writes to Kirsten Halleck, *I stopped being afraid. But now there's an emptiness where fear would be. Where fear used to be.*

He has become a connoisseur of shorebirds and gulls, sandspits and sand dunes. The moods of the ocean. The sky, the fog, the rain that falls in sheets, or so delicately that it does not appear to fall at all: but to hang everywhere in suspension, wonderfully silent.

Do you understand? he asks Kirsten, who does not reply. *Do you feel the same emptiness?*

He walks along the edge of the ocean in nearly all weather, with difficulty—often with a cane—but he *does* walk, a mile or more at dawn, toward the old ruin of a lighthouse; and again at sunset. Bearded and gaunt and "inconspicuously" dressed—as one journalist described him. His skin has gone ruddy, bronze, leathery; it appears at times to glint with near-invisible particles of sand or mica. The beard, grayer than his hair, is not a stylish or even a very attractive beard—it gives him a morose yet subtly amused grandfatherly look. And he wears old clothes: a shapeless khaki rainhat that once belonged to his father, found in a closet at the cottage; a sheepskin-lined windbreaker in cold weather, a maroon coat-sweater in warmer weather, obviously once belonging to a heavier man.

In disguise?—not really. For "disguise" is now pointless. Though of course one or two unfriendly neighbors, year-round inhabitants of the little island, might think so. And unfriendly journalists, in the first siege of their interest the previous winter.

Nicholas Martens, fifty, the former Deputy of the Commission for the Ministry of Justice, in "retirement" on an obscure island off the coast of Maine after an attempted assassination by a radical left-wing organization, and his subsequent surprising confession to several violations of . . . Refusing to explain his actions to reporters. . . . Living alone in a seaside cottage, in disguise as a . . .

Interpretations vary. He is a penitent, he is a hypocrite, he is a disgraced and shattered man; he is very ill, he is convalescing, he is bitter, or, on the contrary, vastly relieved to have left public life. Surely he is plotting a comeback of some kind—perhaps he will enter politics? Or are his attorneys' statements correct: in a few years he may return to private practice as a consultant, or then again he may not, but in any case he will never return to Washington. Those days are over.

He is gravely ill, it is said. He will never recover physically from the attack on his life.

Naturally he is emotionally unbalanced—he will never recover psychologically from the attack on his life.

Is he suicidal? Does the ocean attract him? The mist, the fog-horns, the gigantic rocks, the high cliffs of Mount Dunvegan's north shore . . .

Nick Martens, former Director of the Commission for the Ministry of Justice, lives in self-determined exile . . . a Napoleon in voluntary retreat on his own St. Helena. Infrequent trips to a nearby town for groceries and supplies . . . incognito . . . in disguise as an eccentric Maine islander . . . a hermit with a bushy beard. Crutches, a cane. Intermittent ill health. The prognosis for recovery from such a violent trauma, Dr. Felix Staub of the Georgetown Medical School faculty states, is poor. Asked about local reactions to the romantic and controversial figure in their midst, Mount Dunvegan Islanders were surprisingly reticent. He minds his own business and we mind ours, the proprietor of MacLeod's General Store said. Another party who asked to remain nameless stated: As long as he doesn't bring gunmen or F.B.I. men out here he can stay as long as he wants. It's a free country.

He does not question the interpretations, the charges. He has stopped reading most of the material his attorneys send him, which has anyway subsided to a trickle—for there are new Washington scandals this season, new tragedies and diversions. He does force himself to read items about "Nicholas Martens" sent him by former acquaintances and associates and members of his own family, wishing to arouse his anger, or perhaps simply to wound: he scans the articles, notes the underlined passages, has come to see that his "forgiveness" of his attackers has

inspired the most professional and public repugnance, and not his confession of bribetaking in high office. (But the confession itself is suspect.
Made from his hospital bed, so desperately, so dramatically—wasn't it
simply a recapitulation of Maurice Halleck's disjointed confession of the
same crimes?—the attempt of a badly shaken man to exonerate an old
friend of wrongdoing.)

Most peculiar of all—and this story nearly *does* arouse Nick's
anger—is an interview with General Morton Kempe published in the
National Review. The piece began with a brief but highly laudatory
synopsis of the general's wartime career; mentioned the undeniably
interesting fact that Kempe was given only a ten in ninety chance of
surviving his particular form of cancer, yet did survive several operations—and at the present time has a "clean bill of health"; allowed
Kempe to state in his own declamatory words his opinion of Nicholas
Martens's misfortune: The man has had a lengthy career as a fellow-
traveler, in disguise as a patriotic American. . . . Involved with secret
leftist groups throughout the sixties and seventies. . . . American desert-
ers in Sweden and Denmark; Palestinian thugs; Communist-front organizations here in the States. An ingenious double agent. But the record
speaks for itself. The record of READ BETWEEN THE LINES UNLESS YOU
ARE BLIND. The attempted assassination was nothing more than a private Communist feud, an internecine squabble, and if the F.B.I. had any
powers remaining they would see the logical connection between Martens's underground operations and the tragic deaths of Isabel and Maurice Halleck and their son Owen, and would *arrest Martens immediately and charge him with first-degree murder as well as common
treason against his country.*

After I died, Nick writes to Kirsten, who is, so far as he knows,
still with the Kuhns in Minneapolis, *I became suddenly generous—but
I have very little to give away. And no one who wants it.*

Black-winged gulls, ungainly creatures, with their low haunting
hungry calls. Jellyfish drying on the sand, in the sun, evaporating before
his eyes to a few terrifying threads. Rain. A great deal of rain. In which
he sometimes forces himself to tramp, wearing rubber-soled boots and
his father's hat. There are days in early April when the sky is the color
of dirty concrete and does not lighten until dusk, when it reveals a moon
almost too intensely white, and too close. Other days, when the sun
glares so fiercely in the dry white air that even dark-tinted glasses do
not help. His sensitive eyes contract, his head aches. He knows himself
an invalid.

The elation of solitude. The despair of solitude. Days and nights and days of silence which he must not fill with his old hammering voice. *I did this and I want this and I am responsible for this and I am the man who . . .*

He leaves the medicine cabinet door open, against the wall, so that he need not be startled by his own reflection when he enters the bathroom—reminded of his own "personality." The cottage's other mirror, in what had been his parents' bedroom, he simply takes off the wall and places at the back of a closet.

(Who was it, he wonders suddenly, a friend of Isabel's, yes certainly a friend of Isabel's, who had stopped looking at himself in mirrors one day . . . ? Nick asks himself the question before having time to think, to censor his thoughts. For he does not think of Isabel Halleck now except at certain prescribed and premeditated times. There is no "Isabel" of whom he might think without thinking of "Nick Martens" as well —a topic not so much forbidden as simply repugnant. A violation of the sanctity of Mount Dunvegan Island.)

It is erroneous to believe that he is a recluse, a crank, a genuine island eccentric who never returns to the mainland: in fact he drives to Augusta or Portland every week or two to visit with his daughter Audrey (she has never expressed any interest in visiting her father on the island, and he is relieved at her tact) and to buy books and records and other supplies not available on Mount Dunvegan. But in general he stays in one place. A fixed spot. Not precisely "home"—he does not think of it as "home"—but neutral territory.

He is reading about the coast of Maine, its geological history; the migration of seabirds; the great ocean with its incalculable forms of life, its monsters and prodigies. (He has also laid by a stock of other books. Books he has not read since Harvard, books he has been meaning to read all his life. There is a great deal of time now. There is a paradisaical abyss of time.)

He sits in the dark listening to recordings of piano music by Mozart, Beethoven, Chopin. Several recordings of the same piece, by different pianists. Sometimes the music excites him so greatly he has to shut it off.

The elation of solitude. The despair of solitude.

Mornings when he wakes to feel almost "himself" again—physically; mornings of bone-aching unspeakable sorrow when he understands that he *has* died . . . but still his body survives.

Death surprises with its appetites, infrequent as they are, he tells Kirsten. *But perhaps the "appetites" are only memory—tissue-memory, deep in the muscles and nerves.*

He writes to another man's daughter a thousand miles away who does not answer him. His letters are censored by the people who have newly taken her up, for her own good—or she rips them into pieces without reading them—or she reads them, in silence, and sets them aside. *You've given me my life again. But what am I to do with it?*—sealing the envelope and affixing a stamp and never mailing the letter.

Convalescing. At the edge of the ocean. The tide has swept everything away but has, for some reason he can't comprehend, failed to carry him out with it.

Inland he would mourn his dead, like anyone else. But at the edge of the ocean the "dead" are both present and obliterated—obliterated in the sense of never having lived. He thinks of Isabel; he thinks of Owen; and of Maurie. They are present though bodiless—just outside the cottage door, strolling along the beach, sitting at the dining room table with him. At the same time it is reasonable to believe that they have never existed: or that their existences, like the jellyfish that is both animal and flower and yet *really* water, were too fleeting, too precarious, to be measured. Mount Dunvegan Island is postglacial but even the postglacial shore is very old. Very old indeed.

The predatory birds draw his attention, he feels a certain kinship with them, a bleak consolation that has something to do with their crude calls and their hooked bills and their evidently insatiable appetites. And the dunes, the extraordinary dunes of Mount Dunvegan, some as high as eighty feet: a wilderness in which he might wander for hours, for days, transfixed by distortions of distance and scale, and a vertiginous sense of constant motion. (He returns again and again to the dunes of the island's northeast tip. Walls and valleys and smooth dry surfaces and glinting rippling surfaces, burning to the touch, or unaccountably cold. Hills and mounds, slopes, spits. Sand particles shaded with garnet and black mineral in eerie designs—flowers, trees, human figures. The wind is voracious, the wind is a continual exhausting whine, delicate as the smallest of camel's-hair brushes; or clumsy and violent as a sudden shove. The dunes of course are shaped and reshaped by the wind. By that voracious appetite. Built up to small mountains and then worn down again to riblike peninsulas, in constant motion, in a kind of ceaseless migration—oddly, from west to east. Because he has a good deal of time he watches them shift and change shape. Slowly. Very slowly. Like waves, like the mounds and bars and white-capped hillocks of the Atlantic. The entire landscape is fluid. Yet everything is exaggerated: shadows, footprints, even leafprints: the glaring sun, the bone-chilling dark. Nick takes note of the low scrubby vegetation—the beach heather, the beach grass, the stunted pines; he takes note of dun-colored grasshoppers and spiders and tiny flies and larval cocoons spun in the dead trunks of long-submerged forests. It is all a riddle, he is certain that it is all very significant, but its truth for him is merely truth—the emptiness and beauty of a world uncontaminated by, and unguided by, human volition.)

He nearly died, nearly bled to death. And the others did die— Isabel and Owen. And that unfortunate Mrs. Salman. He was still in Mount St. Mary's, though no longer in the intensive care ward, when positive identification was finally made by a team of pathologists: an identification of bodies that involved, in the case of Isabel and her son, not only fragments of jaw but fragments of teeth. The front part of the house had been almost completely demolished; the rear had collapsed; the shock of the explosion was felt for blocks on all sides. *The sentence of death without appeal. Vengeance for the People!* Everyone thought, naturally, that the bombings and the attempt on Nick Martens's life were "senseless." Except perhaps Nick.

And Kirsten, who was to remain inaccessible to him.

(After the disaster at 18 Röcken, with its staggering complexities, its snarls and riddles and unthinkable paradoxes, Kirsten—the "daughter," the "child," the "surviving member of the Maurice Halleck family" —was hospitalized in a private clinic in Bethesda and then, some months later, taken up by her Kuhn relatives out in Minneapolis, who were evidently greatly moved by her predicament, and anxious to rescue her from the Halleck—that is, the Washington and East Coast—contamination. And the Hallecks surrendered her because they might have agreed, or reasoned in any case that *Washington* and *tragedy* and *Halleck* would certainly prolong the distraught young woman's period of convalescence.)

Nick spoke of his attackers in the plural, but failed to describe them except in the most general, confused manner: several young men, three or perhaps even four, forcing their way into the house—overcoming him—taking him completely by surprise—and using their knives at once. The doorbell was rung and a bearded young man in his twenties asked to use the telephone because his car had broken down and Nick hesitated and was about to relent when the young man pushed his way forward and was joined by others and—and suddenly Nick was attacked —at some point, half-conscious, he was carried upstairs—he had no idea why unless perhaps they had intended to keep him as a hostage—or kidnap him—or—

But it all happened too quickly. It was a nightmare, a blaze of terror, he simply couldn't remember. Why there was no blood downstairs, in the foyer, he didn't know. He couldn't remember the sequence of events but he was fairly positive—he insisted, for some reason, on this point—that they had begun stabbing him immediately. Downstairs.

And then carried him upstairs?—into the bedroom?

Evidently.

Did he recognize any of them?—of course not. Did they announce themselves as "revolutionaries"?—he couldn't remember, he didn't think so. Did they tell him he was a "fascist capitalist criminal" condemned to death?—no, there wasn't time.

The F.B.I. interrogated him at length in the hospital, when he was sufficiently recovered, and showed him photographs of various persons —radicals and otherwise. He made identifications and then changed his mind. He stammered, he faltered and lost the thread of what he was saying, he clearly wasn't well; it could not have occurred to his questioners that he was lying.

Why was he in the Rock Creek Lane house, they asked, though surely they had already questioned the man to whom the house belonged, and Nick explained in a vague toneless neutral voice that he had been going to meet someone there—a woman—but she had telephoned to say she couldn't make it and he had decided to stay the night there, alone: he'd planned to get drunk, in fact. Who was the woman, they inquired. I can't tell you, said Nick. A married woman? they asked. He shrugged and looked away. He said, sullenly: Of course. A married woman. With a reputation. With her own life.

It remained something of a puzzle—it was always to remain something of a puzzle—how Nick Martens's assailants knew exactly where he was, that night.

And why the police were eventually summoned, hours later.

They changed their minds, evidently, Nick said. Or one of them did.

A woman, it was a woman who telephoned: did you know that?

A woman, no, I didn't know that, Nick said evenly, vaguely, I wasn't under the impression that there were women involved, there were only men—I saw only men.

Then they changed their minds. Or one of them did. But *why* would they change their minds, under the circumstances—?

I don't know, Nick said flatly. I can't imagine. —But they were amateurs, weren't they. After all. Hacking at me like that. Unable to finish the job.

The bombs weren't the work of amateurs, he was told.

But I can't hate them, Nick said slowly. I can't feel anything against them.

Which means?—his interrogators asked, with a certain measure of pitying contempt.

That I can't hate them, he said, it's as simple and as irrefutable as that. He was so drugged, and consequently so removed from his own pain, that he seemed to be gazing upon himself in the hospital bed from a distance: without physical substance, without the weight of physical emotion.—I can't feel anything, he said.

So he made his confession. Calmly at first. And then with increasing emotion.

He had accepted money in installments. *He* had accepted money —not Maurie Halleck. It was paid to him by an agent for the company—a man whose name he was never told—no, he was no one Nick knew—yes, a stranger to Washington—GBT was never directly involved, naturally GBT was discreet, their methods were sophisticated and nearly foolproof—they had done this sort of operation before, no doubt many times. But it was he and not Maurie Halleck who had dealt with them.

The money, the money. $250,000. With another $150,000 promised. Yes, he could prove he had acquired it illicitly—his salary at the Commission, after all, was only $75,000 a year—and he hadn't any other source of substantial revenue, only a few stocks and investment certificates and some rental properties in Philadelphia, inherited from his father. The money was split into three savings accounts, in Washington, Chevy Chase, and Bethesda.

He began the confession coherently enough. Though his voice was oddly hollow, and his eyes glassy, as if he were not inhabiting his body—not entirely. But soon his words tumbled over one another and he faltered and went silent and began again, impatiently and defensively. How dare they doubt his word!—when he was telling the truth at last!

A very distraught man. A very frightened man.

But then of course he had almost died. . . .

And why so defensive, if he *was* telling the truth? For he refused to name names—he would not even acknowledge Tom Gast—the near-mythical Tom Gast who had disappeared from the States, and had not been sighted anywhere in the past eighteen months. Nick refused to involve this "Gast" though the man's role as go-between had been unofficial public knowledge even before Maurie Halleck's death.

I don't know the name, Nick said stubbornly. Names weren't important. Only money.

So he repeated his confession. He insisted upon his guilt. He was belligerent with his interlocutors; he was haughty with his own attorneys. Clearly a most disturbed man—perhaps in need of psychiatric treatment.

Why are you doing this, June asked, coldly bemused, I mean why are you suddenly so concerned for Maurie's reputation?—he's been dead, after all, for over a year.

Nick had no answer. He lay in his hospital bed in a cocoon of queer suspended absent pain—*he* felt nothing, registered nothing, but he understood that his body was still writhing and struggling to escape a pain so great, flashing upon him from so many directions, that it would never be overcome. —It doesn't suit you, June said, the role of penitent. It isn't really your style, you'll make yourself ridiculous. And lose all your friends.

I haven't any friends, Nick said. They're dead.

(When he was released from the hospital in October charges were brought against him to which he pleaded nolo contendere on his attorneys' advice rather than *guilty*, as he had wanted; though the legal proceedings had interested him in the abstract, and though he had anticipated the courtroom sessions with a great deal of excited anxiety, when the first day arrived he was bored, his mind wandered, he tapped his fingers impatiently on the table before him . . . for of course he would not be punished sufficiently: this court hadn't the power. And when, weeks later, he rose to hear from the judge the amount for which he was being fined and the number of months' suspended sentence handed down to him, it was difficult for him to maintain even a tactful concern.)

The irony of the situation, which June took pains to explain to him, before leaving Washington to return to Boston (where, she hinted with a touching admixture of arrogance and diffidence, there was a man she would "probably" marry) is simply this: Nick's story was believed around town, more or less, the story of his own guilt: but Maurie Halleck's "innocence" was another thing. The only people who firmly believed that he had had nothing to do with the GBT money were people who had known him closely—but then of course they had never believed he was guilty in any case. (I certainly knew Maurie wouldn't do such a thing, June said vehemently, he couldn't have even *considered* it—he was so infatuated with his own purity.) As for the others, the thousands of others—they simply assumed that both men must have been involved, in a singularly messy and clumsy situation, and that one had cracked under pressure before the other.

That sort of thing, June said, is hardly uncommon in Washington.

And some months later June—dear June, considerate June— sends him a clipping from the *New York Times* with *I thought this might amuse you* scrawled in red ballpoint at the top, and Nick knows before scanning the brief article that it will not amuse him in the slightest. Anthony Di Piero, it seems, has been appointed "Special Financial Consultant to a permanent subcommittee of the World Health Organization," and is to establish residency in Geneva, Switzerland.

Nick reads the article twice, grimaces, grunts, crumples the clipping and tosses it on the floor.

And what of Gast, "Tom Gast"?

Has he fled the country, is he living in Europe under an assumed name, with a forged passport?—is he living comfortably right here in the States?—was he, perhaps, not "Tom Gast" at all but a fictional concoction, a sleight-of-hand insubstantial as the joker in a deck of cards, and just as capriciously potent?

I must telephone Isabel, Nick thinks.

In the nights Kirsten visits him: a frenzied angel of wrath, lunging and slashing at him with that incredible knife.

In the days he sees her, by accident, and always mistakenly—a tall young woman striding along the beach, sometimes alone, more frequently with friends: and he freezes where he stands, leaning trembling on his cane, staring.

After I died, Nick writes, *I found myself remembering peculiar things—memories dislodged from the past, floating up—vivid and alarmingly "real"—for instance your father and I as boys, at Bauer —just talking—sitting in one of our rooms and talking—we'd both been studying Latin and we had both read about some brutal religious practices—secret rites—rites of what we would now call initiation—in which young men were terrorized and exhausted to the point of hysteria, so that they lost their sense of the self's boundaries, and identified with the very victim of the sacrifice—sometimes it was an animal, sometimes it was human—and they would evidently tear at the living flesh with their hands—guzzle blood like hyenas—they passed over into what they were killing—they were the victims—it was a form of sympathy we can't understand—not even their contemporaries could understand—the sects were outlawed. Your father and I talked about this and I don't remember most of what we said but I know one of us said something that has stayed with me all these years: that it might be the case that all personal struggle, personal suffering, is an illusion—a deception—*

He seals the envelope, stamps it, lays it on the windowsill in the kitchen. Contemplates it for days. In the end he does mail it out—he makes the effort, the corners of his mouth turning downward with amused self-contempt—and though he tries to picture Kirsten Halleck opening it, and reading it, he cannot "see" either her or the gesture. She can only come upon him, it seems, unanticipated. By accident.

In the dunes and along the windswept beach he experiences jarring distortions of distance and scale. It must be a consequence of the starkly white light, or a warring permeation of dry and moist airs: but in any case Nick cannot attribute it to his own subjectivity because he remembers the phenomenon from the past—he remembers it even from childhood.

A trotting dog in the dunes can acquire, within a fluid instant, the size of a deer; a tern dipping overhead, the proportions of a hawk. Algae in a puddle trapped on a ledge might be darkly scarlet as blood, and then, as the light shifts, as the clouds pass overhead, it reverts to the hue of seaweed, and suddenly there is nothing to see.

Nick cannot be surprised any longer by such changes. One minute he is dwarfed by the immensity of sand, the next, he feels himself towering ten feet tall, his shadow bobbing like a clown's.

He can't be surprised, he tells himself. But he is usually mistaken.

One morning, for instance, after a storm of some ten hours, he slowly approaches a creature thrown up on the beach—a baby whale, perhaps; or a human body, grotesquely discolored—no, it is a harbor porpoise, stub-headed, black-backed, weighing perhaps seventy-five or eighty pounds, quivering with life: except, as he draws near, he sees that the poor thing is dead, and not quivering at all.

Another morning he tests his strength by climbing the old Tower Rock of his youth, and, sweating profusely, panting for breath, turns to see, a few hundred yards up the beach, two people strolling hand in hand —a man and a woman—lovers—who in the next instant dissolve to nothing—shadows caused by wind-blown grass.

It is on a sea-cliff overlooking a pocked ledge of glacial kettle holes, one June afternoon, toward dusk, that he writes his final letter to Kirsten Halleck: after he has spent upward of ten minutes staring, like a fool, at a swimmer trapped in the milky churning water just off the ledge: a girl or a young woman, it was, swimming desperately, her arms flailing, her head ducked, a wraith that disappeared as he approached, shouting at her.

No swimmer, no girl: nothing but seaweed and frothy churning water and an accident of light.

So he sits at the edge of the sea-cliff and writes his final letter to Kirsten. *I won't ever attempt to find you,* he tells her, *I see that our exiles can never touch, I can't even imagine you now:* and this letter too, badly stained by the salt spray, he seals, and stamps, and lays on the windowsill, to contemplate.